CATHERINE'S MERCY

A NOVEL

By Nicole Evelina

chalice
stories

Print: 9780827207509
EPUB: 9780827207516
EPDF: 9780827207523

ChalicePress.com

Printed in the United States of America

EPIGRAPH

Suscipe (Act of Resignation) of Catherine McAuley

My God, I am yours for time and eternity.
Teach me to cast myself entirely
into the arms of your loving Providence
with a lively, unlimited confidence in your compassionate,
tender pity.
Grant, O most merciful Redeemer,
that whatever you ordain or permit may be acceptable to me.
Take from my heart all painful anxiety;
let nothing sadden me but sin,
nothing delight me but the hope of coming to the possession of You,
my God and my all, in your everlasting kingdom.
Amen.

To Nancy Dixson, my Dublin partner in crime,
and for Sr. Roch, who would have been proud of this book (I hope).

CONTENTS

Prologue

CATHERINE MCAULEY

April 1809
Coolock House
Outside of Dublin, Ireland

"Comfort comes soon after a well-received trial."

The words of the priest's homily from last Sunday came to me unbidden as I stepped out of the carriage, ready to meet my new employers and explore my new home. Those words certainly fit my situation. After years of uncertainty, of depending on the generosity of others, and of constantly uprooting my life as I relocated from one dwelling to another, I finally had a home—and steady employment.

The two-story gray mansion called Coolock House welcomed me, its tall, gleaming windows and bright red front door signs of its master's wealth and standing in the community. On the top step of a small staircase leading to the entry stood my new employers, William and Catherine Callaghan. Though his brown hair was liberally streaked with gray, William still had the straight, aristocratic bearing befitting a man who served as secretary and treasurer of the Apothecaries Hall, but Catherine's shoulders were beginning to stoop beneath her shawl and she walked with a cane—assistance she hadn't needed the last time I saw them.

William met me at the foot of the stairs and escorted me to Catherine's side. She embraced me warmly.

"Thank you so much for agreeing to live with us," she said. "It is my hope that over time we will become like family to one another."

"I hope so, too," I said, meaning it.

It was entirely possible we would grow to love one another, as the Callaghans were not strangers to me. The last family I lived with, the Armstrongs, were good friends with their family and mine, and I had attended many balls at Coolock House. At one such event, Mr. and Mrs. Callaghan, childless and both in their sixth decade of life, let it slip that they were considering hiring a live-in companion to care for them as they aged. My name was mentioned and the Callaghans agreed I was the perfect candidate.

"Come, come, now," Mr. Callaghan coaxed. "Allow me to show you to your quarters."

He took me to a small room adjacent to Mrs. Callaghan's bedroom, just down the hall from his own. It wasn't much, only large enough for a small bed, a dresser, a desk, and a wash basin. But to me it was grand; I hadn't had my own bed, much less my own room, since my father died when I was five and my family's fortunes plummeted. Plus, it was ideally suited for my roll, being near enough to both bedrooms that I could hear either one if they called for me in the night.

On our way back toward the stairs, two liveried servants passed us, each holding two grand silver candelabras. I followed them with my eyes, wondering where they were scurrying off to in such haste. Then a woman emerged from the kitchen carrying a large decorated cake. All three disappeared into a long room just beyond the drawing room that I recalled as the ballroom.

"We're hosting a small event tonight," Mr. Callaghan said, by way of explanation. At the door to Mrs. Callaghan's room, he turned away, saying with a sly grin, "I will leave you women to do whatever it is you do."

His wife beckoned me inside. She was holding an elaborate red ballgown, fluffing its sleeves and fussing with the roses at the décolletage.

"Would you like some help putting that on?" I asked her.

"Me? Oh, no, dear. This is for you."

"What?" She wasn't making any sense.

"We can't have a beautiful young woman like yourself missing a party thrown in your honor."

"My ...what?"

"We want to celebrate your new role here and be sure you are introduced to everyone in our social group. That reminds me, would you honor us with a song, perhaps?"

"I ... of course." I had sung many times before in their home at both formal and casual events.

"Who knows, you might even meet a handsome young man," Mrs. Callaghan elbowed me playfully. "You're what, twenty? Yes, you are the perfect age to find a match. After all, we don't expect you to live here forever."

PART I

CONSEQUENCES

Chapter 1

CATHERINE

January 1822
Coolock House
Outside of Dublin, Ireland

I stared down at the small writing book resting on the table before me. It was where I kept my meditations on God, faith, and anything else that was troubling my mind. But years ago I had dedicated a small section in the back to those I had lost—it was my memory book, my way of keeping them alive, if only in my heart. There had been so many; first my father, then the priest who was my first confessor. My eyes lingered on the most recent entry, made only two and half years ago. Catherine Callaghan. Now it was time to add another.

It was hard to believe two decades had passed since the Callaghans had welcomed me into their homes and hearts. Over the years, they had become like surrogate parents, instructing and correcting me when needed, but also encouraging my dreams of helping the poor. I cleaned and cooked for them, read to them, and tended to their needs in their final illnesses. In turn, they made it clear I was not just a companion or nurse; they viewed me as a daughter.

The one sticking point between us, however, was religion. Though the worst of the Penal Code had been lifted and Catholics were free to openly practice our faith once again, the Callaghans were staunchly opposed to it. It was a blessing they did not force me to renounce my faith, but Mr. Callaghan, a staunch Protestant, and his wife, Mary—God rest her soul—an ardent Quaker until secretly embracing Holy Mother Church on her deathbed only months ago, barely tolerated my faith at first. They allowed me to attend Mass, say my prayers in private with Aoine, their only Catholic servant, but we couldn't possess any outward signs of our faith, like crucifixes or rosaries that others might see. "Believe what you will, so long as Christ is at the center of your life, but keep at that Popery and superstition outside of these walls," Mr. Callaghan had said on my first day here.

Over the years, his rigidness had softened, mellowed certainly by the grace of God, but also perhaps by our many spirited debates about faith and philosophy by the fireside on long winter nights. For all his bluster, Mr. Callaghan was an upstanding man who truly believed in his duty to the poor as a Christian. "To whom much is given much is required," was one of his favorite verses to quote from the Bible. Ireland may no longer have fiefdoms and serfs, but he took his role as the wealthiest man in the area to heart. Many times I accompanied him around Coolock village as he enquired into the health and welfare of its merchants, families, and especially those who had fallen on hard times. During sickness, drought, or bereavement, packages were loaded into his carriage and left on doorsteps. He had even once funded a young man's entrance into the military, confiding in us that it was the best opportunity the boy could hope for to rise in the world.

With a sigh, I added William Callaghan's name to the list. *May the Lord have mercy on his soul.* With my last employer gone, I had no idea what my future would hold. At forty-two, I didn't have many options. I was now both too old and too poor to marry, a dream I had given up decades earlier. As a young woman, I would have happily accepted the hand of a man who respected my determination and shared my faith; but such men were a rarity, especially given my family's deteriorating financial state, constant change of address, and ever-shifting social circles as we sought to stay off the streets and keep body and soul joined.

Yet I could not live alone. Not only was it unseemly, it required means I did not have. Thus far I had depended on the kindness of family and friends, but what would I do when that ran out? My brother and sister were both wed and certainly did not want their spinster sister interrupting their lives. With no husband to protect me, where was I to go? What was I to do?

All I knew was I felt still that ever-present tug at my soul, that deep down yearning to do good. The school I ran on the Coolock House grounds was a good first step, but it was not enough. It was like a thirst I could not quench, an ache that no amount of prayer would relieve. Day after day I begged God to show me the way. I knew with the certainty of my own name that he was calling me to something, that my life had purpose and he had a mission for me. Only I had no idea what it was or how to accomplish it.

In my mind's eye I kept seeing the faces of those I encountered regularly when in town. The rotation of prostitutes at the quay never ended, but I knew a few on sight. Most were teenaged girls from the countryside or the orphanages or workhouses who had been disowned or turned out and run out of ways to feed themselves. Others were abandoned wives or widows, some former domestics who lacked either experience or character references to find additional work. As sad as their plights were, it was the families who affected me most. Mothers and fathers often begged for a few coins to feed their children or heat their homes. They were the lucky ones, for they were hale and whole enough to make the trek from their little dwellings into the city; hundreds more could not do even that, due to illness, drink, or loss of limb. So many men had been mutilated in the Bloody Rebellion and discarded into the gutters like the contents of a chamber pot.

What could I do in the face of such abject poverty and suffering? I was only one person, and a woman at that. I could not run for office or influence politics like the great Liberator Daniel O'Connell, had no financial means to donate large sums to charity like the wives of the politicians in Merrion Square, and God knew I had no desire to become a nun. I shuddered at the mere thought. Spending my days on my knees in prayer, trapped in a place I neither wanted to be nor could ever flee was akin to a living death.

I looked up with a start, my musings interrupted when the door to the receiving room banged open. I quickly closed my book and stashed it the inner pocket of my dress before turning to greet the newcomer.

Mr. Callaghan's relative, Mr. Richard Powell, was the first face I took in, his jaw clenched, his brown eyes stormy. But before I could form a rebuke for his rude entrance into my home, my gaze flicked to Patricia, my chief maid, whose cheeks were ruddy with exertion.

"Forgive the intrusion, Miss McAuley," she said, dropping her chin to her chest. "I tried to get them to wait in the foyer while I announced them, but he," she titled her head toward Mr. Powell, "insisted they were expected."

They? It was only then that I looked beyond Mr. Powell and Patricia. Behind them stood Marianne Powell, Richard's wife, her spine ramrod straight, chin tilted up slightly, a haughty expression on her face. Her eyes roamed the room as though she were calculating the value of every item. Hiding behind her voluminous sage skirts were two little girls so alike in curls and dimples, they could be twins.

Returning my gaze to Mr. Powell, I pursed my lips. "Indeed." I infused my voice with frost. "I was expecting the Powells for the reading of Mr. Callaghan's will, but not quite so soon. Why, the attorney isn't even here yet."

"No sense in putting off the inevitable," Marianne said.

Ignoring her, I gestured toward the door. "Please, won't you follow me to the parlor?" There will be more room there once all parties arrive." As I passed Patricia, I added, "Bring us some tea, won't you, dear?"

Over the next half hour, people trickled in, mostly family from the McAuley side—distant relations I hadn't seen in years. The grandfather clock in the corner struck the hour before my brother James arrived, and by then the men had requested whiskey and Mr. Powell sucked on a foul-smelling cigar. Not long after, Patricia showed Mr. Johnston into the room. The gentlemen extinguished their cigars and everyone took seats around the room as the attorney arranged his papers and donned a slim gold pair of spectacles.

After reading through the attestation of Mr. Callaghan's soundness of mind and judgment, dispensing with the formalities of executors of the will, and addressing certain business matters, the lawyer read the section on the distribution of property, land, and other assets.

"To my kind and affectionate friend Miss Catherine McAuley, who resides with me," the lawyer glanced up at me, before returning his eyes to the paper, "for her many kindnesses and attentions I give, devise, and bequeath the four several annuities heretofore mentioned on the lives of Ross Thompson, Lord Howth, Christopher Robinson, and Robert M. Fishbourne, with the several policies assurance connected with the same and all benefit and advantage arising therefrom, together with such arrears of said annuities as may be due at my deceased."

This was not a surprise, as Mr. Callaghan mentioned he would leave me something. But instead of moving on to the next beneficiary, Mr. Johnston continued reading, adding to my inheritance.

"I also leave to the said Catherine McAuley all the grand canal stock or loans which I may have at the time of my death, together with all arrears of interest that may be then due on same. I do hereby appoint the said Catherine McAuley sole residuary legatee of all my estate and effect, real or personal, subject to specific legacies mentioned in my will and I do hereby publish and declare this as and for a codicil to my will and direct it to be taken as such."

What? Could I have heard correctly? Sole inheritor of Coolock House and its assets? A shrill ringing began in the back of my mind, threatening to overwhelm me. I gripped the table to keep myself upright.

Around me, oblivious to my distress, Mr. and Mrs. Powell, several Callaghan relatives, and my brother shouted, creating a collective roar of indignation that drowned out whatever came next.

"Now see here," a man declared.

"What? No! It is unfathomable," Marianne yelled.

"Let me see that paper," my brother demanded, reaching to pluck it out of the attorney's hand.

"Please, calm down, everyone," the lawyer shouted above the din, curling in on himself to protect the document and inching out of William's reach. "There is more. If you will but let me continue."

As the congregation of relatives slowly regained their decorum, my heart continued to gallop as though it would leap through my skin and go cantering off down the lane. I sank back into the fine mahogany chair—my chair, I corrected myself, seeing the entire room in a whole new light. No wonder Marianne was anxious to begin appraising the house. The entire room was made of simple, yet fine things: from the hand-made lace sheers that dampened the light to the thick rugs beneath our leather soles. Why or how I had failed to notice them before remained a mystery; the best I could speculate was that I'd never had reason to. This was simply my home. But now it was a grand estate. And I stood to inherit it.

I struggled to take a deep breath, finding instead that my lungs would only fill to half compacity. I excused myself on account of needing some fresh air. I snuck through the still bickering crowd and had nearly made it before Mr. Johnston's hand came down on my shoulder, not in rebuke but gently, like a concerned uncle.

"There is one more thing, Miss McAuley," he whispered into my ear. "Mr. Callaghan asked that I give you this once you became aware of the considerable inheritance he left you."

The lawyer sipped a folded paper into my palm and I instinctually thumbed it father up my sleeve so no one could see it. "He asked that you read it alone, think it over, and then draw your own conclusion."

"What is it?" I asked in reply.

He shook his head. "I do not know, but whatever it is, it was meant only for your eyes."

I bobbed a small curtsey to him and looked around to be certain no one else had seen or heard, but Mr. and Mrs. Powell were deep into an argument with the Callaghans, and my relatives were squawking amongst themselves about contesting the will in court, which I had no doubt they would do.

On silent feet perfected over years of coming and going from the Callaghan's sickbeds, I slipped out the door and into the garden. As soon as it closed behind me, I leaned against the sun-warmed stones and heaved a great sigh. Try as I might to comprehend the last few minutes of my life, my brain stuttered to a complete halt.

Then I remembered the paper tucked up the bell of my left sleeve. Maybe it would yield some insight. Pushing away from the house's outer wall, I began tracing one of the many paths leading through the gardens. This one began amid the skeletons of herbs like basil, rue, and lavender in the kitchen garden and continued on through what would be in spring more formal flower beds. But now, all was silent, with only the occasional breeze shaking the hibernating plants beneath a light dusting of snow.

I found my favorite fountain, a simple round, three-tiered basin that tinkled like the finest crystal or like icicles splintering after a deep freeze. I sat on its edge and removed the note. Mr. Callaghan's elegant script greeted me.

My dear Kitty,

If you are reading this, then I have gone home to the Heavenly Father and my dear wife. Do not grieve for me, for you know just as well as I that to be free from this world and its suffering is the greatest reward.

I felt I owed you an explanation for the shock you surely received when my will was read, but it was not something I felt the others needed to know, so I commit this information to you alone. It is your choice whether or not to share it with others. You know I always intended to see you well looked-after upon my death. In its original form, I split the profits from my estate between you and the Powells, just as we had discussed. However, not long ago I overheard the most disturbing discussion between them.

One of the days they came to call, you were away at Mass, and having tired, I asked them to take a turn about the garden while I rested. They obliged, but lingered on the back terrace and had a lengthy discussion about my health, which they did not know I could hear through my open window. That I forgive them for, of course my condition would be of concern to them. But what they said next shocked and saddened me more than I can say. Mr. Powell mentioned that he had word from a reliable source that I was entertaining the idea of making you mistress of Coolock House. (Who would have told him that I cannot guess.) Mrs. Powell laughed quite haughtily and responded that the idea was too absurd to be entertained. He, in turn, agreed, saying I may as well leave the house to my favorite horse.

After a few more moments of such talk, they finally took the footpath toward the orchards, leaving only my hurt and betrayal in their wake. I resolved then and there to amend my will, doing exactly what they thought so outrageous. The more I thought on it, the more I realized the Powells were exactly right; no one else cared about our home so much or would put it to as good of use as you. After committing the decision to God in prayer, I dreamed that you would use the estate for your good works. I summoned my solicitor and had a codicil added to my will the very next day.

That is why, my dear, you are now inheritor of our family home. No words can express my love for you or my appreciation for your companionship all of these years.

With all of my love,

William Callaghan

Vision blurred with tears, I seated myself on one of the stone benches overlooking the frost-bitten canes of last summer's roses. A second page listed out exactly what I was owed according to the codicil: ready money in the form of bonds and loans in the name of one Frederick Moore of Mountjoy Square, a barrister whom I assumed held this money in trust for Mr. Callaghan; the house itself plus its outbuildings; it contents, including furniture, plate, and linen; and various other property, including the Callaghan carriage, horses, and farming implements, plus annual income. The sum at the bottom of the page was staggering: nearly £30,000. That was a substantial sum for any man to inherit, let alone a woman who was no blood relation, and a spinster at that.

I stared across the fields, listening to the giggles and shouts of some of the local children as they played stick ball; these were the true inheritors of Mr. Callaghan's munificence. They would reap the rewards in learning, religious education, and skills, and go on to lead respectable lives that would otherwise be out of reach.

I glanced back up at the house, where, through the large glass windows, the Powells were still gesticulating wildly at the poor barrister. There was no doubt this would only be resolved in court, and if needs be, I would reveal Mr. Callaghan's private correspondence to put an end to it.

A smile crossed my lips. In that very room was the one thing I would insist the Powells take with them as part of their inheritance: an oil painting of Cuchulainn, Mr. Callaghan's favorite race horse.

Chapter 2

MARGARET KELLY

January 1822
Lord Montague's Townhome
Dublin, Ireland

So many girls. So many eyes on me. Some little more than dull pools sunken with hunger, others sparkling with cunning and competitive pride. Most bloodshot or rimmed with purple from early rising and late nights, a sign of our occupation just like our calloused palms and ragged fingernails.

We stood shoulder to shoulder in the alley behind Lord and Lady Montague's Merrion Square townhouse, a towering red brick mansion that soared four stories above us, unseen chimney pots puffing gray swirls of smoke into the Dublin fog. Whether little girls of seven seeking their first employment or women of twenty or more with years of experience, we were all here for the same reason. We sought a position in this esteemed house.

I clutched the wrinkled advertisement torn from the pages of the *Irish Times*. By now I had read it so many times, I could recite it from memory.

Wanted

In a gentleman's family of Dublin, a good PARLOUR MAID. She must be accustomed to the care of plate, glass, and waiting at table. There are four sitting rooms to keep, with stoves. A thoroughly respectable, steady young woman, of religious character desired. No Catholics. Apply for name and address at the office of this paper.

A house of this size must employ dozens of servants. How many of these women were applying for the same position as I? Surely, they all had more experience and were more likely to be chosen. What must they see when they looked at me? A naïve sixteen-year-old scared to death of being rejected? A few dismissive looks from dark-haired beauties in fine store-bought uniforms told me they surpassed me in knowledge, skill, and sheer willpower. They had likely been serving in fine houses since their adolescence, whereas this was my first interview at a grand city house.

At least I wore the proper attire. Thanks to the generosity of Mrs. Witcombe, the wife of my current employer, a merchant living on the outskirts of Dublin. Both husband and wife had encouraged me to seek this position after he saw the advert in the newspaper. They had fallen on hard times and were going to have to dismiss me, but kind-hearted souls that they were, didn't want to do so without first seeing me securely employed. When I pointed out that the advertisement specified no Catholics, they dismissed my fears, saying all I had to do was pretend to be a Protestant and no one would be the wiser.

The future deception weighing heavy on my heart, I agreed anyway. What choice did I have? Mrs. Witcombe prepared me for the interview, including sewing the dress I was wearing.

"Margaret Kelly." The stern voice that interrupted my musings had a tone of command, not question. It was my turn to be interviewed.

I turned and approached the green-eyed woman who had called my name, elbowing my way through the crowd with mumbled apologies, praying the terror that squeezed my heart was not visible in my eyes. Struggling to keep my expression neutral and my voice from shaking, I stood before her. "I am Margaret Kelly."

Her gaze flicked from my eyes down to my scuffed boots and back up to my worn bonnet. She turned and took a step inside. "Follow me."

A cloak of heat enveloped me as she led me into the kitchen, where three women were busily preparing the noontime meal, the thwack of a knife on a wooden cutting board and the moist pounding of dough its own kind of rhythm by which all life moved in this world of steam and smoke. We passed a large open hearth where a joint of meat hissed and popped on a spit turned by a young boy. Another darted between us, a large ceramic pot supported by one hand, lid held on by the other, hurriedly fulfilling the cook's call for more flour.

The woman leading the way opened a plain wooden door and ushered me inside. I blinked rapidly. As my eyes adjusted to the relative dimness, I beheld a long, dark wood table with benches parallel on either side. A maid was dressing it with plate and utensils. This must be where the servants took their meals. The table was worn smooth in places a little over a meter apart, presumably from years of arms and hands polishing it as bread sopped up gravy and meat was sliced with dull knives. Pray God, tomorrow one of those places would be mine.

We passed through another door and into a small room lit by several tapers. A rectangular window faced us, flanked by bookshelves filled with neatly arranged volumes. In the center of the room a desk dominated the remaining space, an empty chair in front, and seated behind it, a middle-aged woman with perfect posture, her graying brown hair held in a bun and a pair of wire spectacles perched on her thin, bony nose. She did not rise to greet me, but gestured to the vacant chair. With a nod, she dismissed the other woman.

I sat carefully, minding my every movement so I didn't do a single thing wrong, and flattened my palms on my skirt in an effort to hide their shaking.

The woman looked me steadily in the eye, her expression revealing no emotion. "I am Mrs. Gallagher, the housekeeper," she said by way of greeting, the way she shortened the "o" in "housekeeper," a clear indication her people hailed from the north. "It is my duty to oversee all of the females employed by this house, and therefore also to hire those best suited for each role. How old are you, Miss Kelly?"

"Sixteen."

She picked up a quill, dipped it in ink, and scribbled in the journal laid flat on the desk before her. "And you hail from what part of Ireland?"

"Howth."

Her quill scratched the page. "So, your family is nearby. I suppose you'll be wanting a few days a year to see them," she said, more to herself than to me. Mrs. Gallagher laid her pen down and folded her hands a top the journal. "I think it prudent to advise you before we begin that there has been a change in the position you are applying for."

She paused and my heart sank, a lead ball in my stomach. What if I would be dismissed without uttering a word? I had enjoyed my work for the Witcombes, but not only was it coming to an end, now that I had seen a bit of Dublin, I wanted more. I wanted to know where every lane and alley ended, who lived behind each brightly painted door; most of all, I wanted to know what life might hold for me here. It had to be better than marrying a farmer like my father—that was my only option back home, if I could ever piece together a dowery.

"We recently lost one of our kitchen maids, so we find ourselves in need of someone who can handle working both in the parlor and in the kitchen, a between maid who can do whatever is needed."

I had heard tell of "tweenies," as they were called among those in service. It was a demanding role, for you never knew what your duties would be when you woke up in the morning and they could change at any time throughout the day. But because of this, tweenies were paid slightly more than low-level parlor or kitchen maids. That meant I could save a little money of my own in addition to what I sent back to mam and da.

Mrs. Gallagher gave me an appraising gaze. "What is the nature of your experience in service, Miss Kelly?"

I swallowed, trying to remember how I had rehearsed this answer with Mrs. Witcombe. All of it was true, but it was important that I portray myself in the best possible light. "I began my training caring for my younger brothers and sisters and taking care of my family. I learned to cook basic meals and tend our household while my mam took in laundry and other odd jobs. I had some education while I cleaned the houses of the other farmers outside Howth. I am good at needlework and can read and do basic sums." I smiled, unable to keep the pride from my voice. That was much more than most other country maids could say. "When I finished school, I was taken in by a merchant family who lives in the city. They had me as a maid of all work, so I can do anything you need me to. I can light fires, clean floors, work in the kitchen, polish plate, and I know how to turn a house in spring and for the winter."

Mrs. Gallagher's expression was dubious, a deep v forming between her brows. "But you have never worked on a large estate?"

I dropped my gaze to my hands, which were fluttering in my lap, and laced my fingers together. "No, ma'am."

"Mmmm." The noise she made was not comforting. My heart sank a little lower, resting now on my pubic bone. "Lord and Lady Montague will be spending the season here in Dublin and then retiring to their much larger country estate. I believe you might be able to get along here, but I fear you will be overwhelmed at the summer manor. Perhaps it would be best if you return to us in a few years when you have worked in a larger household."

I closed my eyes, fighting back burning tears. So that was it then. A few words about what I had and hadn't done and back to Howth it was. How disappointed my parents would be; they had been counting on this job to provide room and board, and I know my mother secretly hoped that having a child employed in fashionable Merrion Square would elevate the family somewhat and perhaps provide better opportunities for my siblings. Now I would have to return home to tell them I had failed, a burden on their already overtaxed lives.

A chime jangled behind Mrs. Gallagher and I started. I hadn't previously noticed the row of bells behind her. The older woman cocked her head and said, "Ah, that would be the lady of house. Come on girl, I'll show you out on my way upstairs."

I stood and Mrs. Gallagher brushed my shoulder with her hand, steering me toward the door. We passed through the empty dining area and back into the kitchen. Instead of the loud cacophony that had greeted us before, the room was silent, save for the crackling of the fire and the burbling of boiling soup in a large iron cauldron. Every person stood perfectly still, eyes cast downward. Even the boy had ceased turning the spit.

"Ah, Mrs. Gallagher. There you are," a statuesque woman in a ruffled cream dress held her hand out to the older woman.

Mrs. Gallagher stepped forward. "How may I help you, Madam?"

Madam? My eyes widened with shock and I quickly lowered my gaze to the stone floor. That was why everyone else stood at attention. This was Lady Montague.

"I need to speak with all of you urgently," she said, her voice kind, but stern. "I have just been informed that the Duke of Wellington has been called back to London. He leaves at first light but wishes to dine with us tonight, as he has urgent matters to discuss with Lord Montague. Needless to say, we will need to completely change the menu."

The kitchen staff exchanged concerned glances, but held their tongues in the Lady's presence.

The lady of the house gestured to the head cook and head housekeeper. "Please, Mrs. Gallagher, come with me—you too, Mrs. Donahue—and we will discuss what needs to be done."

"But what about all of them?" Mrs. Gallagher gestured to the throng of women still waiting for their turn in the alley outside. "There is no way I can interview them and oversee the preparations."

Lady Montague let out an exasperated sigh. "Send them away then. Tell them to come back next week. But hire one of them. We need additional hands tonight." Her gaze fell upon me for the first time. "Was this girl in with you when I rang?"

"Yes ma'am, but ..."

Lady Montague approached me and leaned down so her face was level with mine. I inhaled her delicate scent, something like soft powder and jasmine. "Can you serve at table? Can you cook?" she asked, speaking a little more slowly, as though she was afraid I was a simpleton.

"Yes, ma'am." I dared to glace up at her. "Both."

She smiled, her wide brown eyes glowing with relief. "Well then. It seems you are just what we need. Put her on the books and meet me upstairs," Lady Montague commanded.

Mrs. Gallagher pulled a small notebook from a hidden pocket within her skirts, wrote something down, and said so rapidly I could barely understand her, "Don't count your eggs, deary—you aren't hired yet. But we need your hands tonight." She pierced me with an unyielding stare. "We will start you out in the kitchens. Consider this a trial. If all goes well, you will officially join us in a week. Mind you, this job is also probationary. Do you know what that is?"

"No ma'am."

"It means it is only yours until the missus says it's not. If, after the season is over in mid-March, you're doing well, Lady Montague may choose to hire you on. If she does, then you'll make the journey to the country estate where we spend most of the year. But that is two months away. Let's focus on now. If we ask you to come back next week, at that time you will be entered as an official part of our household, paid regularly like everyone else, and given a ration of sugar, butter, and tea for your own personal use. You are responsible for your own clothing. We can go over the other particulars later. Do you understand?"

I nodded, though what was happening was anything but clear. My mind was whirling with the suddenness of it all. I was hired, yet not. I would be working in the kitchens, but only on a trial basis. How had a simple interview turned into this?

"Grace," Mrs. Gallagher called. "Please show this one around and give her a task while Cook and I talk with Madam."

"Yes, Missus," came a voice from one of the three servants still posed behind a large wooden worktable.

A beautiful woman a few years older than I with blonde hair tied back into a braid wiped her hands on her apron and approached me. "Hello. I'm Grace, second assistant to Cook."

I shyly introduced myself, overwhelmed by her looks and comportment.

"Welcome to the Montague house."

Chapter 3

GRACE RYAN

March 25, 1822
Lord Montague's Townhome
Dublin, Ireland

"What a wretched day to bring on new staff," Mrs. Donahue grumbled as she passed through the kitchens on her way to bring Lady Montague her breakfast—two four-minute eggs, toasted bread, and a small jar of strawberry preserves from the estate's own gardens. "Grace, be sure to fill the large teapot. With this cold she'll be wanting extra tea."

Outside, heavy raindrops just on the verge of snow spattered loudly on the stones, nearly, but not quite drowning out the slight note of condescension in the head housekeeper's voice. Normally this would be the duty of her ladyship's personal maid, but she was laid low with a fever and a cough the entire house prayed wasn't catching. Perhaps Mrs. Gallagher could be forgiven on the grounds of extra work and pressure if this wasn't the only incident, but I was beginning to believe she simply didn't like me.

There was no way she could know, was there? No, Lord Montague was much too careful for that. Or at least that's what I told myself as I filled the cream pitcher and set it next to the sugar so she could take the tray above stairs.

Though Lord Montague hadn't been careful enough to prevent other things. I skimmed my hand across my still-flat belly. It would be another month or so before I would know for sure, but I was fairly certain I was with child by my master, and not by my own doing. It was an open secret among the younger servants that Lord Montague did what he willed with whom he willed. Those who couldn't or wouldn't stand for such behavior either fled, if they were lucky, or learned exactly how strong a hold Lord Montague held over those in his employ. I wasn't sure if Lady Montague chose to turn a blind eye to our plight or had deluded herself into believing her husband wasn't capable of such sins. Mrs. Donahue had to know, but her loyalty was that of a well-tended hound; her fealty was to her master through and through.

But I had not the time to think on such matters now. Soon enough I would be able to devise a plan for remedying my situation, but now I had to be certain all was in order to receive the new maids, footmen, and other estate servants who came to us at the beginning of each social season, a tradition that had been in place for centuries. I had signed my own contract at the beginning of such a season three years earlier, and I had only a two years remaining before I was free. Once I had earned my independence, I would ...

"Watch out, you daft cow," Deirdre, one of the servants filling in for Lady Montague's personal maid, called as she descended the stairs carrying the night's chamber pots for emptying. She nearly plowed right into me. Her determination forced me to flatten myself against the wall or be trampled.

I shook my head and forced my mind back to where it belonged— on my job.

Earlier this morning, a new maid named Margaret had come to us to begin her employ. She had proven herself nimble and obedient on the night of the Duke's surprise visit, but she still had so much to learn. Surviving in a house this size took skill and fortitude she had not yet developed. It was up to me to show her how Lord and Lady Montague liked things to be done and train her up right. If I did, it was possible they would take a month off my contract or perhaps even give me a small bonus come Boxing Day.

The bells of St. Andrews tolled nine times. I slid into position behind Mrs. Donahue and the others who would be responsible for the new members of our household. As soon as the last vibration faded into in the sky, the housekeeper opened the door to the kitchen and beckoned to the small, wet group of men and women and two very young girls. "Come in now," she called. "Madam and Sir wouldn't take too kindly to a quarter of their staff catching their death on their first day."

The newcomers happily flocked toward the kitchen's warmth, created by a large oven, a fireplace with open flame, and an iron cookstove that had been installed some years before. As if in obeyance to some unspoken command, they stood in a row, eyes to the ground, ducklings differentiated only by their uniforms, which were already beginning to dry. Their small bags of clothing lay at their feet. Cook and Mrs. Donahue inspected them one by one, straightening a lapel here, tucking in a stray curl there.

Finally, Mrs. Donahue spoke. "Those of you who will be working in the front house are under my watch." She gestured toward the door which led above stairs. "Come with me." They followed her out of the kitchen, the established servants and butlers bringing up the rear.

"The rest of you will remain here until I give your first assignments," Cook said.

Margaret watched both groups hesitantly, usure who to follow. I came to her rescue with a gentle tug on her arm. "You're with me," I whispered.

Picking up her bag, she followed me up the bare stone stairs. I walked slowly, hoping she could see well enough in the lantern light, although soon enough she wouldn't need it. She'd know these stairs in complete darkness, having traversed them many times half asleep and having learned which one was shorter than the rest, which had a particular indent that might trip her, and how to use the wall to guide her when her eyes could not.

"First thing's first, I'll show you our room—you will be sharing it with me—and we'll get you dried off."

Margaret didn't respond, but her hesitant footfalls told me she was still following me.

In no time, we reached the top of the stairs and turned into a hallway lined with six wooden doors. I opened the second from the left and bade Margaret to enter before me.

As she slowly took in the room, my mind drifted back to the first time I'd seen this tiny space. Was she seeing it as I had, as a blessing, for it meant a reliable place to sleep and relative safety? Or was she disappointed that it didn't live up to the image in her mind? Surely, she understood that all servants lived in attic rooms with high ceilings, but cramped quarters. I, for one, was as grateful today as I was three years ago when I first beheld the small iron bedsteads against each wall and the wooden pegs protruding from the wall above. Between them was a small window about the length of my forearm and twice as high, the only source of light and cause of the shiver that fizzed down my spine. We had no heat beyond a small coal-fueled brazier and we had to use our own allowance to feed it, but it was better than completely freezing to death in these bitter months.

Margaret turned to me. "Which one is mine?" she asked, indicating the beds with a nod of her head.

"The one on the right."

Margaret took a few hesitant steps toward her bed, placed her bag on it, and then opened the small wooden box sitting below the pillows. She peered to its depths and then back at me.

"It's for your personal items. You may take it with you if you leave." I gestured to mine, set along the opposite wall. My box was long and narrow, more like a toolbox than the chest in which Margaret was now placing her things.

I took a towel from the washstand and handed it to her. "Dry your hair as best you can. Then I will go over your duties with you."

*****

"Well, if it isn't just who I was looking for," Lord Montague's rich voice interrupted us. "Margaret, isn't it?"

Startled, both Margaret and I whirled around to see him leaning against the doorframe, a partial smirk on his lips and a glint in his eye that made every instinct I had stand at attention. Without conscious thought, I stepped in front of my young charge, shielding her from him. I bowed my head, praying the girl remembered to stay silent until Lord Montague said something requiring a response. She had been here a fortnight now and was adjusting well, but this was an easy command to forget when you were addressed rhetorically.

He took a few slow steps toward us. "Grace, you may leave us."

My head jerked up. No. I couldn't leave her alone with him. It was inevitable this would happen eventually, but not today, not while she was still so new and vulnerable. My heart begged me to stay, to find an excuse to watch over her. Yet I couldn't go against his wishes. What kind of example would that set for Margaret?

"Go on." He shooed me away like a cat too long underfoot. "I'd like to get to know our newcomer here." Far taller, he leaned forward to be level with her sightline.

She looked up and nodded. "Yes, sir." Her voice was small, wavering. It betrayed her youth and innocence better than any direct questioning ever could.

"Don't be afraid," he put a reassuring hand on her shoulder. "Please, sit." He guided her backward toward a chair. "I only want to talk with you."

This time. But that was always how it began. This was how he gained your trust. It was not so long ago he said similar words to me. His eyes took on a glint that she would no doubt take as encouraging, but which really meant something very different.

He called over his shoulder to me, "Tell Mrs. Gallagher I have given this girl a task and she will be detained until luncheon." Then, as though I was already a distant memory, he sat down opposite Margaret and began speaking with her.

"Well, Margaret, it is nice to finally meet you. My wife says kind things about you. I have no doubt you will soon find yourself at home here."

Yes, open with a compliment. Just as you told me I came highly recommended by the vicar's wife. It was a powerful antidote to my fear. As I watched her, Margaret relaxed incrementally, blood returning to her white knuckles and her grip loosening ever so slightly on the arms of the chair.

Lord Montague smiled, his expression guileless. "You are in good hands with Grace," he glanced up, a grimace clouding his features for only a moment before the light returned. "She will teach you everything you need to know. But you must understand one thing—and normally this wouldn't require speaking aloud, but I understand you are young and this is your first time serving a family like ours, so I will say it anyway." He pinned Margaret with a solemn stare.

Yes, turn those paralyzing eyes on her. She may as well be a specimen pinned to a board in his study. At the memory of his expression when I sat before him, my own body grew heavy and force seemed to prevent me from even blinking.

With both of us in this thrall, he went on. "Though I am a generous master, I demand much from those in my employ. Foremost among these is obedience. You will do as I and Lady Montague say, whether we deliver our wishes through Mrs. Gallagher or Mrs. Donahue or speak to you directly."

His voice was directed at Margaret, but his eyes were on me.

Very subtle. Yes, I know you told me to leave. I sighed inwardly, out of excuses to linger. With one last glance at my charge, I curtsied to my employer and turned toward the door.

I only made it a handful of steps before Mrs. Donahue appeared.

"Beg pardon, my Lord, but is that our new tweenie with you?"

The intensity dissolved from his face like a drop of ink in a pond, replaced by a mask of warm curiosity. "Indeed it is. However,

I have need of her at present. I will send her to find you when we are through." Without another word, he turned back to Margaret.

"Forgive me, sir," Mrs. Donahue interjected. "But it is madam who requests her presence. The inspection..."

Oh yes, Lady Montague's bi-annual assertion of dominance. I had forgotten that was today. She would be waiting in the parlor for all of the female servants to gather for her instruction. She would then critique our performance and release those who were not meeting her standards. I inwardly rolled my eyes. Anyone who had been here at least six months realized it was Mrs. Donahue who really wielded the power; this was a mere formally to make Madam feel it was she who held sway over her household.

Dread shot down my spine. *No, that wasn't the only reason,* a little voice inside my mind reminded. It was also her chance to rid herself of anyone who displeased her. Rarely did a Lady Day or Michaelmas inspection go by when some poor girl wasn't sacked. I desperately searched Mrs. Donahue's eyes for a reason I hadn't been requested as well. *You know why,* the voice goaded.

"Go on then," Lord Montague said through gritted teeth. "Both of you."

"Oh no, my Lord. Grace may stay with you. She was just promoted so Madam does not need to see her."

I nearly sighed aloud with relief. But then I realized it meant I would not be there to support Margaret. Crossing to her, I took her hand and squeezed it. "You will be fine. You have done nothing to warrant any suspicion." Her amber eyes flicked to mine. "I will see you at luncheon."

When the two had left, Lord Montague returned to his work, completely ignoring me. After a few moments of silence, he looked up. "Why are you still here?"

"Don't you think I should wait a bit to make it look like you had a reason for keeping me? Otherwise, why was I here in the first place? You could have sent for Margaret alone if she was all you wanted."

He glowered at me. "That tongue of yours will be the death of you."

"I don't recall you saying such after the Duke's dinner party," I sneered back without thinking.

Lord Montague shot to his feet. "Speak to me like that one more time ..." he warned.

"Or you'll, what? Dismiss me without a reference?" I crossed to stare him down over the desk. My hands shook on the smooth, polished wood. "You've already gotten me with child! What more can you do?" The words slipped out on a tide of rage and frustration; I hadn't meant to say them.

Lord Montague marched to the door and slammed it shut, growling as he returned to tower over me. "I said to guard your tongue!" He pulled back his arm and let his fist fly at my face. I tried to evade the blow, but it was too late; my vision shattered as his fist met my left eye and the side of my head exploded with searing pain. The force of the blow knocked me to the side and I stumbled, but Lord Montague caught me, his fingers digging painfully into my upper arms.

"You'd better thank God the women are off with my wife," he thundered. "If someone had heard you ..."

Caught in his grip, all I could do was roll my pounding head in his direction. "What if one of the men heard?"

"I will handle them. Unlike you, they know the meaning of the word obedience." He shook me like a rag doll. "And as for your revelation, take care of it."

"Take care of it?" I repeated dumbly. That was certainly not the reaction I had imagined.

"Or I will," he added, tossing me away like an unwanted toy.

I knocked into the chair, sending it toppling and my hip banged the wooden slats of the floor, my head barely missing the damask-covered wall. For a moment, I couldn't breathe. As I struggled to take in air, my mind whirled. What did he mean? Was he going to let me go? If so, why not make up a lie and have his wife do it publicly today? He certainly wouldn't send me to the country to give birth in private like his mistresses. But he was not remanding me to a workhouse to give birth or die from my travails. What was I to him?

Lungs working again, I struggled to my feet. "That is it? You command it, so this unwanted thing just disappears? Is that truly how you believe life works?" I knew I was overstepping now, but it no longer mattered. I had nothing left to lose.

He was nose to nose with me in the time it took me to blink. "In my position," he growled, picking me up by my neck, "that is exactly how life works."

He tossed me aside like a dirty handkerchief and stalked out, not even looking back when my skull cracked into the wall.

Chapter 4

MARGARET

March 26, 1822
Dublin, Ireland

"No, that will never do," Grace said, gently tracing her fingers over her swollen left eye, reflected in a freshly polished silver tray. She sighed. "Margaret, you will have to serve dinner tonight in place of me."

I nodded. I might not like it, but unpredictability was part of my job now. "Does Mrs. Donahue know?" I asked, pulling on the chain to slowly hoist the freshly lit crystal candle chandelier back into place. It swayed as the chain moved, casting shadows over the mahogany table where, soon, Lord Montague would sup with one of Dublin's up-and-coming elites—the Catholic reformer Daniel O'Connell, and his wife, Mary. The two were on opposite sides of the battle over the future of Catholic rights in Ireland—Lord Montague wanted to keep the old Penal Laws and Mr. O'Connell wished to abolish the remainder—but tonight was an important attempt at an accord, or so Mrs. Donahue had explained when we received our assignments that morning.

"No, I've avoided her so far today, but with the dinner hour approaching, she soon will."

I narrowed my eyes and stepped around her to light the candles on the sideboard. "It is only a black eye. I don't understand why you believe Mrs. Donahue will be displeased. You certainly can't be the first injured woman she has ever had on her staff."

Grace waved away my words like they were spider silk and gestured to her already bruising eye. "There is no way she would allow me to show my face in front of the guests like this. Cook might confine me to the kitchen, but I could never serve. It would shame her to have such a disreputable woman on her staff, and what's worse, it would be an embarrassment to Lord Montague and his whole house.

If his reputation were threatened ..." She shivered, not needing to complete her sentence.

And if I put a toe out of place, Lord Montague will send me back to Howth and my family will have to repay the money he gave them even though it ran out last month. I can't do that to them.

Lord Montague's temper was legendary. Even before I came here, my kinfolk in service to the Irish peerage warned my parents against him, having heard his name bandied about by their employers. Unlike his gentleman father, the younger Montague had a taste for vice—women, drinking, dice, blood sport, and the like.

But what man of rank didn't? That was how my parents justified their decision to send me off.

If they only could have heard the gossip in the carriage about him, they might not have been so hasty. All it took was one woman asking my destination, and they were off, telling me all sorts of stories about my prospective employer. It seemed he was something of a local notable and everyone had their own opinions of his very public vices. By the time the conveyance stopped a few miles from the estate, my ears were blackened—and possibly my soul as well—with gossip that implied Lord Montague wasn't a strict adherent to the sixth commandment and even more so that he harbored a dark temper.

The most often repeated tale took place a few years previous. Lord Montague flew into a rage when a business associate accused him of cheating on the terms of a contract. He challenged his associate to a duel. Instead of settling the matter with sabers so that only first blood was required for satisfaction, Lord Montague insisted on pistols. His associate's obituary appeared in the papers the very next day. As if that wasn't enough, tongues wagged, when Lord Montague was later convicted of manslaughter, he claimed the privilege of peerage to escape punishment. That meant, in essence, I was living with a murderer.

I regarded Grace with renewed suspicion. I might be new to service in this house, but I wasn't a fool. Exactly who had given her this bruise? She claimed to have been hit in the face by a door when another servant opened it as she was approaching, but now that didn't ring so true. One of the footmen had heard her in a heated discussion with Lord Montague the previous day. If she said something that threatened his carefully crafted way of life, if the rumors were true ...

My gaze dropped to the white cuffs of Grace's shirtsleeves, which were resting not in her lap but on her belly. Was it my imagination or did it protrude a bit? Was her dress tighter in the bosom? I glanced at the side seams. Yes, the material on either side was a shade darker, less worn than the rest. It had been let out. Certainly, she could have gained weight, but we took all of our meals together. Grace ate sparingly.

This was not about a black eye at all. It was the consequence of a larger problem. But surely, he hadn't suggested ... Surely, he wouldn't ask her to commit a grievous sin?

My eyes locked on hers. "Grace, is your eye the only thing weighing on your mind?" I lowered my voice even though no one else was near. "You can tell me. I will keep your confidence."

Grace's normally pale countenance flared pink. "I have no idea what you have gotten into your pretty little head." She examined her ragged fingernails, picking at one. "As I was saying, tonight I will plead a megrim and remain confined to my room so no one will be any the wiser."

"Mhmm," I muttered, imagining she would not be in her room at all, but on her way to a clandestine meeting with a disreputable doctor in a dark alley. "What about the next day? Surely a condition such as yours will take more than one night to heal." I turned away and removed the glass chimney from an oil lamp, filling its base. As much as I was concerned about Grace, I couldn't let her problems keep me from my tasks, especially not with Mr. and Mrs. O'Connell arriving within the hour.

"I'll sneak out early to the market, and when I return, I'll tell Mrs. Gallagher I was set upon by ruffians with untoward intent. That will explain my eye and any other soreness I might be unable to hide." Her gaze was flinty, but an unspoken admission hovered behind her bravado, braided into the second conversation that lay just beneath our words. We had at last come to an understanding.

I couldn't imagine being in her place, but she had to know there were other options. She could ask for a leave of absence to attend to an ill relative and bide her time in the country, giving the child away to an orphanage, or even seduce one of the footmen and claim it was his. That was a lesser sin, surely. What she was saying—or rather not saying—didn't just imperil her employment status. It affected her very soul. She would be committing a mortal sin, one that would condemn her to hell. "Perhaps you could …"

"No." Grace held up a hand to halt my suggestion. "Lord Montague made it very clear what would happen if I didn't follow the instructions he gave me to remedy the situation. This is the only way forward."

I looked into her blue eyes, which had welled with unshed tears. How could I in good conscience refuse her? "Very well. If Mrs. Donahue approves, I will take your place at dinner. But promise me you will go to confession tomorrow on your way home from the market."

*****

Standing at attention around the perimeter of the dining room required more stamina than one might think. We had to be certain not to lean on or even brush the walls, all the while remaining perfectly still and keeping a sharp eye out for the needs of the guests. We were to respond to the slightest command, even the flick of a finger or a discreet cough, but not listen in on the dinner conversation.

At first, that was easy. During the early courses of soup and fish, I was so caught up in doing my duty correctly that I could not spare a thought for what was being said. But by the time the roast goose with apple and herb stuffing had been distributed, my shoulders had relaxed and I breathed a little easier. Facing the couples around the dining table, my back to the yellow damask wall covering, I retreated into the shadows. While my eyes flitted from wine glass to plate, waiting for one to need refilling or the other removal, my ears became attuned to their words. The conversation had shifted from the airy topics of social gossip over the early courses to a heavy religious and political debate along with the progressing meal.

"I hear you're still campaigning for the Papists, eh Daniel?" Lord Montague remarked, spearing a piece of fowl with his fork, but not looking up at his guest.

I shuddered at the slur. The Penal Laws had been in effect for the last century and a half, splitting our country in two and robbing Catholics of our land, our liberty, and our right to openly practice our faith. As a result, the gentry were now nearly all Protestant and most Catholics were poor … as desirable as mold. Men like Mr.

O'Connell had helped ease the stranglehold of the laws a wee bit, giving us back our ability to own land and vote, but there was much progress left to be made.

"Still siding with our oppressors, are you?" Mr. O'Connell retorted, his gaze directed squarely at his host.

"Why should I care about the Catholics? They should do what my family did two generations ago and convert. It would solve all their problems," Lord Montague said, as though no other option was even worth considering.

Mr. O'Connell sighed. "James, faith is not something most people can discard like a soiled stocking, only to replace it with a new one as suits. The very fate of our souls is at stake, yet you speak as though we are asking you to offer an opinion on the proper color of our waistcoats for Sunday dinner."

Lord Montague shook his head. "You are wasting your time throwing in your lot with the lower elite and those who hang on their coattails. Your passion for Parliament tells me you intend to seek a place there one day if the law is changed."

"I never said ..."

"Don't deny it. I can smell ambition—though you do a fine job in cloaking yours in frankincense. I'm telling you, this latest idea of a Catholic Association is a stain on your political reputation. No one wants a populist in Westminster."

Mr. O'Connell lay down his knife and fork gently, leaning into Lord Montague and softening his tone. "Perhaps *you* don't, but thousands of your fellow citizens would disagree. They need a voice. Time and again I have heard you complain about the nuisance of beggars in the streets. Abolishing these antiquated laws would reverse their fortunes. If I don't represent them, who will? You? I've seen your maneuvering. It's clear you'll one day seek a seat in the House of Lords."

Lord Montague regarded his political and religious enemy coolly. "Believe what you will."

"I will and I do. For all our differences, I know one thing—we both wish to be acknowledged by those who hold sway over the future of this country, and I believe we would both fare better in their eyes if we could work together rather than be constantly at loggerheads. Even the Marquess Wellesley sees the wisdom in Catholic freedoms being restored while preserving the rights of

Protestants. We don't seek to take anything away from you. Is there no way for us to compromise?"

Lord Montague snorted. "That is like asking when the lion and the lamb will lie down together."

"You are the lion, I presume?"

Lord Montague nodded and bit into another forkful of food.

Mr. O'Connell sighed. "James, if no one is willing to bend, Catholics and Protestants will never live in Ireland as Christian neighbors, not really. There is too much inequity. I realize you benefit greatly from this arrangement, but can you not see what holding all the power in Protestant hands is doing to the Catholics? You may as well have enslaved us."

Lord Montague swallowed a mouthful of food. "You have done well enough, with your law degree and notoriety."

"I am an outlier," Mr. O'Connell said. "But you have a point. I can use my position to my advantage and so can you. Please, join with me in supporting my new association. If the peerage sees an influential Protestant is involved, they will take us much more seriously."

Lord Montague scoffed. "And betray my own? That would be political suicide. And for what, the support of a few social climbers? Not even if you offered me the keys to Heaven itself."

Before Mr. O'Connell could offer a rebuttal, Lady Montague piped up. "Perhaps you should ask Miss Catherine McAuley to join your group. You seem two sides to the same coin."

"Yes, both of you are keen on folly," her husband chuckled darkly.

Mr. O'Connell wrinkled his brow. "Who is this?"

"You do not know?" Lady Montague responded, his voice ripe with scandal. "This spinster inherited a veritable fortune in Coolock House—surely you know where that is?" Her tone dripped condescension.

Even I knew where it was, about an hour outside the city on foot. If only I had known of its owner's good fortune a few hours earlier, I could have recommended Grace plead aid from this Catherine rather than risk her life and her reputation as she was currently doing. I raised my eyes to the ceiling as though I could see through it to her attic bedroom. Was she yet at her appointment, or had she returned? *Lord bless her and forgive her for she knows not what she does.*

When Mr. O'Connell indicated he knew the place, Lady Montague continued. "Well, she is talking to anyone who will listen about how she wishes to open a school or foundling house or some such nonsense on the property. This Popish spinster, this woman who came from nothing, whom no one knew until she became an heiress, inherited more money than her family could hope to see in six generations and *this* is what she does?" Lady Montague turned to Mrs. O'Connell, clearly expecting a mirror to her outrage.

Instead, Mrs. O'Connell merely blotted her lips with her napkin and gestured for one of the other maids to remove her plate. "She has the right to live her life as she pleases."

Lord Montague lifted his glass slightly, my signal to come forward and replenish his wine. "Only because the father is dead and her brother is weak-willed," he muttered. "She needs a husband to direct her."

"That's just it," Lady Montague turned to her spouse. "She shows no interest in acquiring a husband. What does she believe she can do on her own?"

I cleared a few more plates, and their voices receded as I descended the stairs to the kitchen, two maids trailing behind me. The cook was just plating the individual blancmange jellies when the door shut behind us. When we returned with dessert, Lady Montague was still railing.

"Thank goodness she lives outside the city," she said. "I hear she has already taken in a few runaways in addition to the children of relatives. As though a single woman could teach them anything." She tittered as though the thought was ridiculous.

"Well, I think she is very brave," said Mrs. O'Connell.

"As do I." Mr. O'Connell slapped the table decisively. "I will visit her on the morrow to inquire how I might assist." He gave Lord Montague a pointed look.

By the time I stepped in to remove Lord Montague's plate, his fist had tightened on the arm of the chair and his neck was flushed— telltale signs of his temper rising. Mr. O'Connell likely didn't know him well enough to notice, but the other maids, footmen, and I exchanged worried glances.

Lady Montague must have been aware of the subtle changes in her husband's demeanor as well, for she dismissed us with a polite nod and swiftly rose. "Mrs. O'Connell, will you join me in the parlor for a digestive?" She held her hand out to her guest. "We should leave the men to their whiskey and conversation."

*****

I wiped away the sweat from my brow with the back of my forearm and blinked, forcing my blurry vision clear again. Along with serving at table came the washing up, and as I was the newest, the other maids were allowed to retire long before I. Finally, even Cook headed to bed after assuring herself the cookfire was safely banked for the night.

I had just finished drying the last of the cookware when the hall clock chimed once. My shoulders sagged with fatigue. I would have to be up in four hours and I still had to see to the lamps in the dining room. I also wanted to check on Grace. Even if she was sleeping, I needed to assure myself that she had returned hale and whole, especially before the dramatics she intended at daylight. Drying my hands on my apron and hanging it on a peg by the door, I snuffed out all the candles save the one I used to light my path, and trudged up the back staircase.

I pushed open the door to the dining room, wincing at the additional light. I lowered the chandelier and snuffed out the candles, plunging the room into deep shadows illuminated only by moonlight. Next, I turned down the wicks in the oil lamps until they were extinguished. After making one more circuit of the room, I knelt to tend the fire, but found it already tucked under a blanket of ashes, its soft orange glow ready to be awakened with the dawn.

Turning toward the door, I covered my mouth with a hand to stifle a yawn.

"Stay a while, Miss Kelly."

The masculine voice startled me and I turned to find Lord Montague ensconced in a chair cloaked in darkness save for a ray of silver light illuminating a diagonal slash of his face. In my haste to complete my duties and be abed, I had failed to notice him.

I bobbed a quick curtsey, hand still clasped to my racing heart. "Lord Montague. Forgive me; I did not see you there. Is there something I can do for you?"

Lord Montague stood, steadying himself on a cane he kept mostly for show, watching me with glazed eyes, a nearly empty cut crystal glass of whiskey in his left hand. "I'm certain there is." His voice was husky and slightly slurred, giving his words a lazy drawl, as though they were as weary as he appeared. He raked his gaze down my face to my breasts and then back again.

Hopefully he wouldn't notice I had removed the white smock meant to cover my black dress and reprove me for being out of uniform. Surely, he would understand given the lateness of the hour. However, the longer he leered, the clearer it became it was not the uniform he was staring at, but my body underneath. Suddenly self-conscious, I crossed my arms over my chest as though I was as naked as his eyes wished me to be.

He came toward me. I took a step back, trying to maintain a respectable distance, once, and then again, until my hips bumped the long end of the dining table. I tried to step sideways around him and out of his path.

"Allow me to refill your glass," I said, reaching to take it from him, anything to remove myself from the orbit of the lust reflected in his eyes. I was not about to become another casualty of this rich man's disregard for those in his employ.

Lord Montague moved the glass out of my reach like a schoolyard bully. He downed its contents in a single gulp and chucked the glass onto the table, not even flinching when it shattered. His eyes never strayed from my face. "I wasn't referring to another drink," he purred, running the tips of his index and middle fingers up my neck to my chin, and leaning in, forcing me to bend slightly backward, my forearms on the table. "I was thinking of a different type of assistance."

My limbs were shaking, muscles trembling from my own weight, nerves urging me to run. I swallowed hard, forcing myself to look him in the eye. "I'm sure I do not know of what you speak."

He chuckled darkly. "Oh, but I think you do." He tossed his cane aside and reached around me, placing a hand on my waist, the other still resting on my jaw. He breathed in deeply, as though inhaling my scent, which after a night of serving and washing, couldn't possibly be pleasant. But he didn't seem repulsed; if anything, he seemed to enjoy it. "These ladies with their powders and their perfumes all smell like over-gilded lilies." He unbuttoned the top three buttons of my blouse, rubbing his cheek against the exposed tops of my breasts. "But you, no—you smell like a woman, that mixture of sweat and musk and pure femininity."

Bile rose in my throat and I squirmed beneath him, trying to dislodge myself. "Lord Montague, you must stop. Please. This isn't proper ... your wife ..."

His gaze snapped to mine, thunder in his eyes and a storm billowing across his features. "My wife is no concern of yours," he snarled. He grabbed my chin, squeezing hard before shoving my head back. It hit the table with a thud and a few small shards of crystal lodged into my scalp. "I am Lord of this house and what I want, I shall have. Do you hear me?" He jerked my face back toward him. Without waiting for me to answer, he continued. "When I hired you, I told you your first duty was to me, did I not?"

This time he apparently wished me to reply, for he loosened his grip upon my throat. "Yes, my Lord." I croaked. He must have bruised my vocal chords.

My subservience appeased him. "Good. I knew you were a smart girl." A self-righteous smile curved his lips. "Now, let's take a look at you."

He ripped open my blouse, sending its buttons flying and exposing my corset and the small, single decade rosary tied within its ribbons. His eyes widened as though he had discovered I was really a man in disguise. He ripped the rosary from my stays and held it up between us, shaking it at me, the crucifix and finger loop glinting in the low light.

"What is this?" he roared. "You little Papist whore! You lying little bitch! All this time you've been eating my food and using my fuel and you are loyal to that demon in Rome!" His palm met my cheek with a crack that sent an instant wave of pain radiating through the side of my face, momentarily blinding me. My head whipped to the side, one hand instinctively covering the injury, the other striking out at him in self-defense.

Lord Montague grabbed my fists and had both arms pinned above my head before I could react. I lay on the table, crushed beneath his weight. He pressed himself into me, his intentions clear as the bits of crystal slicing into my skin.

No. That was one sin he would not commit with me. *Mother Mary, save me. Virgin of Virgins, protect me.* I struggled, trying to kick out, to find purchase before he could lift my skirt or fumble with his trousers. He pressed his lips to mine and I turned my head, trying to preserve what modesty I could. There, next to my temple, lay a large chunk of crystal, the half of the glass that had not broken upon impact. If I could just free one of my hands, I would have a chance.

I twisted my wrists in his grip and when he came toward me for another rough kiss, I sunk my teeth into his lip until I could taste the metal in his blood. He cried out and staggered back a step, clutching at his mouth. I grabbed the jagged chunk of glass and swung it at his head. It connected with his temple with a thud, ripping a mighty gash that stained the tablecloth crimson before he hit the floor.

Chapter 5

GRACE

Margaret burst through the door, jolting me from nightmares of dark back streets and shadowy women holding sharp objects. For a befuddled moment, I thought they had been thrust through the veil between sleeping and waking with me, but then I realized Margaret was hissing my name.

"Grace! Grace! Wake up!"

I raised my head from the pillow. "What? What is going on?" I squinted at her in the dim moonlight. She was on her knees beside my cot, hair wild and loose when it should have been tucked under its cap. Crusted tracks of tears marred her cheeks. And when she removed her hand from my shoulder, a smear of blood remained. My heart gave a thump of alarm. "You're bleeding! Tell me what happened."

She shook her head. "I can't. There's no time." She glanced over her shoulder toward the door. "They'll be after me soon." Fresh tears started to fall. "I panicked. I didn't know where else to go."

Jesus, Mary, and Joseph, what had she done? Fully awake now, I gripped her chin firmly between my thumb and forefinger, forcing her to look up at me. At this angle, her left cheek appeared swollen. "Margaret, I need you to tell me what happened so I know what to do."

She merely shook her head and dropped her eyes to the bedclothes.

I took a deep breath, trying to calm the impatience and anxiety bubbling in my chest. "Did Lord Montague do this to you?" I asked, brushing my fingertips over her cheek.

She flinched, then nodded.

"And did you fight back?"

Another nod.

Now we were getting somewhere. She was here, so she had escaped, but why was she so scared? "You said 'they' would be after you ... not 'he' would be after you. Is there a reason why Lord Montague can't pursue you himself?"

Her head bobbed up and down and her shoulders began to shake.

I cursed under my breath. "Is he ... did you ... is he dead?" I could barely force the words past my lips.

"I don't know. I don't think so."

"But he is injured?"

"Yes." The word was little more than a whisper.

I breathed out again, this time loudly through my nose. She had to get out of here, that was certain. I may have slept through it—copious amounts of whiskey to chase away my earlier sin and numb the pain had seen to that—but the other servants would have heard the commotion and would be rising to investigate.

"Where did this happen?"

"The dining room."

Inwardly, I groaned. That was only two floors below us and easily accessible. If even one footman had gone in search of the sound, he had likely already found Lord Montague. She had to leave before they quarantined everyone for questioning. But she was such an innocent little lamb, she likely wouldn't know how to make it out of the house unscathed, much less get to full safety.

I shook the covering off my pillow and held it out to her. "Here's what you're going to do. Put anything of value you own in here." I swung my legs around, wincing as a bolt of pain sliced through my abdomen, and began to rise.

She put out a hand to help me up. "What are you doing?" she asked as I pulled on my uniform dress over my nightshirt and slipped my feet into my boots.

"What does it look like?" I asked, tying my robe over my clothes and gesturing for her to do the same. "I'm helping you escape."

To her credit, Margaret asked no more questions, just followed me out into the hallway, which was teaming with whispering servants. Normally, that would alarm me, but tonight it might provide the extra cover we needed to escape undetected. After all, if the other servants were milling about, at least they could say they'd seen us.

Snippets of rumor reached my ears as we descended the stairs.

"Lord Montague ... injured."

"Attempted robbery, that's what I heard."

"No, don't wake her Ladyship. 'Tis best she does not know."

"Dazed and angry as a hornet, but very much alive."

I breathed a small sigh of relief as we reached the kitchen, which was blessedly empty. We were so close now, and Margaret hadn't killed our employer. *Thank you, Lord.* I paused at the hearth and reached into the jar where we kept a small amount of money for market incidentals.

Margaret grabbed my hand before I could pocket the coins. "Grace, what are you doing? You'll be sacked for sure."

I shook my head at her. "Mrs. Gallagher won't notice until morning and when she can't find you, she'll think you took it for the morning shopping." I lit a small lantern. "By the time she figures it out, you'll be far away." I shed my robe into the basket where we placed the soiled towels and motioned for her to do the same. "Put on your cloak."

*****

Once out in the foggy night, Margaret and I slipped down through the silent garden and made our way into town. The usual night watch was out, but in the dense fog, it wasn't difficult to evade them. In truth, I appreciated the excuse to pause in the shadows; my belly cramped occasionally and I suspected my undergarments would be soiled red in the morning. Sense urged me to return to the manor where I could lie still and heal, but I wanted to see Margaret to her final destination at this McAuley woman's home in Coolock, where she had just told me she hoped to seek shelter.

"Do you know the risk you are running ... the danger you are putting this stranger in? Lord Montague could have you arrested and flogged. Or even worse—if he insists you tried to kill him, you could be hanged." My voice came out thick with fear. "You'll be compromising this woman's reputation, you know. No one who harbors a fugitive of justice can be looked on with respect."

"What else would you have me do?" she snapped, beginning to shake. "My family would never allow me back under their roof if I left this job in dishonor. I have nowhere to go and I couldn't let him have his way with me. That would make me ..."

I stopped abruptly, whirling on her. "Would make you what? A slattern like me?"

Silence hung between us until she put out a consolatory hand. "I'm sorry. I didn't mean ..."

I waved her away and resumed walking, rubbing a sore spot on my abdomen. "We each make our own choices. Now we must protect you from yours. What will you do if this Catherine refuses to help you?"

She shrugged. "From what Lady Montague said at dinner, she's open to taking in girls who need help. I have to at least try." She sighed. "It is this or pray I can afford passage back to Howth."

We walked in silence for a while. I briefly entertained the idea of staying with her if Miss McAuley had enough space, but then quickly dismissed it. My place was with Lord and Lady Montague. I had only a short time left on my contract and then I could seek employment where I willed. Maybe I could even send for Margaret then, if she hadn't found other work.

A plan was just taking shape in my mind as Coolock House came into view.

Wrought iron gates barred the path to the gatehouse and the main house beyond. We would have to wait until morning to make our inquiries. No matter. I sank to my knees and leaned my forehead against the cool metal. Margaret slumped beside me, her back against a stone pillar, eyes closed. I snuggled against her and soon we were both asleep.

The trill of a robin woke me at dawn. Light was just beginning to slash the blue-black sky with streaks of gold, illuminating the land beyond the gates. On either side of a dirt carriage path, acres of greening lawn spread out toward the horizon and in the garden, sprouts poked out their heads from soil, awakening from winter slumber. The face of the gatehouse, save for a door and two windows, was covered in tiny green shoots beginning to poke through brittle brown cascades of ivy. Inside, light flared, and was followed by a steady warm glow as its caretaker lit an oil lamp in preparation for the day.

When I turned back to Margaret, she was awake. "I should leave you now," I said, standing and placing a reassuring arm on the small of her back. "The servants are beginning to rise, so someone should be with you soon."

Margaret turned to me, confusion clouding her weary eyes. "What do you mean? Aren't you staying with me?" She clutched at my hand. "I thought we would both seek shelter here."

A wan smile played at my lips. "No. I merely wished to see you safely off. I'm due to pretend I've fallen into a scuffle in the market, remember?" I squeezed her hand tightly. "If both of us are missing, the whole household will notice. But if only you are gone and I distract them with my dramatic early morning encounter, it will buy you a few more hours of safety."

"But you mustn't ..."

She was cut off when, on the far side of the gate, the gatehouse door creaked open and a man emerged clad in knee breeches, a dark shirt, wool stockings, and heavy boots, ready for a day of work. He kissed a woman who stood on the threshold and she set out for the main house, while he turned our way.

While Margaret was distracted watching them, I hugged her and slipped a few coins from the purse I had stolen from the kitchen into her hand. I would need the rest to pull off my ruse. "If you have need of me, send word and I will meet you at the Fitzwilliam Street gate. I promise the same." I hugged her tightly. "Goodbye, my friend. May God bless you."

Before she could respond, I turned and fled into the trees, brushing hot tears from my cheeks.

Over my shoulder, the caretaker greeted Margaret, and she told him she was there to see Miss McAuley. My steps slowed, ears pricking. His reply was too low for me to hear, but the rattling of the gates as he bid her to enter was all the answer I needed.

Chapter 6

MARGARET

The sun had nearly cleared the treetops when the woman we had glimpsed earlier ushered me from the foyer into the main house. My eyes were immediately drawn to a narrow, curving staircase with bright red carpeting, tracing it as it spiraled upward several stories. Peering over one white rail were four pairs of eyes, all less than eight or nine years old. These must be the nieces and nephews Lady Montague mentioned.

The servant followed my gaze to where the children watched us curiously. They had stepped into the light, and now it was clear they were still in their nightclothes. "Always up with the sun, those wee ones." The woman shook her head and introduced herself as Mrs. Doyle, the head housekeeper. "Miss McAuley will see you before the household departs for Mass."

I followed her into an east-facing parlor lined with windows, providing an excellent view of an orange and gold sky. A set of cherrywood chairs faced a small table, on which a tea service had been laid out. In one chair, a straight-backed woman sat reading a small book. When she heard us, she looked up, her blue eyes bright with joy. She crossed herself with her rosary crucifix and set the book aside.

Mrs. Flynn introduced us and poured me a cup of tea, which I really did not want, her husband having graciously allowed me to partake of their oatcakes and tea while we waited for the appropriate hour for guests to call. But it would be rude to decline, so I took the cup and focused my attention on the slim, blonde woman before me.

Miss McAuley grasped my hand warmly. "Please, won't you sit? It sounds like you've had a harrowing night. Tell me what I can do for you."

The woven rush seat of the chair creaked and gave slightly as I settled into it. I met Miss McAuley's gaze again, expecting to see suspicion or censure there, but found only kindness. Still, I fumbled with the pleats of my black uniform, suddenly seeing a bloodstain I hadn't noticed in the darkness. My eyes flitted about the room as I listened to the sounds of her household beginning their day, acutely aware of how much I was interrupting and inconveniencing them.

"I ... I ..." I couldn't find the words to begin. I cleared my throat, trying to dislodge the lump of anxiety rapidly forming there. "Mrs. O'Connell said you were a kind woman," I began. To my horror and embarrassment, tears spilled uncontrollably from my eyes as words tumbled from my lips ... the events of the night revealed in a rush. The only detail I held back was the name of my employer; if this woman couldn't help me, it would do no good to make accusations that might get back to him.

Miss McAuley handed me her handkerchief and stood, wrapping me in a warm half-embrace. Once I had dried my eyes, she knelt beside me, my hands clasped in her own. "Don't worry yourself anymore. I am certain we can find refuge for you. Why don't you come to Mass with us in Dublin? Entrust your fate to the Lord there and we can begin inquiries as soon as the service is over."

I rose with her and bobbed a curtsey. "Thank you so much for your kindness, ma'am."

Miss McAuley smiled. "Oh now, none of that. And please, call me Catherine."

*****

Two hours later, Catherine and I sat in the parlor of St. Teresa's Convent, our backs straight, hands folded primly in our laps, as we waited for the Mother Superior to join us. While Catherine looked expectantly at the grille, the thick bars that separated the nuns' Carmelite enclosure from the outside world, I stared at the polished wooden floor. *Lord, please let them know of a place that will take me. I beg of you. Have mercy on me, a poor sinner. I am but a weak woman, unworthy of your grace.*

My head shot up at the sound of a curtain swishing back behind the grille. Before us sat a nun dressed in brown robes from neck to toe with a black muslin veil covering her face. To my untrained eyes, she was more wraith than angel. Instinctively, I reached for Catherine's hand. She took it, but didn't flinch as I had.

"Praised be the Blessed Trinity," came a pleasant voice from beneath the veil.

"Now and forever. Amen," Catherine responded.

"What brings you here today, daughter?"

"Mother Superior, this girl's virtue is in danger at her current place of employment. She came to me seeking help and I was hoping your convent's domestic asylum might take her."

The nun shifted in her chair. "On your recommendation, certainly. However, the committee of ladies who hear cases does not meet again until Monday. She will have to return then."

"But, Mother, you do not understand. Her case is a desperate one, I assure you. It is dangerous for her to ever return to that house, much less abide there for two more days. Can you not admit her at once?"

"*We* never admit anyone," said the nun, affronted. "We are cloistered and our job is prayer. Only the secular ladies' committee handles such matters."

"Can't your lay Sisters help? Can you call a special session?" Catherine leaned forward, hands grasping the grille just as mine had her front gate only hours ago. "Please. You have been so helpful in the past."

"I am sorry, but there is nothing I can do." Turning her head toward me she added, "I will pray for you, my dear."

*****

We inquired at several more religious houses, including the Sisters of Charity of Our Lady of Refuge, a ladies' charity group run by Protestant wives, and even at the Quaker meeting house, and were told the same thing at every turn: Nothing could be done until Monday.

"The poor need help today, not next week," Catherine muttered angrily as we left the government building. They had nearly laughed us back down the front steps.

Once we were in the carriage, Catherine pressed her fingertips to her temples. "I cannot think of anywhere else to enquire today. We will have to wait until Monday."

I opened my mouth to object, but she stopped me with a glance. "It is getting late." She peered out the carriage window. "It will be dark soon. Is there somewhere in particular you'd like me to take you for the night? I want to see you safely lodged before returning home myself. You can come to Coolock House again tomorrow. Perhaps then I can find a safe, quiet place for you until Monday."

I blinked at her, unsure I had understood her correctly. "I don't wish to overstep, madam, but mightn't I stay with you tonight?" Surely her house was large enough for one more person, even with the four children and the servants currently in residence. "I'll sleep on the floor or in the hallway if I have to ... in the barn or a garden shed ... anywhere. Please don't send me back. I can't go back there." My voice rose in pitch with each word as I imagined Lord Montague's horrible reaction. He would kill me. The flashing rage in his eyes when I had struggled beneath him was enough to prove him more than capable.

Catherine gently removed my fingers from her skirts, where I had twined them without realizing it. She stroked my cheek. "Of course not. I would never ask that of you. I was wondering if you had friends or other relatives who might take you in for the night, that is all."

I shook my head.

She frowned. "I have family arriving tonight with their children and servants in tow, so I have no spare space; I am giving my bed to my sister, and even Mr. and Mrs. Flynn are taking in additional lodgers. But by the morning, we should know what is what, and be able to sort something out. Do you trust me?" Her blue eyes begged me to say yes.

"Yes."

"Good. I know a shelter on Love Lane that will take you in for the night. They don't accept long-term lodgers, but they will provide what you need tonight." She gave the driver directions to a Dublin address and we set off. "I will return for you on the way to morning Mass."

*****

I was taking a meager meal of small ale, bread, and a hunk of dry cheese when a boy I vaguely recognized, but couldn't place, pushed open the shelter door letting in a blast of cold air. I shivered as he scanned the faces, clearly looking for someone. His eyes lit with recognition when he saw me, and he trotted in my direction.

"Miss Margaret, thank God I found you. Been through most of Dublin lookin'." He took my free hand—the one not grasping my dinner as though someone was going to snatch it away—and tugged me toward the door.

That was when I recognized him. I didn't know his Christian name; the servants all called him Smiddy because he was the blacksmith's junior apprentice at Lord Montague's estate.

His tug grew more insistent. "You hafta come with me. It's Grace."

I leapt to my feet. "Grace? What happened? What is wrong?"

"Don't know, Miss. She was bleedin' when I left and out o' her mind with fever. Asked for you."

My hand flew to my mouth. Oh God. It must be the aftereffects from that procedure. I shouldn't have let her accompany me to Coolock House. I should have tried harder to convince her to stay with Catherine—at least we would have ended up here together, where I could find help for her. I should have …

Smiddy shoved me toward the door. "Let's *go*."

My stomach flipped at the thought of returning to the townhouse, of facing Lord Montague and the consequences of my actions. He couldn't see me. If he did, this would all be for naught. I stopped short, forcing Smiddy to pause as well. I looked down at his round, soot-stained face. "No one can know I am there. Do you understand me? Can you get me in one of the back entrances?"

He gave me a gap-toothed grin. "What's it worth to ya?"

I rolled my eyes and reached into the inner pocket of my gown, producing one of the coins Grace had given me. "This enough?" I gestured to the dingey room around us. "As you can see, I'm not in the best fortunes at the moment."

His smile widened and he saluted me before scampering out into the night and calling over his shoulder. "Leave everything to me."

*****

The lamplighters had finished their rounds by the time the house came into view. I hadn't ever seen it from the road at night, always indoors busy with chores at this hour. I shivered, suddenly grateful for the warm fire that lay just within the walls.

I made for the servant's entrance out of habit, but Smiddy steered me toward the garden through which I had fled the previous evening. "Best you go in this way. Less chance you'll be spotted," he said with a tap to the side of his nose.

He ran off toward the carriage house, and I took the opposite path to the house through the kitchen garden. I was just rounding a hedge when an arm shot out and grabbed me. One hand muffled my scream as the other dug into my upper arm, forcing me into the shadow of a thick evergreen.

"I knew you'd come back for her," Lord Montague scoffed, the woodsy scent of gin on his breath mingling with the pine sap. For a moment, my senses swam and I swayed with fear and disbelief. Lord Montague? What was he doing here? I wriggled until I could turn to face him.

His eyes were cold, glinting like the darkened windows in the moonlight. I bit down on one of his fingers to free my mouth and he sucked in air, cursing as he recoiled to suck his bleeding finger. I opened my mouth to scream for help, but before I could, he tackled me, sending me sprawling. My head hit the ground hard enough to momentarily blind me as pain radiated through my veins, but soon the world swam back into focus.

Lord Montague towered above me, kneeling on my legs so I couldn't hope to free myself. "You really thought you could simply run away and escape the consequences?" He clicked his tongue reprovingly. "No, that is not how the system works. Allow me to demonstrate."

He picked up his cane from where it had fallen in our tussle, holding it not by the handle, but in the middle. "You see, when I hired you, I made clear that I had certain *expectations* from my staff." The word was heavy with inuendo. "Foremost among those is obedience." He raised the cane so that the metal head caught the light. "You not only disobeyed me, you attacked me." He turned his head so I had a clear view of the jagged slash that marred his temple. "And now you have to pay. I will not have any servant thinking she is superior to me."

I flinched, squeezing my eyes shut and curling up like a pill bug to shield myself from his blows. And come they did, raining down on my arms, my chest, and head. Each one was like taking a direct hit from a cannon.

Eventually, he stood but I remained still, sensing that trying to run would not only be painful and likely end in failure, it would make the situation worse. I swiped at a matted strand of hair coated in blood that had stuck to my eye, and tried to speak, but all that emerged from my split and bleeding lips was a groan. I lay still for a few moments, breathing and gathering my strength. Finally, I croaked Grace's name.

Lord Montague sneered, understanding my question. "Don't worry about her." He glanced up at the top floor, where all the windows were dark. "She's asleep in her bed, 'recovering' from the beating she took in the market today. Clever idea, that. And it *almost* worked."

He took slow steps around me, circling like a wolf, deciding how to go in for the kill. "When Mrs. Gallagher reported you missing, I realized Grace must have helped you escape and used her 'experience' at the market to cover her actions. But don't you worry, I made sure she really is in pain tonight."

"The Devil take you," I spat blood, a tooth hitting the ground along with it.

"Wish it all you will, but you'll be the one meeting him tonight." Lord Montague shook his head. "It was almost too easy to lure you here. Smiddy was more than willing to say whatever I told him, provided his purse was a little heavier for his efforts. And you—so trusting. What is it about women that makes you want to see the best in everyone? Both you and Grace would be much better off if you hadn't grown attached to one another."

"Don't blame her for caring about me. It's more than you've ever done."

Lord Montague yanked me to my feet. My muscles screamed in pain, the sinews in my arms threatening to pop free of my bones and leave me a defenseless ragdoll.

We were so close, I could taste his bitter breath. "At least she will live to regret it." He swung his cane twice in quick succession, sweeping my feet from beneath me and then bringing it down onto my skull.

Chapter 7

GRACE

A crack like lightning striking a tree startled me from a dreamless sleep. Instinctively, I sat up, seeking the source of the sound. Pain lanced through me, radiating from just below my belly outward in all directions until my vision swam with white-hot stars.

"Grace?"

My name reached me from far away, echoing as though I were underwater.

"Grace."

I blinked rapidly, trying to clear my head. Blackness overtook me for a moment and then Mrs. Donahue was there, matronly and motherly, more so than anyone I had ever known.

"Grace, dear, do lie down. You will strain your stiches."

I smiled, wanting nothing more than to please this woman, whom I knew, but didn't. For a few moments I floated there, unaware of anything but the pain slowly abating. When I could breathe again, I asked, "What was that sound?"

Mrs. Donahue hovered over me. "What sound?"

I shook my head, trying to describe it. "It … it was like lightning. Is it storming?"

She turned her head, presumably to look out the window. "No. The moon and stars are shining."

"But I heard …"

"You were probably dreaming, having a nightmare. With what you have been through today, I shouldn't be surprised."

"What I …" I whispered. What was she talking about? What had I been through? The last thing I remembered was leaving Margaret at Miss McAuley's estate. Then … nothing.

"Yes, dear." Mrs. Donahue stroked my forehead and temples lightly. "You've had quite a shock. You were set upon at the market. Don't you remember?"

Remember? I searched the back of mind for something, anything, that resembled the words she was saying. No. There was nothing.

I recalled sneaking out of the house and down Dublin's back lanes. There I met a woman, who took me into her dank residence and promised me she could fix everything. I gave her some of the coins I had stolen from Cook's expenses tin.

Then everything was sound and fury. I cried out as something blunt was shoved between my thighs. Strong arms held my wrists and ankles, preventing any escape from the pain. Then the scraping began. I screamed and screamed and screamed. I felt as though my stomach was being pulled out from between my legs. I feared my heart would explode from the strain.

Then I was home again in my own bed. Margaret woke me and I took her to a house, some grand affair from my daydreams. But then I left her. I would never do that, would I? Why did I leave her? Did I leave her? Oh Margaret, where are you?

I reached out to Mrs. Donahue. "Where is Margaret? I want to see Margaret."

"I don't know, my dear. She's been gone for quite a while now. But don't you worry. Lord Montague is looking for her. Here, take this." She held a small vial to my lips and tipped it back, urging me to swallow the sweet liquid that immediately soured on my tongue.

Lord Montague. His name stirred something in my mind. Margaret. He was the reason she left. She had injured him. But then why did I seem to see his face in my mind, leaning over me, hands wrapped around my throat?

I lay back on the pillow and closed my eyes, trying to reconcile the rest of my memories with Mrs. Donahue's account. On my way back to the townhouse I passed through the market. That much I recall. I don't remember being accosted like Mrs. Donahue said, but yet ... I must have been. Flashes of memory, jagged recollections of blows and bruises played through my mind. A shouting male voice telling me I should have listened. I should have remembered my place.

And then that sound. That dreadful noise, like bone breaking. I had heard it before. I struggled to recall where, but I couldn't seem to catch my thoughts. My mind was growing fuzzy around the edges, thoughts melting together like butter and sugar in cake batter. Beaten ... beating ... my head spun dizzily until I thought I would faint, or perhaps wretch. Blessedly, sleep took me first. But not before I placed the source of the sound.

It was Lord Montague's cane.

Chapter 8

CATHERINE

May 1822
The River Liffy
Dublin, Ireland

My stomach had clenched when Margaret failed to meet our carriage for Mass on Sunday morning. Now, weeks later, as the constabulary dredged the Liffy, it threatened to jump out of my mouth entirely.

If only I had allowed her to come back home with me that night, I would not be standing here, and she wouldn't be ... what? Alone and afraid? Wandering the streets? Holed up with a stranger? Back with her abusive master? Dead? I had no idea the fate that had befallen her. How could I, who prided herself on charity toward the poor, not have found a scrap of carpet or a blanket on which she could lay her head for a single night? I was as bad as the innkeepers who turned away Mary and Joseph before the Christ child was born.

I will do everything I can to find her. I repeated the vow I'd made to myself several times a day since it became clear something had happened at the inn. The proprietor remembered her, but did not see her leave. It had been a busy night, he claimed, and when he looked up, she was gone, away to the common room to sleep, he assumed.

I had paced the halls of Coolock House for the remainder of Sunday, hoping Margaret would appear, sheepish for missing our meeting. I was eager to inform her that I had found a place for her. The following day, I began asking around the village, but no one had seen her. She hadn't given her employer's name, so I had no way of knowing which house to call upon. All I could do was hope someone would report her to the authorities as a runaway servant in the hopes of finding her quickly, even if it was her much-dreaded employer.

To that end, I visited the Royal Irish Constabulary a few days later. After asking if they had heard of any woman matching her description and receiving a negative answer, I asked them to notify me if that changed.

"What business is it of yours? You clearly are not her mistress or her mother, so why do her whereabouts matter to you?"

"I feel responsible for her welfare. Isn't that enough?"

He snickered. "Not according to the law." He scribbled something in the book on his desk, flipped to a previous page, and then looked up at me again. "You smuggling them? She one of yours?"

"Of course not!" I instinctively defended myself. But he was right to ask. Poor women were not only contracted into service in Dublin but also shipped illegally to the United States for labor or marriage, or sold for even darker purposes to clients in the Orient.

I had been thinking about these unfortunate women a lot lately. Coolock House was a blessing but, as Margaret's plight demonstrated, it was limited in capacity. If I was truly going to make a difference, I needed more space. To that end, I hired an agent to help me scout land in Dublin.

Taking a deep breath, I told the Constable about my plans to build a refuge for just such women, which would keep them off his streets and out of jail cells because they would learn meaningful work.

"Ah, a do-gooder. Just what I needed."

I closed my eyes, sensing I was getting nowhere. "Constable McCarthy, I haven't all day to debate with you. Perhaps a donation to your department would fix my name in your memory if you hear any rumors of a woman who might be Margaret?"

The officers carried the body of a young woman up the steep embankment on a stretcher. To preserve her modesty, they had covered her whole body in a cloth, so I could not discern her identity from a distance, but still my hands shook on my rosary beads. As another bead slipped through my fingers and I added silently, *Holy Mary, Mother of God, whomever this girl may be, safeguard her soul and commend it to Jesus' mercy.*

"Miss McAuley." One of the officers beckoned me toward him, the silver buttons on his blue coat gleaming in the sunlight. When I reached his side, he fixed me in a stern gaze. "I strongly object to you being here. This business is nothing for a woman. Send your father or brother in your stead. Men are much better equipped to handle such things."

I stared him down. He was not the first—and would likely not be the last—man to balk at my independence. "With all due respect, officer, I am a spinster, so I have no husband. My father is dead and my brother knows better than to interfere in my business. So, if you please ..." I gestured toward the stretcher.

"Nosy woman. Damn constable's gone soft," he muttered under his breath as he lowered the sheet, revealing the girl's bloated face.

It was not Margaret.

Nor was the next, or the girl after that, or any of the others over the next two years.

PART II

OPPORTUNITIES

Chapter 9

CATHERINE

April 1824
Merrion Square
Dublin, Ireland

By the time Mr. Callaghan's will finally made its way through probate, two years had passed, and I knew the passages of the court buildings as well as the halls of Coolock House. Mr. Powell and several Mr. Callaghan's relatives had tried to contest it on grounds that were at least somewhat plausible, such as it being incorrectly filed or that Mr. Callaghan was unduly influenced to name me as his heir, or as flimsy as that as a woman—and an unmarried Catholic at that—I had no legal right to inherit.

Although my lawyer, Mr. Andrews, assured me I had nothing to be concerned about—the probate process would simply take time—at first I was troubled by the idea those avaricious men would find a loophole in the law that would take away everything I had just gained. Memories of growing up indigent persisted and I felt weighed down by guilt that I might once again be a burden to others. At night I dreamed of sleeping on the cold, hard floor of a relative's house as I had as a teen or having to beg my brother for bed and board as I did before the Callaghans took me in.

Yet I knew deep in my soul the rightness of Mr. Callaghan's will. If I had learned nothing else in my decades in their service, it was that he left no details to chance. As an apothecary, he understood the important of proper measure down to the milligram, so he would have been just as exacting in his legal affairs. Trusting in this and in God's divine providence, every morning I banished the lingering fear of my nightmares through prayer, lifting my troubles up to Heaven for Jesus to solve so that I could focus on more immediate needs.

My proudest accomplishment was that the school at Coolock House was thriving. Claire had completed her studies and was off in France, studying teaching methods under the patronage of a wealthy family who planned to hire her as a governess, and Johanna had become my assistant. Thanks to a sum of money set aside that was not part my contested inheritance, I expanded the school, taking in girls from farther afield and instructing the nieces and nephews who had lived with me for the last several years.

Most of my daylight hours were spent with them, but at night I found myself a sought-after member of Dublin society. Even though my inheritance was still being decided by the court system, it elevated my social status in ways I never could have imagined. I had been a fixture at the Callaghans' parties and balls for as long as I lived with them, but that was always because of my relationship to them. Now I found myself included in events at other grand homes, my name the one written in graceful looping script on the invitation and announced upon my arrival.

On the last night of the season, I arrived at the home of the infamous Lord Montague, a minor member of the noble class who thought himself akin to a duke, from what I had gathered from the local gossip, which was impossible to avoid at market or even after Mass on Sundays. I had debated whether or not to attend, given his reputation, but many important people would be there and if I had any hope of achieving my dreams once the bequest was settled, I was going to need connections in the upper echelons of society.

I was ushered inside a tall brick townhouse on Merrion Square by a beautiful parlor maid, a girl not too much younger than Margaret had been, but whose eyes glinted with naked ambition. I had seen her type before. No doubt she was carefully cataloging the names, ranks, and estimated worth of everyone who passed through the doors. She would do well, this one. No life of servitude lay in her future; she was simply biding her time to find someone who could lift her up into respectability where she felt she belonged.

My arrival was announced to the guests in the drawing room and I was free to mingle as I chose. Many of the faces were familiar to me from past dinner parties, but I knew neither the host nor the hostess and required a formal introduction to approach those with whom I was unacquainted. Fortunately, someone found me.

"Miss McAuley?" A jovial voice I knew well called my name from over my shoulder. I turned to find myself looking into the eyes of The Liberator himself, Mr. Daniel Connell. We had met several years earlier when he came to offer his condolences after Mr. Callaghan's death and then again after he heard of my desire to expand the school at Coolock House. We shared a passion for the rights of Catholics, especially the poor, and were in frequent correspondence.

I held out my hand for him to take. "Mr. O'Connell, it is so lovely to see you again." I turned to his wife, Mary, and greeted her warmly. We were well acquainted from our visits as well as several ladies' groups at St. Teresa's, where we all attended Mass.

"And you as well. How are things at Coolock House?" Mr. O'Connell asked.

"Busy as ever. We have a dozen students now and my eldest nieces are helping me teach." I beamed, proud to my core of how they were thriving under my affection.

"If I may be so bold, how is probate progressing?"

"There has been little change, I'm afraid."

Mr. O'Connell frowned. "I'll see if there is anything I can do to expedite matters." He winked. "I may know a judge or two."

I laughed. "That would be much appreciated. "Now, tell me, how is your work with the Catholic Association? I've heard you will soon be opening membership to the poor?"

Mr. O'Connell sipped his drink. "Yes. They can be a part of the movement for only a penny a month. Even the poorest can beg that amount or even find it discarded in the gutter. I want all Catholics to have a voice. Mark my words, one of these days, the forty-shilling freeholders will choose to vote their consciences rather than following their landlord's wishes, and then we will have a true insurrection on our hands."

"On that day we shall all fear for our fortunes," a tall man with a pale, willowy woman on his arm put in with heavy sarcasm as he approached.

"As you should, Lord Montague," Mr. O'Connell retorted.

So, this was our illustrious host. I regarded the man with keener interest. Like many of the male guests, he wore a tailored black frock coat nipped at the waist over a matching waistcoat and pantaloons, though his were trimmed in elaborate gold embroidery and his cuffs and jabot were frothy white lace. His wife was a vision in a high-waisted, dusty rose taffeta dress that ended in twisting flounces and frills at the hem. Her hair was pinned in an intricate twist topped with feathers, and jewels sparkled at her throat and ears, leaving no doubt these were people of wealth and power.

"Pay him no mind," Lady Montague said, swatting at her husband's arm. "He likes to be surly when you are around," she added to Mr. O'Connell.

Interesting. Clearly these two knew one another well, though town gossip painted them as mortal enemies—the Protestant gentry seeking to preserve the status quo and the Catholic upstart bent on revolution. They certainly did not appear so now, teasing one another and exchanging pleasantries, issues of religion and politics temporarily put aside. Could it be they were two of the rare few who had seen their way past their differences into mutual respect?

Mr. O'Connell caught my eye. "Excuse me," he said to our hosts, "but I would like to introduce Miss Catherine McAuley, heir to the Callaghan fortune."

We exchanged pleasant greetings and the wives excused themselves to freshen up. Mr. O'Connell offered to fetch us both a drink, but I declined.

"Ah, that is right, you do not drink alcohol," Mr. O'Connell said as he turned away. "I will bring you some punch then. I hear it is very good."

"You do not imbibe?" Lord Montague asked, surprised. In a lower tone, he added, "How unusual."

"I do not feel it is healthy for the body or the mind, to say nothing of spiritual peril to which it can lead." I should have stayed silent, for there was no need for me to justify my choices to this man, but something in his tone provoked me to speak.

"I see you are a woman of strong opinions, just as they say." Lord Montague regarded me with something akin to admiration.

"And am I to believe the rumors about you as well?" The question came out more chiding than I had intended.

He pretended not to understand my meaning. "Which ones? Those that sing my praises as a future member of the House of Lords? Yes, those are true." He grinned, his blue eyes sparkling with vanity.

Though not compelling to me, I understood how so many women were enthralled by his good looks and charm. "Come now, Lord Montague, I know what you have been saying about me, that I am ungoverned and in need of a man to control my fortune. However, I assure you I can manage it very well on my own."

He narrowed his eyes and looked down his nose at me, as though unconvinced. "Can you? If the courts find in your favor, is it true you will spend your wealth on the poor?"

I titled my chin up slightly so I could return his gaze with calm assurance. "It is."

"Unbelievable," he muttered into his nearly empty glass. "This sort of well-intentioned but disordered thinking is why women will never hold public office."

"Is that so?"

"Yes. Men have the education and experience to know that by giving hope to the poor, all you are doing is perpetuating a cycle of misery. God has pre-ordained our stations in life and we are meant to remain in the sphere in which he placed us—and for women, that means at side of their husbands."

"And if I do not agree? What will you do then? I am none of your concern." I counted off on my fingers. "I do not live on your lands, I am not employed by you, nor am I related to you or a business associate. Yes, we reside in the same city, but so do thousands of others, yet you don't take an interest in them."

"You are a very attractive woman when your blood is up. Do you know that, Miss McAuley?" The grin he gave me contained so much carnality my stomach flipped in response.

"You're deflecting. I must have hit a nerve. That is why you oppose me so much, isn't it? Because you can't control me. I, an unwed female, dared to rise from poverty to wealth—however accidently—and enter your sphere spouting opposing views. Now you must stop me because you see me as a threat. Well, hear me now. I am not. Just as I do not speak against your political ambitions— though I believe them unwise—so I would kindly ask you to leave my affairs to me."

Lord Montague closed the space between us. "And if I do not, what will you do? Send me to confession? Order me to pray the Rosary? Face it, Miss McAuley. I hold all the cards. I can keep your will tangled up in probate for years if I so desire. I can ensure no contractors work on the projects you dream up. I can have you struck from the registries of society so that no one will speak to you again, much less grant you favors. I may not directly be your Lord, but I can end your ambitions with the snap of my fingers."

"I'd like to see you try."

*****

Mr. O'Connell proved to be a man of his word. In early April, my lawyer and I were called before a judge for the final time. The last challenge to the will had been heard and the judge was about to rule. As I stood next to Mr. Andrews, the long nightmare of my inheritance came to end with the words I has waited two years to hear:

"I see no reason why the will of Mr. William Callaghan should not stand as written. Miss Catherine McAuley is its sole beneficiary. This case is dismissed."

After thanking the judge, I turned to Mr. Andrews. "Well, now that is over, might you recommend a good leasing agent? I am looking to acquire some land."

Over the next month, I walked the whole of Dublin and back at least three times, or so it seemed, looking at parcels of land and buildings to lease. Where to place my new venture was a vexing issue. At first, logic won out and I looked at areas on the river and around the docks, neighborhoods where the poor usually congregate. Even though I was accompanied by my lawyer and my brother, my mere presence drew curious stares. Why were three people of means—and one of them a woman—visiting the paupers and the penniless? While the people I wished to serve called this place home, it was no place for a woman of fashionable society; there was no way anyone would volunteer in these areas, much less give donations to support my cause.

Next, we traveled to the business district, but no one wanted to rent to a woman who would be housing the poor right next door; it was bad for business, they said. Privately, I began to wonder if Lord Montague was making good on his threat.

Even my own brother urged me to give up and try to find another approach.

I didn't want to start over. I wanted to see the plan I held in my mind come to fruition, and I wouldn't stop until it did. One lesson from my father I held onto all these years was to keep moving forward in pursuit of a noble goal.

Disappointed, I turned to my only source of comfort, God. Kneeling before the Blessed Sacrament at St. Teresa's, I begged God to show me a sign that this is what he wanted me to do. I had been so sure for so long, but now with so many doors closed to me, doubt crept in.

What if I had misinterpreted everything? Here I was believing that God was giving me a way to fund my life-long dream of a school and the women's refuge I had longed to build in the wake of Margaret's disappearance. But what if I was wrong? What if God had nothing to do with this and I was simply a fortunate woman who had benefited from the munificence of her employer? I now had more than enough money to retire to the countryside and live out my days entertaining and contributing to charitable causes. But when I tried to imagine that life, something was still missing.

I opened my Bible to the gospel of Luke and began to read. Jesus was teaching the disciples and those who had gathered to hear him speak using parables, trying to make them understand that worry is useless and that they should trust in God, for as long as they remained watchful and did good with what they were given, they would be rewarded. One line in particular caught my attention: "For unto whomsoever much is given, of him shall be much required: and to whom men have committed much, of him they will ask the more."

I meditated on this verse as the carriage transported me to back to Coolock House. This felt like the sign I needed to continue. I had been given much and God wouldn't have put the dream of the house in my heart if I wasn't meant to take action on it. But I was not the only one to whom much had been given; I knew dozens of wealthy Dubliners who might benefit from practicing the principles of this verse through volunteer efforts or donations.

That was it. I needed to locate the house somewhere the poor wouldn't be afraid to approach, but where the wealthy would also be comfortable being seen. That narrowed down my search area considerably.

Later that day, as I examined a map of Dublin, drawing circles around areas where the rich and poor lived only a lane apart, I began to giggle. It was slow at first, but built as I eliminated potential plots that were too small to suit me. By the time I had only a handful left, I was outright cackling. I would be shopping for real estate practically in Lord Montague's backyard. Depending on my final choice, we might even be neighbors.

Chapter 10

GRACE

May 1824
Montague House
Dublin

With the promise of spring just on the horizon, the Montague family prepared to depart for their country estate in Killiney. Outside, wagons held trunks of clothing, small items of furniture, and linens, ready to make the two-hour journey. Our breakfast had been cold meat, cheese, and bread, the remnants of the larder that could not be packed and transported. Even Mrs. Gallagher's precious pans had already been loaded and she stood guard with them, among the first servants to depart.

I stood precariously on a small stool, reaching for the curtain rod to determine why the heavy fabric had snagged and the curtains would not close. Lord Montague planned to rent his townhome while the family resided in the country, but had yet to find a suitable tenant, so we were closing the house up as for winter. I wrestled with two hooks that had somehow become entangled. If I were only a bit taller, this wouldn't be such a struggle.

"Miss Ryan?" Lady Montague called up to me.

I immediately stopped what I was doing and stepped down. "Yes, madam?"

"I would like to have a word with you." Her voice was stern, devoid of all warmth.

She gestured for me to follow her toward the parlor, which had already been prepared for the move, and my stomach twisted. When Lady Montague wished for privacy, the outcome was never good. Around us, sheets had been placed over every item of furniture, including the chandeliers, to protect them from dust. The curtains were drawn and the shutters locked, making it difficult to see and I had to fight to avoid getting my shoe caught in the fabric covering the floor. Why would she bring me in here? Better yet, why would she speak to me directly at all? Mrs. Donahue handled the household affairs, so if I was in some sort of trouble, wouldn't she reprimand me?

I stood in the gloomy room, eyes cast downward, but noticing every shaft of light that managed to squeeze in between the slats of the shutters and make its way around the edges of the curtains. It cast menacing shadows on the floor and gave the room an eerie glow as it diffused into darkness in the corners.

"Miss Ryan, I am here to inform you that your services are no longer needed in this house. You will not be joining us at the manor this summer or ever again."

My head shot up and I had to swallow the incredulous question of "What?" that rang through my head. Did I hear her right? Why was she doing this?

The confusion must have shown on my face, for she answered, "It brings me no joy to do this, for you know as well as I we need more servants in the country, not fewer. But I cannot have you in my employ after what you have done."

What I had done? I had been a model employee since Margaret disappeared, taking over her duties in the scant weeks remaining before the move. I even ceased to fight back when Lord Montague came to me, the Devil's urge upon him. Though that happened less now, ever since young Bess was hired to replace Margaret by day and supplant me at night, or so it seemed. Unlike her predecessor, Bess had none of Margaret's guileless warmth; she possessed a cunning that sharpened her eyes and froze her humanity. She was going to be trouble.

"What am I said to have done?" I asked quietly. She had not addressed me, so I should have remained silent, but what did it matter now?

Lady Montague's frown grew even tighter. "Oh, you truly have had us all fooled, Miss Ryan. You ask with such innocence I am half-tempted to believe you truly are unaware." She regarded me closely, squinting her eyes as though she were weighing the options before her. "If you must know, it has come to my attention that you have been engaging in lewd behavior, even going to far as to try to seduce my husband." At these words she plucked an invisible thread from her sleeve and let it fall to the ground. "Therefore, you are hereby dismissed—without a character."

I could contain my fury and confusion no longer. "But without a character I will not be able to get another job," I cried, desperation sweeping over me like a wave. I wanted to run to her, to fall to my knees and clutch at the fabric of her rust-colored traveling gown and beg for mercy.

"Maybe you can put your acting skills to use on the stage," she retorted.

"Please, madam. I have only a few months left on my contract. You will never see me or hear my name again after that. I promise you. But I have done nothing. You must believe me."

Her eyes flashed with so much anger it was like a whip to my face. "I *mustn't* do anything." She paused, chest heaving with anger. "Do you think I didn't know? That story you concocted about being attacked in the market was as transparent as egg whites. I know the signs of a botched abortion when I see one."

Fleetingly, the question of how a lady such as herself would know such a loathsome thing danced across my mind, but then more practical matters took the lead. "So, you will just leave me here?" My voice cracked as I fought for control. "Where will I go? What will I do?"

Lady Montague stepped to one wall and pulled the tassel handing from the ceiling. A bell sounded.

Bess came bustling in with my old carpetbag in one hand and my bonnet in the other. She smirked at me as she dropped the bag at my feet with a thunk. She handed my bonnet to Lady Montague, who passed it to me in a final gesture of dismissal.

"I had Miss Bannon gather up your things. And lest you think me completely heartless, you will find the wages you are owed inside. That should tide you over long enough to get settled. Goodbye, Miss Ryan."

She nodded to Bess, who grasped my arm above the elbow and began leading me toward the front door, which was closer than the servant's entrance. Heads turned as we rushed through the drawing room and foyer.

Before I could even fully understand what was happening, Bess had pushed me over the threshold, the door already propped open. I stumbled, catching myself just before I would have tumbled headlong down the three stairs to the sidewalk below. As I brushed myself off, the quiet assailed me, every person having stopped what they were doing to gawk. Straightening to my full height, I returned their gazes with a smile, tied my bonnet securely, and set off down Fitzwilliam Place as though I had planned this all along.

*****

When I reached Merrion Square Park, I slipped inside and hid behind a hedgerow. Not only did this give me a relatively safe place to count my coins, but it hid me from the judgmental eyes of the wealthy who frequented the park. The last thing I needed was to be robbed of the last of my money by a misguided thief or accused of stealing it and arrested. Then I would be sent to the gaol or the workhouse for sure. I shivered. There was no way I was going back to the workhouse ever again. I'd die on the streets first.

I opened the carpetbag and plunged my hand into the fabric, past my spare uniform, a few other items of clothing, and one pair of boots. My fingers touched a small irregularly shaped pouch of soft leather. I withdrew it to find that, as promised, it contained my wages. I counted up eight and half pounds. Most boarding houses charged around two pence a night, so including food and other necessities, I had enough money for at most three to four months.

That night I secured a room in a cheap boarding house run by an eccentric woman named Mrs. MacGregor. In her establishment, the kitchen was a communal hearth with a single saucepan, a gridiron, and a frying pan we all shared. Tea was served not in fine china or even ceramic, but in glass jars that threatened to burst if the liquid inside was too warm. While the female tenants took turns cooking and gossiping with Mrs. MacGregor, the men lazed around, smoking or reading the newspaper. Those who were illiterate played at dice or cards—both of which Mrs. MacGregor was banned from playing because she had a tendency to cheat.

"I don't cheat," she'd insist. "I follow me own rules."

Though the constant threat of robbery or rape loomed from outsiders, the long-term lodgers quickly built up a tacit trust and my new life took shape. Meals were simple affairs of bacon, herring or sausage, paired with bread and some tea or beer. Sometimes we pooled our resources to make a stew. After our evening meal, we each retired to our own tiny room, barely large enough to hold a palette and chamber pot, and tried to sleep despite our neighbor's snoring and the scratching of rats in the walls and skittering of roaches across the floors.

From first light until the dinner hour, I answered every ad for a domestic listed in the *Times* and the *Evening Post*, but no one would even see me without a character. Tired of having doors slammed in my face, I began to enquire at taverns, shops, and churches if anyone had heard of available work. My fellow lodgers asked around as well, but every lead turned into a dead end.

Within six weeks, unexpected expenses had taken a chunk out of my meager savings. I had known I'd need to buy my own food, but I hadn't counted on the additional cost of necessities such as crockery, utensils, and soap, not to mention medicine and candles. Soon I was forced to take in clothes for mending, using my valuable candles late into the night to earn enough to keep body and soul united.

Mrs. MacGregor was a surprisingly compassionate proprietress. Even when my rent was late, she always had a good bit of gossip and a warm cup of tea. Despite having a building full of lodgers, I think she was lonely. She often popped in at night to help with the mending or offer me a leftover heel of bread coated in drippings or some cheese. She even occasionally let me work for her, cleaning, running errands, or minding babies or children of clients. It wasn't steady work, but anything helped.

I dreaded the day I would have to say farewell to Mrs. MacGregor, but the lack of coin in my purse didn't lie. Soon I'd have to be moving on. I'd miss that strange old woman.

Chapter 11

CATHERINE

June 1824
O'Malley Real Estate
Dublin, Ireland

As I descended the carriage outside the offices of a real estate firm in downtown Dublin, I felt, more than saw, the stares of those on the street around me. It was not the usual course of things for a woman to walk into a legal or business establishment when she wasn't following her husband. But here was I, alone, doing exactly that.

Pausing in front of the closed door, I took a final moment to contemplate the momentous step I was about to take. When I affixed my name to that contract, there was no going back. Most of my sizable fortune would be gone. I wouldn't be the wealthy heiress suddenly so in demand within Dublin's social circles after years of being ignored or treated like a worthless commoner. I would be a female investor in both land and real estate, something few others could claim; but the true owners of the building I envisioned would be the homeless servant girls, women without hope, and abandoned children who would seek refuge there, and the poor and sick whom we would visit in our homes. This wasn't simply a contract signing; it was a kind of transubstantiation in which my unexpected inheritance became the hope and salvation of lives in the name of mercy.

I shook my head to clear it of such fantasies. I was deluding myself with such lofty thoughts. I was no saint, no heaven-sent prophet declaring the way of the Lord. I was merely a Catholic concerned with the plight of those around me—and a woman at that. A woman who needed to learn to tame her pride. I would build my house amid the stately wealth of the Georgian row houses surrounding Merrion Square and trust that the Lord would take care of the rest. After all, it was his idea; I was merely the instrument through which he worked—the pen in the hand of the Creator, as my beloved St. Teresa of Jesus would say.

I took a deep breath, and as I exhaled, sent up a prayer. *Lord in Heaven, guide my hand this day that I may do you work. May all that I do please you.*

Inside, we were greeted by my spiritual advisors, Fathers Michael Blake and Joseph Nugent, as well as Father Edward Armstrong, the priest administrator of the nearby St. Andrews Chapel—all three of whom would become superintendents of the construction in my stead and have oversight of the building of the house. Behind them stood my chosen architect, John B. Keene, Dennis Lenehan, the builder, and John Curran, the carpenter with whom I had contracted.

"This is a truly selfless and wonderful thing you are doing, Miss McAuley," Father Armstrong said, once the clamor of welcome and introductions had settled. "The entire area will be better for it."

I pushed a breath out through my lips. "You truly believe so?"

He nodded. "I do. And so does he." He gestured beyond the ceiling and sky into the heavens.

"Gentleman, madam," a man I did not know called us to order. "I am Mr. Degnan, representative of the Earl of Pembroke, from whom you are leasing this land." He inclined his head slightly toward me.

"Thank you, Mr. Degnan," my lawyer said. "I would like to review the specifics of the contract one final time so that all parties are clear on the terms." He unrolled the deed and read aloud. "The lease herein is for the term of 150 years from George Augustus Herbert, Earl of Pembroke, to Catherine McAuley, spinster, for a plot of land, 100 feet by 175 feet on the corner of Baggot Street and Herbert Street in southeast Dublin, formerly owned by Richard Viscount Fitzwilliam. The annual rent for said property is 60 pounds." He looked up, removing his glasses. "Are we all in agreement?"

A chorus of "ayes" answered.

"Very good. I wish to note one addendum here that states that should any of the tradesmen involved in this project— Mr. Keene, Mr. Lenehan, or Mr. Curran—fail to produce adequate work, any of the rest of you may submit an individual or collective notice in writing of the deficient and, upon notification of such, they are bound to either correct the stated defect or forfeit payment for such. Any objections?"

To a one, each man shook his head and I replied, "no."

He picked up a quill and dipped it in ink. "All being in agreement, let us then sign."

Mr. Degnan was the first to take the pen, then the priests, and finally it was in my hand. Carefully, I signed my name and title, "Catherine McAuley, spinster," to the deed. Mr. Degnan poured a circle of hot wax next to his name and embossed the stamp of the Earl, giving his approval by proxy.

It was done. My dream was coming true.

*****

I returned home that night to Coolock House in high spirits, planning to celebrate with Aoine, Bridget, and my adopted nieces and nephews. I had been saving up some delicacies for just this occasion: cheese, some bread, a flagon of wine. Mrs. Flynn would have procured a smoked salmon and roasted a leg of mutton to grace our table in thanksgiving. The adults would toast with a little wine, while the children and I drank grape juice from the same tall goblets.

"Mrs. Flynn," I called. "Is it time to call the children? Father Armstrong gave me the loveliest bottle of wine to toast to our new venture."

When I opened the parlor doors, however, it wasn't my maid I found there but my brother, James, contemplating the fire, his hands laced behind him, back toward me.

I removed my bonnet and gloves and reached to embrace him, but he backed away. "James, what is wrong?" I asked, genuinely concerned. It was unlike him to avoid me like this.

"So, it is done, I hear," was his only reply.

My brow wrinkled. "What is? What are you speaking of?"

He glowered at me. "Kitty's Folly has become a reality," he scoffed. "Lord help us all."

I fought the urge to roll my eyes at him. "This, again? James, really. You know my thoughts on the matter."

"Yes, and that is why I raise the issue again." He placed his hands on my shoulders. "Kitty, I love you. You know I do. Do you have any idea what people are saying about you? About me? To go this alone is madness."

"I asked you to partner with me when I made my decision, remember?" I couldn't keep my voice from shaking in frustration and that only infuriated me more. "You refused. That was when you first called this venture 'Kitty's Folly.'"

James closed his eyes for a moment and breathed before responding. "This isn't about me. You need a husband." His voice was sterner than I'd heard it in some time.

I gave a mirthless little laugh. "And because my older brother says so, it must be."

Shaking his head, James crossed to the small table near the door where incoming correspondence was kept and picked up a small stack of envelopes. "Herbert, Guinness, Eyre, O'Farrell, McNamara," he read off, shuffling the envelopes like a deck of playing cards. "All nobility and all in want of wife. Yet you refuse to even entertain them."

I hugged myself, hackles up. "I see no sense in pretending interest I do not have."

James turned toward me, dropping the envelopes back on the table. "You haven't even *met* them."

"And I shall not. Where were they when I was in the flush of youth, when I could have led a very different life?"

Memories of those days came to me unbidden. Laughing and dancing with all manner of young men at balls the Callaghans hosted, my cheeks flushed with excitement and wine; singing at more intimate parties with neighbors and friends, hoping to impress a certain gentleman; glancing flirtatiously over my cards at a handsome whist opponent on a Sunday afternoon. Three had courted me in earnest, and two even proposed. But in the end, my lack of dowery was too much for their families.

The images faded. Now the widowers and confirmed bachelors of these same families were so wealthy they needn't worry whether or not a woman had a dowery; they sought to enrich their coffers even more with my inheritance. I swallowed the bitterness poisoning my blood so that my brother wouldn't hear it. "They can smell money. That is all." I gave a careless shrug. "As of today, most of it is committed anyway."

"That is exactly my point. Invitations like these will dry up as word goes around. If you could but charm one of them now ..."

"It wouldn't be too late? Is that what you were going to say, brother?"

His lips twisted in chagrin. I had called him out. "Why couldn't Daniel O'Connell be single? You would be a matched pair." He mumbled.

"Even then it wouldn't matter," I said firmly. I took a deep breath, steeling myself to reveal what I decided not long after the reading of Mr. Callaghan's will.

"I am afraid to ask why."

I squared my shoulders and forced the words past my lips. "I have decided to remain single."

James' eyes bulged. Had he been sipping wine, he would have spit it out in shock. He took a moment to collect himself before speaking. "I have long known there was something wrong with you, but I never thought to hear you say it aloud," he said, more to himself than to me. "Are you to become a nun then?" The distaste in is voice was as though he swallowed vinegar.

"Hardly," I replied on a laugh, heart lightening at the absurdity of the idea. "I may be a Catholic, but the Devil take me before I kneel at the feet of Mother Superior and kiss her hem or lay in the refectory doorway and allow the other sisters to trod upon me for my sins."

"Then what *are* you going to do, Kitty?" My brother's exasperation was plain.

"I am going to live my life—just like I always have. As I am doing now." Why was this so difficult for him to understand?

"Will you continue living here? Or will you live in your new … what did you call it? … asylum?"

I shuddered. "That word is so distasteful. It brings to mind a dour place where people go to die, or at least be forgotten. No. It will be a home, a house of love and mercy."

James shook his head again, mumbling something about "female fantasies." After a moment he added, "You do realize what you a proposing, a group of lay women gathering to minister outside of cloister walls, has never successfully been done before."

"Of course it has. The French and Belgians had their Beguines."

"And they were eventually absorbed by the Church."

"What about Nano Nagle or Mary Aikenhead?" I asked, recalling tales of the foundresses of the Presentation Sisters and the Religious Sisters of Charity, once lay women like myself.

"Both were forced to become nuns. You know that. Selective memory doesn't help your argument any, Kitty."

More than forty years old and I wanted to stamp my foot like a petulant child. "Someone has to be the first!" I declared. "Why can it not be me? I'm not looking to change the world, James. I simply want to help people." Tears welled in my eyes. "Why can no one understand that?" I collapsed onto a settee, the fight suddenly gone out of me.

James came over and sat beside me, pulling me into the warmth of his arms as I wept. "You were always one for living life on your own terms," he said into my hair, rocking me like a child. "I suppose there is nothing I can do to change that."

I meant to agree with him, but amid my tears it came out as a very unladylike snort.

He pulled away and looked at me, eyes shining with love. "Be careful, Catherine McAuley. That is my advice to you." He kissed me on the forehead, then looked around. "Now, what was this I heard about wine?"

I rang for Mrs. Flynn and she quickly appeared, wine glass already in hand, having anticipated the request. Once James had taken a hardly mouthful, I turned to him. "While I am being honest, I may as well tell you everything."

My brother's arm stilled, glass midway to his mouth. He regarded me warily. "There is more?"

I nodded. "I've been thinking quite a bit on the school I wish to be part of my house and I feel I need further education as a teacher. Learning as I went was fine for our little manor school, but to teach large groups, I feel like I need to study under other educators, those who have been formally trained and who use different methods."

James set down his glass. "Is that all?" He let out a sigh. "I thought you were going to give me another shock. I can easily arrange for you to tour the country." He looked off into the distance, already making plans. "Let's see, there is Nano Nagle's school in Cork, the Ursuline Sisters have schools on Hennessey Road and in Newtown ... oh I could join you in Waterford—I have business there anyway—and you could see how the Christian Brothers teach at Mount Sion." His face was glowed with excitement.

I hated to dim his joy just when we'd found a subject on which we agreed. I had to tread carefully, be sure not to devalue the offer he had just made. "That is a perfect first leg to the journey," I said, meaning it. "But I would like to advance my education beyond this country." I swallowed hard, forcing the words past my lips. "I have decided to go to France."

James jumped to his feet, sloshing wine all over his suit and onto the floor. "France?!" he bellowed. "Why?"

"France has made great strides in education," I explained. Under its last two leaders, Napoleon and Louis XVIII—whose brother Charles was a great believer in learning—thousands of students learned the Catholic faith, conformity to the rule of country, and practical education. "The Church even approves of their methods. Several French priests have predicted that their educational system will raise the strongest generations of Catholics even seen in France. Think of what such principles could do for Ireland."

James pinched the bridge of his nose, as though trying to ward off a headache. "Nothing I say is going to stop you, is it?"

"No."

"Please at least let me arrange for a proper chaperone—for your safety."

"Of course."

"How long will you be away?" he asked on a sigh.

I looked away, not wishing to see his eye light with fury once again. "I was planning on two years, beginning in August. I will leave just after the cornerstone is laid. You will be in charge of the construction of the house while I am away."

*****

Sweat poured down my back in sticky rivulets as three priests trudged around the four corners of the foundation of my house on Baggot Street, blessing it with incense and holy water and kicking up dust as they moved. Though July was far from an ideal time to have such a ceremony, construction had moved fast, and nothing could proceed until the cornerstone was laid. Already, the foundation was dug out and the future building prepared to receive its walls and windows. The builders still anticipated two to three more years before the structure was complete, but this was a promising start.

I wiped a bead of sweat from my brow with my glove before it could roll into my eyes. Looking around the crowd—a few hundred people, at the least—it felt as though half of Dublin had turned out to witness the blessing of the cornerstone and the beginning of the above-ground construction the whole town would see rise as they passed it on a daily basis. While there were certainly a number of friendly faces in the crowd—Father Armstrong was smiling the widest—I was not foolish enough to believe they all wished me well. No, this was no indicator of what I could expect on opening day any more than my nan's creaky joints predicted rain. More than half of the people were either vehemently opposed or simply looking for a distraction that might provide good fodder for gossip at the tavern that night.

I caught Lord Montague's eye in the crowd and he tipped his hat toward me in a mocking greeting. He had to be eating his heart out right now. Despite all of his public protestations, my ministry was moving forward. No doubt he would blame it on Catholic magic and popery.

I smiled back at him beatifically and inclined my head, half trying to infuriate him and half in genuine prayer that the Lord might soften his heart.

I turned away then, refocusing on the ritual at hand. The priests were now blessing the well that would provide for our food and washing. Looking up, I imagined the completed building before me; I had looked at the blueprints so many times, I could overlay them with the space before me without struggle. The foundation would become a basement that would hold both cold and dry storage, the refectories for our workers and residents, and, eventually, a laundry. But that would come later; if we were to ever open the house and begin our ministry, we had to focus on the necessities, like the first-floor schoolroom and chapel. We might not be nuns, but we were women of faith whose ministry was grounded in the teachings of Christ, so being able to receive the Sacraments was of utmost importance. Above these would be the infirmary and another schoolroom, and the top floor would be reserved for dormitories and a small water closet.

Even only in my imagination, this building paled in comparison to the opulent mansions surrounding it, but it would meet our needs. If a woman expected luxury, she was better off seeking out a wealthy neighbor's hand in marriage than extending one in mercy here. Our coin was stored in heaven, not on this earth.

By the time I roused myself from my heat-induced daydreams, the priests had completed their circuit and were standing behind the cornerstone. I shielded my eyes with my hand to better see them.

Father Armstrong raised his arms above the large white stone, which glimmered in the relentless sunlight. Father Blake followed suit. "'The stone the builders rejected has become the cornerstone,' declared our Lord, Jesus Christ. May this stone, which we now bless, mark the first of many acts of mercy to the very people the world rejects." He passed the thurible over the stone three times in the shape of a cross.

I made the same sign over myself, as did all of the other Catholics in the audience.

"Boo!" someone yelled.

I turned, but was unable to locate the source of the heretical mockery.

"Take your cornerstone to the docks. It belongs amid the rest of the filth," someone else across the crowd yelled.

"Better yet," a third man interjected, "throw it in the Liffey."

A chorus of laughter followed.

My cheeks flamed. How dare they interrupt a solemn occasion such as this to mock good works? How could these men call themselves Christians?

Doing my best to keep my expression neutral, I focused on the cornerstone, repeating the Beatitudes to myself, several of which seemed especially relevant in this moment. *Blessed are the poor in spirit, for theirs is the kingdom of heaven.* These are the people to whom we will minister. Lord, guide our every thought and action. *Blessed are they who mourn, for they will be comforted.* Lord, help me to find comfort in you. *Blessed are they who hunger and thirst for righteousness, for they will be satisfied.* Please, help these people see that this work is done in your name and for the good of all. *Blessed are the merciful, for they will be shown mercy.* Please watch over all who minister here. Give us an excess of patience, charity, and love, that we may pass them on to the people we serve.

Before me, the priests were sprinkling the stone with holy water. I crossed myself as they evoked the Holy Trinity.

"I don't know why they are botherin' to clean it," one man whispered to someone behind me. "The lads and I are plannin' ta piss on it tonight anyway." He snorted. "See how far their blessings get them then."

I ground my teeth and continued my prayer. *Blessed are they who are persecuted for the sake of righteousness, for theirs is the kingdom of heaven.* Teach me humility, oh Lord, for pride is my greatest vice. *Blessed are you when they insult you and persecute you and utter every kind of evil against you because of me.* Lord, how did you utter not a word when the Romans mocked and derided you far worse than what I suffer now?

"Lord God Almighty, in whom every act of love has its source, and by whose grace it is multiplied and spread, grant, we beseech Thee, that this work, which we conduct in the holy name of Jesus, may be fulfilled through the guidance of your Holy Spirit."

I crossed myself a third time as they anointed the stone with holy chrism.

"Popish witchcraft," a woman yelled. "See how openly they defy God!"

The the crowd began to grow restless, shifting from foot to foot and grumbling around me. No one had thought to arrange for security, but I found myself wishing we had. It would take only one ill-timed act to turn these people violent. Men around me clasped and unclasped their fists, their wives and daughters sneering ill-intentioned words to one another, faces wrinkled in hate.

We had planned to have Father Blake place the cornerstone as part of the ceremony as well, but now it appeared prudent to do so in private. Better end the whole thing now. If someone didn't do something, the whole event could be ruined, and along with it, any hope for the future of our ministry.

Swallowing my fear, I stepped over to the cornerstone and, praying I wasn't defiling it, hoisted myself upon it to be better seen and heard. "Ladies and gentleman, I thank you for being here today to witness this solemn occasion," I projected my voice as loudly as I could. "Though not all of you share our faith, I ask you to please respect ours as we respect yours. Those who wish may join us now in a procession to St. Andrews where we will celebrate a Mass of thanksgiving. I ask that the rest of you please depart in peace."

Those gathered watched me warily as Father Armstrong helped me down from the stone. The priests flanked me on either side, effectively blocking the stone from desecration. Finally, the Protestants began to drift away, while the Catholics huddled near us, waiting to begin the long walk to the church.

Men of all ages filed past us, along with women, some with babes in arms or leading small children by the hand. Most wouldn't look at us, but some glared in open hostility. I started as an elderly woman opened her mouth and spit in my face, the warm liquid oozing down my nose and cheek. Chortled laughter followed as I attempted to clear my eyes and remove her spittle with my sleeve.

Lord Montague stopped before me, holding his handkerchief out with a flourish. "Let it never be said I am not a gallant man."

Pursing my lips, I reluctantly took it from him and cleaned my face.

He leaned in and lowered his voice so that only I could hear his words. "This is only the beginning, Miss McAuley. Continue down this path and you will find yourself in the brambles indeed."

I tried to return his handkerchief, but he waved me away. I wanted nothing of his in my possession; I would have to burn it in the fire tonight.

"Oh," he added as he made to continue on. "Just know that I can end this little charade any time I wish. I know things that could bring all of this," he gestured to the stone and debris around us, "tumbling down like the Tower of Babble." He winked and began to walk away, whistling as he went.

Chapter 12

GRACE

Late August 1824
House of Industry
Dublin, Ireland

I was fortunate to find summer work in the fields outside of Dublin, but with harvest already upon us, I needed to secure arrangements for the winter. That was easier said than done, however, because so did all the other seasonal workers.

As I walked home from another failed interview, my thoughts strayed to Margaret. If I had only stayed with her that day, sought out Miss McAuley with her, I could be warm and happy right now instead of wet and shivering in the late autumn rain. For the first time in months, I wondered where Margaret had ended up. Perhaps she could help me. Maybe if I visited Miss McAuley, she could tell me where Margaret had gone.

The next morning, I donned my most respectable dress—the only one that hadn't started showing signs of wear at the elbows and wasn't dotted with stains—and set out, hope rising with each step. I recalled the route out of Dublin to Coolock House fairly well, making only a few wrong turns along the way. By the time the stately manor came into view, I was certain I'd made the right decision.

The iron gates we had waited at two years prior were open. I started up the long drive to the main house, but not even a third of the way there, a matronly woman called out to me from what I could only guess to be a carriage or gate house. At her inquiry about my business there, I introduced myself and told her I was seeking to speak with Miss McAuley.

She shook her head. "I'm sorry, my love, but she is not at home presently."

"Well, when will she return?"

"She's taken up temporary residence in France for the next two years, I'm afraid, so it will be a while before she returns."

"Two years?" My stomach dropped to my feet. "But ... I really need her help. Now." I bowed my head. There was nothing I could do. I had to go back home to my last night in the boarding house and figure out a way forward.

The next morning I swallowed my pride and rented out a tiny cellar in a less-than-respectable area of town. Accessed by a trapdoor in the floor of a rundown house, it was primitive at best, with a dirt floor and cold stone walls that afforded me only enough room to lie down. I had to supply my own candles or coal if I wanted light or heat, and there was no running water or sanitation. I had to sneak to one of the city's fountains before dawn if I wished to bathe or collect water for the day. Good thing I had stolen my chamber pot from the boarding house, or I would not even have a place to relieve myself. Not that it would have made much difference; the cellar was prone to seepage from the sewer, especially when it rained.

My reduced circumstances made it more difficult than ever to find work. The stench of rot and piss clung to my clothing and I wasn't always able to complete my ablutions before the night watchman came along and chased me off. If he found me one more time, he threatened to put me in shackles.

As the days grew colder and my meagre income from sewing and other odd tasks proved far too little to heat my tiny cellar, desperation gripped my mind. The last thing I wanted to do was sell my body, but it was rapidly becoming my only option. The problem was that I didn't have anyone to recommend me at the nicer brothels, so there was no way the madams would let me in, much less offer me employment. I could always work the docks or around the bars and alehouses, but if it became known I had been working on the streets, any hope for the finer establishments was gone.

Every day, foundations for new construction projects were laid, shops opened, and vendors set out carts selling food to passersby, yet I could find little gainful employment. I survived for a while by cleaning at an inn, but as soon as the proprietor realized he couldn't offer me to his clients, I was sacked.

Finally, I had no choice but to pawn the last of my possessions, even my clothing, leaving me with a single dress, a cloak, and one pair of worn boots. I took to begging on market days and situating myself near the fashionable shops by day, in hopes one of the wealthy ladies might spare a coin or even a crust of bread—or better yet, that one might recognize me and offer me work. At night, when the temperatures dipped well below freezing, I sneaked inside the glass houses, seeking the heat of their embers, wondering how, within six months, my life had plummeted so drastically.

Looking around at the other bodies sleeping around me, children piled on parents like pups, I realized one thing—come the depths of winter, these sandy, ashy illegal beds would not be big enough to meet Dublin's needs.

If I wanted to live, I had to make a choice, and soon.

*****

I breathed in deep through my mouth, trying to keep the nausea at bay. I hadn't eaten in two days, so what my stomach could be using to protest was a mystery to me. The very sight of the lime-washed walls of the House of Industry on James's Street brought back flashes of memory—of a time when the inner side of the workhouse's walls trapped me within their shadowy heights, rather than offering sanctuary as they did now. But then again, I was much smaller in those days, only just able to form lasting impressions of my world. If I let myself travel back in time, I immediately tasted the bitter bite of slightly-turned milk and encountered the resistance of stale bread—our first and sometimes only meal of the day—and found myself rubbing the muscles in my hand, the ghost pain of so many hours scrubbing and cleaning filling my joints with burning shards of glass once again.

But then again, without such an upbringing, I likely wouldn't have survived so long without work. If nothing else, growing up an orphan taught me to be resourceful, and doing so here gave me at least rudimentary education, along with basic skills in cooking and cleaning. It may not have been the level of experience many girls had, but it was more than the street urchins had; therefore, I wasn't picking pockets or prostituting myself then or now.

The line to be admitted to the workhouse slowly advanced, step by miniscule step. My stomach rumbled and my head was beginning to feel hollow. If I didn't eat soon, I might pass out right here on the cobbles. I doubted there would be any mercy for me then; if one person was allowed to skip the line from fainting, within moments every person in the queue would be on the ground. I shook my head to clear it. Each person had to be processed in the central building before being assigned to one of two perpendicular dormitories, and I would wait as long as it took.

The nearby church bells of St. James tolled the hour twice before I stood before the porter, a young, trim man with black hair and a thin mustache, attired in an official-looking black suit with silver braided trim at the cuff and lapels.

"Name?" he asked without looking up from the log book open on the desk in front of him.

"Grace Ryan."

"Age?"

"Eighteen."

He glanced up at me then, his gaze evaluating. He must have believed me, because eventually he nodded and moved on.

"Are you married?"

"No."

"Religion?"

"Protestant."

As expected, this seemed to please him. "Occupation?"

"Domestic."

"Last residence?"

I gave him Lord Montague's address. His eyebrow shot up; he was no doubt wondering how I had fallen so far.

"Have you been housed here before?"

"Yes. I was born here and lived within these walls for ten years." A memory of the day I left to take on my first job in a household tried to push its way to the front of my mind, but I pushed it down. There would be plenty of time for reminiscing once I was inside with a full belly.

"And why are you seeking shelter here?" He looked up again, poised to record my story.

I told him of the hardship of the last several months.

His pen scratched the page but his face remained impassive as he wrote. At this point I had been through the timeline so many times in my own head, I could recite it without really thinking. Watching his hand move across the page, I couldn't help but wonder about *his* life. What other tales of woe and misery had this man heard? Did they make him grateful for his home, his wife, his children? Or did they serve, as they did for so many others, to inflate his sense of superiority? I prayed it was the former but expected the latter.

"One last question, Miss Ryan." The porter's voice drew me back from my reverie. "What is the name of your nearest relative?"

For a moment, confusion clouded my mind, but then I remembered they needed to know who would stand for you if you became unruly or who would claim your body if you died. What *would* become of me if tragedy struck? I didn't know my family. Margaret would have been appropriate to name, but I had no idea where she was. "I don't have one," I finally admitted.

I watched him write "none," on the final line of the form. With a sinking heart I realized that meant either a lunatic asylum or pauper's grave could be my end. No. That would not happen. I wouldn't let it. The very fact that I was here right now meant one step closer to a new life.

"Step over here, please." The porter gestured to his left, where a guard waited.

The uniformed officer made me remove all my clothing, save my shift. He passed my clothes off to another guard, who inspected them and then placed them in a wicker basket. "You'll get it back when you leave," the first guard said, making me wonder if everyone had the same question at this point in their intake process. He then ran his hands over my body, likely searching for bottles of spirits, opium, or other contraband. His sharp squeeze to both breasts startled me, but it also prepared me for his more thorough inspection to come. I was used to being fondled without my permission and I couldn't help but smile— not from any pleasure, but from picturing the indignant response of Mrs. Donahue or Lady Montague if they were treated the same way.

Once the guard had his fill of me and was convinced I wasn't carrying anything illegal, he sent me to a back room to endure a medical inspection. There, I was asked to remove my shift and stood shivering as a doctor peered into my eyes and mouth, inspected my teeth, felt my glands, and examined every inch of my skin, cataloging the sores he found from bedbug and flea bites. He then picked through my hair with a thin comb, finding the lice he expected. Thankfully, he didn't seem inclined to check for venereal disease, so I escaped the worst possible humiliation.

Dressed and out in the hallway once again, I was directed to another room containing rows of metal tubs and about a dozen women, residents and workers included. A young girl stationed at the door took my shift and an older woman of about forty guided me to one of the tubs. I glanced at the water warily, remembering the cold baths after five other girls had already dirtied the water, but to my surprise, the water was clear and steaming.

"We don't do it that way anymore," my caretaker said with a knowing smile. "I remember those days, too. I'm Martha, by the way."

"Grace," I replied, feeling I had made my first friend on the inside. I lifted one leg into the water and then the other. A groan of pleasure rose to my lips, but I stifled it. I couldn't recall the last time I had had a proper bath. Though this was a matter of necessity rather than luxury, I couldn't help but feel Martha took her time lathering and rising my hair and body with a strong soap she said would kill the vermin. Finally, after she had poured a last pitcher of warm water over my head, it was time to get out.

I dried myself with the coarse towel provided, then stepped into the gingham shift Martha gave to me. Over that went a petticoat of linsey-woolsey and a coarse grogram gown. I pulled on a pair of worsted stockings and then skipped my feet into woven slippers. By then, the heat of the baths had mostly dried my hair, so I twisted it into a bun and secured it beneath my new day cap. Finally, Martha placed a second shift, this one of a softer calico, into my arms. I noticed it had a number stitched into it, as well as a tag that declared it property of the workhouse. No one would be able to remove it without causing a noticeable hole in the garment. Come to think of it, each piece of clothing had had the same identifiers, but I had been in too much of a hurry to notice. That was certainly one way to keep the items from being stolen and sold for profit.

Martha led me out of the bathing area and into a large, empty rectangular room. Beds lay on the floor perpendicular to each of the long white walls, a fireplace crackling at one end and a communal privy at the other. To my great relief, she led me down the narrow center aisle away from the stinking hole and closer to the heat. She pointed to a straw mat. "That one is yours. I'd make it now and place your nightclothes under the pillow. That will show the others it is taken. Can't be too careful while you're in confinement."

She was right. In a place where women cycled in and out on a daily basis as they were released with a bill of clean health into the general female dormitory or sent to the infirmity to suffer through whatever catching disease they developed, not even one's one bedding was safe. Every person did what she must to mark one small scrap of space as her own.

On top mattress lay a pile of linens. "Do they still make the beds sheet first, then the blankets and coverlet?" I asked, my hands beginning to do the work without conscious thought.

Martha nodded. "It's remarkable how quickly it comes back to you, isn't it?"

I was about to ask her about her previous experience here, when a bell rang in the distance. Martha looked up. "That is the dinner bell." She bustled over to me and helped me finish making my bed. By now I had noticed even my sheets bore the same number and markings as my clothing—not that that would stop anyone from trying to claim them for her own use.

"Be thankful you came to us on a Thursday," she said, leading me to the refectory. "Tonight we eat ox head porridge. Tomorrow they are serving plain, with only vegetables and a bit of seasoning. Tastes like glue," she said with a small laugh.

The very thought turned my stomach. I never did develop a taste for the sludge-like dish. I would have to remember to try to eat extra supper on beef days and breakfast on plain days.

We stood in line in the refectory, listening to the buzz of conversation all around. Once we reached the front, a woman spooned a ration of slop into a bowl and I held out my hand for my allotted piece of bread and cup of small beer. Martha led me to a long table where three other women, similar in age to me, were already rapidly consuming their meal. I sat at an open seat in the middle, nodded a greeting to them, and picked up my bread. Though the hunger pains had long ago subsided, I was lightheaded, like a hive of bees had taken up residence in my ears. I grabbed the bread, but before I could bring it to my mouth, Martha had stayed my hand.

"Wait." She squinted at the three dark-haired girls. "Did you say grace before eating?" After moment of silence, she shook her head. "I thought not."

At a look from her, three spoons clattered to the table, three pairs of fingers were interlaced in prayer and six eyes shut. I hurried to follow suit.

"Dear Lord, we thank you for the meal we are about to eat. We thank you also for the opportunity to do your work this day and for bringing Grace to safety here with us. Give her strength and guide us all in your holy wisdom. Amen."

A chorus of "amens" followed.

When I opened my eyes again, all three girls were staring at me.

"Ladies, don't be impolite. Introduce yourselves." Martha said as she brought her first spoonful to her mouth.

"I'm Isadora," the girl farthest to my left said, flipping an auburn braid over her shoulder and offering a small wave. "Everyone here calls me Isa."

"Jane," the middle one said, smiling down shyly at her plate.

"I'm Cressida. It means 'gold,'" the third added, watching me carefully through long dark eyelashes. "My mother named me that because she wanted me to be wealthy, and I intend to be."

"Then you are in the wrong place," Isa noted.

Jane giggled into her cup and Cressida scowled. "In here everyone calls me Wren," she added.

"Because you are small?"

"Partly, but I'm also clever and I hide my secrets well." Her eyes glimmered.

"Not to mention she has a beautiful voice," Martha said, sounding just like a proud mother.

"Surely you could use that gift to lift you out of poverty," I said.

"It takes more than a beautiful melody to get you on a stage or to secure a patron. You need training and that costs money, which I don't have." Wren fell silent a moment and muttered into her cup, "And even then, you're still considered a harlot."

Isa shook her head at her friend, then turned her attention back to me. "Have you gotten your assignment yet?"

I looked to Martha for guidance. "My assignment? No."

Martha smiled indulgently. "She's asking where you'll be working while your here. The matron might assign you to the infirmary, the nursery—which is where Jane works—or have you sew or clean. What skills do you have?"

I swallowed the spoonful of porridge I had just put into my mouth. "I can cook and clean. I've been in service for years."

Cressida leaned toward me. "Oh," she said, drawing the word out like I'd given her a juicy piece of gossip. "So how did you end up here?"

Martha swatted at Cressida and gave her an admonishing look. "Don't be rude, girl." She turned back to me. "They will likely put you in service here, too. Not a bad job. You'll find out in the morning."

I regarded my new companions. "If you don't mind me asking, how long have the three of you been here?"

The girls looked at each other. "We all arrived last month," Isa volunteered. "I work in the spinning shed."

"I was in service, like you." Jane said. "But my employer experienced a downturn in his fortunes so he had to let several of us go. Now I care for the children."

When Cressida didn't immediately answer, I glanced up at her. "Cressida?"

She sighed loudly. "My mother brought me and my sister here after my father died. He owed his employer a lot of money, so we had no choice but to seek shelter here."

"Where are your mother and sister now?" I looked around, attentive for a face with similar large brown eyes or generous lips.

"They're dead," she said without emotion.

"What?" I cried. "Wait—didn't you say you just arrived last month?"

"Yes," Isa cut in. "They developed a fever the night after being placed in probation."

"I fell ill as well," Cressida said in the same monotone. "But I survived. They didn't."

I looked from her to Isa, to Jane, then at Martha and back again. Was I missing something? Why wasn't Cressida sad? I would have been heartbroken in her place.

Cressida finally met my eyes. "They are the lucky ones. Believe me, if you'd come from where we did, you'd consider death a blessing, too."

I shrank back in my chair, embarrassed to have read the situation so wrong. After a few bites of bread in silence, I asked Cressida, "How do you plan to make your fortune?"

"What?"

"You said you intended to become wealthy. How?"

She shrugged, "I don't know yet. But I'm taking you lot with me when I do."

*****

Two weeks passed quickly, and before I knew it, Martha had somehow arranged for the four of us to be assigned to the same dormitory. The days melted into nothingness, with little time for thought beyond our work, the plain meals, and sleep. We rose each day when the bell tolled eight, put on the uniforms for our positions—mine included the white apron and cap of a domestic, just as Martha had predicted—and made our way to the rectory to dine on either stirabout or a mush of potatoes and milk. The next ten hours were taken up with work, save for a one-hour break for dinner, and then prayers before the bells ordered us to bed once again.

Sundays were the only reprieve from this grueling routine. While many of the residents spent the day in prayer in the refectory-turned-chapel or catching up on sleep, those who were Catholic and those with hardier constitutions—like the domestics, nurses, and nannies, who were used to long days, hard work, and unpredictable schedules—used the time to gossip, work on personal sewing and stitching, and relax as much as possible around the dormitory fire.

"You girls better find a way out of here by spring," Martha advised, her hands moving seemingly of their own accord as she wove pieces of torn blanket in and out of each other, finishing them in knots, until she had a much thicker and more useful blanket.

"Why do you say that?" I asked.

"There are plenty of people here right now to run this place," she said, her eyes drifting from a trio of older women praying the rosary to a gaggle of young mothers who were either nursing or encouraging their children to play with one another. "But come late spring and especially by early summer, most will have left to find work in the fields or at country estates. There won't be enough of us to maintain it to any level of sanitation. It happens every year, but no one seems care. Besides," she added with a hint of mirth, "by then you'll be well and truly tired of the food."

"What about you? Won't you come with us?" I asked.

Martha shook her head. "No. I'd sleep better at night staying in here and caring for the elderly women and the new lasses like yourselves. Someone has to, and besides, I wouldn't last long out there. Too many mistakes, too much past." Her voice held a regretful note.

"What would we do? How are we to survive?" I asked, only now realizing that in my desperation to escape my current circumstances, I hadn't thought about ever leaving the workhouse. "They don't pay us here, so how will we afford food or a place to live?"

Wren snorted. "You really are a sweet young thing, aren't you?"

Hardly, but she didn't know that.

"We already have everything we need. These ..." she wigged her fingers, "and this ..." She gestured at her body.

My heart sank. "You don't mean—"

"Yes, saint Grace, that is exactly what I mean. We use what we have to, at least in the beginning. We may not be able to take anything from here, but there are plenty of women among this lot who would be willing to teach us to steal—and maybe even help us—if they knew we were building a future for all of us."

Isa looked up from her knitting, interested for the first time. "Building a future? How?"

Wren let out a sign of frustration. "Do I have to figure out everything? I've been listening to the stories of the new residents, and there is talk of a group of women outside of Kildare who have united to protect one another from the dangers of plying their trade."

"Like in a brothel?" Isa asked, keeping her voice low. Speaking of prostitution in here was considered the precursor to doing it, and if the wrong matron overheard, you could be punished for engaging in lewd conversation or inciting immorality.

"Yes and no. They live completely in common—money, food, everything. What happens to one of them happens to all. I get the impression they are completely self-sustaining. We could do to the same. Between the four of us, we already have enough skills to get started. Grace, you can keep house and cook. Jane can assist with the cooking while you are entertaining," she winked at me, "and see to our health needs. She has as much training as any nurse. Isa, you can continue your sewing so we have items to sell for honest income." Wren's eyes were shining with anticipation.

"You could sing, as well," Isa said.

"This is all well and good for dreaming, ladies," Martha put in, "but what of reality? When you leave here, you will start from the dirt. Say you manage to steal your food without getting arrested, you still will need clients. You could start on the docks or at the barracks, but you'll be known quickly and not by the clientele you are looking for. Where will you live? We're in the middle of a city where the night watch doesn't take kindly to women who attract that kind of attention."

"You're right," Wren said, chewing on a fingernail. "We need the captains and officers as our benefactors, not the sailors and soldiers any woman can snare."

"Or even better, the nobility," I said.

Wren laughed. "Grace, you know as well as I that is near to impossible."

"Not necessarily. It wasn't only his servants my employer consorted with."

Wren scoffed and Martha gave me a dubious look.

"Hear me out. If there is one thing I learned in my years of service, the rich will patronize anyone they believe can benefit them. If we have connections in most areas of trade, we can use them to continuously snare bigger fish. What we need is something that makes us special, so that we are the ones men want to patronize over others," I said.

"What could we possibly provide that men can't get elsewhere? Sex is sex," Wren said.

"Maybe," Isa said. "But that is not the only reason why men take up with that type of woman."

I heard their exchange, but only just. I was wracking my brain for what might set us apart. "The thing those men value most is their reputation. No woman in this trade wishes to be caught, but we need to become their best-kept secret, like an exclusive club you can only access with approval … from us. And they can only find out about us by recommendation."

"That's it!" Wren snapped her fingers. "Unlike the high-end brothels, they won't have to go to us. We will already be where they are. It's less risk to both of us. We need to be accessible to our clients but untraceable by the authorities. If the men don't vary from their routines, they won't arouse suspicion."

"What if we move around at first while we're building a reputation? We skip the base workers of any trade and begin at the parties held for their superiors. We move up from there," Isa suggested.

"And use different names with different groups. That will make us more difficult to find, but also keep each group in the dark about the others," Jane added.

"We can use the upcoming social season to find out who the key players and competition are," I was thinking aloud, warming to the idea. "Then we'll have ten months to cultivate our contacts and build out our plans. We should spend that time outside of the city; it will be safer for us to move around, plus the men we aim to attract spend most of the year in the country. If we can find a toe hold there, we'll be the ones they will seek out in the city. A year from now, you may well have your fortune, Wren."

PART III

FRUITION

Chapter 13

CATHERINE

January 1827
Coolock House
Dublin, Ireland

I arrived home from France to find the ladies and gentlemen of Dublin society had cooled toward me while I'd been away. At first, I attributed the lack of invitations and visits to being out of the country for the last two years. The rich, I had learned, were easily distracted. When they saw me regularly, I was top of mind, but once their eyes had time to be dazzled by something else, I was forgotten. They were like kittens chasing moonbeams or dancing rays of sunlight.

But I soon learned there was much more to their sudden change of heart. As I skimmed through back issues of the newspaper, I traced the development of Lord Montague's ire since the cornerstone blessing. While I had been gone, he had progressed from a nuisance to a full-fledged threat. Writing negative opinion pieces and hiring people to protest at the construction site was one thing, but then I found a letter from Mr. Andrews informing me that Lord Montague would be challenging the Earl of Pembroke regarding my right to lease the land on Baggot Street. That was going too far.

It was time to pay that man a visit.

When I rang the bell at his Merrion Square townhome an hour later, I was met by a dark-eyed young servant who held herself with the confidence of a woman of much higher rank. When I enquired about seeing Lord Montague, she informed me he was not available and that I should make an appointment and return at that time. When she tried to close the door on me, I stopped it with my foot.

Two male voices carried to the entryway, so there was no doubt she was telling the truth, but I was not about to leave and come back. I wanted answers. Now.

It wasn't the maid's fault that Lord Montague was detained, but he was the kind of man who would only respect others if they showed they would not be cowed. I regarded the haughty girl with distain, as though I were any other lady of rank. "Please inform Lord Montague that Miss Catherine McAuley is here to see him and will do so now, regardless of whom his guest may be." When she didn't move, I made a shooing gesture at her. "Go on. I'll wait." I slipped past her and took a seat in the parlor.

The maid disappeared. A few moments later, she came back and gestured me to follow her.

When I was shown into the drawing room, I found Lord Montague sitting across from Father Mathias Kelly, administrator of Saint Andrews Chapel on Townsend Street. Both were drinking whiskey and smoking cigars.

"What have we here?" I cooed, not waiting for a formal introduction, as I was well acquainted with both. "Might we read of a peace accord between Catholics and Protestants in the evening paper?" I asked, sarcastically.

"May God be so gracious," Father Kelly responded.

Lord Montague smirked up at me, though his tight lips betrayed his annoyance. "Miss McAuley, to what do I owe this surprise visit?"

I thrust the letter at him. "I rented that land legally. How dare you accuse me otherwise!"

Lord Montague held up a hand to the priest, as if saying, "I will handle this." It did not escape my notice that he failed to offer me a seat as decorum demanded.

"I have no doubt you did. However, the land is not his to rent. When the Viscount Fitzwilliam bequeathed that land to the Earl a decade ago, it was not taken into account that this land was improperly seized from my family decades prior. That part of the legal issues does not concern you and would be going forward no matter who tried to lease the land."

"Then why involve me at all?"

Lord Montague exhaled loudly, as though I was trying his patience. "The Earl is profiting from your lease, and because the land is mine, that money is legally mine. So, I tell you as a courtesy, but also because as your landlord, I am not in agreement with what you are doing with the land. Until my solicitor can prove in a court of law that I am the rightful owner, my only recourse is to discredit your ministry."

I couldn't believe what I was hearing. "You are telling me that because you are squabbling over land with the Earl, you are willing to risk the lives of the citizens of Dublin by depriving them of much needed resources? What kind of devil are you?"

Lord Montague glared at me with such venom that it was clear that had a priest not been present he would have struck me. "Miss McAuley, let me be perfectly frank. That I dislike you and your ministry I have made no secret. The poor need to remain on the outskirts of the city where they belong, not venture into the neighborhoods of their betters. Secondly, you are a woman who stumbled into a fortune without anyone to advise you, and now you believe you can change centuries of societal tradition by sheer force of will. What's more, you believe you can go around the laws of your own Church to do so. There are so many reasons for me to oppose your venture I cannot pick only one."

I opened my mouth to reply, but Father Kelly spoke up instead.

"If I may interject," he held up a finger like a student in a classroom and addressed me. "While this is a complex matter with legal implications, let me remind you that there are ecclesiastical considerations as well. I am here today representing the spiritual authority in the parish where your ministry is being built. Like Lord Montague, I have grave concerns about your fitness for the role you have undertaken. I am also worried how it will affect the parish and the members of our flock. Your intentions may be good, but I am not sure you are going about this in the best way."

I was rapidly losing my patience with both men. "And what would be the best way?" I asked, trying to contain my irritation.

Father Kelly looked down, a gesture that evoked a humility I doubted he possessed. "I wish you had consulted me before going off on your own to begin this undertaking. There is little precedent for what you are doing, and I fear the Church authorities will not let it stand. If you would at least consider working in collaboration with me ..."

"So, you can tell me how to run my house just like you dictate the lives of the Sisters of Charity? Not a chance." I closed my eyes, willing myself to address Lord Montague more patiently. "Is there anything I can do to make you stop opposing me at every turn?"

The men locked eyes for a moment before Lord Montague said, "Cease your efforts. It is the only way."

Chapter 14

ANNA MARIA DOYLE

April 1827
Baggot Street
Dublin, Ireland

Gulls dove in and out of the early morning fog as I turned from Grafton Street onto Baggot Street. Before me, St. Stephen's Green bloomed in a riot of red, yellow, and pink tulips, competing with the first buds of spring for my attention. This was one of my favorite parts of Dublin and I couldn't resist a slight detour through the park.

Gravel crunching under my boots, rays of sun peeking through the fog warming my face and neck, I soon became lost in thought. After Mass at St. Teresa's, I had stayed behind, praying for a solution to the issue vexing my heart. Jesus was everything to me; I longed to devote my life to him as a Presentation Sister, as my sister had done. Now she was secreted away behind cloister walls clear across the country in Killarney. She was fortunate indeed.

I stopped to admire the intricate conical flowers of a lilac and breathe in its heady scent, more divine to my mind than any incense. Its perfume cleared my mind and warmed my heart. I chewed my bottom lip as I continued on. With my brother off in London working as an artist, that left me as my parents' only caregiver. If I was to enter the Presentation convent, even the one here in Dublin, they would be left to fend for themselves. I couldn't do that to the people I loved more than anything in this world, who had insisted I attend the best schools like my brother, even as their business suffered because we were Catholic.

They had raised me follow God's will, and it seemed God wished me to care for them as they aged. I tried to submit myself humbly and accept this as my fate, as Father Blake advised, but sometimes the pull in my heart toward the convent was so strong it brought me to tears. Today, the Eucharist was enough to quench my thirst and I felt the wisdom of Father Blake's words, "If your vocation is true, it will still be there when your parents are resting in the arms of the Lord. Then your way will be clear to take the veil." In meantime, he advised, I should offer myself to Our Lady's protection and emulate her example of saying "yes" to anything God asked me.

I paused one more time at the far gate of the Green. A tangle of trained rose vines looped and curled from bushes on either side, forming a canopy above. Most of the plant was still young leaves and thorns, but here and there a few ambitious buds had formed. Near my eye level, one had only recently burst into bloom, it's white petals delicately unfurling, while still protectively cupping the delicate pollen within. A smile slowly turned up my lips; this tender bud was a visual representation of how I felt—mature and ready to drink in the sun, to explore my life, but still sheltered within the embrace of my family. I lovingly stroked the tip of the bud, and prayed, *Holy Mother, Mystical Rose, show me what God wants of me.*

Continuing on down Baggot Street, I was greeted with tipped hats from carriage drivers as they ferried the wealthy who made their homes in and around Merrion Square out from the city center to business or social events. I smiled and waved to those I knew, nodded my head to the others. Lost in my own thoughts, I paid them only passing attention—that is, until an approaching buggy slowed at my side. When it came to a stop, a gloved hand emerged and waved in my direction.

"Anna," a voice from within beckoned. "Anna Doyle? Is that you?"

I stepped closer. A tow-headed figure was seated inside, grinning warmly.

"Tom!" I exclaimed, surprised to find him here of all places. "I was not expecting to see you again so soon."

"Nor I." He opened the door and stepped out, gracefully donning his hat. "May I walk with you?" He held out his arm.

I looked at it, hesitant to agree. I cared very deeply for Tom, but I didn't want him to think this meant more than it did. Only four days ago, Tom had asked if he might court me. I knew I should say yes. It made sense. I was of marriageable age, we were well acquainted—his first gift to me at the age of six was a dogfish he had caught fishing with my brother—and perhaps most of all, my family needed the money his could provide.

It would be so easy to say yes, to announce our intentions by dancing exclusively with one another at the next ball, and to accept when he eventually proposed. It would be a good life—he would never hit me or allow a hurtful word to escape his lips—but a sedate one, lacking adventure or any real substance. I felt it deep down in my soul that I needed to do something to make a difference in the world, and being married to the heir of a shipping magnate would offer little opportunity in that regard.

Smiling, I accepted, taking his proffered arm and heading in the direction of the Bank of Ireland, which was across the street a few blocks down. After exchanging pleasantries, he asked the question I had been dreading, "Have you thought any more about what I asked you?"

I had escaped giving a firm answer when he asked to court me because the musicians began a new tune and my promised partner came to collect his dance. Now, I glanced around at the men and women of Dublin going about their business; this time there would be no conveniently timed rescue. "I have," I said, stopping where we stood and taking both of his hands in mine. "I care about you very much Thomas, and I have no doubt you would make an excellent husband." His eyes burned with hope that I was loathe to douse. Nervously, I began to play with the gold crucifix hanging around my neck. "But I don't think it is fair for me to accept your offer when my heart already belongs to another."

Tom took a step back, as if I had struck him. A range of emotions played across his face. His eyebrows knit together in confusion, then his jaw clenched and his eyes hardened—no doubt at the idea of another man—and then his expression cleared as he understood my meaning.

"Ah." That was all he said before urging us onward. After a few steps of silence, he added, "I had heard rumors you were inclined to the religious life. I think I may have a solution, though."

"Really?" I giggled. "Have you convinced the Pope to allow nuns to marry?"

"No," he chortled back. "But I would allow you to take on whatever devotions and charity work you wish as my wife. Should you wish to attend daily Mass, my carriage stands at the ready. Long to join a charity board? I will contact the husbands of those in charge. Would you like to build a chapel in our home, you have only to speak and my architect will come to call."

This time it was Tom who stopped us in the middle of the pedestrians. "You *can* have it all," he said. "I find myself falling in love with you, Anna. I think I have been since the day you brought me a posey of wildflowers and then skinned your knee running away out of embarrassment. Please say you will allow me to take the next step."

I looked from Tom's grey-blue eyes to the clearing sky and back again, unable to force either "yes" or "no" past my lips.

Once again, I was saved from answering when we were jostled by two burly men carrying long cords of wood.

"Watch out now," Thomas called after them, shielding me with his body.

The men either didn't hear him or didn't think the situation worthy of response.

"I say, does no one have manners in this town?" He brushed himself off and straightened his suit.

I barely noticed him, transfixed by the sight before me. We had reached an intersection. The way before us was blocked by horse-drawn carts laden with wood, rock, and all sorts of debris, plus scores of men whose labor could be counted in the white brick building rising before us. Three, maybe four stories from the look of it. Many, many large windows, which indicated many rooms inside. It was too big to be a private residence. Another hotel perhaps? Or a boarding house? But no, a stone cross graced the triangular portico above the front door. A seminary, maybe? Dare I hope for a convent?

Following what felt like a magnetic pull to this place, I crossed the street, heedless of Thomas's calls for me to wait and let him help me cross safely. I approached the nearest worker, a muscled man perhaps in his early forties, who was standing back, observing as a trio of other workers hoisted a glass windowpane to the second floor using a system of ropes and pullies.

"Excuse me," I called over the growling of saws and the rhythmic thwack of hammers. He didn't seem to hear me, so I called out again. "Excuse me. Sir?"

He turned and looked down at me, regarding me with no small amount of suspicion. It wasn't hard to guess why. Women were a rarity on any construction site, especially one who was not yet twenty. Before he could say anything, unplanned words tumbled out of my mouth. "What is this place? It's so very beautiful."

The compliment must have done the trick, for all trace of suspicion vanished and he smiled. "Why, this is the building all of Dublin is buzzing about. Surely, you've heard?"

I shook my head, aware suddenly of Thomas's presence behind me.

"It may not look like much now, but it's going to be a kind of shelter for the poor, especially women and children. Some people are raising a stink over it, but I'm in favor of it. The woman who owns it is a beautiful soul. I know she will do wonders for the city."

His gaze flicked to Thomas. "I'm Dennis Lenehan, the overseer." He held out a dirt-stained hand to Thomas, who politely shook it.

"And who is this woman who has such lofty dreams?" he asked after giving his name.

"Miss Catherine McAuley. She inherited a fortune and is using it to build this place."

I gazed at the building, a million questions galloping around my mind.

"What is she, a nun or some charitable Protestant leader's wife?"

The worker lit a cigarette produced from his pocket. "Oh no, sir. She's a spinster. A Catholic, but there will be no convent for her. She wants nothing to do with nunneries. She wants this place to be run by women like herself who have a genuine passion for helping those less fortunate. Married, single, widowed, it don't matter." He shrugged. "You don't even have to be Catholic. She'll take anyone with a good heart."

Was it possible? Could this be the answer I was seeking? It seemed like the perfect solution to my predicament. If Miss McAuley would have me, I could spend my days in Christian works of charity and my evenings with my parents. I'd even be close enough to visit them during the day, if needed. A peace I'd never before known settled over me at mere thought of working in this special place.

My face must have lit up with the same joy that made my soul buoyant because the overseer laughed good naturedly. "Your wife sure seems interested in what we're doing here. Would you like to see inside? Only a portion of the building is finished, but it will give you an idea."

"She's not my wife," Thomas was quick to correct him. "We are merely companions."

Was it my imagination, or did I hear a note of melancholy in his voice?

"Yes, we would love a tour, wouldn't we, Thomas?" I squeezed his arm.

"Yes, yes of course," he said, rousing himself from introspection.

The overseer led us into the construction area, bidding us to watch our steps. A chill fizzed up my spine as we crossed the threshold. I was meant to be here. Over the next half an hour, he led us through the receiving parlor and through a chapel large enough to put some country churches to shame. We toured rooms meant for education, where women would learn to sew and children to read. There was an infirmary and more bedrooms than I could count. It appeared people would live here around the clock, making it more of a sanctuary than a soup kitchen or school.

When the tour was over, we thanked Mr. Lenehan for taking time away from his work to entertain our interest. Thomas tried to give him a donation toward the ministry, but Mr. Lenehan refused. "You give that money to Miss Doyle, here. She can give it to Miss McAuley when they meet." He caught my eye and held it. "Call on her anytime at the royal hospital in Kilmainham. She lives there with her brother-in-law's family most of the time. Tell her Mr. Lenehan sent you."

"I will. Thank you so much."

He tipped his hat to us and turned away, heading back to his work.

"That was kind of him, don't you think?" I said to Thomas once we had resumed walking. He had gone quiet, his expression pensive.

"Indeed," was all he said.

We walked another half block before I finally stopped him. "What is wrong? I know when something is bothering you," I added when he failed to answer my question.

He gave me a bittersweet half smile. "You were never mine, were you?"

The question was rhetorical and I was glad, for I couldn't have summoned an answer in that moment if I had to. The look of sorrow in his eyes closed the pathway from my mind to my throat.

"And now I've lost you, not to another man, not even to Christ." He reached out and took my hand, rubbing its top with his thumb. "Miss McAuley and her ministry have taken your heart."

I made to respond, but he continued. "You don't need to tell me. I saw it in your expression as we walked the halls of that building. You were brimming with happiness and awe; I've only ever seen that light in you once, when we attended Mass together." He gave a rueful little sound. "I wish you would turn that light toward me, but I know you cannot. I could insist that you marry me and I would give you permission to volunteer with Miss McAuley, but you wouldn't be happy. We both know that. You have to give your whole self, body and soul, to the causes you believe in. I would only stand in your way."

I reached up and moved a lock of hair that had fallen over his left eye. "Oh Thomas, I am so sorry."

He took my hand as I moved it away and kissed it softly. "Do not ever apologize for following your heart. I followed mine and it led me to you, which was a great gift, even if I didn't get what I wanted. Now it is time for you to see where yours takes you."

We stared into one another's eyes for a moment, alternate futures unfolding before us: one with us and husband and wife and the other that God had preordained. It was no accident that Thomas and I had met on the street today; if he hadn't been here, I would never have had the courage to ask the overseer about the building. I could have taken a different route and might not ever have seen it at all.

"You will always be my angel, you know that, right?"

"Yes."

"Call upon me if you ever have any need, large or small."

Tears welled in my eyes at his generosity, even as I was breaking his heart. "Thank you, Thomas. I will. You will forever be in my prayers."

He nodded and smiled ruefully. "I suppose I should take my leave, then. Goodbye, Miss Doyle."

I swallowed hard. My reply came out as a croak, the word suck in my throat. He was already striding back toward his carriage when I was finally able to whisper a clear farewell.

Blinking to clear my vision, I looked around me, trying to orient myself. Mr. Lenehan had mentioned the royal hospital in Kilmainham. That would be my next stop. This Miss McAuley was someone I had to get to know.

*****

Stepping out of the carriage, I inhaled sharply. Towering above me were stone walls better befitting a fort than a hospital. Maybe it was designed that way to make its first residents—well-off retired soldiers of the Royal Army—feel at home, but it certainly didn't give me a restful feeling. The thick walls, and even the steepled clocktower, seemed to press down on me, keeping me in mind of my insignificance in God's grand design.

Thankfully, my destination laid not inside these four imposing walls, but within a square home built on the north end of the hospital complex to house the Adjutant-General, the role Miss McAuley's brother-in-law now held. Built in the French style, its cream-colored stone rose two stories above me, but even with a sharply pitched slate roof and three chimneys, it was dwarfed by the building behind it. I skirted a manicured garden to reach the front door and pulled the rope hanging before me. A bell tolled above—once, twice, three times. A moment of silence followed in which the fragile chirps and tweets of yellow finches dipping and swooping between the tree branches captured my attention. Then the metal doorknob turned and I found myself looking into the eyes of a liveried servant.

"May I help you?" He intoned solemnly.

"Yes. Miss Anna Doyle to see Miss McAuley." I handed him my card. "Mr. Lenehan recommened that we meet."

He looked down at the card, then back at me, before gesturing me inside. "Wait here, please."

The pale green walls around me reflected the French influence evident outside, set off by immaculate white crown molding, chair rails, and baseboards. The wood floors were polished to such a high shine the light from the crystal chandelier above glanced off their surface. I was just beginning to inspect a gilt-framed painting of a somber older gentleman when the servant returned.

"Miss McAuley will see you in the parlor." He led me down the hall to a large room decorated in a similar style, save the walls were the deep blue of clouds in a summer sunset and the room was dominated by a large white fireplace. At our approach, a trim woman with blonde hair looked up from her place seated at a small mahogany table. Her blue eyes regarded me with gentle curiosity as she rose to greet me.

We exchanged introductions and Miss McAuley called for tea. After a few cordial pleasantries, she came to the purpose of our meeting. "Miss Doyle, I assume because Mr. Lenehan suggested you come here that you took an interest in my Baggot Street project?"

"I was drawn to the spot in a way I cannot explain," I admitted.

"God has a way of guiding people where they need to be," she said with a soft smile. "Tell me, what is it about my plans for the space that most interests you?"

"All of it," I replied, feeling my face flush when I thought of the future possibilities. I explained my hopes and dreams of entering the Presentation order and the impediments I'd encountered. Miss McAuley listened attentively, interjecting a question here and there, but for the most part happy to simply let me tell my tale. When I had finished, she sipped at her tea in silence for a few moments.

"What would you like your role to be in the order, if you had your choice?"

It was an odd question, given that nuns were assigned rolls by the Mother Superior without their input, but I had to admit I had my preferences. "When I imagined myself as a nun, I always thought I might be trained as a nurse infirmarian. Or perhaps help to keep the books. I am well educated and very organized."

"Are you now?" Catherine sat forward on her seat, leaning toward me. "Tell me, where did you receive your education?"

"It started out in the usual manor, with tutors and governesses teaching me basic skills like reading and arithmetic, but when I was thirteen, my parents sent me to study in France so that I might have a more well-rounded education than what is typically available to girls here. As a result, I am fluent in French and German. In fact, I only just returned a few months ago. That is why I hadn't yet heard of your venture."

"Indeed, you are fortunate. I myself spent time in France studying their educational methods," I said.

"Really?" she asked. "What was your favorite?"

"It is really a moot point because the bishop has informed me I am to use the Lancastrian monitoring system, but if I had my way I would employ a blend of that and the one in place at St. Cyr. I like having the colored ribbons as rewards for good work to keep the women wanting to advance, but I also like the small groups of the Lancastrian style."

"I wish we were free to develop it."

She gave me a conspiratorial look. "Don't count it out, yet. Perhaps after a few years we can quietly make some changes. Now," She clapped her hands, bringing us both back to the matter at hand, "you said you are organized. That is a skill I desperately need as we get closer to opening. How would you like help me?"

My excitement must have shown on my face, for Catherine held out a hand as if to stave off an overreaction. "Hear me out before you agree to anything. This work is not for the faint of heart and will not be easy. Mr. Lenehan assures me that we will be ready in early autumn to begin taking in boarders. At first our operation will be small, for there will only be so much completed space for us to work in. But I don't wish to delay opening our doors any longer. The poor have had to wait long enough."

I nodded, unable to keep a wide grin from spreading across my face.

"I will be very busy over the next few months as the building progresses. I am currently acting as an adoptive mother to several children, plus helping my sister and brother-in-law with their household here and overseeing my own home at Coolock House. I have been trying to figure out how I could begin my ministry without neglecting my familial duties. And now Heaven has given me the answer in you." She looked up at me, hope evident in her eyes. "That is, if you are willing."

I had to school myself to keep from leaping from my chair to embrace her. "I am. Tell me what you need and I will see it is done."

Over the next half an hour, Miss McAuley, who insisted I call her Catherine from here on, explained what she required, from the ordering of provisions to outfit the kitchen, dormitories, and classrooms to the accounts that needed settling and letters written to secure permission to house the Blessed Sacrament in our chapel or to coax a priest to lend his support at the opening day Mass.

"Knowing you will be attending to such things will be a big weight off my mind," she concluded. "But please know I am not expecting you to do this all on your own. My cousin, Catherine—we call her Kate to distinguish between us—will accompany you. I will meet with you at least once a week, and you may always send a messenger to me if you have urgent questions. Is that agreeable?"

"Most certainly, yes."

"Good." She stood and extended a hand to me. "Come, let me show you the papers you will need."

I followed her down a long corridor. When we reached her study, Catherine stopped in front of a large writing desk strewn with papers. "I wish you to see yourself as my equal in all things to do with this ministry. It may have been my idea—or rather divinely inspired— but you will have just as much invested in it as I do. I want us to be able to say with absolute certainty that our work commenced with two—you and I. God has brought us together for his greater purpose."

Chapter 15

GRACE

June 1827
Montague Manor
Countryside outside of Dublin, Ireland

In the three years since we left the workhouse with no more than a rough plan and a dream, the Doves of Dublin, as our group came to be called, became some of the best known, yet most elusive gentlemen's companions circulating among the city's elite. We were in attendance at balls, state functions, and even occasionally at intimate dinner parties, with the wives of our clients none the wiser.

As we grew in renown, we agreed to do all we could to maintain our anonymity. To that end, we chose to keep opposite living schedules of our clients—we lived in town during the off season, when everyone else retired to the countryside, and during the social season, we flitted from one engagement to the next with no fixed home. It didn't take long for all that moving about became tiresome, and we decided we doves needed a place to nest.

I knew exactly where to begin. On midsummer Lord Montague was known to hold a large garden party to show off the grounds of his sprawling country estate. When one of my clients asked me to accompany him, I seized the opportunity. As we descended the stone steps into the garden, my stomach flipped, a combination of excitement and fear at witnessing Lady Montague eat her words. She had been so clear that I would never set foot on their property again, yet here I was, and much enriched as well.

We joined a small group of people clustered around our hosts. I recognized the Duke and Duchess of Wellington from the first night Margaret had served with us. Also present were the O'Shay sisters, Eliza and Regina, a pair of raven-haired troublemaking twins who were each married to government officials, and the elderly widower Lord Sullivan. They were all peering over their wine glasses at a blonde woman who was deep in conversation with Mr. and Mrs. O'Connell.

"Can you believe the Earl of Pembroke leased her his land on Baggot Street? What must he have been thinking? That is one of the most fashionable areas of the city," Eliza said. "It belongs to monied lines, not to a woman whose fortune was based on a lucky inheritance."

"That's the English for you," Lord Sullivan scoffed. "Willing to make any deal in order to make a profit."

"Surely he had to know she is a Catholic," the Duchess said.

"Perhaps, perhaps not," Her husband responded. "Her family has nearly all converted, so he may not know she is the lone holdout."

"What is she doing with all that land?" Regina asked.

"Running some kind of refuge, I think," Eliza added.

Ah, so the woman in question must be Miss McAuley. Her new venture, which no one traveling through the center of Dublin could fail to see, was the topic *du jour* at every society party the Doves attended. No one liked a newcomer, it seemed, especially not a Catholic.

All I could see was a glimpse of the bun pinned atop her head, but suddenly I was overwhelmed by the urge to run to her, to ask her what happened to Margaret. As far as I knew, she was the last person to see her. I placed a gloved hand on my chest, willing myself calm. I had to remain poised. My past had nothing to do with why I was here tonight; the gossiping nobles in front of me, however, might well enhance my future.

When I brought my attention back to them, Lady Montague seemed to be answering a question I did not hear. "The same thing all those high-minded women do—take in strays, feed them, train them, and the like. They will be producing Catholics faster than rats. Then we will have to deal with them blocking the walks and asking for work while we try to conduct our affairs."

"Lady Talbot said two of her daughters are interested in joining Miss McAuley's cause," the Duchess said. "No girl of mine will set foot there, I assure you. I am having tea with the mayor and his wife two days hence. You can be sure I will voice my displeasure. Who ever heard of a single woman doing such a thing?" She clucked her tongue.

"She must be starting a religious order, then," Lord Sullivan concluded.

"No. That is the juiciest part. She wants the house to be run entirely by laywomen." Lady Montague widened her eyes to emphasize the incredulity of that statement. "In fact, a few of them have already joined her at Coolock House to begin their work while the building is constructed."

"You act as though that is somehow scandalous," Eliza said, looking bored. "The women of my church run charity houses all the time."

"Yes, but the Catholics don't follow the same rules," the Duke explained. "You know how their priests and bishops are—they want to control everything. They can control the nuns, but they have no direct authority over laywomen, so she would be acting outside of their influence."

Regina rolled her eyes. "Those Catholics are so strange."

"And yet they may soon be in power." The Duke nodded toward the man and woman conversing with Catherine. "Mr. O'Connell is campaigning for the House of Commons next year, or so I heard."

"Not if I have anything to say about it," Lord Montague said through gritted teeth—the first words he'd spoken since we'd approached them the group. "I plan to declare my intentions to run for the House of Lords. Trust me, by the time I'm through, he'll look like the Pope-controlled marionette he is and I will be in a place to ensure his downfall."

He took a long slug of whiskey from a cut crystal glass similar to the one Margaret had assaulted him with all those years ago. "And I will take Miss McAuley down along with him."

*****

Later that night, when Mrs. Montague was distracted by other guests, I approached her husband with a proposition—but not of the sort he expected; I would never agree to lay with him again. Instead, I unfurled my lace fan and whispered in his ear, "How exactly do you intend to pay for your political campaign? From what I hear, your star as fallen while mine has ascended."

He barely turned his head, as though he didn't wish to be seen talking to me. "Miss Ryan, I thought that was you earlier. How lovely to see you again." His polite tone was betrayed by the tension in his jaw, something only someone who had known him for years would notice. "Tell me, what lips have been telling you such lies?"

"It isn't lips you should concern yourself with, my Lord, but ledgers."

He raised an eyebrow, pretending nonchalance by sipping his drink. "Is that so?"

"Mmmm-hmmm," I purred in his ear. "Your friends are rather lax with their records, leaving them unsecured in places interested eyes can easily see them."

"And what is it you think you've seen?"

I circled around him, his inability to stand still entertaining me just as much as the light sheen of sweat that was beginning to form on his brow. "Does Lady Montague know you are ruined, or is that another secret you've managed to hide from her?"

"I have no idea what you are talking about."

The musicians began a new song, a waltz, which was perfect for my purposes, as it would keep us close enough to speak yet arouse no suspicion among the other guests. "Ask me to dance," I commanded.

"What?"

"You heard me."

With a grimace, Lord Montague held out a hand to me and bowed, asking if my card was free.

Once I had accepted and we were whirling around the floor, he said, "I didn't think servants knew the waltz."

If he was trying to unnerve me, he would have to try harder. "I didn't know they attended balls, either." Catching his eye after a turn, I added. "Much has changed since we last met, but you are still a master at deflecting subjects you don't wish to discuss. We were talking about your gambling debts and how you've lost practically everything."

He glanced from side to side at the other dancers. "Keep your voice down."

"This can be a short conversation. I know a way you can secure a regular income."

"And what is that?"

"I need a place to stay and would like to rent out your Merrion Square townhome."

Lord Montague opened his mouth to respond, but I cut him off.

"I know for a fact it sat vacant last year because no one of your set wishes to remain in town outside of the social season. Well, I do."

The song came to an end and we retreated to a settee to catch our breath.

Lord Montague narrowed his eyes at me. "Exactly how have you amassed enough wealth to afford such a desirable property?"

I snapped open my fan and began waving lightly, effectively dismissing his query. "You might say it is family money that is on offer."

He looked me up and down, eyes pausing on my left ring finger as though searching for a wedding band. "I thought you were an orphan."

"I am, but I have sisters now, all of whom have their own fortunes." I watched as he processed this information and began to understand the subtext behind my words.

"So, I would be your landlord. But I thought you ladies were nomadic."

"Even doves need a perch," I countered.

"And if I wish to invest in your business in other ways?"

I let the question linger, thinking through the possibilities. This was a man who could not be trusted. Any more than the simplest agreement and he would find a way to try to control us. That he knew my identity was dangerous enough. "I'm afraid we aren't interested in any more at present. But I'll let you know if that changes. Do we have a deal?"

While he did his own mental calculations, I surveyed the room. Lady Montague was watching us with a bemused expression, as though she not only wondered why her husband was still talking to me but was trying to place why I looked familiar. I leaned over, whispering, "Your wife is growing suspicious. Unless you wish to answer questions about why you have been entertaining me overlong, I suggest we conclude our business quickly."

Lord Montague followed my gaze to where his wife was sitting, chatting with a small group of society ladies. A shock jolted me when, rather than turning away from them, he beckoned his wife to us.

"You may have the house under one condition."

"What is that?"

We both watched Lady Montague approach.

"Take Bess into your fold."

"Tired of her already?" I chirped.

"Long ago. And I need to be rid of her." He looked me square in the eye for the first time all night.

"How exactly does this benefit me?"

"You take her in and no one needs to know who you are or what your business is in my house. I will make your excuses."

"And they are?"

Lord Montague breathed an audible sigh of relief as the O'Shay sisters caught his wife's attention, waylaying her progress toward us. "I don't know." He thought a moment. "You can be a group of ladies looking to engage in charitable work, perhaps with that McAuley woman."

"I thought you didn't approve of her."

"I don't, but that could work in our favor. If people think you are spies I sent to infiltrate her organization, they won't be watching for the signs of what you really do."

I eyed him warily. This a was a power grab if ever I had seen one. "Let me guess. If we don't play along, you'll have us arrested?"

He nodded. "And ruined." His voice was as cold and stiff as the grass at dawn in February.

"But if you unmask us, I'll have no choice but to reveal your debts. I know exactly with whom and where the evidence lies. I could end your political ambitions with a single word."

His eyebrow quirked again, followed by a wolfish smile. "You have learned well. Then we have deal?"

Lady Montague had broken away from the crowd and was nearly upon us.

I searched his eyes for some sign I was making a bargain with the Devil, but all they revealed was his usual sensual charm. "We do."

When his wife reached us, Lord Montague introduced me under a false name. "May I introduce Lady Grace Devaney, three years a widow. She has just agreed to rent the Merrion Square house until the season begins. She and her sisters are new to the city and looking to begin charitable work. I suggested our home because it is near to the Society of Friends, as well as to the ministry on Baggot Street."

His wife scoffed, "That eyesore." She met my gaze, not an ounce of recognition in her eyes, even though I was in her employ for years. That told me exactly how much she valued her servants. "You don't wish to work with those Catholics," she said the word like it tasted of sewage, "do you, dear?"

"Oh, I don't know, my Lady," I feigned ignorance. "Lord Montague was just telling me of the variety of choices we have. We aren't members of the Society of Friends, but their work sounds very rewarding, as do the plans of Miss McAuley. I hear she accepts anyone, so that may be a good place for us to start."

Lord Montague cleared his throat. "Indeed. Lady Devaney also mentioned she and her sisters were in need of a new maid of all work, so I recommended Bess. Provided she is willing to go, of course." The last was added as an afterthought, for we all knew Bess had little choice in the matter. I wondered how she would react to hearing her beloved master had pawned her off on me so easily.

The expression of relief on Lady Montague's face told me everything I needed to know about Bess's relationship with her master and mistress.

"How very generous of you, my Lord," she responded. To me, she added, "You may return to collect her on Monday."

*****

When I rang the bell at the Montague estate two days later, Mrs. Donahue greeted me, Bess at her side, trunk in hand. They must really have wanted to be rid of her. I introduced myself under the name Lord Montague had given me and Mrs. Donahue gave me a knowing look, quite similar to the one on Bess's face.

So, neither one was fooled. To Mrs. Donahue she said, "I believe Miss Devaney and I met briefly years ago when she was visiting her sisters in town."

The little viper hadn't changed. She knew exactly who—and at least suspected what—I was. But she would not gain the upper hand. "Now that you mention it," I pretended to recall that fictional encounter, "I believe we did. I look forward to introducing you to my sisters as soon as we arrive in Dublin."

I pinned her with a stare as tight as a mounted butterfly. "After all, you are one of us now."

Chapter 16

ANNA MARIA

August 1827
Coolock House
Outside of Dublin, Ireland

The sun-drenched days of summer were upon Dublin, but all I could see were storm clouds. God had filled me with the sweetest wine by placing Catherine in my life, but then just as quickly forced me to drink the dregs. A letter from the Presentation convent in Killarney arrived at my home in early August informing me and my parents that my sister, Catherine, had died of consumption in May.

My mother and father were inconsolable in their grief. He locked himself in his room while she wept and wailed amid a crowd of friends and family.

My body ceased functioning all together. I couldn't move from my bed, only stare off into the distance, seeing nothing. My sister had gone home to God four months before, and we were just now finding out. The date on the letter showed it had been written shortly after her passing, so the letter must have somehow been waylaid. That meant we missed the opportunity to say farewell to her, even in death. The vigil, funeral Mass, and burial all had taken place without our knowledge, and because the Presentation cemetery was located behind the cloister walls, we couldn't even visit her grave.

My parents were so absorbed in their own grief that no one noticed I was missing from meals or came to check on me. I was roused from my stupor several days later only when a servant came to tell me that Catherine was at my door.

Upon seeing me, Catherine rushed to my side. "Anna Maria, when was the last time you ate? You are so thin." She said something to the servant and the next thing I knew she was undressing me and pacing me a tub of warm water. I laid back, unable to sit up, and she thrust a cup into my hand.

"Drink this. You will feel better."

I took a sip of the hot liquid and grimaced. It was rich like tea, but with a bitter edge.

Seeing my expression, Catherine explained, "I may have added a dram of whiskey. It's what my mother would always do when one of us had a great shock. She called it a 'comfortable cup of tea' because it settles you down and makes you feel more comfortable."

I took another sip, the alcohol less astringent on my tongue now that I was expecting it. It warmed me from the inside out as I swallowed it, bringing feeling back to my limbs and slowly thawing out my heart and mind.

While I drank, Catherine washed my hair and body. "When Kate told me you hadn't been to the House in four days, I knew something had to be wrong. I made inquiries and heard about your sister. I am so sorry." She squeezed my shoulders. "I will do everything I can to help your family."

Once I was out of the tub and dry, Catherine dressed me and wrapped me in my warmest cloak until I shed it of my own accord. While we shared a simple meal of bread and broth, I told her what Mother Superior had written and how my family reacted.

She nodded sympathetically. "I'm afraid," her voice quavered, "that I will be in your place very soon." She went on to confide that her sister, Mary, was suffering from the final stages of tuberculosis and that she was caring for her.

"The only consolation I have is that she was received into the Church in a secret ceremony last Sunday. The only other person present was her daughter. We couldn't tell anyone else because the rest of my family is Protestant, especially her husband, William. He hates Catholics so much, he would lose his mind if he knew. I know it isn't right to deceive him, but I would rather carry her secret with me knowing that she will die with the Sacraments and with her soul right with God. That is what matters in the end."

Catherine insisted that I lay down for a nap after our meal, although I was eager to hear more of her sister. When I woke up, the sun was in a strange place in the sky; it took me several moments to realize that I must have slept all the way through the night and into the next day. I donned my robe and stumbled into the kitchen, where my aunts were busy peeling potatoes and one of my mother's friends was plucking a still-bloody chicken.

"What is all this?" I asked, mystified.

"Your friend Catherine brought us a bounty from a place called Coolock House. She said that even though we missed the formal funeral ceremonies, we should still celebrate your sister's life and mark her entry into Heaven as a family. She suggested making her favorite meal and sharing memories over dinner. The idea brought both of your parents out of their seclusion. Your mother is making Chicken Colcannon Cottage Pie. She is out at the market now getting the spices. Your father is down at the pub and promises to bring back some stout to toast Catherine with."

"What can I do to help?"

*****

A fortnight later, I arrived at the House of Mercy, only to find Kate descending the front stairs, the door closed behind her.

"What is going on?" I asked.

Kate looked up. Her cheeks were blotchy and her eyes red-rimmed as though she'd been crying.

"It's Mary ... Catherine's sister," she added when I didn't recognize the name right away. "She died during the night. I'm on my way to her home in Stillorgan Street if you'd like to come with me."

I hurried to catch up to her. "Yes, please. We can use my carriage. It will be faster."

We found the house still and silent, a cloak of mourning drawn heavily around it. Someone had already affixed a black ribbon to the front door and covered the doorbell clappers in black fabric so as not to disturb the family.

Kate knocked softly on the door. The maid who answered didn't even speak, just ushered us inside, gesturing to the room where we would find Catherine. She was arranging flowers around a coffin that was propped up on two sawhorses. She turned when she heard us enter and dissolved in our outstretched arms with a watery smile.

"How are you holding up?" I asked.

"Not so well," Catherine admitted, her shoulders beginning to shake.

"How are William and the children?" Kate asked after a respectable silence.

Catherine looked up, wiping tears from her face. "Heartbroken. I'm really worried for the little ones. They don't understand that their ma is never coming back. And how can they be expected to when I, who am so much older, can barely grasp that I will never again dance with my sister or hear her laugh?" Tears sprang to her eyes anew.

While Kate sat with Catherine, I found the woman who had greeted us and asked what I could do to assist the household. She gratefully accepted my help and put me to work covering the paintings and mirrors in black cloth, stopping all the clocks at the time Mary had died, and other mourning rituals.

Catherine found me later that night and asked if she could speak with me. We sat in the drawing room because the family was keeping vigil in the parlor. "You have been so kind today. I cannot thank you enough for all of your help."

I started to demur, but Catherine stopped me.

"I'm afraid I am going to ask for a little more, if you are willing."

"Of course, anything."

Catherine swallowed, fighting back a fresh wave of tears that made her eyes glisten. "I am going to need to rely on you and Kate to complete the final preparations for the House. I know we talked about me needing your help previously, but recent events have made it such that I would like to turn that over to you. You already know what needs to be done. You can contact me with any questions. I will either be at Coolock House or with William and the children at Kilmainham. He doesn't know how to care for them, so I will do so until more permanent arrangements can be made."

I thought back to my last inspection of our supplies and list of outstanding items and gave her a report. For the next several hours we talked about what furniture and other necessities could be borrowed from Coolock House. Catherine insisted we obtain the painting of William Callaghan from the main hall and give it pride of place at the House—without his generosity, the House would not exist. We had enough dishes, utensils, and bedding for Kate, me, and about fifty women, but we'd soon need more, so I added contacting local houses to my list. By the time darkness fell, we had a plan.

I was just leaving, when Catherine called over her shoulder, "Oh and Anna, please see that that horrible choir grate or grille or whatever they are calling it is removed from the chapel. I saw it yesterday and I will not stand for it. No matter what Father Kelly thinks, the House of Mercy is not a convent. I will not have iron bars separating my volunteers from those who come to the chapel to pray."

Chapter 17

GRACE

July 1827
Merrion Square
Dublin, Ireland

Despite her initial reluctance, Bess surprised all of us by settling into her new life quickly and taking change of our safety. Though the rest of us had lived on the streets for long periods, Bess had an uncanny sense of danger and how to avoid it or extricate herself if she had to. She never spoke of her life before Lord Montague employed her, so I had to wonder if whatever she had seen in her formative years caused her to develop keen instincts at an early age.

She mapped out at least a dozen routes for us to use to access and leave the house so that no one would notice our comings and goings and it would be difficult for anyone to follow us home. We agreed upon safe meeting places throughout the city, and each of us learned to coo like a dove as a signal of distress to one another. Bess even created a schedule for us to keep up the ruse of being ladies of charity by ensuring we appeared regularly at the right events and helped at various organizations.

Being young, vivacious, and charming—not to mention new to many of our clients, who hadn't given her a second look when she was merely a servant—Bess was more in demand than the rest of us, who relied on our regular customers and the occasional visitor to town to earn our living.

I was under no illusion that Bess's presence in the "dove cote," as we had taken to calling our house, was an accident or happenstance. She was a spy for Lord Montague, and we all knew it. It came as little surprise, then, when I walked into my room—I had taken over Lady Montague's room—to find her digging through my bureau.

"Bess." I addressed her calmly, but firmly enough she would know she'd been caught.

Her hands stilled and she turned around. "Yes?" She wouldn't meet my eyes.

"May I ask what you are looking for?"

She said nothing, only clasped her shaking hands in front of her and looked down.

"Bess?" I said again, gently. "Please, be honest with me. There may be no honor among thieves, but there are also no lies among sisters."

She looked up, revealing a blackened eye. Her nose was crusted with blood.

I was in front of her in three large steps, tilting her chin up toward the light. She flinched at my touch. "Who did this to you?"

Stubbornly, she pulled away. "Who do you think?" She clasped her arms around herself, hugging tightly.

"I know it was one of your patrons, but which one?"

"The one we can't escape. Not as long as we want to keep living here."

"Lord Montague? Why?"

"I ... I overheard him talking about plans to bring us to heel. He was trying to frighten me into silence, but I got away." Tears bubbled up and poured down her cheeks.

"Oh, my poor girl." I embraced her carefully, unsure where else she might be injured. "Every woman who has ever crossed his path has felt the sting of his fists—more than once." I guided her to the bed and we sat. "Can you tell me what happened?"

She sniffled. "I met him as we had agreed for our usual assignation. When I got there, he was drunk. He started raving about how we owe him more than rent. He demanded that I give him anything valuable I could find in the house or he would turn me over to the authorities."

"So that is what you were searching for, then?"

She nodded. "I'm sorry, I know that violates the trust that holds us all together. Please, forgive me."

She looked into my eyes and I saw genuine fear there, a reflection of the terror I had felt many times when facing his wrath. "I do. But you know we will have to deal with this as a group, just as we do with all things."

Bess nodded again. "I know. I will tell everyone tonight after dinner."

"Good. Now go on. What did you overhear?"

"He mentioned something about teaching us our proper place, which is not above men, but beneath them, which could mean any number of things. I don't know exactly what he is going to do, but it is going to be bad."

I squeezed her hand. "Whatever it is, we will face it together."

*****

A letter arrived the very next day, threatening not only our livelihoods but our very lives. It was a cheap ploy, one more likely to have come from one of Lord Montague's associates rather than from the man himself. Not only was it not his style, it wasn't his handwriting either.

Still, if the Doves were going to remain in control, we couldn't let such a gesture pass without a response. I may have let it slip to one of my clients that he should look into Lord Montague's finances.

That night we were all scheduled to attend a party given for a Dublin lord who was soon to be wed. We were used to this rowdy kind of event in which each man attempted to prove his masculinity to the others by bedding as many of us as possible. It wasn't the most pleasant experience, but it paid well, so on occasion we agreed to such an arrangement.

I can't explain why, but my gut twisted as soon as I arrived at the house, one of the many new mansions on Merrion Square, not far from the Dove Cote. Perhaps it was the unfamiliar location, but my instincts were telling me to turn back. But I ignored them. The Doves were women of our word; when we agreed to be present, we would be.

I was the second to arrive, behind Wren, who was already in the arms of one of the men. Given how intoxicated he was, I assumed him to be the groom, which meant Wren was in for a difficult night. At these events, the groom had the right to do whatever he wished with the woman of his choice in honor of his final night of freedom. Silently scanning the room, I counted five other men, all eyeing me with interest. Even the groom-to-be looked up, assessing me as though he was trying to decide if I was a more attractive prospect than the woman he had already chosen.

Over the next quarter of an hour, I accepted their offer of libations—that always made the loathsome task more bearable—and watched the men's reaction as Isa and Jane arrived. Once all four of us were present, our hosts exchanged smirks, each moving to the side of one of us, as though by a prearranged signal none of us could detect.

Two men I hadn't previously been aware of, large and muscular, emerged from the shadows. One, tall and completely bald, I recognized as an associate of Lord Montague, although I couldn't call his name to mind. He strode purposefully to the front door, turned the lock with a click that reverberated like that of a tomb, and stood solidly in front of it, hands behind his back, military-style, as though daring anyone to try to get through him.

I turned just in time to see the other man heading toward the terrace doors, where he did the same, turning to face us with an expression like granite. A shiver ran down my spine. As far as I had seen, those were the only two entrances and exits to the building. I exchanged worried glances with the Doves. Jane had gone pale, her eyes darting around as though trying to find a way out; Isa clung to her as though in doing so, she could stave off whatever was to come; Wren, accepting her fate as the groom's chosen, simply swallowed the whiskey in her glass and gestured for another. No matter how I looked at it, we were trapped.

Usually, such parties involved feasting and music, but now that I had a chance to really see my surroundings, neither musicians nor food was in sight—just plenty of booze, couches, and chairs.

Before I had much chance to contemplate what that might mean, a commotion at the top of the main stairs drew my attention. Lord Montague emerged onto the landing, dragging Bess behind him, though she fought valiantly to wrest herself from his grasp. Once at the bottom of the stairs, Lord Montague shoved her in the direction of one of the men, who immediately claimed her in a possessive choke hold from behind.

It was only when Bess turned that I could see one of her hands was bleeding. I wrested myself from my client's grip and raced over to her, taking her hand in mine. One of the few rules we had was that if anyone harmed our girls, we all left, even if it meant forfeiting our payment. I lifted Bess's hand so that I could inspect it. The source of the blood was a brand placed over the veins and tendons on the top of her hand. I smeared the blood away with the hem of my skirt and found the imprint of a dove burned into her skin.

I looked up at Lord Montague. "What is this?"

He smirked, fully confident in his dominance. "I told you I would find a way to make you mine. Now everyone knows who and what she is, and she can't hide it unless she wants to scar her hand beyond repair."

"But she could always wear gloves," I retorted.

"And risk potential clients mistaking you for refined ladies? I think not."

I looked at Bess, horrified. The wrath she had shown on the stairs had faded and she was shaking. She looked like she wanted to cry, but was too scared or shocked. She pulled her hand from my grip and brought it to her mouth, sucking her wound like a child.

I turned back to Lord Montague. "You are a monster!"

He chuckled. "Face it, Grace. I own you and your little enterprise."

"No!" I shook my head violently. "No one owns us. Not now, not ever."

I cocked my head in the direction of the door, silently commanding my girls to run. We were outnumbered, but perhaps if we all rushed the door at once, at least some of us could escape.

We raced for the opposite door of the one I had pretended to indicate, a prearranged signal we had agreed upon for our safety. The man guarding the door quickly stopped Wren, but Jane managed to get past them, as did I. She unlocked the door and my hand closed around the knob. I flung the door open, but before I could step outside, I was seized by the ankles by one of the men, who sent me sprawling. My knee and elbow broke my fall, taking the brunt of the pain.

"Jane, go!" I yelled. "You know what to do."

With a final nod at me, she turned and fled. We had an agreement that if we were ever in danger, whoever was able would summon the constabulary. Not that any of these illustrious men would be arrested; but the distraction would be enough for us to get to safety.

My assailant dragged me backward, my knees burning as they bumped over the carpet. One of my nails bent backwards and then broke as I clawed for purchase, trying to stop my inexorable motion away from freedom. I was hoisted to my feet and I turned, expecting to see the man who had claimed me earlier, but found myself instead looking into the thunderous eyes of Lord Montague.

"Where do think you are off to, little dove?" His smile was that of a wolf who has sighted the jugular and is waiting to make the kill.

"As far away from you as possible," I spat, shoving vainly against the strong arms that held me immobile. "You can have your house. If this madness is how you are going to treat us, our deal is off."

Lord Montague forced me to walk with him to one of the couches. He removed a long iron stick from the fire. As he brought it to the top of my right hand, I realized what it was. A branding iron. My turn had come.

Behind us, one of the men cried out as another Dove struck back. Lord Montague turned, and it was enough for me to bite into the hand holding the brand. With a yell of his own, he dropped the metal and blindly struck out, hitting me in the face and causing my nose to gush blood. All thoughts of escape left my mind. The pain was so great that for a moment I saw stars, and even when they cleared, all I could do was clutch at my nose.

Lord Montague pushed me onto my back, holding me down with a knee on my chest. "You will obey me!" he yelled, spittle flying from his lips to land on my cheek. "And to ensure you do, I'll make sure everyone knows exactly who you are. That way, all I would have to do is tell the authorities to be on the lookout for women with doves on their right hands and they will find you right away."

I screamed when the glowing orange iron seared the thin flesh protecting the top of my hand, ripping open a trail I would never be able to hide. The government no longer branded thieves, but Lord Montague had taken justice into his own hands.

Gasping through a haze of tears and burning pain, I stuttered, "You have given me a gift, you know?"

"And how is that?" Lord Montague's brow was beginning to sweat.

A manic laugh escaped my lips. "You've taken the last thing I held dear—my anonymity. Now I can tell the world who you really are."

I reached out, grasping blindly for anything I could use as a weapon. I vaguely recalled seeing a statue on the end table. Now, if I could only reach it…

Before I realized what was happening, Lord Montague had the handle of the iron at my throat and was pressing it into my larynx, gagging and suffocating me. "You may threaten to speak, but I could kill you right now. Give me one reason not to," he growled.

Without thinking, I pressed my lips hard against his. If he had one weakness, it was lust. If I could only convince him this was what

I really wanted. He kissed me back even harder, his lips grinding into mine, tongue prying my lips apart and desperately searching my mouth. I managed to wiggle out from under him and flipped him onto his back, so that I was straddling him. If I had more strength, I could have snapped his neck, but as it was, the best thing I could hope for was that he would loosen his grip on the brand.

Lord Montague was just beginning to relax into his passion beneath me, when someone screamed. Concern for my girls strengthening me, I shoved Lord Montague off me and sat up, searching for the source of the sound, only to find Wren holding a brand in her hand, eyes flicking from it to the bloody wound on the groom's temple. She must have hit him with it. He wasn't moving, so it was very possible he was dead. I had to get her out of there before anyone else could react, or we would be joining him in the afterlife.

Jumping over the back of the couch, I pulled Wren to the door. The guards were busy tending to the groom, so our path to freedom was unimpeded. I turned back to Isa, when I caught sight of a dark-haired form on the floor. Bess lay prone not far from the groom's feat, completely unconscious.

"What have to you done to her?" Wren screamed.

By now, Isa had caught up to us and was urging us out the door.

"No," I fought back. "We can't leave Bess. I won't leave anyone behind."

"It is her or all of us," Wren hissed. "Let the authorities deal with her when they get here. Right now, we have bigger problems."

"Plus, she never really was one of us," Isa said over her shoulder as we ran, seeking any place we could hide.

Shouts started to pursue us, the lords like a pack of angry hunting dogs, when the crunch of carriage wheels caught up to us from the front drive. Jane must have found the authorities.

We dove for the shadows, knowing, thanks to Bess's obsessive preparations, which alleys would lead us to safety. But we weren't quite fast enough. From a distance, an officer shouted, "You there. Stop!"

We ran, hair flapping in the wind, silk shoes quickly growing wet as we trounced through puddles and gutters. But it didn't matter. All that mattered was escape. Brick walls and wooden doors blurred past. I tried to listen for the sound of pursuers, but all I could hear was my own ragged breathing and pounding heart. In the distance, a cry went up at the house, as the police—I assumed—entered uninvited. Ahead, Wren called my name.

I came to a halt at a tall wooden gate topped with jagged finials. Locked, it was the only thing that stood between us and safety. Wren picked up a fallen brick and started pounding on the metal casing. Less than a dozen strikes later, she had loosened the plate holding the lock in place. We all shoved at the gate at the same time and, with a splintering of wood, the locking mechanism broke free and we tumbled out onto Baggot Street.

Wren immediately collapsed, but she was still conscious and breathing so Isa and I carefully hoisted her to her feet and helped her to walk between us. We needed to put as much space as possible between us and the mansion, and preferably, find a hiding place where we could rest before seeking safety.

"What are we going to do?" Isa asked, her eyes wide, voice shaking. She was normally so calm and collected, but the evening's events had pushed her near to hysteria. "A lord is dead, Bess may be too, and we're all marked. No doubt Lord Montague has a bounty on our heads."

We walked in silence for a long while, listening for sounds of pursuit.

"We scatter. Go wherever you feel safe. Hide."

"That will keep us safe for a while, but we can't hide forever," Isa pointed out.

"I know. I have an idea, but it will take some time. If you can stay alive and out of jail for a few months, I will find you," I said.

"How?"

"We know where we hide. I know where to look."

"So does Bess," Isa pointed out. "We have no idea what Lord Montague will do to her to find us. She may tell him our safe places. There is no way he will let us go now."

She had a point.

"Then we build new nests. Stay out of site until we can get under the protection of someone just as powerful as he is."

"Who is that?" Wren mumbled, just conscious enough to follow along.

"Catherine McAuley."

Chapter 18

CATHERINE

September 24, 1827
64A Lower Baggot Street
Dublin, Ireland

A small crowd had already gathered by the time my carriage arrived at the House of Mercy from Kilmainham. The workers had paused in their labors and were standing in vertical lines like manor house servants welcoming their master home from the city season. At their head were John Curran and Dennis Lenehan, the carpenter and architect. A small crowd of supporters were gathered behind them, including two priests. To one side, a group of women waited, dressed in plain gowns, their hair pulled into messy buns, arms crossed and heads inclined toward one another in conversation, clearly uncomfortable being part of the spectacle around them. Some had babies in their arms or children hiding in their skirts. Anna Maria had assured me enrollment in the school was strong, so these had to be our first students.

I squeezed Kate's hand and she returned the gesture, blessing me with one of her radiant smiles. With unrulily brown curls and plain features, Kate wasn't the most beautiful girl, but the joy that radiated from her could melt anyone's heart. If I was to choose the ideal person to put wary women at ease, it would be someone just like her. I prayed our ministry here would be enough to satisfy her religious calling. Just as Anna Maria had wanted to become a Presentation nun, Kate longed to join the Dominicans, but she had agreed to put off her calling in order to help begin operations at the House.

"Are you ready?" I asked her, the slight nervous tremor in my voice audible even to my own ears.

"Are *you*?" She asked, raising a bushy brown eyebrow.

I took a deep breath. "Almost. Let us thank our Lord that this day has finally come." Together we offered a prayer of gratitude and recited a Hail Mary to Our Lady of Mercy, whose feast was today and to whom I dedicated our work.

As I descended from the carriage, red ringlets caught the light as Anna Maria turned toward me, offering her own grin and a deferential nod of the head. How many months would it take her to stop treating me like her superior? As far as I was concerned, we were equals in this venture, she and I, and someday I would make her see that, too.

The crowd parted to let Kate and me through. I stopped to greet Mr. Lenehan and Mr. Curran before ascending the four stairs to the small front portico. "You have both done a wonderful job," I told them, taking each of their hands in mine. I looked up, astonished at the progress they had made since I had visited in August. Then, the House had been a mere shell, but now the walls and roof were complete, and inside, two fully furnished rooms waited for our ministry to begin.

Mr. Lenehan handed me a set of metal keys, nearly thirteen centimeters in length. He went through each—there were only three at the moment—and explained which locks they fit.

We joined Anna Maria before the bright red front door. Once hugs were exchanged all around, I turned to the crowd. "Thank you for being here today to witness the fulfillment of a dream—not only my own, but that of Mr. William Callaghan, without whom none of this would be possible."

A light smattering of applause followed.

"This building, which we christen today the House of Mercy, will serve as a refuge for all women and children who have nowhere to turn and for those who wish to better themselves. May they be received here with the same tenderness and compassion with which we would welcome the Lord himself. In the name of Our Lady of Mercy, we commence the work God has given us."

I placed the key in the lock, and Kate and Anna Maria wrapped their hands around mine. We counted out three heartbeats and, as one, turned it, opening the main entrance for the first time. We whooped and hugged one another as a cheer went up from the crowd behind us.

After three years, much anxiety, and even more prayers, God's work had begun.

Chapter 19

ANNA MARIA

September 24, 1827
House of Mercy
Dublin, Ireland

Catherine wanted to begin our ministry straight away, so as soon as the front door was unlocked, I escorted two dozen waiting girls into the long, rectangular room that would serve as our school. They naturally clustered together in scared groups, with one or two left out to fend for themselves. Poor dears. I had been one of them as a child as well.

"Good morning. I am Miss Doyle, your teacher. Please line up here when I call your name." I motioned to the open area in front of me. I went through the list Catherine had prepared, from Étaín Ahern to Abigail Young, and they lined up.

Our school was taught in the Lancastrian system, in which an adult like me or an older student led small circles of students gathered around her based on ability. The same subject was taught to all groups at once, but at different levels, and we switched topics approximately every hour. It would be difficult right now, with only me to teach all of the classes, but soon the advanced students would distinguish themselves and I'd be able to assign them to groups of younger or struggling students so they could instruct them while I oversaw the running and discipline of the classroom.

I had just assigned the oldest girls to each group to teach various aspects of religion, from Sacrament preparation to basic prayers and Bible study, when a knock sounded at the classroom door. Kate stood there, a thin envelope in her hand. "This just arrived for you. I thought you would want to see it straight away, given the postmark."

A mumbled a distracted "thank you," to her, already opening the envelope, which was marked with the seal of the Presentation Convent in Killarney, where Colleen had taken her vows. What could they want? They had buried my sister before even letting us know she was dead and given her few meager possessions to the poor. There was nothing left of her for us. But that was how it was done behind cloister walls. Once you took your vows, you never left, even in death.

I removed a sheet of paper, immediately recognizing the precise handwriting of Sister Mary Aloysius Ryan, the Mother Superior. It was the same perfect script that had broken my world apart only a few months earlier. I hesitated for a moment before allowing my eyes to fall upon her words, scared of what I might read.

Glory be to Jesus Christ most holy.

> *My dear Anna Maria, I wish you all of God's blessings and pray this letter finds you well. I write to you with glad tidings and news I know you will receive with a grateful heart. It is my great joy to share with you that our congregation voted in our last chapter meeting to offer you your sister's place among us. We know how strong your vocation is, and we can extend this opportunity without burdening your family, because they already paid for Colleen's dowery. We would be happy to receive you on the Feast of Christ the King, which should give you ample time to prepare. Please reply as soon as possible.*

I stopped reading, letting the single page float to the classroom floor. I looked up, not really seeing anything but knowing where I needed to be. Excusing myself, I fled blindly down the stairs to the chapel, pushed through the opening in the grate, and flung myself onto the cold stone floor at the foot of the crucifix that hung above the altar.

Bent double, my forehead nearly touching the ground, tears coursed down my face and I gasped for air as great sobs wracked my body in uncontrollable bursts of emotion. All I could think was, *Why now God? Why today of all days?* I was the punchline to some cruel divine joke, or at least that was how it felt.

As my sobs subsided and I began to breathe normally, I peered up at the Host in the monstrance, which we believed was the true Body of Christ present with us on earth, seeking the face of Jesus. *Why did you do this to me? Have I not been begging you for years for the chance to be yours as a Presentation Sister? Why answer me today, when I begin my work here with Catherine? Why place this cup before me?*

Was it a temptation, an attempt by the evil one to lure me away from the good I might do here? Or was this letter a sign that this was not where I belonged after all? My mind chased itself in circles, my heart more torn every single time I returned to my starting point.

If I left here and joined the Presentation order, I would be fulfilling a lifelong dream. Yes, my place was already paid for, but that still meant I would be leaving my parents alone. They wouldn't dare interrupt my brother's life in London, even for this. Whereas if I continued my work here, they were provided for and I still was able to help those in need.

Was it really fair for me to take a highly coveted place when there were plenty of other girls who knew with complete certainty that the Killarney convent was meant to be their home for the rest of their days? There were so many other girls like me who longed to become nuns but whose families couldn't afford a dowery. Perhaps giving my sister's place to one of them would be the right answer.

On one hand, the choice was obvious: Remaining at the House of Mercy would be best for everyone involved. But on the other, turning down the offer meant formally putting an end to any chance I had at becoming a nun. There would be no second chance. The hope of being a bride of Christ had been such an important part of my life for so long, it felt like part of my identity. Who was I without it? Did I owe it to myself to at least see if it worked out in the Presentation cloister? If so, I was where God wanted me; if not, perhaps Catherine would take me back.

Catherine. We had become so close over the last six months. The thought of never seeing her again was so painful that I burst into tears again at the mere thought of losing her friendship. The idea of facing the world without her compassionate strength behind me was more than I could bear. As she had said, this ministry commenced with two and it would continue with two as well.

Images of the students I had met less than an hour earlier flashed on the inside of my closed eyelids. I might not know them yet, but I wanted the chance to get to know them, to watch them grow and learn. My work here would allow me to see the effect my efforts were having on them. Comparatively speaking, spending my days in prayer inside the convent enclosure, hoping that God granted my requests according to his holy will, suddenly didn't seem as appealing as it had a few months ago. I wanted to be where I could help people directly.

"Miss Doyle?" A little voice reached me from a side door leading off into one of the hallways.

I quickly dashed any remaining tears from my face, trying to mask the fact that I had been crying. I looked up to see a small brunette girl, one of the youngest from my classroom. "Yes, dear?"

She hung back in the doorway, as though afraid to enter, one finger in her mouth. "I had to use the water closet," she explained, still chewing on her finger. "I got lost."

I rose, my knees popping in protest after so long on the hard floor. "Well then, we'd better get you back to where you belong, shouldn't we?"

She slipped a clammy hand into mine and my heart lifted, suddenly weightless as a cloud. *Thank you.* I directed the thought to Heaven as I turned to lead the girl back to the classroom. *We'd best get me back to where I belong, as well.*

I made up my mind then and there that as soon as I had a break from teaching, I would reply to Mother Superior, expressing my gratitude, but also my regret, and requesting that my space be given to another girl in need. The House of Mercy was my home now, and these women and children were my family. To believe otherwise was sheer folly.

*****

When I had a moment between classes, I tentatively knocked on Catherine's office door. I couldn't keep something as momentous as this to myself. I had to confess my temptation to leave. She needed to know I was weak.

Catherine bade me to enter and I sat down on the opposite side of her desk. Looking up into her eyes, I told her everything, about how Sister Aloysius contacted me and I turned her down and about my vow to remain at Baggot Street. "I'm sorry," I said to her when I had run out of words. "I don't know what came over me."

Catherine came around the desk and embraced me. "Between the excitement of the opening, teaching your first class, and this, you have had a very unsettling morning."

She smoothed her black skirts and sat down next to me.

"You renounced the life you'd been planning for since you were a girl in favor of one that is radical and unpredictable. That would be enough to upset anyone. You've spent your entire life identifying as a future Presentation Sister. And today, without warning, you rejected that part of yourself. It's natural to feel confused and hurt and yes," she stroked my hair, "even a little guilty. But you have nothing to feel guilty for. You were honest with yourself and with Sister Aloysius, and that is all God asks."

I sniffled. "Sister Aloysius really despises us." I had gone back and read the rest of the letter, which was brimming with ire and hateful accusations that we were rebellious, prideful, and dangerous not only to the Church but to the entire Catholic community of Dublin. Her closing line made her position perfectly clear: "I will pray for you and everyone in that cursed House. But do not expect my support when it all tumbles down like Babble."

Come to think of it, she sounded a lot like Lord Montague.

Catherine sighed. "Oh, I am aware. You are not the only one to receive letters from her. Between her, Father Kelly, and Lord Montague, I fear we have raised the ire of a very unholy triumvirate."

I laughed.

"All because we are trying to help others. Sister Aloysius is jealous because we are doing what her order was intended to do but lacks the courage for. Father Kelly is showing himself to be very concerned that the monitary donations to our ministry might take away from St. Andrews. And Lord Montague," she paused, looking out the window at the cross atop the portico, "well, I don't know why he hates us other than that we are Catholic and doing what he will not ..."

"And we are females," I added. "They refuse to admit women can be chosen by God to do his work in the world."

"There it is then. Our own trinity of 'sins.'" She smiled at me. "We cannot change other people's hearts by force. Believe me, I have tried. The best we can do is pray God will move them with his grace and they will see our sincerity through our actions."

Chapter 20

GRACE

September 24, 1827
House of Mercy
Dublin, Ireland

"Hello. How may I help you?" A friendly young woman with bushy brown eyebrows greeted me at the front doors of the massive white building on Baggot Street before I'd even had a chance to ring the bell.

I glanced up at her shyly, well aware of how reduced I must look in comparison, the result of hiding for the last two weeks, trying to survive until I could seek refuge here. Her clean hair was pulled back into a tight braid that wrapped around her head, while mine, snarled and greasy, hung limply down my back. Her black British merino dress was crisp and fell into perfectly straight pleats; my shirt and calico skirt were caked with dirt and sweat and likely smelled, too, and my shawl was frayed. For a moment, I considered turning back, but then I looked into this woman's eyes. Instead of the usual pity or distain, I found only concern and genuine warmth. "M-my name is Grace. May I please speak with Miss McAuley? Please, I have nowhere else to go."

The seconds between my request and her answer stretched for what felt like hours as I braced myself for rejection, but she only smiled. "Of course, come in, Grace." She stepped back to allow me inside. "Please forgive the sparse furnishing. We have just opened and don't have everything in place yet."

I looked around in wonder. The floors, though coated in a thin layer of sawdust, were finely tiled; the walls were painted or papered in rich hues; gas lamps lit the rooms and corridors; and, perhaps most importantly, the slate roof kept out the cold and wet. Compared to where I had been living, this place was nicer than Dublin Castle.

"I know," I said in response to her remark about the opening, "I have been waiting for this day for three years."

For a moment she looked puzzled, but then she smiled sweetly. "Won't you please take a seat? I will let Miss McAuley know you are here. Please, help yourself to some tea."

I lowered myself gently into the rush-seat chair she indicated. Once she had left, I carefully selected a cup and saucer from the service on the table and began to pour. At the touch of the smooth ceramic handle, memories of pouring tea for guests at the Montague estate came rushing back, reminders of the woman I had been before. Recalling that I had not always lived in abject poverty with memories and knowledge that could get me killed, I straightened my spine. I had been comfortable once and would be again.

I had only just sweetened my tea and taken my first glorious sip when the pocket doors to my right slid open to admit the woman I had glimpsed at Lord Montague's garden party. She was dressed in similar fashion to the woman who had greeted me, in a plain black dress. She certainly didn't look the part of an heiress today. "You must be Grace," she said warmly. "I am Catherine McAuley. Welcome home."

I noticed she didn't say "welcome to *my* home," but greeted me as though I already belonged here.

"Thank you, madam."

Miss McAuley smiled, her cheeks coloring slightly. "Oh now, none of that. You and I are equals here. Please, call me Catherine."

Heat rose in my cheeks so quickly I thought they might burn. "Thank you for your hospitality, Catherine." I took a deep breath. "I am here to beg for your help. I have nowhere left to seek refuge and I would very much appreciate the chance to rest my head somewhere safe. I have skills. I can cook and clean for you, if you'd like." I was rambling, desperate for her to say yes.

"No begging necessary. All you must do is ask and that you have done." Catherine cocked her head and examined me closely. "You don't speak like one used to living on the streets, do you?" She said more to herself than to me. "Why don't you tell me a little more about your situation."

I intended only to tell her in broad strokes what had happened over the last several years, but as soon as I started speaking, the entire story came out, starting with my aborted pregnancy and my time at the Montague house. When I mentioned Margaret and how we had fled to Coolock House, Catherine's eyes widened and she sat forward in her chair.

"I apologize for interrupting your story, but I remember her."

"You do?" Momentary relief washed over me before my whole body tensed, preparing for her answer to what I was about to ask. "Do you know what happened to her? The last I ever saw of her was at your gates."

Catherine looked down into the teacup cradled in her palm and shook her head. "I'm afraid I do not." When she raised her eyes to me, they were brimming with unshed tears. She relayed everything that happened once she met Margaret, including her long search for her and her ongoing hope that Margaret would one day find her way here.

I slumped back in my chair. "So, you know no more than I," I said, more to myself than to her.

Catherine reached out a hand to grasp mine. "Please know that taking her to that inn is one of the biggest regrets of my life." Her voice shook and she wiped at one eye with her free hand. "I have asked God's forgiveness every day since. Now it is time that I ask yours. Can you forgive me for abandoning your friend in her time of need? For putting her in danger when I should have given her refuge?"

Catherine was crying in earnest now, her face pink and blotchy. Tears rose to my own eyes, their stinging pressure a reminder of all I had lost. I had cried many times since that fateful night, but never for Margaret, always holding out hope. Now that Catherine had confirmed Margaret was missing, the tears were free to flow down my cheeks.

Deep in my heart, the small remaining ember of hope was doused. Margaret was gone, likely forever. Part of me wanted to rage at this woman and hold her accountable for her uncharitable actions toward my friend, but her broken expression told me there was nothing I could say that she had not already accused herself of. She held the heavy heart of one condemned anew each day to a penance more severe than I could ever mete out.

The devil on my shoulder urged me to wallow in the betrayal I felt by holding a grudge. *If Margaret had been safe at Coolock House*, it hissed, *she could have rescued you before Lady Montgomery turned you out and all that has happened wouldn't have occurred. Why should you forgive her?* It was tempting to believe this tale, but the angel on my other side reminded me that my fate was not dependent on Margaret's. *You don't know that she would have come for you. Do not hold Catherine accountable for your choices.*

I took a deep breath, willing the tears to cease and forcing my mind back to the present. "There is nothing to forgive," I said to her, realizing as the words came out that I truly meant them. "You made the best decision you could at the time. That is all anyone can do. God knows I have experience in that."

Catherine squeezed my hand. "Thank you. You cannot know what this means to me. Perhaps one day I will be as merciful to myself as you have been."

She refreshed both of our cups and I continued with my tale, telling her about my time at the workhouse, the formation of the Doves, and all of the highs and lows since—minus any crimes committed. This woman might be kind, but I didn't trust her not to call the authorities. By the time I finished speaking, my heart was lighter, my shoulders had unknotted, and a soaring sense of hope I hadn't felt in ages lifted my spirit.

Catherine sat back in her chair, clearly absorbing all I had relayed. "My dear, you have been through a lot, haven't you?" She fell silent, lost in thought. Just when I began to fear I had said too much, she continued, "You are exactly the type of woman I had in mind when I first dreamed of this house, and it is clear God has been guiding you in this direction for years. I am honored to offer you a place here."

I jumped up, a grin spreading across my face, and Catherine instinctively stood as well. Forgetting all social niceties, I encircled her in a tight embrace. "Thank you so much. You have truly saved my life."

"I don't know about all that," she said demurely when I finally released her. "Come, meet my companions and they will show you around your new home."

*****

That night, after a grand feast provided by Daniel O'Connell himself, Catherine led me up to her private bedchamber. "You are the only one who would truly understand this," she said as she opened the door.

The room was dark, save for a small hurricane lamp sitting on the street-facing windowsill that illuminated a circle of the knotty pine floorboards.

Catherine walked over it to it, fingering the glass shade. "I intend to keep this burning at all hours of the day and night as my signal to the women of Dublin. I want them to know ..." She cleared her throat and tears sprang to her eyes. "I want her to know—Margaret, and all the others like her—that they can come to us any time, day or night, and find refuge here. No one will ever be turned away again, not by me or by any of the women who work in this house. I won't allow it."

"You still hold her in your heart, don't you?"

She nodded, pressing her lips together to avoid sobbing. "I regret not doing more. I will carry that sin of omission as long as I live—no matter how many absolutions are granted to me."

I turned back to the lamp, drawing solace from its warm glow, so much like Margaret's trusting heart. It was a fitting symbol indeed. I could almost see her smile reflected in its glow. My own eyes began to sting.

"I pray for her every day," Catherine continued. "I pray that she knows how sorry I am. Wherever she is, if I keep this light on, she will come. Someday, she will see it and know I have made a place for her."

Chapter 21

CATHERINE

January 1828
House of Mercy
Dublin, Ireland

Our ministry quietly celebrated the turning of autumn to winter and welcomed the joyful season of Advent alongside dozens of new residents and students. By the time Mr. O'Connell blessed us with a whole pig to roast for our Christmas Day celebration, the butterflies in my stomach had settled in to rest.

That is, until I picked up the newspaper one morning. My cheeks grew increasingly flushed with each line I read. That man had some nerve. And in the *Irish Times* nonetheless!

"Charity is a noble effort that is to be lauded, make no mistake about that. Our city suffers from an overpopulation of beggars, prostitutes, and other criminals who need to be dealt with in one way or another. But I am certain that drawing them into our most wealthy neighborhoods is not the answer.

"Yet, this is exactly what Miss Catherine McAuley has been doing for the last four months. And what gain have we seen from such activity? An increase in crime and vagrancy, for one. For another, the residents of this area—of which I am one during the season—cannot go about our daily lives and activities without being accosted by the women of this house. They beg us for employment, money, food, just about anything they can think of. If they do not get those things under Miss McAuley's roof, what is the purpose of her building?

I have personally interviewed several of them and can say from experience that they are woefully unprepared for working in service. Many only use the House of Mercy as a night shelter and spend the daylight hours clogging our streets and doorways. In short, they are a menace. Rather than helping improve Dublin's vagrancy problem, all Miss McAuley has done is ruin one of the few safe areas left. In my opinion, her House should be shut down, or at the very least moved to another part of the city where such people gather."

I laid the paper down and gazed out the carriage window. We were close to Baggot Street and I had to be prepared to address this anonymous editorial. Though it was unsigned, there was little doubt who penned it. It was mid-morning already, so there was no way Grace and Kate hadn't already seen the paper. No doubt they were as troubled as I. This was one of the downsides of traveling back and forth between the hospital, Coolock House, and Baggot Street each day. So often, by the time I arrived at one place, something had already happened. If I could only complete my duties as executor of my sister's will, I could move out of the hospital. Then I could sell Coolock House. If I lived at the House of Mercy full time, I would be able to address things as they occurred rather than spending the rest of my day trying to catch up.

The carriage slowed, then stilled, and I got out. As soon as I stepped over the threshold, Anna Maria was there, flinging the newspaper down in a fit of temper.

"He has gone too far this time," she exclaimed.

"Good morning to you, too," I responded, amused by her uncharacteristic outburst.

Grace followed us, taking my coat, gloves, and bonnet as I shed them, years of experience rendering the gesture automatic.

"How dare Lord Montague speak ill of our women like that?" Anna went on. "He can say what he likes about us, but they are innocents. If this keeps up, no one will want seek help here."

"Oh, I wouldn't go that far," I said, struggling to keep my voice calmer than I felt.

"I would," Kate chimed in, handing me the morning mail.

"As would I," Grace said. "Lord Montague is a powerful man."

"But he's not the only one. As infuriating as this is, I doubt it has much to do with us," I said.

"How do you figure?" Kate asked. "He mentioned you by name."

"Be that as it may, he is simply upset that Kate and Betsy O'Connell have agreed to be daily helpers here. Grace, you know more than anyone about his odd acquaintance with their father. If I didn't know Daniel so well, I'd say he encouraged his daughters to volunteer their time just to upset Lord Montague."

Grace laughed. "I only know Mr. O'Connell from afar, but he does have quite a sense of humor, I'll grant you that."

"So, what are we going to do about it?" Anna wanted to know.

I looked up from the envelopes. "We will do nothing."

At least not now. I longed to give that man the tongue lashing he deserved next time I laid eyes on him.

"We will continue our ministry as though we never saw his editorial. He is merely posturing to try to win the favor of the Lords in the upcoming Parliamentary election. What we do here depends not on any man; it is God's work. Always remember that. God is charge and will do as he wills. Our only responsibility is to the women and children who need our help."

"I wish I had your faith," Kate muttered.

I patted her on the shoulder. "It will come with time. I was not always this confident, and there are days still when I doubt everything."

I handed the unimportant letters back to Anna to handle, holding back two I wished to address myself. One was from Mr. O'Hanlon at the Carmelite monastery, and the other from Father Blake, who had been helping me establish rules for our way of life.

"I will be in my office if anyone needs me," I announced, headed for the large winding staircase at the center of the first floor.

Once situated at my desk, I glanced over to the oil lamp to ensure it was burning as it should be—why I worried, I don't know; Grace had made it her personal mission to tend the lamp in memory of Margaret, wherever she may be—and said a silent prayer that anyone who needed help would put more stock in its welcoming light than in Lord Montague's vile words.

I opened the first letter, from Mr. O'Hanlon. He inquired as to our welfare and then asked how the Carmelites might help us. God bless him and all his nuns. They did more for us from inside their enclosure than most of Dublin's wealthiest did in the fullness of their freedom. I removed my leather-bound ledger from the desk drawer. The school children already numbered in the hundreds, and that wasn't counting their mothers and the other women who sought shelter here. As we faced the depths of winter, they all needed new clothes, heavier coats, and new stockings and shoes. Perhaps the Carmelites could help us organize a fund drive or donations for them.

Or maybe it would be more prudent to ask for their help in recruiting volunteers who could then solicit funds or donations themselves. Lord Montague's scathing assessment of our ministry echoed again in my mind. I shook my head to clear it. *Jesus, Mary, and Joseph, grant me peace of mind. Holy Ghost, inspire my heart with the will of God.*

I stared out the window, my eyes gazing on the Bank of Ireland but my thoughts far, far away. All that money in one place, yet our children shiver and suffer in the cold. How was that fair? But then again, Jesus wept over the city of Jerusalem and he had the power to heal all ills. Who was I to assume I could do anything more? And God had just blessed us with two new volunteers. There would be more to come; where Daniel O'Connell's daughters went, others followed. We already had more than doubled our daytime staff, taking on a few of the girls from my old Coolock House school, although Kate, Anna, and Grace remained the only ones who lived in the building overnight. It was small progress, but it was better than nothing.

I turned to the second envelope. Father Kelly, originally a supporter of the House, had been growing more disgruntled with our operations—or maybe just with me—since we opened. Like Lord Montague, he did not approve of my decision to begin this ministry without Church approval—something I was sure I had not heard the end of yet.

He also wanted to know what rules had been established for our volunteers. In truth, there weren't many. We all wore the plain black dresses, but that was more out of a sense of egalitarianism than anything else. We didn't want the wealthier volunteers to show up in their finery and jewels and unintentionally intimidate those seeking our help. The volunteers also lived at home, but eventually, as the rest of the House was completed, that would change for those who desired. Compassion and charity were to be foremost in our minds, and every woman promised to treat each she met as though it was Jesus himself.

But Father Kelly wanted more. What was our daily schedule? When did we pray? When did we eat? At what times were the ladies away from the House? Who was our custodian? Our cook? Did one woman hold that role, or did we rotate duties? Honestly, we had been so busy setting up the school and tending to the needs of our wards, we hadn't had the time to sit down and discuss such formalities. We simply did what needed doing.

But I couldn't put Father Kelly off forever. I named Anna Maria my assistant and the head teacher, with Kate acting as her protegee;

Grace as the teacher of women seeking domestic training, a job she had taken on happily; and several other women to fulfil the needs of the House. I was just beginning to draw up a sort of schedule when a soft tapping at my door interrupted my thoughts.

"Yes?" I called.

Grace poked her head around the door. "I hope I am not disturbing you."

"No, of course not. Please, have a seat."

Grace sat down tentatively, perching on the edge of the chair as though she were afraid to commit to sitting or standing. At my inquisitive look, she took a deep breath.

"I've been thinking a lot about what Lord Montague said in the paper."

"Don't pay him any mind. I understand how what you have been through with him might make you skittish, but I assure you I have faced more formidable men than he."

Grace rubbed the back of her hand, where the brand of a dove had been set into her skin. "When you so kindly accepted me into this place, you told me that any woman or child who was in need was welcome here. Did you really mean that?"

"Of course. Certainly, you have seen that for yourself by now."

Grace nodded vigorously. "Yes, I meant no disrespect. I only ask because he complained so vigorously about the character of the women here." She cleared her throat. "I only ask because I have had word from the other Doves. They are still in hiding from Lord Montague, and I was hoping the House might be their way out of danger."

I mentally went over our ledgers in my mind. "There are, what, six of you?"

"Five, including me. I know where they are all hiding, except for Bess. I'll keep looking, but she'll likely have to come us."

I steepled my hands in front of me. "We are a shelter, yes, but you know we don't offer security. I cannot guarantee their safety."

"They have a much better chance here than on the streets."

"I still have to interview them, but I'm sure they will all be candidates to join our educational program or maybe even work in the House itself."

Grace reached across the desk and placed her hands over mine. "Thank you so much. You have saved our lives."

I smiled, embarrassed at the high praise. "I will do all I can for them."

With another thank you and a wave over her shoulder, Grace departed.

I took a deep breath and let it out slowly. Picking up my pen, I added to the list for Father Kelly, "Anyone is welcome at the House of Mercy, be they volunteer or asylum seeker, provided they learn a trade so they are able to provide their living expenses. We do not count a person's past or present against them. Their poverty, illness, crimes, or reputation are of no concern to us, provided they do nothing illegal on our grounds. As for any sins, it is God's job to judge and forgive; we merely tend to the body and mind so the soul may grow and flourish."

Let him do with that what he willed.

Chapter 22

GRACE

March 1828
House of Mercy
Dublin, Ireland

"Goodnight, Mr. O'Leary," I called, waving to the drunken man who had mistaken our front door for his—again. I'd pointed him in the direction of his home and watched until he stumbled out of sight before closing and locking the door.

In the distance, the bells of St. Teresa's tolled twelve times. Exhausted, I rested my head against the wood and immediately my eyes closed; they felt weighted with lead. Being night porter was my least favorite position at the House, but it one of the most important. So many women were only able to come to us under cover of night, and we had to be alert to receive them; but no one, including Catherine, had yet made it a full night without falling asleep at least once.

Sometime later, a gentle tap on the door woke me from a light slumber. I opened the door, still half asleep, and for a moment, I thought I was dreaming. There was Wren, standing in front of me, dripping with rain. It wasn't until she lifted her right hand to push her sodden hair from her face that I saw the brand on her hand and realized it was really her. It took all I had not to scream her name as I pulled her into a long, hard embrace and tugged her inside, calling to Isa and Jane to join the reunion. At last, all of the doves had come home to roost.

We kept a small store of clothing, towels, diapers, and other necessities in the reception room for just this reason. While Wren dried and changed, I stoked the fire to life, feeding it fresh kindling and wood. Soon it emitted a glorious warmth and should help Wren relax and stave off any chill she may have caught. If not, the tea brewing on the hook above it should help.

Once Wren was settled and seated as close to the fire as safety allowed, I pulled the pocket doors mostly closed to give us privacy, but left them open enough that I could hear if anyone came to the door.

For a long moment we simply stared at one another, marveling that we were together once again. Finally, I broke the silence. "Are you hungry? I can get you some bread and cheese, if you'd like."

She shook her head. "Not quite yet. I am happy with the tea for now. Thank you."

Catherine always taught us not to rush the women to tell their stories, but this was Wren, not a stranger. I hadn't seen her for nearly six months and I was bursting to know where she had been. But it was her story to tell in her own time, just as the others had done.

As soon as Catherine had given permission for the Doves to seek refuge at the House, I had whispered to a handful of people they might turn to that they were welcome here at any time. As they slowly found the House of Mercy, I learned their stories. Jane was the first to join us when she saw me washing the windows of the ground level one day and dared to inquire. Isa found us through Martha, who was still happily employed at the workhouse and wouldn't hear of leaving. And now, finally, Wren was here.

That left only Bess, whom I feared was either in jail for the groom's murder or long dead. I scoured the newspapers every day, assuming the arrest of a young woman for the murder of a Lord would be reported, but I had found nothing that sounded like her. I doubted the police had helped her leave the city, so that meant that she was either still under Lord Montague's control, running from him, or dead. If the pure evil in his eyes that night was any indication, the latter was the most likely outcome.

"I tried," Wren said, breaking the silence, her voice more a croak than clear speech. "I really did."

I reached out to her, but she flinched, so I put my hand on her knee instead.

"What did you try?"

"To find Bess." Her voice broke. "I should have come here months ago, but I was determined to find her, to bring her here with me." She sobbed into the cloth napkin I handed her. "I wanted us to all be together again."

She told me how she'd left Dublin, hidden in the first cargo cart she could find, and when she was discovered, found herself forcibly ejected onto the side of the road just outside Kingstown. Between the men at the fort and the sailors enjoying leave in the port, she'd had plenty of work, but she couldn't stop thinking of Bess. So, she had used her newfound contacts to ask around for her when they went into Dublin. She even ventured back herself a few times, but she could found no trace of the girl.

"What caused you to come here tonight?" I asked.

"One of the men found me. I don't know who it was; my memories from the night of the party aren't all that clear. It wasn't Lord Montague—I'd recognize him—and it couldn't be the groom, since he is dead. But I was in a tavern and when I reached out to accept my cup, a hand seized mine. It belonged to a very large, bald man. He yanked off my glove and when he saw the scar, he told me to come with him. I pretended to obey just long enough for his grip to slacken the slightest bit and then I broke loose and ran. Thank God, Bess taught us all those ways through the back alleys of the city or I would never have lost him. It was only when I stopped in a maze of side streets that I remembered hearing that not only canaries were welcome here; the House of Mercy took in crows, seagulls, and doves, too."

"And even the occasional Wren," I added, hugging her. "I am so glad you are here. You are safe now."

*****

At dawn, Kate relieved me at the door and I was free to rest for a few hours, but I had given Wren my bed and I was still too excited to sleep. After checking to make sure Wren was sleeping soundly, I took the back stairs to the chapel.

The room was still not complete—and much to Catherine's chagrin, the grille still split the vast room in two—but I could think of no better place to go at this moment. I needed to express my relief and gratitude to God. I may have been raised with only the basics of religion and no real faith at all, but this place was changing me from the inside out. I was learning to see God's grace in action and feel His hand guiding my life. I may have made many mistakes and committed many sins, but I repented of them and was trying to be better, so I slept well at night, confident in his forgiveness and mercy.

After all, I saw both every single day in my work and in the women staying here.

To my great relief, the chapel was empty when I entered, the workers not yet making noise. I passed through the grille and knelt in my customary spot, on the left side, three stalls from the front, where I had a clear view of the stained-glass window depicting St. Zita, the patron saint of domestic workers like me. Catherine had commissioned the window long before we met, but she confided in me once that she knew there would be many who would need St. Zita's guidance. Sometimes I would come in here and find on the floor beneath the window scraps of paper with prayers written on them or little tokens—acorns, wildflowers, seeds, a coin, a button, anything the woman could spare as an offering of petition or thanksgiving. Catherine had even given me permission to collect them every night and add them to a wooden chest she kept next to the perpetual lantern upstairs. We burned these offerings every April 27, St. Zita's feast day, and used the ashes, mixed with a little oil, to bless the women who went out in search of domestic employment.

There was one petition I asked her not to burn, however. When I joined the House, Catherine and I both wrote fervent prayers to God for Margaret's safe return to us. We promised to keep them until the day we found her.

Now I added another to wooden chest.

Thank you, Lord Jesus Christ, for watching over the Doves and keeping us safe. We may be sullied women, but we ask you to forgive us our trespasses as you did for the Magdalene. My eyes flicked over to the image of the fallen woman from the Bible depicted in one of the windows. In the dawn light, her dress glowed crimson, but so did her halo. *Please, dear God, watch over Bess and bring her to safe harbor here.*

I prayed in silence for a while before the creaking of the grille gate brought me back to myself. I looked up to see Father Armstrong, Catherine's confessor and the priest at St. Michan's on the north side of the city, approaching the altar. Instead of heading straight for it, or pausing to pray at the kneeler in front of it, he sat down in the stall next to mine.

"Forgive me for interrupting your prayer," he said by way of greeting. "I was looking for you, and Catherine said you might be here after your eventful night."

"Yes." My cheeks flamed at having been caught at my personal devotions. "I have a lot to be grateful for."

"More than you know," the priest said, gesturing at me with his breviary.

"Oh?"

A grin spread across his face. "I spoke with the Archbishop today. He believes you are ready to be received into the Church at Easter."

"What? So soon?" This was as overwhelming as Wren's appearance at our door last night. I had been studying catechism with him since shortly after arriving here, but I had expected a much longer course of study. Now, after less than half a year, I was joining the religion I had come to find so comforting, embracing the God—Father, Son, and Holy Ghost—who loved and cared for me so much more than anyone in the world had ever done, not to mention finally having a mother in the Blessed Virgin, and true confidants in Saints Zita and Mary Magdalene.

Father Armstrong's grin was that of a proud grandfather. "Yes. This Wednesday is Ash Wednesday. You will walk with Christ throughout Lent and then, during the Vigil Mass of Easter, you will be baptized, receive your first Holy Communion, and be confirmed as a life-long Catholic."

"Oh my," was all I could say. My mind was spinning with this unexpected good news on top of very little sleep.

"We can discuss the details later. I simply wanted to tell you the good news." He stood, leaning on a cane I hadn't noticed to help him rise. "Catherine asked me to tell you one of the O'Connell girls will take your place at the school today so you can get some rest."

"Yes," I spluttered, still in shock. "Yes, of course I will."

Father Armstrong left the stall and made his way down the center aisle. He put his hand on the grate, stopped, and called over his shoulder. "Do give some thought as to which saint you will take as your patroness, for she will guide you for the remainder of your life."

From the wall opposite, St. Zita's image glinted in the sunlight, making it appear, just for a moment, as though she was winking at me.

"Thank you," I whispered to the ceiling and the heavens beyond. "For everything."

Chapter 23

CATHERINE

June 1828
Coolock House and House of Mercy
Dublin, Ireland

Saying farewell seemed to be the theme of the summer. Red, puffy eyes greeted me each morning when I looked into the mirror, and I closed raw, gritty ones to sleep each night. How much could one heart bear?

First, Father Armstrong died. We had been friends for less than a decade, but the intimacy of trust our made it feel like three times that long. He had advised me in my exploration of my own faith before Mr. Callaghan died; supported me through the legalities and strife of building this House; and, most importantly, was a constant in a world of change over the last year as our ministry was birthed and took its first steps. As with so many others who have gone home to Heaven, I was there with him when he took his final breath, praying him into the loving arms of Jesus, where I hoped he would pray for me for the rest of my life.

As my confessor, it was Father Armstrong who taught me to trust in God alone, a lesson I clung to now as I said my goodbyes to Coolock House, which I had called home for nearly thirty years. I said a silent farewell to the memories of the Callaghans evoked by every room, marveling how it had lost its warmth and character when we sold or transferred its goods to Baggot Street; now it was a hallow, cavernous space waiting to be brought back to life by a new family, one headed by Mr. Henry Brooke, the new master of Coolock House.

I said a prayer for the new owners, then stepped outside onto the front stairs for the last time. I scanned the horizon, drinking it all in, so grateful to have lived the balance of my life in such a magnificent place. To my right, the sea sparkled beyond orchards beginning to fruit. To my left, the mountains rose above a vast green lawn. In the distance lay the carriage and caretaker's houses, where I had first held my tiny school for girls, never imagining it would blossom into a place of learning for hundreds on Baggot Street.

This was my past. In front of me waited my future—three carriages holding Mrs. Doyle, now a widow, my remaining students, and my nieces and my goddaughter, all of whom would be taking up residence at the House of Mercy with me. Yes, I would miss the beautiful views, familiarity, and comfort only home could bring, but it was time I made a new, permanent life on Baggot Street with the women I now called family.

*****

Less than a week later, the House of Mercy buzzed with even more activity than usual, thanks to more new residents. Daniel O'Connell's daughters and two of their cousins were moving in. Between the servants helping them, the well-wishers, and the hangers on who came to wish them well, it was impossible to move without literally bumping into someone.

"Oh, I am so sorry," I said without looking up as I rounded a corner, on a mission to find Grace, my mind set on remembering what I had to tell her rather than on what or who was in front of me.

"Miss McAuley? Good, I was hoping to find you."

Wrenched from my own thoughts, I looked up into the cheerful face of a young woman, perhaps eighteen, who was holding a suitcase in one hand and dragging a steamer trunk with the other. Her skin held the olive tone of the Mediterranean, but her voice said she was a born daughter of Erin. Behind her was a smaller girl, thin, fragile, and meek, like a little mouse. She, too, held a traveling bag, but seemed to be doing her best to blend into this woman's shadow.

"Hello. Yes. May I help you?" I asked.

"My name is Frances Warde," the taller girl said confidently, offering me her hand. "I am a friend of your niece, Mary. You wrote to me some weeks ago about joining you here?"

The mention of Mary's name brought conversations we'd had by letter to the forefront of my mind. "Yes, you are the orphan who needs employment and board."

"I am." She gently urged her friend forward. "And this is Elizabeth Harley, my dearest childhood companion. She wishes to be of service as well. I know you were not expecting her, so I apologize for any inconvenience."

I would have to ask Grace to make up another bed, but we were used to receiving people without notice. "Please don't. We're happy to have you. Welcome. Please let me take that." I reached for the trunk at Frances's feet.

"That is the contents of our doweries," she explained. "Inside you will find black dresses similar to your own, shoes, a few personal belongs, and, of course, payment for the first year of our keep." Her crisp tone was reminiscent of that adopted by military leaders, and I couldn't help but wonder if her relatives in Abbeyleix or the family she had been living with were veterans.

"I ... well, thank you." I was taken aback by the offer, which was required at convents, but not here. "We do not ask such things of our volunteers, so if there is anyone in your family who can make use of it ..."

Frances shook her head. "We are fortunate to come from wealth," she said matter-of-factly. "Please, we wish to pull our weight. Use it as you see fit."

This unexpected blessing would help us more than she could know. I led the girls to the dormitory, which was slowly beginning to fill with live-in volunteers. While Elizabeth took in her new surroundings, Frances selected a bed and began unpacking without asking for a servant—rather unusual, but very welcome—which meant she would be a self-sufficient woman, a trait much needed in this House, where servants were only allowed to help women move in; once they were settled, they had to learn to tend to themselves.

Elizabeth followed her friend's lead. I had a feeling she often looked to Frances for her cues.

"Miss Warde ..."

"Please, call me Frances."

"And please, call me Catherine. We do not stand on ceremony here. What area were you hoping to assist in? What skills do you have that might be helpful?"

She turned, already nearly finished unpacking, and regarded me with a serious expression. "As you can see, I am very organized, and I know a little of business and finance from my family. My father was a successful merchant who indulged my curiosity." Her voice held the same hint of guilt many educated woman seemed to have about learning above their prescribed station. "So, if you need help running the house or someone to teach maths, I can assist there. I have also been told I am good at religious instruction. I spent some time teaching at the House for Homeless Children before coming here."

I stifled a giggle, because Frances spoke as if she were applying for a job, though I knew she was just being who God made her.

"And you, Elizabeth?"

"I will help however I am most needed. I will be happy anywhere," she assured me.

That was exactly the answer I expected from her. "Right now, I am most in need of another teacher, so I can't tell you how much it pleases me to hear that. Would you be comfortable in that role?"

Elizabeth's face lit up. "Oh yes, I love children."

"Wonderful. I also need another assistant, as I am still working out how to run the House as it grows. Frances, you seem capable of holding this office. Would such a thing please you?"

Frances grinned. "Very much so."

"Ring for me when you are finished settling in. I will take you to meet Anna Maria, my other assistant, and the four of us can talk."

"I am ready when you are, Miss McAuley ... er, Catherine." She corrected herself.

"As am I," Elizabeth echoed.

*****

We returned downstairs to an even more chaotic scene than when we'd left—something I hadn't thought possible. Around us, women had their heads bent together, talking in rapid exchanges, and a crowd had formed in the reception room; the space was bursting with women. Several times I heard the words "Catholic," "oath," and "victory," but I could not for anything understand how they could be connected. As each woman saw me, the crowd parted, allowing me to reach the innermost circle relatively quickly. There I found Kate and Betsy O'Connell with their two younger cousins. Grace and Anna Maria were there. Next to them stood a liveried messenger, beads of sweat collecting on his brow, trying to look anywhere than directly at the women surrounding him.

"Does your employer require a response?" I whispered to him as I reached his side.

"Only to know that his message was safely delivered and received," he replied.

"Then you may go. Please tell him Catherine McAuley sends her best."

With a nod, the man scurried off. I'd seen mice chased by cats move slower.

I approached the women with great interest, making no effort to hide my presence. "Ladies, it seems you have attracted quite a crowd. To what do we owe this distraction?" I kept my tone light but chose my words carefully, so they knew this sort of spectacle would not be tolerated.

"We have received the most wonderful news," Betsy said.

"Shall we read it to you or would you like to read it yourself?" Kate asked.

"Please summarize it for me."

The girls looked at one another and broke out into the most radiant twin grins I had ever seen. "Papa won his election in County Clare!" Betsy declared.

I had forgotten the Parliamentary elections had taken place a few days before. I counted back in my head. Yes, this was the right time for the results to come in. That meant that their father was the first Catholic Parliamentarian since James II fled to Ireland in 1688. What a wonder. No one in seven generations had hoped for such a thing. Was it possible then … ?

I couldn't even finish my thought before Kate added, "He is already refusing to take the Oath of Supremacy."

This did not surprise me in the least. Daniel O'Connell would be the last person to voluntarily acknowledge the King as "Supreme Governor" of the Church, even over the Pope. No, to him remaining union with the Catholic Church was worth any price—even his life. And it might come to that if men like Lord Montague had their way. Legally, the remaining Penal Laws still forbade Daniel from taking his seat in the House of Commons, but anyone who knew him, or even knew of him, knew he would not let that stop him. We were so close to being equal citizens with the Protestants once again.

Between this news and fact that four of his closet female relatives now called the House of Mercy home, we prepared for an onslaught of volunteers. Anna Maria taught Frances how to accept and interview applicants so I wouldn't be tied up all day speaking with them; Grace prepared the dormitories so we could receive those who wished to live here at a moment's notice. And Wren, who had chosen to reclaim her birth name of Cressida, helped in the kitchens. She had a particular talent for baking that had not gone unnoticed since her arrival.

As un-Christ-like as it was, I couldn't help a small inward grin of satisfaction when I heard that Lord Montague had lost his bid for the House of Lords. Between that and our rise in both fortune and popularity, he should be well and truly cross. But there was a downside to that: If he was to continue his campaign against us, he would have to resort to more drastic measures than poisoning our neighbors' minds against us, and I had no doubt he would think of something dreadful.

Chapter 24

GRACE

November 22, 1828
House of Mercy
Dublin, Ireland

We huddled in a circle outside the front doors of Sir Patrick Dun's Hospital on Grand Canal Street. In our matching black cloaks and dresses of merino wool, we must have looked like a flock of shivering ravens to anyone who observed us from the street—or, God forbid, nuns. It would be an easy mistake to make, especially if that person simply glanced up, not taking the time to notice we wore bonnets on our heads instead of veils. I chuckled to myself. That was quite the thought. Me, a former prostitute, a nun. Ha!

"Remember, not a word that we are Catholic," Catherine hissed to Anna Maria, Frances, Kate, and me. "If they find out, they will bar us from ministering here, Archbishop's permission or no."

"Why would they think otherwise?" I asked in a low voice. "I thought everyone knew ..."

"My friends and family are all well-known Protestants, and we have many volunteering and supporting the House. It's a matter of letting them think what they will for the greater good."

Kate, who often saw the world in black and white, scowled. "I still don't like it." She crossed her arms over her chest.

I rang the bell again, anxious to get inside, out of the cold, and divert this argument before someone took the carriage back to Baggot Street in an unnecessary huff. "They probably won't even ask," I said. "Catherine isn't asking you to lie if questioned, just to not be open with the information. Because the Penal Laws haven't yet been stricken from the record books in Dublin, she's only making sure you adhere to the law."

"In a very roundabout way," Kate muttered.

She was prevented from saying more when the door finally opened. A balding man with spectacles and a broom-like red mustache leaned toward us. "May I help you?"

Catherine stepped forward, making it clear she was our leader. "Yes, sir. We are women of charitable work and we have come to inquire about nursing your patients. May we please speak with your administrator or chief physician?"

"You would have to gain permission from our board of physicians, but you are fortunate they are meeting today. Come and I will see if they have time for you."

After a lengthy session answering questions, the board agreed they needed the help, and they approved our visits on Mondays and Thursdays. Frances stayed behind to speak with the nurses on staff to find out what was needed of us and what we should be prepared to do.

This process was repeated at Dublin's two other hospitals, with Anna Maria remaining at the Hospital for Incurables in Donnybrook and Kate at the Combe Lying in Hospital. As such, it was left to Catherine and me to begin inquiring in the slums, or "the ancient parts of the city," as they were referred to by the gentry.

We returned to Baggot Street to obtain some basic provisions for the poor and set off again on foot. As we left the fashionable areas of town and traced the path of the River Liffey west, the houses grew smaller and noticeably less maintained. Whereas in St. George's Square, one would never so much as see a dead leaf on a tree, here in the narrow streets, the masonry was crumbling, windows and doors were missing completely, and often people were lying on the steps—asleep, passed out, or dead, I couldn't tell, and honestly didn't want to know. But soon that was going to be my job: to minister with another volunteer in the very streets in which I had once lived. It would be my responsibility to persuade these people, who were skittish and distrustful by nature and experience, to put their faith me and let me do what I could to alleviate their suffering.

"My, how you've come up in the world." A scratchy voice greeted us as we turned into Bull Alley, which was bounded by St. Bride Street and St. Patrick's church.

I turned toward the sound to see Mrs. MacGregor, the proprietress of the first boarding house where I stayed after the Montagues dismissed me from employment, standing in the doorway of a broken-down brick dwelling. It seemed she had seen hard times as well.

"I've been in the muck but am currently in much better circumstances," I said. "And you? Still cheating at cards?"

"I don't cheat ..."

"I know, you play by your own rules. I remember."

She grinned at the old joke. "I've seen a bit of muck myself. Lost the old place near the park. Now the best I can do is charge a few pence for a dirty mattress and a cup of thin broth in this shithole," she gestured to a decaying building behind her. There was no sign of interior light, nor any water pump nearby. A crude pile of charred wood and ash on the floor was the only evidence of heat as well.

"Well, Mrs. MacGregor, we'd like to help you if we can. We're from the House of Mercy ..."

"Oh, that big ol' white building down by the canal? That's rich, ain't it? Now that you got yourself a castle, you come down here to feed the peasants. I remember when I was the one feedin' you." She spit in my direction. "Piss off."

I jumped back to avoid her spittle. "Damn your pride, woman! Think of it as me paying you back. We just want you to know that there is a place where you can get food, rest ... maybe learn a new skill if you ever get tired of the grind of being a proprietress. You were there for me when I had nowhere to turn. Now I am in a position to help you." I looked deep into her eyes. "If you will let me."

I took a loaf of bread from the basket Catherine was carrying and held it out to her.

"Think about it. We'll be back a few times a week. And you know where to find me if you need me."

Mrs. MacGregor took the bread with no small about of reluctance. She was about to turn away, but something stopped her. She looked up at me with alarm in her eyes.

"That mark on your hand," she said. "A girl who stayed here recently had one just like it."

Bess ... it had to be Bess.

I pretended confusion. "Are you sure? What did she look like?"

"How many girls you think have a bird burned onto their hand?" She went on to describe Bess perfectly.

"Is she still here? Where did she go?"

She shrugged. "Three men came in and dragged her off."

My heart plummeted to my toes.

"They looked right angry." She turned around, but called over her shoulder, "You ladies be careful, you hear?"

Catherine and I looked one another. She must have seen the fear on my face, because she put an arm around me. "Don't worry. You are not Bess. There is a reason those men accosted her. Whatever it is, you were with me in the House. You were not involved, so they will not seek you out." She whispered in my ear. "And if they do, I will stab them with my hatpin."

Despite her reassuring words, a chill ran down my spine. Maybe it wasn't such a great idea for the Doves to participate in the community aspect of our ministry. If someone was after Bess, it was likely Lord Montague and his friends. After all, we were witnesses to a murder and we knew about his finances, both of which were enough to ruin him, not to mention that we could expose him for his involvement in our establishment.

All of that added up to a good portion of the Doves being in danger. I couldn't tell Catherine everything, could I? She would certainly show us the door before my voice stopped echoing off the walls. That would leave as all out in the cold and vulnerable. No, it might be a lie of omission, but one more venial sin on my soul was worth it to minimize the risk to everyone else.

Chapter 25

CATHERINE

December 25, 1828
House of Mercy and The Royal Hospital Kilmainham
Dublin, Ireland

Between spending six days a week at the hospitals—two at each—and nearly every day in some of the ancient parts of the city, autumn passed us by quickly. Our school and the number of women seeking us for training grew faster than we could keep up. More volunteers joined us in both part-time and live-in situations, but the demand was still overwhelming.

So, when our second Christmas in the House of Mercy was finally here, everyone—students and workers alike—were exhausted and eager for a few days of peace. The holy feast began much the same as it the year before. We spent the wee quiet hours of the morning in mediation by candlelight, adoring the newborn baby Jesus, who was reverently placed in his crib by Anna Maria. At dawn we celebrated Mass, with a special blessing for all of the women and children, whether they remained with us for the holiday or were off visiting family. We broke our fast together in joy and friendship.

By eight o'clock in the morning, well-wishers began to drop by, some in person, others through their messengers, often leaving beef roasts or joints in their wake or filling our table with fresh fruit or candies. Many stayed, intending to attend our Christmas feast, which was becoming a fixture on the social calendar.

Daniel O'Connell, now an official MP, and his family joined us once again. When I picked up the knife to do the carving, which was my right as host, he gently cleared his throat. "Madam, if you wouldn't mind, I would like to keep my role from our previous dinner. To serve such beautiful souls as these"—he used the knife to indicate the women and children present—"not only brings me joy, it keeps me humble. I so often take for granted the blessings in my life, and so on this one day a year, when Christ assented to be born in a manger, the least I can do is serve these fine women their daily bread."

I smiled warmly, passing the fork to him with a shake of my head. He was a born orator. No wonder he had accomplished so much.

Anna Maria's parents were among our guests that evening, insisting they wanted to see the place and the people that moved her to give up the convent life she had so long planned. I expected to have to convince them of the worthiness of our mission, but one look at the women and children dining at the fine mahogany tables and being served by the volunteers—instead of the other way around—wiped away their concerns.

When Mrs. Doyle saw Anna cutting food for a little girl of maybe five, her whole expression lit up. "I always knew she would make a good mother. When she announced her intention to join the Presentation Sisters, I will admit to being disappointed that I wouldn't have any grandchildren from my daughters, but seeing her like this ..." Anna Maria was laughing at something one her students said, "shows me I do have grandchildren. Hundreds of them, just not through my bloodline."

One face I was not expecting to see as I made my way through the tables, wishing everyone Happy Christmas and making sure there was nothing they might need, was Lord Montague's. When I first caught his eye, I was so shocked I couldn't speak. To give myself some time to compose my mind and school my features, I retreated to the kitchen, where Grace was removing another batch of scones from the oven.

"You will never believe who is here." I said quietly.

She glanced in the direction of the stone stairs that led from the main hallway to the kitchen. A flicker of hope passed over her face— she was likely thinking of Margaret and Bess, the return of either would be the best possible Christmas gift anyone could ever give her.

"Lord and Lady Montague," I said, through clenched teeth.

"I'm surprised they didn't burst into flames as soon as they crossed the threshold," Grace joked.

"Give them time," I retorted. "The night is still young."

She laughed and nearly dropped the pan of scones.

"I wanted to warn you not to go upstairs if you don't want to see them." I smoothed down my skirt and checked to be sure my hair was still in its tight bun. "And … I needed to place to collect myself before facing him."

"You'll be fine," she said, setting down the pan. "Actually, you'll be better than fine—you'll be gracious and he won't be able to stand it." She came over to me and gave me a hug from behind. "Good luck."

Upstairs, I worked my way down the opposite side of the table and back up the other, shaking hands and exchanging warm greetings with each couple. When I finally approached Lord Montague, he turned and regarded me with mock surprise, as though he hadn't been glowering at me for the last half an hour.

"Miss McAuley! How lovely to see you." He flashed his most charming grin.

"You as well," I ground out.

Turning to Lady Montague, I greeted her as well.

She smiled radiantly, as though we were the best of friends and there was nowhere else she'd rather be. "I hope you have had a blessed Christmas so far," she said with false warmth.

All was well until the two of you showed up. "Indeed. And you?"

"It has been lovely," she cooed. Her eye was caught by someone at another table. "If you will excuse me, there is someone I must see." She was up and walking away before I could respond.

She enjoys my company just about as much as I enjoy hers. With Lady Montague gone, I hoped to be able to slip away easily, but Lord Montague was too savvy to let an opportunity to insult me to my face to pass him by. I had just turned to move on when his hand brushed my arm. I bristled.

"Really, Catherine, what do you hope to accomplish here?" he asked, sitting back in his chair, swirling his whiskey in his glass, relaxed like we were old friends.

"It's *Miss McAuley,* if you please," I said, emphasizing my formal name. "I did not give you permission to call me by my Christian name."

"Christian. Is that what you are? Because from where I stand it looks like you are a Papist who doesn't respect the rules of your own religion or society. You go about doing whatever you please, no matter who tells you not to. It's not bad enough that you attract a certain unsavory element to this neighborhood. Now you have to go and seek them out. I've seen you in the streets, encouraging those filthy beggars and inviting them back to your 'house.' Really, *Miss McAuley*, what is wrong with you?"

"I might ask the same of you. Who or what wounded your heart so badly that you are now incapable of empathy? Do you feel nothing when you pass by the poor on the streets? Do you give them a second thought or some spare change? Or do you just keep walking and turn a blind eye? You, who have so much, but give so little."

"You have no idea where my charitable pursuits lie," he shot back. "I am here, am I not?"

I put my hands on my hips. "Yes, why is that exactly? Your lot don't typically frequent Catholic events. Shouldn't you be licking the boots of some MP or other?"

"Perhaps I should take a lesson from you, beholden as you are to the Pope and your parish priest. You can't even crack an egg without their permission."

"And you ask permission of no one. See where that got you—a failed bid at Parliament and a crumbling legacy."

Lord Montague's eyes raged like a stormy sea. He shot to his feet and grabbed my wrists. "What do you know? What has that little viper told you?" He shook me just slightly, not enough for others to notice, but enough to frighten me and jar my confidence.

I refused to react. He wanted me scared and submissive. I forced a knowing grin onto my face. "So, you *do* have a secret ... or maybe more than one. That explains so much ..." I let my voice trail off as though I was putting together the pieces of a large puzzle.

And in many ways, I was—just not the ones he thought. I understood in that moment that I and my ministry posed a threat to him, although I wasn't yet sure how. I understood he felt the need to eliminate anything that endangered his sense of power and control. And most of all, I understood why Grace and the Doves were so afraid of him. The man had a dark side so powerful it possessed him; in moments like this one, he truly was capable of anything.

I looked down at where he still gripped my wrists, his fingertips digging into the sensitive skin. "If I were you," I said in a voice completely devoid of emotion, but unmistakably commanding, "I would remove your hands from my person. Then I would gather up my wife and leave this place. I never want to see your face in my home again or I *will* destroy you."

I yanked my arms from his grip more dramatically than necessary. I wanted those around us to wonder what was going on.

Lord Montague sneered, keeping his voice low. "You are proud of your words, are you not, Miss McAuley? But they are nothing but empty threats. You think you can bring me down? Go ahead and try. Greater women than you have learned why I am not to be crossed."

I raised an eyebrow at him. "Your bluster may intimidate some, but I am not one of them. One word to Mr. O'Connell about the way you have treated me tonight or the myriad other things you'd rather remain in the dark and you would lose everything. Your day is coming, Lord Montague. Justice may be blind, but she never misses her mark."

Lord Montague took a step back. People were beginning to stare. Realizing what he had done, he compensated by towering over me.

"Is it a war you want, Miss McAuley? I thought you were an emblem of peace and love, but if it is a battle you want, you shall have one. You are forgetting that you aren't the only one with secrets. You may not directly be a part of it, but guilt lurks within your walls. How would you like it if the public knew exactly what kinds of women you shelter here? I don't think the law or the Church would look kindly on someone guilty of aiding and abetting criminals. It would be a shame if you lost your life's work, your whole inheritance because of the company you keep."

With that, he raised an arm and motioned to his wife, who was at his side in a flash. In a voice loud enough to ensure all around us heard, he said, "Thank you for an enlightening evening, Miss McAuley. I am afraid we must depart. I wish you the blessings of this holy day." He bowed slightly.

"And I, you," I managed to choke out.

When he was out of sight, I slipped into a storage room near the foot of the stairs. I leaned against the closed door, welcoming its strength. All the energy and fight drained from me, like water sluicing off the brim of a hat. I propped my head against the cold stone. Dear God, that man was evil. What had I just started?

*****

The following day, I took the carriage back to the Royal Hospital to visit my brother-in-law and his children. This was only our second holiday without my beloved sister, Mary, and it would be easier on all of us if we were together.

That night, as we were preparing dinner, my niece, also called Mary, put down the whisk she had been using to mix gravy and regarded me seriously. "Aunt Catherine, can I tell you something?"

"Of course, dear." I checked one more time that nothing cooking on the stove was likely to burn if neglected and ushered her into the next room, where we could sit and talk. "You can say anything to me."

Mary sat down on the velvet-covered settee. Several moments passed in silence while she stared down at her hands, clearly working up the courage to speak. I kept one eye on her and the other on the large clock in the corner, still concerned about the food. Finally, she blurted, "I'm going to become Catholic!"

"Oh Mary, that is wonderful!" I cried after a moment of stunned silence. I hugged her tightly. All the grief I'd experienced growing up for refusing to give up my faith along with everyone else was worth it when I saw so many in my family embracing it once again.

When she pulled away, Mary's face was as red as if she'd been standing over a boiling cookpot and her cheeks were wet with tears. "I have been thinking about it since Mother died. Her own conversion was so beautiful. We spent a long time talking in those final weeks and she asked me to seriously consider my faith and decide what was right for my soul. I've been praying about it and secretly talking to our parish priest. Papa doesn't know that I snuck out last night to attend midnight Mass, but it was there I knew for certain. I asked Father Blake after Mass if I could be received into the Church and he said yes."

Peace and joy shone in her eyes. She really had been touched by the grace of God. "Oh, my sweet girl, this really is a miracle. I am so happy for you."

"There is one problem, though."

She didn't have to say it. William—my brother-in-law, her father. He was nearly as anti-Catholic as Lord Montague. There was no way he would consent, and he held powerful sway over Mary, both emotionally and financially. He controlled the purse strings not only of her daily life but of the dowery she would have to offer a future husband.

"I will stand by you, however you need me to."

She looked away and then back at me. "Would you be willing to tell him for me?" she asked in a small voice that evoked memories of her younger self.

"I am happy to broach the subject with him. You will have to talk to him about it eventually, though."

"Will you tell him about Mother's conversion as well? She asked me to tell him about her experience if I decided to convert. I think she wanted to show him that this isn't a young woman's whim."

I took a deep breath. She was asking a lot. But I also had experience informing staunch Protestants that their loved ones had become Catholic on their deathbeds. And Mr. Callaghan had taken it fairly well when I told him about his wife's change of faith. William was a reasonable man, so he would, too.

"Yes. But consider this your Christmas gifts for the rest of your life," I teased.

"Oh, thank you!" She enveloped me in a tight hug.

I stood, offering her my hand. "Come on, we have a meal to finish preparing."

*****

After dinner, once all of the gifts and been exchanged, opened, and tossed aside and the children were all sleeping soundly in their beds, I plucked up the courage to talk to William. He had had a fair amount to drink—he seemed to be numbing his grief with alcohol more and more frequently lately, as though each passing day it increased rather than slowly abating over time—so I hoped that would make this confession go easier. When I approached, he was staring into the parlor fireplace, mind far away, a glass of whiskey forgotten in his right hand, left absently stroking the chin hairs of his beard.

"William, there is something I have to tell you," I began, my voice soft, careful. In my mind, I imagined treating him like a wild animal, slowly, offering my hand for him to sniff.

He looked up, clearly shaken out of reverie by my voice. "What is it?"

"It's about Mary."

His eyes narrowed. "My wife or my daughter?"

"Both of them, actually."

"Go on." His tone was cautious. He took a large gulp of whiskey from his glass.

I thought for a moment, still unsure exactly what I was going to say, even though I'd been turning it over in my mind all evening. "I learned something tonight that you should know."

When I didn't immediately continue, William motioned for me to go on.

I decided just to say it. "You wife became a Catholic on her deathbed, and your daughter wishes to convert as well."

My words washed over him like a wave. At first, he didn't move, contemplating what he'd heard. Then his eyes widened as comprehension dawned. Storm clouds passed over his face as he realized the import of my news. Finally, he stood, staring down on me like Zeus from Mount Olympus, lightning in his eyes.

"Two Catholics under my roof? In *my* family? This is all your fault!" Spittle flew from his mouth as he raged, pointing at me, forcing me backward with every sentence.

"This never would have happened had I not let you live here! I should have confined you to Coolock House, where you belong. My wife would have died with or without your care, that much is clear to me now. But instead, you bring Popery into this upstanding Presbyterian house! Then you use your wiles to convince a dying woman she would go to Hell if she did not accept your superstitious faith … and her vulnerable, grieving daughter believed you, too. You will not get your claws into her while I still live!"

I had known William for years, and I had seen his temper on display before, but never had I seen him in such a state. It was as though the holiday, his memories, grief, and the drink had combined into a volatile compound in his blood and the word "Catholic" lit the spark it needed to explode.

I put my hands up defensively. "William, calm down. I had nothing to do with any of this. Your wife and your daughter are capable of knowing their own hearts and what is best for their souls."

I sidestepped the hearth, so that I was away from the fire, my back toward the empty room. "I am simply the mouthpiece of this message. Whatever concerns you have, you need to discuss with Mary. But not now. Tomorrow or another day, when cooler heads prevail."

A low chuckle emanated from his throat. "You *would* want to delay the resolution of this issue. It gives you time to poison her mind further. Well, I will not let you!"

He reached into the drawer of a side table and brought out something metal that caught the firelight. When he moved, it became clear it was either a small dagger or a letter opener. Either way, I did not want its point piercing my skin.

I backed up again, my body focused on protection, my mind scrambling for what to do. No one ever teaches you how to survive when someone you love brandishes a knife at you. I had to get out—that much I knew. And I couldn't leave Mary here with him. The other children would be fine. He had no quarrel with them.

I glanced at the door. I was closer than William and I was sober, so I had a good chance of making it unscathed. But where to go once I was out of the house? At this hour, the hospital proper would be locked, as would the front gates, so I had to find help somewhere within the outer grounds. There was always the keeper's house, but it was on the opposite end of the grounds.

William continued to approach, the knife outstretched between us. I turned slightly as I backed away so that my back was facing the open door. As I stepped back, I bumped my hip on an end table, nearly upsetting a vase of holly and laurel that Dr. James Cusack and his wife had sent to William in celebration of the holidays.

That was it! Dr. Cusack lived in a house similar to this one, not far across the short end of the courtyard. I knew him only in passing, but surely, he wouldn't ignore cries of distress, especially not on Christmas. I just had to rouse Mary and we could seek refuge there.

I fled the room into the hallway, running as fast as I could.

"Mary, Mary! Come down here quickly!" I yelled at the top of my lungs.

Her heavy footsteps overhead told me she had been awake, and before I even reached the door, she had bolted down the staircase, trying to tie her dressing gown as she moved. "What is going on?"

I took her hand. "No time, just run!"

Behind us, William's silhouette appeared at the end of the hallway. He was still waving the knife and calling me all sorts of unholy names. Praise Jesus he had chosen a blade instead of a gun or we'd both be dead.

Together Mary and I barreled out the front door into the frigid night air, William's increasingly unintelligible ravings echoing behind. The cold slammed into me with the force of a wall of ice. Poor Mary had to feel it even more, as she was wearing less and was barefoot as well. We raced to Dr. Cusack's front door and began banging on it furiously, calling for someone to open up. It didn't appear that William was following us, but we needed to be inside, away from the elements, and I sure as heaven was not going back into William's house before we had a chat with the authorities.

Dr. Cusack's butler opened the door, running his hands through his hair and asking what was the meaning of the racket. Mary and I pushed past him, yelling at him to close and lock the door. Once he had complied, we both collapsed in a heap right in the foyer.

"Ay now, what is all the commotion about?" he asked crossly.

By then Dr. and Mrs. Cusack had joined us, each pulling on thier own dressing gown.

I was still gulping air, but tried to explain between heaving breaths. "William ... he has ... knife ... threatened ..."

Mrs. Cusack reached Mary first and attempted to help her up. "Oh, my dear, you are as cold as Satan's soul. Let's get you in front of the fire."

She removed her own robe and put it around Mary's shaking shoulders, then sent her maid to put the kettle on.

I stood of my own accord, still breathing hard but able to form words now. "William threatened us with a knife," I repeated, this time coherently.

"What? Dr. Cusack exclaimed. "Why would he do that?"

I hobbled in the direction Mary and Mrs. Cusack had gone. "It's a long story. I'll tell you over tea. Better yet, if you have any brandy, I wouldn't turn down a glass."

*****

The next morning, Mary and I stayed with Mrs. Cusack and huddled by the library fire while Dr. Cusack and a few of their mutual friends talked William back into sanity. They returned mid-afternoon with him firmly in tow.

When Dr. Cusack told us he was there, Mary and I instinctively clung to one another. As I had been the one to witness the worst of it, the doctor left it up to me whether or not to admit him. I didn't want to see him ever again, but my conscience said he at least deserved a chance to explain himself.

"I will see him, but he must remain across the room and in your control," I finally relented.

When they brought William in, I barely recognized him. He had aged twenty years overnight. New wrinkles lined his forehead and face, and I would swear his beard held more grey. He walked stooped over as though he carried a great weight, and his gait was no longer that of a confident man, but the shuffling step of one who had given up on life.

"What do you have to say for yourself?" Mrs. Cusack prompted, when he didn't appear inclined to speak.

William wouldn't meet our eyes, but instead spoke to the knotted pine floor.

"I am sorry for my actions of last night. The idea of my daughter willingly turning herself over to a religion based in control and folk magic rather than in Christ's teaching as revealed in the Bible sickens me to my very core." He glanced up at Mary. "But I will not stop you. I cannot give you my blessing, but I can promise I will not interfere."

He flicked his eyes to me.

"As for you, Catherine, I leveled several outrageous accusations at you, and I regret each one. You are a respectable Christian woman and deserve to be treated as such. I hope you will accept my sincere apology."

"I will accept it because Christ bids us to forgive those who wrong us," I said softly. "I will not, however, ever forget how you betrayed me last night. After all the years we spent together and the things I did for you, and you repaid me in the most repugnant way possible. I never wish to see you again."

He turned to his daughter, hands outstretched like a beggar's. "Mary, surely *you* understand. I did nothing to hurt you. I would never ..."

"Would you not, Papa? What would have happened if I had been the one to tell you or if I had remained behind after Catherine escaped? You were in such a rage all you could see was your hatred for Catholics. In your eyes, I was as good as dead."

She took a deep, ragged breath, tears beginning to splash onto her cheeks.

"You are the one who is dead to me now," she pronounced solemnly. "I shall become Catholic with or without you."

Mary and I stood, Mrs. Cusack and her maid accompanying us to the door.

"Where do you think you are going?" William asked Mary.

"To my new home," she replied. "I am going to live at the House of Mercy."

Those were the final words William would ever hear from his daughter. Three days later, he was dead.

PART IV

TRANSITIONS

Chapter 26

ANNA MARIA

April 1829
House of Mercy
Dublin, Ireland

After the excitement of Christmas, it was relief to have a few months of relative peace. Catherine had grown more contemplative after her brush with death at her brother-in-law's hand, and I frequently found her scribbling letters or reading official correspondence, but she kept their exact nature to herself. Her lawyer, Mr. Andrews, made frequent visit to the House, consulting with her behind closed doors.

One morning in early spring, Catherine called Kate and me into her office, but would not say why. Mr. Andrews was there as well.

I glanced at him, then to Kate, who shrugged, as oblivious as I as to what this meeting was about.

"We are waiting for one more person," was all Catherine would tell us.

About ten minutes later, there was a knock on the door. Frances stuck her head in to tell us Archbishop Murray had arrived. Catherine invited him in and he took a seat in the empty chair across the desk from her.

"As you all likely know, I am turning fifty in just a few days," she began. "When one approaches such an important milestone, it only natural to begin thinking of the end of life. God willing, I have many more years, but with such a valuable asset as this ministry in my name, it is best to be prepared. That is why I have called you here today.

"The three of you are the people I love and trust most in this world. There is no one else to whom I would want to entrust the House and all we do here. Kate," she turned to her niece, "you may be young, but you are bright and strong, just as I would want a daughter of my own to be. Anna Maria," she smiled at me, "you have been my partner from the beginning and I consider you my right hand in all things. Archbishop Murray, you have long been my confidant and guide. You are a true man of the Church, a priest of Jesus Christ who knows and understands what this community needs.

"If you are all willing to accept, I would like to create a trust with the three of you as parties to ensure the House and its ministry continue on after my death. Kate and Anna Maria, under the terms of this trust, should anything happen to me, it will become yours. Only if you and your successors, whom you may name or change at any time, are unable to fulfill this role will the House, its contents, and it legacy become the charge of the Church through Archbishop Murray. Are these terms acceptable to you?"

"I believe so," Kate said.

"Yes," I responded, a bit overwhelmed at the idea of ever becoming responsible for such a large endeavor.

"Of course," Archbishop Murray said. "You are wise to make a plan like this so that no one can claim right to what you started or try to exploit it."

The lawyer stepped out of the shadows and laid a copy of a legal document in front of each of us, along with a pen. "Please read this and, if you agree, affix your signature to the last page."

The document said, in so many more words, what Catherine had outlined. I signed my name and handed the page back the lawyer.

"Thank you so much," Catherine said. "You have lifted a huge weight from this aging woman's heart."

*****

It seemed God had arranged to give Catherine the greatest birthday present possible for an Irish Catholic of our time. On April 13, Daniel O'Connell made good on his promise of reform with the help of the British Prime Minister, the Duke of Wellington, and Sir Robert Peel. That day, the Emancipation Act of 1829 was introduced in Parliament. It essentially brought to an end the last of the Penal Laws by admitting Irish and English Roman Catholics to Parliament and to all public offices, save a few exceptions. It also guaranteed the civil rights of Roman Catholics in Ireland, undoing 134 years of oppression under Protestant rule.

The Act passed, setting off a series of celebrations and protests across Ireland. While we celebrated with songs, dancing, and recitation of poetry at the House of Mercy, not far away, a group of Protestants gathered to oppose our freedom and equality under the law. The Dublin faction was led by none other than Lord Montague, who sent us a message exhorting us to "enjoy our freedom while we can because it will be, like our ministry, short-lived."

Chapter 27

GRACE

September 1829
Streets of Dublin, Ireland

Was it only two years ago that I had been living in hovels like these, or worse?

Did my cellar apartment really smell this bad? I tried to recall its specific odor as I climbed up the short ladder into the main house and helped Elizabeth up. While she'd lived at the house for some time now, this was her first visit to the poorer areas of Dublin.

"Bye!" called the little girl from down below. Her mother clutched her tightly. Both were frighteningly thin, hip and collar bones jutting out from skin pulled too taunt over them. At least they had a store of bread and cheese, and a special container to keep it in that the carpenter promised would keep the rodents at bay—at least for a while.

On our way out, I stopped the owner who was renting to them. "If I pay you, do you promise to give them one bottle of milk from your daily delivery?"

"Yea, I can do that," said the man. "That'll be nice."

"Don't listen to him," said his wife. "He'll spend it on drink."

The man raised his hand to slap her, but I stepped between them and took the blow. The look I gave him said more than words ever could and he backed away. He would at least think twice before striking his wife again.

As we left, the wife called to me in a low voice. "Talk to the milkman. He's a good soul. He'll be sure to get a bottle to them."

I tried to slip the coins into her hand, but she refused. "There are others who need it more."

The generosity of the poor was something the people of Dublin Castle and Merrion Square could learn from. What was it Jesus said about the widow with her last two coins? No one in these streets deserved their lot, not even the criminals, but there was little we could do. The city was crumbling and those who could afford to help fled to their country manors, leaving the rest of the population with nothing.

"Why did you do that back there?" Elizabeth asked.

It was the most words I'd heard her speak in a row since she'd arrived with Frances nearly a year ago. "What?"

"You let that man hit you."

"His wife certainly didn't deserve it. And it was a way of teaching him a lesson without saying a word. By enduring his violence without complaint, I modeled Jesus's teaching to turn the other cheek. Plus, it brought me close enough to him that he couldn't miss the warning in my eyes."

"What made you think to do it? I never would have."

Because you are too sweet and innocent, my love. "I don't know," I said truthfully. "Instinct? Something I learned along the way?"

We arrived at Mrs. MacGregor's "hotel," to find her outside, hanging washing on a line. I introduced her to Elizabeth, who visibly flinched when Mrs. MacGregor greeted her. I had been coming here for so long now I'd grown used to her heavy accent, her loud way of speaking and general outsized personality, so I hadn't thought to warn poor Elizabeth.

"What do you have for me today?" Mrs. MacGregor asked, peering from my basket to the one Elizabeth held.

I began pulling items from mine. "Bread, as usual, a few eggs, cheese, some apples, the last of our plums—I know how much you like them. Some canned beans and parsnips for the winter. Oh, and Cressida says hello. She really enjoyed meeting you on our rounds last month and looks froward to returning soon. She baked this blackberry pie just for you."

Mrs. MacGregor smiled, revealing several missing teeth. "Give her my thanks. I miss that girl."

"She will come to see you as soon as she can. I'll make sure of it."

Mrs. MacGregor looked at the items sitting at her feet. "You have given me quite a feast."

"It is a fertile time of year."

She shook her head. "It is amazing you are able to produce so much from a small garden right in the middle of the city."

"If you joined us there, you could help tend the garden." I'd been trying to coax her into giving up her failing business and join us at the House for months now. Normally she laughed me off, but this time she gave my offer serious consideration.

"I just may. Not quite yet, but it is good to know the option is there."

She looked at the buildings around us, many of which had crumbling chimneys, broken windows, and rotten boards.

"City isn't the same as it used to be, that's for sure. Started its decline some thirty years ago, when I was a young lass. When there's no rich people in the city to keep it up to impress the rich people from other towns, the city don't care. We've asked, we've begged, and they just say 'no' or 'go to the Church.' You wanna know what the Church said to me?"

"What?"

"They told me come back next month because they had already run through their stores. Richest parish in town and they don't have a crumb to spare!"

"But we do. Remember that." I hugged her tightly. "I'm afraid today has to be a short visit. We have to be on our way."

As we finished our rounds, I couldn't stop thinking of what Mrs. MacGregor said. The rich had abandoned us. The government didn't care about the poor. The Church only had so many resources, and we were facing the same circumstances. Most of Catherine's inheritance went either into the House itself or into keeping it running, so we had to rely on the dowery from each full-time volunteer—Catherine had been forced by circumstance to begin requiring them of new residents—and the bazaars we held a few times a year to afford what we gave away. The priests at St. Andrews gave us nothing but grief, though they didn't correct those who assumed they funded our ministry or turn down donations given under that false impression.

While these circumstances occasionally made our work seem hopeless, for the most part the gratitude in the eyes of those we encountered made up for it. Certainly, there were a few crab apples in every visit—often women too proud to take what we offered or men who felt threatened accepting help from a woman—but by the end of each day, we usually had at least one outstanding story. We made a habit of sharing them during our recreation period between super and bedtime. It was a good way to end the day.

*****

I was washing dishes one winter night when Cressida came in and asked if I'd seen Jane recently.

"Come to think of it, no. The last time I recall was at morning prayer yesterday." When I thought about it, she hadn't been at recreation last night, either. "She usually works in the nursey. Have you asked Frances if Jane was helping her with the girls?"

Cressida nodded. "She was the first person I asked."

"What about Isa? Sometimes she goes into the ancient parts of the city with her."

"Yes. She said she and Jane were delivering clothing on Townsend Street, but they got separated. Isa looked for her but came here when she couldn't find her, assuming she would eventually return."

"But she hasn't," I finished for her.

Cressida shook her head. The expression in her eyes said she was worried, and so was I.

"Does Catherine know?"

"Yes. Catherine contacted everyone she could think of yesterday. So far, no one has seen her."

Cressida started rubbing the dove burned into her skin.

"Are you thinking what I'm thinking?" I asked.

She shrugged. "It's aways possible."

"Let's pray we are wrong."

*****

Body of Young Woman Found in Liffey River

The headline could easily have been missed amid more sensational news about clashes between Protestant and Catholics across Ireland as the "Orange," the Protestant's preferred name, sought to undo the Emancipation Act. But Cressida and I both saw it. The reporter described the woman as thin, with long brown hair and an odd burn on the top of her right hand. It was Jane, it had to be.

I sank down into my chair, trying to understand what could have happened. Jane was always a conscientious woman. She wouldn't have gone off on her own. She was a strong swimmer, so she wasn't likely to accidently drown, and she certainly was not one to throw herself into the river in a fit of melancholy.

The constabulary were calling it an accident, but I wasn't so sure. The Doves were still being hunted for what happened at that terrible party; Jane was the weakest in our flock, so it made sense the snakes would target her first. The natural question was, who was next?

Chapter 28

CATHERINE

January 1830
House of Mercy
Dublin, Ireland

My foot had just touched the first stone step of the spiral staircase leading to the second floor when the front bell rang. I turned around and strode quickly to the door; we always tried to answer it before the person outside rang a second time. I opened the door, expecting to see someone seeking help or one of our neighbors come to call, but instead I was greeted by the sight of Father Kelly in full clerical regalia, a deacon standing submissively behind him.

"Good day, Father Kelly," I greeted him with much more warmth than I felt.

He grimaced slightly at being addressed first, a subtle insult to his authority I took great pleasure in. "*Dominus vobiscum*," he intoned.

"*Et cum spiritu tuo*," I responded automatically. "Please, do come in."

I stepped aside to let them pass, but Father Kelly barreled onward, his black cassock billowing behind him like the tailfeathers of a hooded crow. The deacon scurried behind him, catching the priest's coat and wide-brimmed hat when he tossed them back, never breaking stride.

"Miss McAuley, I must speak with you privately." He called over his shoulder without turning around.

I did not appreciate his tone, much less having to chase after him in my own home. Was he really taking the liberty of heading to my office without an invitation? I stopped. "Then we may do so in here," I said, gesturing to the reception room. I will have Grace bring us some tea and scones."

Father Kelly stopped just short of the stairs, pivoted on one foot and stared at me. I had him and he knew it. To refuse my offer of hospitality would be an unforgivable breech of etiquette; he had to do as I suggested.

When I was sure he was following, I rang for Grace and instructed her to bring the refreshments. Father Kelly chose to sit at the head of the long table, so I took the seat to his right. His deacon stood in the corner, doing his best to melt into the wallpaper. We exchanged small talk until Grace had delivered the tea tray and sweets.

"Please be sure we are not interrupted," I asked Grace. "And take Deacon—I'm sorry, I'm afraid we haven't been introduced," I said to the younger man.

"Deacon O'Brien." He politely bowed his head to me.

"—Deacon O'Brien, to the kitchens and see that he is treated as a valued guest."

Father Kelly opened his mouth to say something, but I cut in, anticipating his concern. "My steward, Frances Warde, is there as well, taking stock of our supplies. They will not be unchaperoned."

Unable to form another objection, he motioned that the deacon was dismissed.

Once we were alone and the tea poured, Father Kelly got right to the point. "Miss McAuley ..."

"Please. Father, call me Catherine. I've asked you this before."

Father Kelly grimaced. "*Miss McAuley*, you have no doubt heard the ongoing protests against your organization—the biggest being that you are neither fish nor fowl. You are not exactly laywomen in that you act like a religious order in your dress, way of life, and ministry, yet you are not under any vows."

"You mean we are not under your control."

The priest's eyes flashed and it was clear that were he not a man of the cloth, he would have hit me. He swallowed hard.

"I prefer the term 'guidance,'" he said, "but yes. You know as well as I that even the great St. Paul wrote that women should remain silent, yet you and your companions are taking the ministry of the Church into your own hands every day. You are walking a dangerous spiritual path and are confusing the people."

He took a sip of his tea. "And now I hear that your women have taken to addressing one another as 'sister.'" He shook his head. "This madness has to stop."

"What is wrong with a few of them calling each other 'sister'? It is a term of endearment, one I heard often enough when Mrs.

Callaghan was alive. The Quakers use it, as does your beloved St. Paul in his letters."

"Yes, that is true. But can you see how it could be confusing to the poor? They are ignorant of many things and when you are caring for them and they hear the term, they think of religious sisters, which you are not."

When I said nothing, he continued, "The way I see it, you have two choices—you can convert this house into a convent and take solemn vows, or I will give it to the Sisters of Charity. Either way, the future of the House of Mercy is as a convent."

He sat back, steepling his fingers in front of him.

For a long while, I could not speak. Then my shock turned to rage. How dare this man come in here and demand such a thing from us? Yes, we resided in his parish, but he had no formal authority over us, thanks to the trust I had drawn up naming Anna Maria and Kate as my heirs and Archbishop Murray as our Church representative. Who, exactly, did he think he was?

I fought to keep my tone even, but rage simmered underneath. "How dare you come into *my* home, the House *I* built on land that *I* lease in my own name and make such demands?"

Father Kelly sipped at his tea as though we were discussing the weather.

"You are the one who placed the House in the hands of the Church," he said smoothly. "Archbishop Murray is the one who thought of this idea as a way to resolve the ongoing strife regarding your ministry."

"The Church only has access to this house if I, Anna Maria, and Kate, are all unable to take care of it," I pointed out. "And I don't believe for one moment this scheme of yours has the Archbishop's approval. He loves this House and our ministry. He would not turn it over to you or make such demands of us without consulting me first."

Father Kelly gave me a look that asked, "Are you quite finished?" He sighed. "Miss McAuley, surely you know your place under the law. A woman needs a man to guard her interests and property. As a spinster, you have neither. As a nun, you would be covered by the Church. Otherwise, you are vulnerable to lawsuits from which you cannot defend yourself in court."

I might not be able to appear in court, but I could hire a lawyer to do so on my behalf. I knew my rights and he was trampling on them. "You will have to sue me then, if you wish to carry out your plan."

"Why must you be so stubborn?" he asked, genuine curiosity coloring his words. "I have given you a reasonable alternative, yet you refuse to even consider religious life."

I slammed my hand down on the table, causing the teacups to jump in their saucers. "I will not entertain a life that is repugnant to me simply because you wish to enrich your coffers so you can expand St. Andrew's. That is what this is really about, isn't it? You speak of 'giving' this House to the Sisters of Charity—an order which you founded, may I remind you— yet we both know money will exchange hands. It has to. This is a business transaction and nothing more."

Father Kelly brought his teacup his lips, muttering something about overly educated women. When he brought his attention back to me, he acted as though I hadn't spoken.

"If you will not respect my will, then I must play a card I was hoping to keep concealed." He sat forward, as though drawing me into more intimate conversation. "I know that you balance on a knife's edge financially. I also know exactly how much this House is worth. I can make your future comfortable or leave you to get by on your own. It's your decision."

I stood, my chair scraping back loudly.

"This house is *my home*," I said through gritted teeth, hitting the tabletop with my index finger for emphasis. "*This* house is the one the Lord built through me, and I will not see you take it away for all the money in the Bank of Ireland. This ministry is one run by lay women for lay women."

I was shouting now, but I didn't care. Let the whole house witness the depths to which this supposed man of God would stoop.

"That was a very deliberate choice, and I will not have you force the veil upon me out of greed."

Father Kelly stood. "If that is your decision, so be it. We will let the courts decide. Daniel, come," he called to the deacon, who appeared from the other room as through waiting on his command. "Miss McAuley, would you be so kind as to give us a proper tour?"

It took everything I had not to tell him to go to Hell. My cheeks flamed, my heart was pounding in my ears, and I seriously thought for a moment my eyeballs might burst out of their sockets. The nerve of the man! First, he tried to force me into a convent, then evict me from my home, and now he wanted the grand tour?

Frances had accompanied Daniel upstairs. One look at my face and she stepped between me and the priest.

"I'm afraid Catherine has an important appointment to prepare for." She glanced at the clock. "Yes, her guest arrives in less than fifteen minutes. Catherine, why don't you go up to your office and I will lead these gentlemen wherever they wish to go."

Father Kelly inclined his head to Frances, but he hung back for a moment when she led the deacon from the room.

"Miss McAuley," he said, "one more thing. Despite what you may think, I am not a complete monster. If staying here means so much to you, you may select a room or two for yourself and we will have a private entrance installed to maintain your privacy. Think about it."

*****

As soon as Father Kelly and the deacon were on the other side of the building, I raced upstairs to my office. My pen was in hand and dipped in ink before I even sat down.

Dear Archbishop Murray,

Over the next two hours, in draft after draft I poured my thoughts out to him, trying to convey the heaviness of my heart. I tried to be polite but still get my point across. I asked him to please meet with me before making any final decisions, but assured him that in the end, I would acquiesce to his will, as he was the representative of God on earth.

By the time I finished a clean copy I was happy with, my head was clouded by a sense of impending doom. I addressed and sealed the letter and placed it on the tray in Anna Maria's office so she would know to post it.

Halfway down the stairs, I ran into Frances ascending them. "How was the tour?" I couldn't keep some sarcasm from leaking into my tone.

"Long, detailed. I think he had that poor deacon record every single item in the house. If I were one to place bets, I'd say they are assigning values to each thing right now."

"Well, he clearly wants this property."

Frances put her arm around me. "Whatever happens, all will be well. Remember, God never lets us down."

*****

The following morning, I lingered in prayer before the Blessed Sacrament, trying to reconcile myself with God's will. Looking up at the stained glass above me, I prayed to St. Teresa of Avila to teach me the abandonment she wrote about in her books. I had never been one to have my head turned by rumors of visions and miracles, but in this moment I wished I could either see the future or have an angel imbue my soul with perfect sanctity.

No matter how many times I wiped them away, tears kept forming in my eyes. A wave of guilt washed over me and I repented sincerely for my caustic words to Father Kelly. Yes, I was angry with him. No, he didn't understand me at all. But that didn't mean he deserved my ire. As a priest, he was elevated above me by God. I had no right to assert my will over his. I shouldn't have any will but that of God. And as the voice of God, I should have listened to him. My pride would be the damnation of my soul.

"Catherine?"

I started and opened my eyes. Anna Maria was standing next to the pew in front of me.

"I'm sorry to disturb your prayer, but you have a visitor, and he is not one to keep waiting."

I stood. "Who is it?"

Instead of answering me, she shook her head.

Confused, I followed her from the chapel into the reception area. Looking out the window was a tall man with a ring of white hair wearing a black cassock with purple flared lace at the wrists. Archbishop Murray. How? There was no way Anna Maria could have sent my letter already. Maybe Father Kelly had told him of our conversation? My stomach turned over, unsure whether to be scared or pleased that he was here.

"Your Grace?"

The Archbishop turned, his face lighting up. He held out his hands toward me. "Catherine. It is so nice to see you." He examined my face like a concerned father. "Your eyes are red. Have you been weeping?"

The compassion in his voice made me nearly tear up again. "It has been a difficult week, Your Grace." I took his hand, kissed his amethyst ring of office, and dipped into a small curtsey.

He raised me up. "I have told you many times, child—formality is not needed between us. Please, sit."

It was strange having him invite me to sit in my own home; I should have been the one to invite him. Nonetheless, I obediently pull out the chair he indicated and sat.

Grace appeared, carrying our best tea set. She set it down and served each of us as though we were her employers and set a small tray of sandwiches next to the teapot. The tea smelled of flowers and nectar, but like nothing I had ever encountered before. Curious, I raised the glass to my nose and inhaled, momentarily swept away by visions of lavender, honeysuckle, and currants. I sipped the hot liquid carefully, the taste of violets and the summer sun tumbling on my tongue.

"It is a blend of my own making," the archbishop said. "Your letter sounded like you needed it."

My gaze flew to his. "My letter? How?"

"Anna Maria sent it by messenger last night. When I read it, I knew I had to speak to you in person." He placed a hand over mine. "You need to know that nothing Father Kelly said was true, far from it."

A weight lifted off my shoulders. "What?" was all I could say.

"Catherine, you know me. Far from endorsing his ideas, I never once entertained the idea of taking the House of Mercy from you or interfering in any way in your benevolent work. Indeed, I hope it will continue and prosper."

This was so far from what I expected to hear, I couldn't speak. Slowly, my mind began to comprehend his words and joy washed over me. "Bless you, Father." Warm tears of joy spilled over my cheeks.

He gave me a few moments to collect myself, sampling the sandwiches Grace had made. Once I had dried my eyes and I my breathing calmed, the Archbishop leaned toward me. "There is one thing I do recommend. You are not going to like it, but is best for the future of your ministry."

I eyed him warily. "What is that?"

"I believe it is in the best interest of everyone here that you found a religious order, one that is completely new and unique to your ministry. Hear me out—doing so will provide for your work in perpetuity and protect you from the venom of your enemies. You need not be confined to the cloister; we can write your Rule in such a way that it permits you to walk among the people and tend to their needs. You can fulfil the dream Nano Nagle started."

"I have heard such horrible things about convents," I confided. Memories of the stories my Protestant relatives had told me as child and those the Callaghans had repeated played in my mind. "Their customs are so strange," I mumbled. "The idea of kneeling before a superior seems so medieval and so wrong. Should I not only kneel before Christ and king? Then there is the requirement to admit my sins publicly every day before the whole order and submit to punishment for them. I thought forgiveness and justice were between a soul and God, through the medium of a priest. Why should I allow another nun to humiliate me and administer whatever torture she sees fit?"

"Not all orders are so harsh, my dear. You will be able to set out exactly what your order will and won't do."

I nodded, still half lost in my imaginings. I shook myself to rid my mind of them. "Father, if nothing else, I am a fifty-two-year-old woman. I am set in my ways. Religious life requires learning a whole new way of life, does it not? I'm not sure I have it in me anymore."

The Archbishop chuckled. "You live more like a nun than you realize. Your critics are right about that. You already live on a regimented schedule with time devoted to prayer, work, and recreation; your black dresses are not far off from a religious habit; and you live in common, dedicated to the same cause. It won't be as big of an adjustment as you think."

"How would this happen? Would we need to enter another convent? Who would keep the House open?"

The archbishop leaned back, thinking.

"I suppose you could conduct your novitiate here, so long as you can remain separated from those who are in active ministry. It is very important that you have the time to contemplate your vocation and really learn what being a nun means."

He looked around. "The House is certainly large enough. But would you be able to keep your mind from being distracted by the other activities going on around you?"

"No," I answered honestly. I knew my heart. I was a leader and I wanted to know everything that was happening at all times. Controlling? Perhaps, but I liked to think of it as being an involved part of the ministry.

"I thought not," he said with a good-natured chuckle. "Then it would be best for you to spend at least a year as a member of another order."

"Which one? And how many of us would go?"

"That is up to you on both counts. You may decide how many you need to remain to keep the House open. Remember that once you take your vows, you can train more women here. As to where, you will need to think about which order's constitutions best mirror what you want your order to be like. It will be easier for you to write your own Rule if you train in one similar to the life you wish to lead."

"One more question, Father. If we did this—became a religious order—what would we be called?"

"Again, that is up to you. But your work and your House are already dedicated to Our Lady of Mercy, so I would suggest the Sisters of Mercy."

A tingle shot down my spine. "The Sisters of Mercy," I repeated to myself. Somehow the words felt right. Was it possible? Was this the best decision for us? Right now, only one thing was clear to me—this was a choice I couldn't and shouldn't make on my own. I would have to talk to the volunteers about this. After all, my life wasn't the only one that would change based on this decision.

Chapter 29

ANNA MARIA

February 1830
House of Mercy
Dublin, Ireland

Within days, the entire House was buzzing with the news that the Archbishop wanted us to become nuns. Catherine may have been hesitant, but many of us weren't. We found a kinship in our shared desire for religious life. At night, Kate and I sneaked into the volunteers' dormitory to talk with the other women.

"When I was a child I wanted to be a Dominican," Kate said, "but to become a nun with my aunt would be an honor."

"Maybe Catherine will chose their constitution to model hers after," Frances said.

"If you find you still want to be a Dominican later, you can change orders," I added.

"Really?"

"Yes. It doesn't happen often, but there is a process. When my sister was in the Presentation convent in Killarney, one of the Sisters left to become a Franciscan."

"Did you want to join the Presentation Sisters, too?" One of the newer women asked.

"For many years. But I am very at home here." A warm feeling came over me at the thought. "I'm curious to see what Catherine has to say when we meet tomorrow."

"As am I," said Margaret Dunn.

"I just hope we aren't put under the Carmelite Rule," Frances added. "Their spirituality is beautiful, but they are so austere. No meat, Grand Silence nearly all day, and half the year they eat only one meal. That is not the life for me."

"I heard they only wash their bed linens every six months," Kate said.

A chorus of disgust ripped around our circle.

"If I wanted to live that way, I could have stayed at the workhouse," Grace said.

"What about you, Grace? Have you thought about becoming a nun? I know you've only been Catholic for a few years, but you must love the faith to come to it as an adult."

Grace looked away. "I don't think religious life is for me. I ... I don't think they would take me anyway. Life hasn't been as kind to me as it has to some of you."

An awkward silence followed, during which I noticed one girl was missing. "Where is Isa?"

The women looked around as though she was present and I simply wasn't seeing her.

Several shrugged.

"She was with us at dinner," Cressida said.

"She's probably in the cellar helping Cook sort the leftovers for the poor. She does enjoy that."

"I'll look for her," Grace volunteered.

My heart went out to her. She didn't speak much about her past, but I gathered she'd had a rough go of it. Her comments made me wonder exactly what had happened, but it wasn't my place to ask. I just hoped she wouldn't let it keep her from seeing the potential of her future.

*****

Isa didn't appear the next day, and we were all growing worried. Catherine reported her missing, but the police said there was little they could do but keep an eye out.

So, we carried on without her. After supper, Catherine called all eleven of us into the parlor, where she had arranged chairs around one of our long dining tables. At each place sat two beans: one white and one black. Resting in the center in neat piles were several stacks of paper.

As the two original founders of this house, Catherine and I sat at either end, she at the head and I at the foot. The other women chose their seats at random.

Catherine wasted no time repeating the details of her encounter with Father Kelly and the Archbishop. "My dearest friends, I have called you here tonight to discuss the future of our ministry. It comes down to two questions: First, should we form a new religious order or remain a lay ministry? And, if we form an order, on what order will we base our Rule?"

She gave us a moment to reflect on her words before continuing. "As to the first question, should we become a religious order, I ask you to indicate your answer by placing a white bean in this jar—she held up a small ceramic jar with a narrow mouth—for yes or a black bean for no. To keep the voting fair, please hold both beans in one hand and keep the one you didn't use in that hand. We will pass the jar around again later for your second bean. Are you ready?"

A few of the heads nodded, so she handed the jar to Grace, who was on her right. Grace hesitated, looking at each of us before depositing a bean in the jar. The next two women voted quickly, as did Kate, but Frances was a little more deliberative. The jar came to me and I deposited my white bean before passing it along down the line. The final volunteer to vote was Cressida, who looked at the jar, at her closed fist, and then back at the jar before the clink of her bean sounded. Catherine voted last. I watched her for any indication of her vote, but found none.

She emptied the beans out onto the table before her and sent the jar back around the table to collect the unused beans. Catherine quickly separated the white from the black and announced the totals: eight white and four black. "Being thus voted upon, I hereby announce the creation of the Sisters of Mercy religious order."

Applause and cheers erupted around the table.

"I want to make one thing clear before we proceed." Catherine looked us each in the eyes before continuing. "Even if you voted 'no' today, you are still welcome here. While most of us will go on to take vows, we will still need lay helpers. And we would still like your thoughts about our constitution."

Catherine reached out and picked up the first pile of paper.

"Now, our next order of business is to choose a Rule on which to base our own. It will also determine the convent in which we complete our novitiate, as well as direct our way of life until our own Rule is completed. I have copies of each for the orders here in Dublin if you'd like to see them, but there are a few I think we can rule out right away. The Ursulines are a teaching order, as are the Dominicans. While we do teach, and there may be things they do that we wish to incorporate in our final Rule, I think they are too far afield from our work."

We discussed and eliminated several other orders before finally coming to the Carmelites. "I especially wish to hear your opinions on their Rule. I am afraid I cannot be unbiased here because they have been intertwined in my work from the beginning. They are eager that we should become a branch of their order, but I am not sure if they are whom we wish to emulate. I will save my opinions until the end of our discussion because I do not wish to sway yours."

We glanced at one another in the ensuing silence, wondering who would speak up first. As far as I knew, Catherine was unaware of our clandestine activities, so had no idea we'd had this conversation already.

Finally, Frances stood. "While we are grateful for everything the Carmelites have done for us, that is no reason to accept their Rule off-handedly. I believe I speak for everyone here when I say that their Rule will be nearly impossible to follow with our type of ministry. What their saints teach has great merit and should be studied by anyone who wishes to have a rich interior life, but their days are built around prayer and contemplation. Yes, we make time for that, but the majority of our time is with others. They spend their days mostly in silence. How are we to continue in work where communication is so important if we have to do it all in writing or using sign language? It isn't efficient."

Catherine nodded, taking in Frances's argument.

"Don't forget what you said last night about their diet," Kate added.

Frances shot her a look that had no place among a group of women contemplating religious life.

Catherine giggled. "So, you've talked about his before, eh? I'm glad. That means you trust one another, and a bond of unity has formed among you. That will be very important moving forward. What is this about their diet?"

"It is very austere," I answered. "They abstain from meat and from the Feast of the Holy Cross until Easter they eat only one small meal a day. That may be sufficient when you spend most of your day in prayer, but we need to keep up our energy. We are walking for miles in the city or standing on our feet for long hours teaching or milling among our students. I spend my days trying to keep up with two very active young ladies. Their way of denying themselves and our way of ministry are not healthy or compatible."

"I agree," Catherine said. "Their asceticism worries me. I understand wishing to tame your body for the sake of your soul, but not when it affects the work we do for the greater glory of God. We will have our own privations—everyone does—but seeking them out is counterintuitive to our purpose."

We discussed other aspects of their Rule, including how we might adapt the prayers of the Divine Office for our busy schedules, whereas they comprised the majority of a Carmelite's day. Catherine also voiced concern that the Carmelite nuns were under the authority of the Carmelite priests, so that meant our order would not be truly free. Knowing Catherine as I did, I would have voted against the Carmelite Rule based on that alone; there was no way she could ever find peace under the thumb of men. By a hand vote we overwhelmingly rejected the Carmelite Rule.

That settled, Catherine picked up the last stack of pages. "That leaves us with the rule of the Presentation order. Many of you are familiar with them and some have even had relatives among them." Catherine winked at me. "But I don't want to you think we must adopt their Rule because it is the last one on the table. If we can't find one suitable, I will go back to Archbishop Murray and we will chart another course."

One by one, all eyes turned to me. My face flushed at the unwelcome attention.

"What? I am no expert on life in a Presentation convent. I chose to remain here rather than join, remember?"

"Yes, but you know it better than anyone," Elizabeth reminded me. "What was it that attracted you to them?"

"Well, the first thing was their dedication to poor. I won't go into why, but I have had tenderness toward them from a young age. In that respect, they are much like us. Their spirituality also attracted me, with its deep devotion to the Sacred Heart of Jesus and an emphasis on justice, especially for families. Plus, I loved the idea of becoming a bride of Christ."

I looked down at this last statement, embarrassed at my own admission, but when Frances said my name and I looked up, several other women appeared lost in thought about the idea Jesus as spouse as well.

"Did you learn anything from your sister that we should be cautious about?" Frances asked.

I thought back to my visits with Mary, which were generally joyful affairs. "Nothing specific. The usual complaints about adjusting to a new lifestyle, novice mistresses who are harsh on the fledgling nuns, believing they are helping them prepare for the reality of religious life, that sort of thing."

Mother Aloysius's hatred for our way of life lay heavy on my heart. She had died several months earlier and I didn't wish to speak ill of the dead, but I was glad she was Jesus' problem now. I chose my words carefully. "The Mother Superior there now is very kind, but the previous one—who influenced many of the nuns—held strong views about solemn vows and enclosure making a woman a 'real nun.' I fear we would take a fair amount of verbal abuse for insisting on simple vows that would allow us to remain in the world as we are today."

"Hmmm …" Catherine hummed. "That is a serious concern. However, it would only be for a year. Look at how many years we've had insults hurled at us from the public and even from our own parish priests."

A murmur of agreement rose from our group.

"If you look at their history, the Presentation order began with much the same mission as we have," Catherine said. "Take away the rule of enclosure—which was only recently added—and you'll find their founding principles are fairly similar to our intentions." She passed a copy of the Rule around the table. "The only reason they didn't adopt the Ursuline Rule was enclosure, the same reason we rejected it."

Catherine gave each of us time to look over the document, as she had with all the previous Rules we'd seriously considered. While the others examined it, I turned the situation over and over in my mind. Was it really possible that God might have found a way to integrate my two great loves? For so long the only future I had imagined for myself was one in which I wore the black-and-white habit of the Sisters of the Presentation of the Blessed Virgin Mary. Then Catherine and the House of Mercy had come along and I had fallen in love all over again with a very different kind of life, one that required me to take part in the world, rather than be sheltered from it. And now, here was the opportunity to train among the order I so loved and then dedicate myself to a life of service like the one I was living now. *Thank you, Lord!* Now I just had to hope the others agreed.

When everyone had finished reading the rule, Catherine called for a vote. Every single woman raised her hand in favor of this constitution, including Cressida and Grace, who had abstained from many of the prior votes.

Catherine let out a deep sigh of relief. "It appears we have come to a decision. Now there is only one more to make—which of us will spend the next year of our life at St. George's Hill learning to become a nun."

"You mean we all won't go?" Kate asked. The disappointment in her voice and in her frown was so palpable, my heart broke for her.

Catherine regarded her with great compassion. "No, my dear. Some of you will need to stay here to keep the House open and continue our ministry. Besides, no convent would have room for all of us."

To the wider group, she added, "When he asked for copies of their Rule, Archbishop Murray also inquired about how many women each convent could accept. Keeping that in mind and thinking through who was essential to the operation of the House, I have decided to choose two others."

Another mummer rippled through the lines of seated women, decidedly less pleased than before.

"I know, I know," Catherine said, "it is not fair, but it is how it must be. I, of course, must go. But the rest of you are free to do as you will. If you already know religious life is not for you but you wish to continue in your ministry here, that is perfectly acceptable. No one will think less of you. If you wish to remove yourself from consideration for the two remaining places, you are free to go and continue about your normal duties. If you have any doubts whatsoever, I advise you to leave now."

Grace and Cressida stood first, followed by two of the newer volunteers, and—to my great shock—Kate and Frances. That left six women, including Catherine. At her invitation, we gathered closer to her, taking the seats the others had vacated.

"Before I name the two who will accompany me, please know how proud I am of each of you and how much I love you. My choice is based on practical matters and has nothing to do with your level of piety or your performance in ministry. Please not do not feel bad if I don't choose you. That simply means your place is here for now. When we return, we will immediately begin training anyone else who wishes to become a Sister of Mercy, so this is not your only opportunity."

Under the table, the five of us linked hands, though we had not planned to.

"My first choice is Anna Maria." Catherine looked at me with a love that reflected our years together. "You have been with me from the first and we will be together until the last. Will you join me in this adventure, my friend?"

Fighting back tears, I nodded. "Yes, you know I will."

We embraced like sisters and I whispered my thanks in her ear. "Don't thank me, yet," she said. "We still have to survive this."

When we had collected ourselves, Catherine turned back to the expectant faces. "My other companion to St. George's will be Elizabeth."

Elizabeth's mouth fell open and mine nearly did the same; of the women present, she was the last I would have expected Catherine to pick. Elizabeth tried to respond, but nothing came out, she was so taken aback.

Catherine came around the table and hugged her. "You have the perfect temperament for a nun. Anna Maria and I could learn from you. Plus, I believe there is a strong woman in there." She poked playfully at Elizabeth's chest. "Religious training will help draw her out."

"What do you say? Do you wish to join us?" I asked. I couldn't tell if her reaction was borne out of natural reticence or if she wished Catherine had picked someone else.

Instead of answering my question, she asked, "When do we leave?" sounding like a girl who couldn't wait to spend the summer with her favorite aunt in some foreign land.

"It will be a few months yet. Early autumn, probably. There are many arrangements to be made, both with the Presentation convent and here. Should you change your mind, please tell me. No one will blame you. I simply need to know to submit another name."

So, there it was. The Sisters of Mercy would begin with three: Catherine, Elizabeth, and me.

Chapter 30

GRACE

When the parlor doors clicked shut behind me, I couldn't decide if it was wiser to run to the water closet to vomit or to the chapel to pray. The women's conversation the night before had touched a little too closely on my worst fear—that I wouldn't be accepted here and would have to return to my former life—and now my stomach was in knots and I feared I would faint.

Swallowing the bile in my throat, I headed for the chapel, which was blessedly empty. I crashed through the gate of the grille and fell to my knees before the Blessed Sacrament, sobbing. My tears came from deep within, from my blood and my bones and my very soul, burning even as they healed me. They were for all the mistakes and missteps of my life, for letting myself become entangled with Lord Montague; for Margaret, Jane, and Isa; for the years I was feral, living on the streets and rutting like a sow for money; for the lies I had to tell and deceptions I had to maintain in order to keep the Doves safe; and for the little girl I once was, who deserved so much better.

The cross atop the tabernacle blurred in and out of clarity as I blinked. Now that the women here were becoming nuns, what would happen to me? Catherine said we could stay, but was that really true? Did someone with a past like mine deserve to live under the same roof as nuns? Could I—was it allowed? I'd never heard of lay women living in a convent. Ice shot down my spine. Catherine only said we could continue volunteering, not that we could continue living here. What if they had to sanctify the building and everyone in it? I had confessed all my sins when I became Catholic, but I still didn't feel clean—like a window with a layer of grease you couldn't scrub off no matter how hard you tried. I probably never would.

I worked for my room and board, not for pay, so how would I sustain myself? Perhaps Catherine would give me a character and I could go back into service in a Catholic household. Now that our religion was fully legal, there had to be some wealthy families who had returned to the Church. That wouldn't be so bad. Perhaps Cressida would even want to come with me.

I picked myself up and moved to my choir bench. From this distance, the candles on either side of the tabernacle made the jewels inlaid in it sparkle like stars. Jesus, what should I do? Mother Mary? St. Zita? St. Teresa? Anyone?

It was probably a smart idea to leave anyway. If anyone ever recognized me on the street and connected me to the Doves, not only would my life be in danger, but Catherine's whole ministry could be as well. I would probably be excommunicated, and Catherine would surely be censured for allowing me to work there. Who would ever trust her again after that? It was a small miracle Lord Montague hadn't betrayed us all already, given what he knew and how much he hated Catherine. My knowledge of his involvement with the Doves must be damning enough to keep his silence. Catherine had had more than one spirited row with him, so perhaps she had her own leverage on him.

But then again, Cressida and I were the only two Doves left, and no matter what explanations the authorities gave about Jane drowning or Isa's disappearance, I would never believe them. Jane had been murdered and dumped into the canal to make it look like an accident. I couldn't prove that, just like I couldn't prove Isa hadn't tired of our life and run away, but I knew it in my bones. And if my own fate was so tied to theirs, the last place I needed to be was here, putting all of these innocent women and children in danger.

A calm sense of certainty gradually came over me as I mulled over my plan to leave. Worst case, I could live with Mrs. MacGregor until I secured a job. But knowing Catherine, she wouldn't let me leave without a place to stay and a few coins in my pocket, even if they were her last. I would speak to her in the morning.

It was my night to serve as porter, so I had plenty of time to rehearse what I would say to Catherine. I played out various scenarios in my mind depending on her mood, changing her reaction so that I would be prepared for any situation.

Around midnight, a frantic knocking startled me from my dozing. I opened the door to find Cressida propping up a badly beaten woman who was barely conscious.

"Oh my God, Cressida!" I reached out to take part of the woman's weight. "Help! Catherine! Anyone! We have an emergency! Help!"

We helped the woman into the parlor and laid her on a couch. As soon as her feet were off the floor, she passed out. Her long hair was sticking to blood on her face and she was covered in scrapes and bruises. Cressida stayed with her, trying to determine the worst of her injuries, while I ran to the kitchen to reheat the kettle and find towels to clean her. Above me, Catherine called for Kate to fetch the doctor, who thankfully only lived a few streets over.

When I returned, Frances was standing over her. "My mother was a nurse," she explained. "I'm the best we have until the doctor arrives." She and I took turns soaking our rags and wiping the woman down.

"She looks to have been whipped,' Frances said in disgust.

"Poor thing. Who could have done this to her?" I wondered.

Frances was stitching up the wounds as best she could and Catherine and others were applying pressure to still bleeding gashes, but the mountain of bloody towels on the floor only grew. Out of the corner of my eye, I caught movement as Elizabeth entered the room, balancing two streaming pitchers and another basin.

I took charge of the basin and positioned it under her head. Elizabeth handed me a pitcher. With one hand, I poured water over her head as in a kind of baptism in death, trying to detangle her blood-matted hair with the fingers of my other hand. She was so pale, somehow sweating and shivering at the same time. "What do we do?" I asked the room.

Frances shook her head. "She's lost too much blood. I doubt even the best doctor can save her now."

I glanced at Catherine, who nodded. "Do what you can, but know we are essentially preparing her body for burial. Treat her with the respect she deserves."

Some of the women backed off, their help no longer needed. Cressida sat down on the floor next to the couch and took the woman's hand. "I'm sorry I didn't find you sooner," she sobbed. "I'm sorry we couldn't save you ..."

Her voice cut off abruptly. Then she breathed my name. "Grace, look at this."

Cressida raised the woman's hand so I could see it. There, on the top of her right hand, barely visible through layers of dirt and caked-on blood, was the unmistakable shape of a dove.

Cressida and I stared at each other. She was one of our lost sisters. I poured another pitcher of water over the woman's forehead and Cressida struggled to loosen her hair without hurting her. She may be nearly dead, but we were still hesitant to inflict pain. Finally, the strands covering half of her face came loose. We gently wiped the blood from her face.

Bess.

There was no mistaking her slightly upturned nose or the mole on the side of her neck. Even the scar on her temple matched my memories.

"Oh Bess, what happened you? I wish you could tell us," I said.

"You two know her?" Catherine asked.

"Yes," Cressida croaked out between sobs.

Bess' breathing slowed. We each took one of her hands. "You were not alone in life and you will not be alone in death," I promised her.

"Doves protect their own," Cressida said.

I bowed my head and began to pray the Hail Mary, begging our Blessed Mother to be the mother in Heaven that Bess didn't have on earth. I didn't know much about God's judgment, but I couldn't imagine that the pain of her death didn't make up for her sins.

A shudder ran through Bess' body and she sighed her final breath. It was a peaceful sound I would never forget. When I raised my head, her eyes were open, staring at eternity.

Kate and the doctor returned less than ten minutes later. Cressida and I were combing out Bess's hair and cleaning her skin as best we could.

"I'm so sorry I wasn't here sooner," the doctor apologized. "I wasn't at home when this young lady knocked. She had to track me down at the pub."

"It wouldn't have mattered," Frances said gently. "She was too far gone."

The doctor removed his coat and hat, which Kate placed on a rack by the door.

"Prepare yourself," Catherine urged. "She died by violence."

I stepped back to let the doctor do his work. He inspected her body, put his ear to chest and held smelling salts beneath her nose. "She is dead," he declared.

"May Christ have mercy on her soul," someone in the back of the room prayed.

"And may she rest in peace," another woman said.

"Amen," everyone in the room responded.

A moment of silence passed before Catherine addressed us. "We have all had a quite a shock tonight. Please, go back to your beds and try to get some sleep. All activities are canceled tomorrow, so take as long as you need to rest and recover."

"I will bring up some tea as soon as it is ready," Kate said.

Catherine put a hand on my shoulder, as well as Cressida's. "Will you two please stay? You as well, Frances." She gestured toward the table, the same one around which we had sat just hours ago discussing religious orders. That felt like a lifetime ago.

"We will need to summon the constable," the doctor said. "Do you wish for an inquest?"

"Yes," Catherine responded. "If it can tell us anything about her killer, we will all rest easier."

The doctor opened a small notebook he procured from an inner pocket of his jacket. "What was the name of the deceased?"

"Bess Bannon," Cressida and I chorused. "Short for Elizabeth," I added.

"And how did she come to be here?"

"I was out for a walk, trying to clear my head," Cressida explained.

"So late at night?" the doctor looked dubious.

"We had a special meeting that lasted until well past dark," Catherine explained.

"I know it wasn't wise, but I had to get some fresh air. I only intended to walk to Merrion Square and back, but once I started walking, I got lost in my thoughts. Eventually I found myself at St. Stephen's Green. I was nearly back here when Bess came stumbling around the corner from Herbert Street. How she held herself up, I will never know. As soon as she saw me, she lunged in my direction. I think that must have used up the last of her strength, because she was barely conscious when I caught her. At first I thought she might be drunk or ill, but then I saw the blood and realized something very bad had happened to her."

"Did you see anyone or hear anything?"

"No. If either of us been even a few moments faster or slower, we would not have crossed paths," she muttered, mostly to herself.

"You knew her name. Did she tell you? Speak to you at all before she died?"

"No. Nothing." I answered. "We've known her for years, used to work with her before we came here." I prayed the doctor wouldn't ask about our line of work. Thankfully he didn't.

"Is there anything else you think I should know before I call the constable?"

We shook our heads.

"You should know he will likely ask you the same questions again. You may have to testify in court, depending on the circumstances surrounding her death. Do you understand?"

We all said yes.

After he departed, Catherine called us to her. "It has not escaped my notice that Bess is the third Dove to die under mysterious circumstances, first Jane, then Isa, and now Bess. Until we find out what is going on, the two of you are staying in this house. You may walk about the back garden, but do not leave this property unless I am with you. I will not have another one of you die when I could have protected you. Do you understand?"

"Yes," we both said.

"Go to bed. It is late and we all need sleep. We will continue this discussion tomorrow."

"What about the blood? Shouldn't we clean it up first?" I was so tired I could barely see, but the domestic in me had to ask.

"It has already ruined everything it's touched. It won't be any worse in the morning," Catherine sighed.

"What about you, Catherine?"

She ran a hand over her face. "I will go to bed once the coroner is done here and Bess is safely on her way to the morgue. Thank you for everything you did to help her. When my time comes, I hope to be surrounded by women like you."

*****

Two days later we received an urgent message summoning Catherine, Cressida, and I to the constabulary station. We were shown inside to a private room much like an office where the constable and a tall bald man, whom I assumed was the coroner, were seated. Relief swept over me that there were no bodies in sight.

"Miss McAuley?" The corner extended a hand to Catherine.

"Yes."

"I am so sorry to make your acquaintance under these circumstances."

"Thank you. These are my friends, Miss Ryan and Miss Finnan. They were friends of the deceased."

He took our hands and inclined his head to each of us. "I'm so sorry for your loss. Please have a seat."

After a moment's pause, the constable addressed us. "I know this is delicate business, especially for ladies, so I will try to be as gentle as possible."

Inwardly, I rolled my eyes. This dandy of a man wouldn't have survived a week in some of the places I'd lived or weathered much of what I'd seen. But if he wished to think me a fading flower, so be it.

"Clearly, Miss Bannon, that is, Bess, died from severe beating with an unknown object. Our best guess is that she was whipped and then struck with a thin, blunt object, like a stick."

Unbidden, memories of being hit and punched by Lord Montague and former clients flashed through my mind. I closed my eyes and lowered my head, willing them away.

"The good news is that we know who killed her."

My head snapped up. "What?"

"Somehow, in the course of the struggle she swallowed this." He held up a small gold object.

I leaned forward to see it better. It was round, with some sort of crest engraved on it.

"What is it?" Cressida asked.

"A cufflink. You may hold it if you like."

He placed it in her hand and she turned it this way and that so that the engraving caught the light. "I don't understand. How does this identify her murderer?" She passed the cufflink to me.

I held it up between my thumb and forefinger. For a moment I thought I would faint or that I had traveled back in time. I knew this symbol. It had been part of my life for years. Engraved on fine china, in wood, even in the silver tip of a cane. "Lord Montague. This is his crest." My voice shook with the shock of recognition. I held it out the them, begging them with my eyes to see what I did.

The constable smiled at me like as though I were a very small child who had just proudly identified the grass as green. "Yes, it is. We went to his house yesterday, and what did we find?"

It was a rhetorical question, but Cressida said hopefully, "It's mate?"

"Yes, indeed. Lord Montague had some very interesting explanations for its absence until I told him it was recovered from the stomach of a dead woman."

"I bet she bit him," Cressida said.

The constable arched an eyebrow. "What makes you say that?"

"Well, he didn't exactly feed it to her, did he?"

"When you've been beaten as many times as we have," I explained, "you learn to do anything to try to break free—to use anything at your disposal to avoid death, even if it is only what God gave you."

The sadness in the corner's eyes was enough to nearly undo me.

The constable, on the other hand, had clearly seen as much, if not more, than we had. His eyes glowed with pride. "Good girl," he whispered, presumably to Bess's spirit. He cleared his throat and looked at Cressida. "You are a very perceptive woman. When we arrested Lord Montague, he had a scar on his right wrist in the shape of a deep bite mark that is consistent with this theory."

"How did he explain that away?" I asked.

The constable shifted in his seat. "His excuse was not something I would be comfortable repeating in front of members of the fairer sex." His cheeks and throat turned a bright shade of pink.

Cressida and I regarded one another, on the edge of nervous giggles. She pretended to bite the air and I nearly lost control.

"He is in custody, then?" Catherine asked, bringing us back to the subject at hand.

"Yes, but I don't know for how long. He is a very powerful man, so he may be able to buy his way out of the gaol."

"Not if his finances are as bad as they once were," I said without thinking.

The constable looked intrigued.

"I used to work for him. I saw all kinds of things, sometimes even those he didn't wish me to see."

He scribbled something down on a piece of paper on the table in front of him. "Is that so? I may wish to speak with you further about this." Seeing my frightened expression, he added, "You are not in any trouble. It would simply help us to know what you do."

I glanced at Catherine, scared this was the moment I had dreaded, where everything would be exposed.

"'You will know the truth, and the truth will set you free,'" she whispered, quoting the gospel of John.

I nodded. "I will tell you anything you wish to know."

PART V

VINDICATION

Chapter 31

CATHERINE

September 8, 1830
St. George's Hill
Dublin, Ireland

The cool autumn breeze off the sea refreshed body and soul as we walked through Dublin from the House of Mercy to the Presentation convent at St. George's Hill, leaving our old lives behind. I must have been more nervous than I realized, because a journey of less than three kilometers shouldn't have been enough to make me break a sweat.

It was Father Kelly who insisted that we walk, even though our few belongings had been sent ahead via coach. He said it would be symbolic of Jesus walking the Via Dolorosa to Calvary and would give us time to transition from our worldly mindset to one focused totally on God.

Personally, I thought he just wanted the time to gloat that he had gotten his way in the end.

I glanced over at my companions. Anna Maria couldn't keep a smile off her face and was nearly skipping, but Elizabeth lagged behind and kept smoothing down her skirt as though the action gave her comfort. I stepped toward her and took her clammy hand in mine. "Nervous?"

She nodded vigorously and swallowed before finding her voice. "I'm excited to grow in my faith but also scared. What if they don't like me or I'm not good enough?" Elizabeth was quite mature, so it was sometimes easy to forget how young she was; the gaze she turned on me then was not that of a twenty-year-old woman, but of a scared teenage girl.

I squeezed her hand. "They will love you. And as far as being good enough, you far outshine me—and I would daresay nearly everyone else at Baggot Street—in virtue, so if they find you lacking, it is their fault, not yours." I smiled at her, feeling very maternal. "Besides, I will be by your side the whole way. I won't let anyone harm you."

"Thank you, Catherine." Elizabeth gave me a half side hug.

"Hurry now, Sisters," Father Kelly called to us from several meters ahead. "We mustn't keep the Lord waiting."

Elizabeth and Anna hastened their step to catch up to the priest, but I kept my pace. I had no desire to get to St. George's any sooner than I must. Unlike the others, I was not looking forward to the next twelve months. Perhaps it was my age that made me recalcitrant—I was fifty-two, after all; most women my age were grandmothers at the very least and spent their days knitting and cooking. Here I was turning my life upside down, something that didn't seem to bother the younger girls. I envied their ability to find such a close connection with God that they were able to embody Jesus' command to "leave everything behind, take up the Cross, and follow him." At moment I felt more like St. Peter than St. John, always reluctantly dragging the Cross behind me, rather than bravely standing at its foot.

What felt like a lifetime later, we crested the final hill and St. George's came into sight. I took small comfort in the fact that its exterior was built in much the same style as our home on Baggot Street, though its brick was a moodier grayish red than our bright white.

As we approached the main entrance, I allowed one final thought of the House of Mercy, reassuring myself it was in good hands. Frances would continue in her usual management of the household affairs and finances, and Grace had agreed to be her assistant, so she would have all the support she needed from someone who had seen all aspects of service. They would be fine without me, I reassured myself, taking deep breaths to try to calm my nerves, which rose with every step.

Despite this being what the Church wanted and what the women of the House of Mercy had agreed to, I couldn't help but wonder if this was really the right choice for our ministry. The whole point of our work over the last three years had been to show that lay women could and should help other lay women—God called all of us to service toward our fellow man, not only the priests. We were doing what they did not. By becoming nuns, we were losing that special aspect of our calling, just has Nano Nagel and Mary Akenhead had before us. It wasn't fair and it wasn't right.

Yet here I was, about to plunge headlong into a future I couldn't even begin to envision. God was teaching me both humility and malleability, I reminded myself. I had to learn to let go of my own will and conform to that of God, not an easy feat for a woman of my age used to doing as she pleased. As I stepped over the threshold, I symbolically left that woman behind. Now I was in a new phase of my life, as fresh and vulnerable as a newborn babe.

Mother Mary Clare Angela Doyle, superior of the convent, met us at the grille separating the cloister from the small public space at the front of the main building. "Welcome, welcome, beautiful souls," she cried. "Oh, there is nothing like the sight of new postulants to spark vigor in the soul. I want so much to embrace you, but that will have to wait a little while longer."

She beckoned us over to a strange wooden panel that stood at waist height next to the grille on one wall. It had an opening like a door or closet, but instead of being empty inside, it contained a round apparatus with three sides, each with different sized openings or shelves.

"It's called a rotary," Anna Maria said. "It turns and they use it pass objects from inside the cloister to the secular side and vice versa. Watch."

I had forgotten Anna Maria knew so much about this life already. Perhaps it was time for the student to become the teacher.

Sure enough, with a slight whirring of gears, the round contraption began to turn. Soon, three piles of black fabric faced us. Mother Mary Clare reappeared behind the grate. "Those are your new uniforms as postulants. Once you have changed into them, Father Kelly will let us know and we can formally receive you." She pulled closed the curtain that separated their seating area from the receiving room, offering us privacy.

Father Kelly handed each of us a one of the stacks. "As you don this first habit of the Presentation order, remember that your role is that of an aspirant. Your first months here are as much meant to see if you are compatible with religious life as they are for the Sisters to judge whether you are a fit for their order. As you are beginning your own order, this is more formality than a true test, but it is still time for you to adjust to your new life. If you think of it in that spirit, you will be happier."

Father Kelly's support was an unexpected surprise. I supposed now that we were doing as he wished, he had no reason to fight us or talk down to us. I decided to take his kindness where and when I could get it and thank God for every moment.

He stepped outside so that we could change into our first habits.

For a moment the three of us looked at one another, speechless. We were finally here. We were really doing this. Then Anna Maria and Elizabeth let out a squeal of joy that I couldn't help but laugh at.

We helped one another into the long black dresses, pulled on our stockings and shoes, and pinned the black veils—which were more like the mantillas we wore to Mass than the long flowing veils of the novices and professed nuns—to our hair. In a short time, we were ready.

"I'm scared," I confided to Anna Maria, while Elizabeth was off getting Father Kelly. I held out my trembling hand for her to see.

"So am I," she reassured me, showing me her own unsteady hand. She took mine in hers and squeezed. "We can to this. We will get through this together."

Father Kelly inspected us, straightening a pleat here or there, but otherwise deeming is satisfactory. "Follow me."

We gathered behind a closed door not far from the receiving room.

"This is the gateway to the cloister. Once you enter, you may not leave until you are a vowed religious or you have formally parted ways with the community. This ritual may seem simple, but it has profound meaning if you are willing to seek it out."

He offered each of us a small book. "Keep this safe. It contains all of the ceremonies you will participate in over the next year. Open it to page four and you will see what you are to do today."

I opened the book and skimmed over its text. This was exactly the nonsense I didn't like about religious orders. So much pomp and circumstance for nothing. It was not like Jesus himself was going to appear because we said the right words or made the right gestures. In this respect, I was inclined to side with the Protestants. This was superstitious nonsense. But I was expected to take part in it, so I would.

We knelt before the door and took the lighted candle Father Kelly held out to us. At his signal, we knocked on the door in unison.

The top half of the door opened to reveal three nuns holding similar books standing behind another grate. Over their shoulders, I could see the rest of the nuns waiting to receive us.

"What is it you seek within?" Mother Superior asked.

"Mother Superior Mary Clare Angela Doyle, these women have requested to be received as postulants to your community: Catherine McAuley, Anna Maria Doyle, and Elizabeth Harley."

Mother Mary Clare responded, "Catherine, Anna Maria, and Elizabeth, during your period of postulancy, you will join us in our daily common life of prayer, work, and fellowship. It is our hope that your experience here will be of help to you as you form the Rule and constitutions of the Sisters of Mercy."

As one, we read from the page, "Like the wise virgins awaiting the Bridegroom, behold, our lamps are lit and we are ready. We knock, we seek, and we ask in the name of Jesus Christ to be admitted into the community of Our Lady of the Presentation, that the way may be opened to us by the Father, all that we seek be found in the Son, and the answers granted to us through the wisdom of the Holy Ghost."

We crossed ourselves in time with our prayer and one of the other nuns sprinkled us with holy water.

"Your pleas have been heard and your wishes granted. Bow your heads and pray for God's blessing as you begin your journey as postulants in our community." She extended her hand over us. "May almighty God bless you in His mercy, and make you always aware of His saving grace."

We responded, "Amen."

After additional prayers and blessings invoking the Holy Trinity and the Blessed Virgin, one of the nuns handed a key to Mother Superior, who used it to unlock the grate. The whole thing swung inward and she flipped a latch on the bottom half of the door, allowing it to open as well.

Standing unimpeded before us, she reached out and I gave her my right hand.

"Catherine, accept this rosary as an outward sign of your postulancy in our community." She wrapped the black beads around both of our hands, binding us. "May it be for you a sign of hope and a source of peace, and may it remind you of the love and forgiveness to be found in the heart of Christ Jesus our Lord."

Without breaking her hold, she pulled me to my feet and through the doorway.

The same words and gestures were repeated for Anna Maria and Elizabeth. Once we were all inside the cloister, Mother Superior turned to the community and said, "Sisters, please welcome Catherine, Anna Maria, and Elizabeth into our midst and help them to embrace our way of life with joy, knowing we live in imitation of our Lord's own mother, offering ourselves and everything we do to God's service."

The Sisters applauded and Mother Superior hugged each one of us.

"Take one final look at the outside world."

We turned and waved farewell to Father Kelly.

"It is no longer your home; you live now in a place that is a kind of heaven on earth. The next time you experience the world, it will be through the eyes of Christ, for you will be united to Him forever and vowed to His service."

The two Sisters who had stood with Mother Superior closed first the door, then the grille, locking them both with one key. They gave the key back to Mother Superior, who placed it somewhere in the folds of her habit near her heart. She held her arms out to us.

"Welcome home, daughters."

*****

Every single day, I was convinced I was going to leave.

I awoke before dawn to the sound the clapper, an annoying wooden instrument meant to rouse us without violating the sanctity of the Grand Silence, a period that began after Compline and lasted until Holy Mass was celebrated at Prime. During those hours, speech was considered a grave sin, as was any unnecessary sound.

I dressed, taking care to whisper the special prayers that went with the donning of each garment. We then hurried to the chapel for the recitation of Lauds followed by a period of silent prayer before Mass. We broke our fast and worked until Terce. After those prayers, while the other Sisters worked, we postulants studied. Then came the midday meal and Sext. Another period of work and study followed, broken only by a remembrance of Jesus' passion and death at None, and continuing until Vespers. After our Vespers prayer, we took our final meal of the day and prepared for Compline, the final prayers of the day, after which we would retire for the night.

Most days, it was rising at two o'clock in the morning for Matins that set me on edge, though I had an advantage over most postulants in that I was used to rising from sleep at all hours to help those in need. Some days, it was the clapper itself that made me want to climb the cloister walls; others, it the expectation of complete deference to superiors—which for us was everyone—or blind obedience to every order given to us. Occasionally, it was something as simple as the rancid smell of the fish market on Boot Lane coming in through the windows or the sound of the carts from the nearby market when I was trying to study or pray, or something one of the other Sisters said or did.

If nothing else had bothered me that day, the evening chapter meeting usually did. I absolutely hated being required to record my sins in a notebook and then confess them publicly before the entire congregation. This practice was supposed to teach us humility and give us an opportunity to both seek forgiveness and practice it toward others. But all it really did was shame us for our weakness and lead to unnecessary and often harsh punishments. I vowed after my first chapter meeting to never allow such a thing to take place within the House of Mercy, much less be required by the Sisters of Mercy. One's sins were between a person and God; they were no one else's business.

This is why, by nightfall, I was usually seriously considering sending for a coach to take me back to the House of Mercy. But each night I overcame that temptation by reminding myself of why I was here: to learn what was needed to establish the Sisters of Mercy. This is what God was calling me to, or at least I hoped so. Mother Superior reassured me God was using the travails of everyday life to polish my rough edges.

Because we were starting a new religious order, our postulancy had been shortened from the usual six months to three, and our novitiate from two years to one. All I was being asked to do was to behave and study my faith for the next year. I could do that without being asked to leave, couldn't I?

Chapter 32

ANNA MARIA

December 9, 1830–December 12, 1831
St. George's Hill
Dublin, Ireland

The sky was just beginning to blush pink on the horizon when we processed into the chapel for Lauds. Catherine, Elizabeth, and I stayed behind in the foyer, for this wasn't just any recitation of the Divine Office—it was the day we would become novices.

"Can you believe it is already here?" Elizabeth asked, brimming with excitement.

"I'm excited to begin our intense study," Catherine put in. "This is what will really help form our new order."

I had the impression that if given her way, she would have begun our training here. But to me, that was learning the quadrille when you couldn't yet master the waltz. Catherine was a woman of action, not contemplation, a Martha rather than a Mary, and even when she tried to hide it, it showed through. That was why only a handful of the nuns understood her and even fewer liked her; her mind worked differently, and in a convent, anything different was considered dangerous.

Yet while we were here, we were invited to sit at the feet of the Master and learn from his teachings. The last three months had served to confirm my vocation and show me the faults I needed to eradicate in order to be a good nun. Today was the culmination of a long-awaited dream. I would finally receive my name in religion and wear the white veil of a novice.

Lauds began with the usual prayers. After the scripture reading, we were led forward to kneel before Mother Mary Clare's chair of office. The nun who had been our director for the last three months said to her, "Mother Superior, after three months of scrutiny, these women—Catherine, Anna Maria, and Elizabeth—seek admission to our order as novices in our way of life."

Mother Superior leaned forward in her chair and asked, "What is it that you seek?"

I couldn't help but imagine it was Christ asking me that question.

"The mercy of God and admission to the novitiate as brides of Christ," we answered.

Mother Superior responded, "Dear sisters, we understand your desire to seek greater admittance to our way of life, but we also know that devils can appear as angels of light. Therefore, we must do as the Apostle says: 'Test the spirits to see whether they are from God.' We must first determine whether you truly seek God, are zealous for the work and Word of the Lord, and are willing to seek it out through obedience and humble service. In fairness to you, we must also warn you of the trials and hardships through which we make our journey to God. Knowing this, I ask you again, are you willing to live in our community and begin the sincere work of seeking God as a novice in our way of life?"

Each of us answered, "I am."

She turned to rest of the community, "Dear Sisters of the Presentation of Our Lady, are you willing to accept these women into our community?"

"We are."

I couldn't help but notice that a few Sisters abstained from answering.

"Hearing both your consent and that of your Sisters, I hereby accept you as novices in our community." She extended her arms over us. "Oh God, it is your voice we hear in our vocation. Hear our prayers and bless these women who wish to undertake deeper service and study of our way of life. Help them to know your holy will, and strengthen them in your service. We ask this through Christ our Lord."

"Amen," the congregation responded.

One of the Sisters came forward and offered a silver pair of scissors to Mother Superior.

"It is said that a woman's hair is her crowning glory. In our way of life, we offer all to God, including our most treasured assets. Are you willing to give up your beauty, your life, and your very identity to follow Christ?"

"I am." My whole heart and soul were in those two words.

Mother Superior snipped one lock of Catherine's hair and held it up for all to see. Two other nuns came forward and did the same to my hair and that of Elizabeth. All three of us bowed our heads in submission. For a few moments, the snick of the blades and the crunch of our hair as it was severed was all I heard. Then the Sisters began singing in Latin a song about giving all to Christ.

After our hair was shorn, Mother Superior presented us with the habit and the same Sisters who had cut our hair helped us to change into it while preserving our modesty. When we were finished, we knelt before Mother Superior, who held a white veil in her hands. "So that you may forever be reminded that your old life is dead, and that you live on only in Christ, today I call you by a new name, pronounced by the mouth of the Lord. May the saints for whom you are now named lead you to the day of your profession and, at the end of your life, lead you to your heavenly reward."

She stood in front of Catherine, holding the white veil of a novice over her head. "Catherine McAuley, may you be known from this day forth as Sister Teresa, after the holy foundress of the Discalced Carmelites." She placed the white veil on Catherine's head and pinned it in place.

Leaning down, she said to Catherine, "May the Lord strengthen you in your resolution." She kissed Catherine on the cheek.

"Pray for me, Mother," she responded, kissing Mother Superior's hand.

Coming to me next, she did the same, saying, "Anna Maria Doyle, may you be known from this day forth as Sister Claire, after the holy foundress of the Franciscan Sisters."

Tears of joy welled in my eyes as the white veil was secured on my head. This was it. Despite the winding road of my vocation, I had done it. I was a nun. I was so caught up in joy that I hardly registered the kiss of peace or Mother Superior calling Elizabeth Sister Angela, after Angela Merci, foundress of the Ursuline order.

We had made it through our postulancy; now the true work would begin.

*****

The greatest joy of the first half of my novitiate was learning about the vows of poverty, chastity, and obedience we would take upon our final profession. More than simply a promise to hold no worldly goods of our own, forgo the pleasures of the flesh, and do what is requested of us by our superiors, these vows had a rich tradition rooted in the Bible and Church teaching.

When I wasn't learning, I worked in the sacristy, a job I considered a great honor. It was my responsibility to ensure the chapel and choir remained clean, to prepare the holy vessels before Mass and clean and purify them after, and to see that the altar cloths, vestments, and other materials were changed out as required by the intricate calendar of feasts held by the Church. I was also charged with the mending of these items as well the sewing and creating of any new ones.

Had things stayed on this course, my novitiate would have been a paradise. However, on May 19, Mother Mary Clare's term as superior ended and Mother Mary Francis de Sales was elected the new superior. Unlike Mother Mary Clare—who treated us with kindness, respect, and if I was honest, a little indulgence—Mother Mary Francis established herself immediately as a rigid disciplinarian who expected absolute adherence to the rules.

She watched our every move and noted our every mistake, issuing punishment in equal measure, at least in her mind, to the severity of the transgression. Flubbing a word during the Divine Office would get one ten Hail Marys while kneeling on a dried bean before the entire congregation at mealtime for every word missed. Failing to clean any part of the chapel or choir to her satisfaction meant doing it again and again until it met with her approval. But the worst punishments were reserved for chapter meetings. If Mother Superior believed a nun didn't confess enough sins or show adequate remorse, she would put her on a food ration or order her to skip meals entirely, usually along with some sort of mortification, like having each of the Sisters slap you or step on you as they entered the refectory. And if someone else accused a nun of a sin before she accused herself, the guilty nun would be forced to stay up all night copying out passages from the Bible.

As a result, I was always on edge, often sleep deprived, and rarely at peace. One day in August, we were studying the vow of obedience with the Novice Mistress when I noticed a tickle in my throat. I coughed, but that wasn't enough to relieve it. I coughed again and then found I couldn't stop. Soon I was coughing up massive amounts of blood. The Novice Mistress carried me to the infirmary and a doctor was called for. By the time I stopped coughing, my lungs burned and felt as though they were going to explode, and my fingers and toes had turned purple, while the rest of my skin was as white as milk.

Convinced I was dying, the Novice Mistress called in Mother Superior and asked her to permit the priest to administer extreme unction and perhaps even allow me to take my vows *in facie mortis*. Mother Superior didn't even bother to fully come into the room, much less examine me, before denying both requests. "She will be fine," she pronounced before turning on her heel and leaving.

The doctor did not have such a blasé attitude. His diagnosis was that I had suffered a severe hemorrhage of the lungs and it was by the grace of God alone I was alive. He ordered me to remain on strict bedrest for the remainder of my novitiate and to avoid all forms of exertion and anything that might upset me.

I thanked God for my safe deliverance through this trial. Even Mother Superior could not contradict the doctor's advice if she wanted to remain in office.

Chapter 33

GRACE

December 1830- June 1831
House of Mercy
Dublin, Ireland

The House of Mercy wasn't the same without Catherine and Anna Maria around to lead it. We did what we could, but so much happened, things quickly spun out of control. Father Redmond O'Hanlon and Father Daniel Burke had promised Catherine they would watch over us while she was gone, but so far they had not made an appearance or answered a single letter we sent asking for help.

The trouble began when we received an influx of new volunteers, all drawn by the fact that we were soon to become a religious order. At first, they entered one or two at a time, but ten women had joined us last month and our dorms were nearing capacity. Each of them needed food and training and jobs, all of which took other women away from their work. The first women Frances recalled from their duties were those who ministered in the streets and at the hospitals. We both felt we had to preserve the House at all costs. It wasn't that the poor were not important to us; far from it. But if we didn't have a stable place to base our work, they would lose us anyway.

On top of that, many of our women took advantage of Catherine being away to change their lifestyle to fit what they thought religious life should be. They tried to be covert, but it wasn't long before we began to notice small changes. A few women regularly fell asleep during prayer, even in the middle of the day. When questioned, they admitted to praying late into the night when they should have been sleeping. As a result, Frances instituted nightly rounds in which the woman on duty would walk the halls from the end of Compline until Matins checking on the women to ensure they were asleep, and another would relieve her and do the same from Matins until Lauds.

A few weeks later, a group of students came to me complaining that their teachers were irritable and yelled at them, something they were forbidden to do. Right around the same time, Frances reported that we had a surplus of food at the end of each meal, which they were giving to the poor to avoid waste. It was quickly becoming a problem and had to be stopped.

Once we confirmed there was nothing wrong with the food, our working theory became that some of the women were starving themselves as a form of mortification. When a monitor fainted in class, I confronted her. She admitted to trying to imitate St. Catherine of Sienna by refusing to eat, in the hopes she could one day subsist on the Holy Eucharist alone. To avoid such behavior, we assigned women to walk around during mealtimes, making sure everyone ate and no one tried to hide her food. At the end of each meal, every woman had to personally present her plate to Frances, and before anyone could leave the refectory, the servants checked for hidden food.

By the time Catherine was allowed to write us at the end of her postulancy, I was wondering whether we were running a nursery school or an asylum for the insane. I told her of everything that was going on and of the deaths that resulted from the austerities these women were inflicting upon themselves. The most tragic was young Cailin Murphy, who joined us last June and had just recently died from her insistence on doing the worst of the work—scrubbing the floors and cleaning the water closets. We had tried to reassign her to other tasks, but found her doing those in addition to the ones we were trying to stop. By the time we were ready to dismiss her, she had started showing signs of consumption, and we were not about to turn a dying woman out onto the streets.

Sadly, it wasn't just the new members who succumbed to religious fervor in Catherine's absence. Ann O'Malley, who had been here long enough to know better, had taken to begging in the streets for blankets, clothing, and money to help those who stayed with us and to whom we ministered in the streets. Her great efforts yielded minimal results and left her exhausted and sunburned by the end of the day. But she kept at it, until one day her body was delivered to us by the same constable who had aided us with Bess. Ann had died from sun fever on a street corner not far away.

Catherine wrote back expressing her concern about these events, but there was little she could do from St. George's. She suggested counseling each woman who showed signs of extremism and reminded Frances and I that we had the authority to remove any woman who showed signs of harming herself or others. Mother Mary Clare of Presentation order, who clearly read each of my letters to Catherine before they were delivered, wrote back with her own advice, most of which was about three hundred years out of date— strange suggestions like changing out the materials our beds were made of, which we couldn't afford, even if we wanted to. We did take her advice on serving beer at dinner rather than water, which helped those who had been fasting to regain weight.

And then there was Hannah Fulham. She appeared on our doorstep as the perfect example of a young woman with a vocation. Blonde-haired with bright blue eyes, she could have passed for an angel. She was demure and polite, yet possessed a sharp mind and keen interest in our work. There was something too perfect about her, in my mind. I expressed my doubts, but Frances had immediately taken a liking to her, so we agreed to admit her for a six-week trial.

About a week into her stay, I was working in the office off the kitchen late one night, preparing for the upcoming feast of Our Lady of Mercy, which was also the fifth anniversary of our ministry. We were trying to plan a large party without spending too much money. I was adding up prices when a rattling caught my attention. It was coming from the scullery. It was well past midnight, so no one should be about and even Dublin's biggest rats didn't make that much racket. When it was followed by the clatter of metal on stone and then a muffled curse, my suspicions were confirmed. Someone was up to no good.

Rather than confront her directly, I quietly padded to the top of the stairs, which were the only exit from the underground level. A few minutes later, Hannah came around the bend in the stairs and smacked right into me. The bundle she had been holding fell to ground, revealing several pieces from a silver utensil set.

"Can you explain this?" I asked, knowing full well she could not.

"Aren't you breaking the Grand Silence by speaking to me?" she challenged.

I gave her my mother's best "don't press me" look.

"I was going to sell it to help the poor," she lied.

"Oh well, then, you may go," I said, sarcasm lacing my voice.

We faced one another silently, me blocking the exit and she trying to stare me down. I could see her calculating the likelihood of getting past me. Sure enough, a few second later she attempted to bound past me, but I grabbed her arm and pulled her back to me.

"We do not tolerate thieves here. I will not force you to leave in the middle of the night, but you should be prepared to go at first light. You will spend the rest of the night in the chapel, where I can keep an eye on you, praying and, I hope, repenting of your sins."

I stood guard at the chapel door. At daybreak, I opened the doors. Hannah was kneeling before the Blessed Sacrament, seemingly deep in prayer. I called her name and she turned. Most of her beautiful golden hair was gone, shorn nearly to her scalp. I looked around for a knife or a pair of scissors, but saw nothing. Also missing was any evidence of the hair she had to have cut off.

"Hannah, what has happened to you?"

Her eyes were suffused with holy light, as though she were gazing into Heaven itself. "Last night when I was praying, St. Clare appeared to me and said I should follow her example in becoming a nun. As a sign to all of you that what I say is true, she cut off all my hair and offered it to Jesus."

"What is going on here?" Frances called when she found us there. Neither of us answered.

Frances's steps slowed as she approached, her posture suddenly wary. "Hannah, where is your hair?"

"St. Clare took it," she replied. "She gave it to Jesus as a sign of my intent to become a nun."

I glanced at Frances, who returned my worried look. The poor girl was either trying to avoid being dismissed or truly believed she had a religious experience and was in need of help.

"This is ridiculous," Frances declared. "Her hair must be here somewhere."

By now, the entire congregation had joined us in the chapel. I explained what was happening and ordered everyone to look for any evidence of what had really taken place. We searched everywhere it might have been possible for Hannah to reach—in the choir stalls, the altar, the tabernacle, inside song books, behind the organ—but came up empty.

It wasn't until Cressida climbed the stairs to the choir loft to begin the service that Hannah finally tore her eyes away from the cross and showed any emotion beyond divine ecstasy. She caught herself and resumed a placid expression, but it was too late; she had betrayed herself. I narrowed my eyes at Hannah while calling to Cressida, "Search very carefully while you are up there. I believe we may have overlooked something."

A few moments passed before Cressida yelled back. "I found something!"

Frances and I raced up the stairs, dragging an increasingly reluctant Hannah behind us.

Cressida was standing in front of the organ, holding a pair of scissors in her hand. "These were in the drawer where I keep my sheet music," she explained.

I took the scissors from her and, sure enough, a few strands of blonde hair were caught in the mechanism that allowed the blades to open and close.

I held them up for Hannah to see. "What do you have to say for yourself?"

"Nothing. That hair isn't mine." Her voice had taken on the sing-song quality it had had earlier when she told us about her experience. "I am not the only resident with blonde hair."

Frances massaged her temple. "This is getting us nowhere and we are already late to begin our prayers. Let's pray the offices of Lauds and Prime, attend Holy Mass, and then we can sort this all out."

Cressida took her place behind the organ.

"Stop!" Hannah commanded. "What are you doing?"

Cressida looked at Hannah as if she was mad. "Playing music. What else does one do with an organ?"

"But you always use the smaller one downstairs."

"Usually, yes, but today is a solemn feast day, so I am using this one." Cressida sounded like it was taking all of her patience even to speak to Hannah. She turned back around and placed her feet on the pedals and her fingers on the keys.

"No!" Hannah yelled at the same time Cressida pressed the keys.

A puff of gold rose from the pipes and thousands of strands of hair rained down on the women below.

*****

Frances arranged for Hannah to be picked up by family living in Black Rock. I watched the carriage carry her away until it was out of sight.

That morning we stopped accepting new volunteers and told those interested to return early the following year, when Catherine and her companions would once again be in residence. It was all we could do to save our ministry and our sanity.

The one bright spot was that Lord Montague had finally been arrested and charged with Bess's murder. According to the Constable, Lord Montague had tried every legal maneuver, lie, and stalling tactic ever recorded, including bribery, to stay out of the gaol. The Constable also warned us that Lord Montague would likely do the same to fight the charges and avoid the public spectacle of a trial, so it may be some time before anything occurred. But I didn't care. That monster was locked up and unable to hurt another woman as he had done with Margaret and me. The rest could come in God's time.

Chapter 34

CATHERINE

August – December 1831
St. George's Hill
Dublin, Ireland

Between the madness at the House of Mercy, Anna Maria's brush with death, and now Elizabeth's worrisome cough, I wasn't sure who to be most concerned about. What I did know what that this new Mother Superior might honestly be the death of all three of us. She forced Elizabeth to work in a cold, damp underground kitchen without any heat, cleaning shoes and cooking utensils. I tried several times to explain to her why this was detrimental to Elizabeth's health, but all I received for my troubles was a swift smack across the face and a week of eating only from others' leftovers. Mother Superior's only response was that if Elizabeth couldn't handle the conditions, she wasn't fit to be a nun.

When Anna Maria was sent to the infirmary, Mother Superior took her anger out on me by assigning me her work in the sacristy on top of my own sweeping floors and serving in the refectory. She took great joy in telling me that Anna Maria and Elizabeth would certainly be received for profession, but that she would see to it I was not.

Finally, the fateful day came when the Sisters voted on whether to allow us to make our final vows. We gathered in the chapter room as usual. Three clear glass jars were set on a table at the front of the room, each with a placard bearing one of our names. We were asked to sit behind the jar with our name on it.

Mother Superior called the meeting to order. "Tonight, we will decide whether our novices are ready to be received for profession, to take their final vows as Sisters of Mercy. I ask you to think long and hard about what you know and have observed about each of these women over the last year. Consider their faults and their strengths, and weigh them against the challenges you know to be part of religious life. Evaluate them individually, not as a group, and don't be afraid to vote differently from one another. When you are ready, come forward and place a white bean in a woman's jar if you believe she is ready for final vows or a black bean if not. I will go first."

I nearly snorted at how backward this woman's attitude toward everything was. A good superior would have cast her vote last so as not to influence the group. But that was exactly what this woman wanted to do. She likely would have said I should have kept my eyes down in deference and prayer for the will of God to be done, but I looked her—and every Sister after her—straight in the eye, so that they would know exactly whom they were allowing or condemning. To the surprise of no one, Mother Superior dropped a white bean in Anna Maria and Elizabeth's jars and a black one in mine.

As the number of black beans in my jar mounted, I consoled myself that Archbishop Murray had promised me after I gave him a lengthy description of what life here was like, that he would receive me into religious life himself if the nuns wouldn't admit me.

Finally, each woman had cast her vote. The jars were overturned so that no beans could fall to the floor or otherwise escape. Mother Superior came forward and counted each woman's beans out loud so there could be no question as to the outcome. It was the work of seconds to see that Anna Maria and Elizabeth would be making their profession. My pile required much more sorting. In the end, my tally was tied and my fate came down to a single bean. Mother Superior and I looked down at the same time. It was white.

A huge grin spread across my face and I looked out into the faces of my fellow nuns who were cheering that they would soon have three new professed nuns in their ranks. I caught the eye of Sister Mary Clare, our first Mother Superior, who had been so kind to me, and she winked.

*****

On December 12, 1831, the chapel at St. George's was decorated in white as though for a wedding. A pure white runner ran down the center aisle, and boughs of holly and ivy decorated each pew. The advent wreath was lit for the third Sunday, two purple candles and one pink glowing brightly.

We stood at the back of the chapel waiting for the appointed moment. Anna Maria, now much recovered, and Elizabeth, still nursing a cough, looked like brides in their white dresses, white veils, and crown of orange blossoms. Out of respect for my age—I was now fifty-three and would look quite silly dressed in white like a young bride—Archbishop Murray allowed me to wear a more matronly gown of a rich lavender brocade, though he insisted I wear a crown of hothouse roses over my white veil.

When the music began, we processed up the aisle, each with one of our teachers at our side. God must have a sense of humor, because it was Mother Superior who gave me into the arms of Mother Church, disgust and displeasure writ large all over her face. Anna Maria was given away by our Novice Mistress and Elizabeth by our Director of Postulants.

After the opening prayers of the Mass, we three prostrated ourselves on the ground in front of the altar on a special mat covered in rose petals, faces to the ground, arms outstretched in the shape of a cross to symbolize our total submission to God. We remained in this state until the nuns finished singing the Litany of the Saints.

The readings and the Gospel were then proclaimed, but instead of a homily, the faithful were asked to be seated while we remained standing. We declared our desire to serve Him faithfully as His brides and Sisters of Mercy and were accepted into the community.

Archbishop Murray then preached his homily. The ending was particularly poignant. "You who are present here today are witnesses to something momentous—the enrichment of Holy Mother Church by the creation of a new religious order. These three women are to henceforth be known as the foundresses of the Sisters of Mercy."

Then the moment came for us to individually profess our vows. With Mother Superior holding out the formula of profession and my hand touching the bottom, I proclaimed:

"In the name of Our Lord and Savior Jesus Christ and under the protection of his Immaculate Mother, Mary ever virgin, I, Sister Catherine McAuley, called in religion Mary Catherine, do vow and promise to God perpetual poverty, chastity, and obedience, and to persevere until the end of my life in the Congregation called the Sisters of Mercy, established for the Visitation of the sick, poor, and charitable instruction of poor females, according to the rules and constitutions of the Presentation Order. On this twelfth day of December in the year of Our Lord one thousand eight hundred and thirty-one."

I signed my name and placed my profession on the altar.

After the others made their vows, our new black habits were blessed and, in the privacy of the cloister, we changed out of our wedding garments and into the habits of the Sisters of Mercy. When we once again knelt before the altar, the archbishop replaced the white veil we had worn for the last year with the black veil of profession. Then he held out a simple silver band engraved on the outside with the words *Ad Majorium Dei Glorium*, "to the greater glory of God," and on the inside *Fiat Volantis*, "May Your will be done."

"Receive this ring, for you are betrothed to the eternal King; be steadfast in faith with your Bridegroom so that you may come to the wedding feast of eternal joy."

He slipped the band onto the ring finger of my left hand. With one final "amen" it was done.

I was a Sister of Mercy.

Chapter 35

ANNA MARIA

December 12, 1831
House of Mercy
Dublin, Ireland

We were so anxious to leave St. George's Hill, we didn't even stay for the celebratory breakfast. The Archbishop loaded the three of us into his carriage and whisked us back to Baggot Street through a lightly falling snow.

The red door burst open before the carriage even stopped, and we were quickly enveloped by hugs and kisses from our volunteers and Catherine's adopted children. When we passed through the entrance, we found women of the house had gathered to welcome us home. Those studying to become domestics had cooked and set a formal breakfast to reward us for the privations of the last year. Tea was in abundance, as were rashers, sausages, eggs, white pudding, soda bread, and potato pancakes.

We dug in with gusto, complimenting the women's skills and answering as many questions as possible. After the most obvious questions about what we ate, what our days were like, and how we stayed awake the middle of the night, the women began to pester Catherine about when she would start her own novitiate for those who wished to imitate her in becoming Sisters of Mercy.

She laughed good naturedly. "I haven't even been home three hours. Give a woman some time to think, will you?"

Once the food was gone—there was plenty for all the women and children to partake of, as well—Archbishop Murray asked the volunteers to meet in the chapel. "There is one more thing we must do to make your new order official."

After we had taken our usual seats in the choir stalls, the Archbishop called Catherine to him. Together they stood in front of the altar. "This more of a formality than anything, but ..." He placed his right hand on her left shoulder. "I hereby appoint you, Sister

Catherine McAuley, as Superior and Mother of the new congregation of the Sisters of Mercy."

The women gathered in the chapel applauded and cheered.

"I do hate the term 'Mother,'" she said, "I may have started this whole mess, but I certainly haven't given birth to any of you."

A giggle rippled about the room. "I am still the same Catherine who left here thirteen months ago, and that is how I wish to be addressed. If you must call me something formal, let it be 'Sister Superior,' or better yet, simply 'Sister.' I'm no better than the rest of you lot."

That may be true, but I suspected the title "Mother Superior" reminded her too much of Mother Mary Francis de Sales for her to ever be comfortable using it.

"My first order as your Superior is to ask the Archbishop to install Sister Anna Maria as Mother Assistant. She has always been my helper and will remain so, come what may."

"A fine idea," the Archbishop said.

I stood and walked over to them. As he had done with Catherine, he placed his hand on my shoulder. "I hereby name you Mother Assistant to Mother Catherine McAuley."

He wrote something down and then handed the booklet to Catherine. "These are the first Rules of the Sisters of Mercy—at the moment it is only a list of things you've told me you do and do not wish to be included in your way of life. Keep it safe and add to it. This is your religious order, the three of you. Shape it as you like. I'll be here to advise you on how to keep within Church law, but let God speak through you."

"Thank you, Your Excellency."

Catherine turned to address the community. "Since we are together, I would like to begin by addressing a few situations that arisen over the last year."

Chapter 36

GRACE

The following day, I tapped lightly on Catherine's office door.

"Come in," she called.

"Do you have time to talk?"

"Always." She set down her pen. "Tell me, how are you? I know you had a time of it while we were away."

"We did. I'm so glad you are back. Thank you for putting some rules in place this morning so we don't have the same situation arise again. I am not meant to lead—I have learned that much."

Catherine frowned. "Don't be so hard on yourself. It isn't easy for me, either. I wonder every single day when one of you will figure out I have no idea what I am doing." She gave a little laugh. "What can I do for you?"

"I ... I don't even know where to start," I stammered.

"You aren't thinking of leaving, are you?"

"Oh no, not at all! Quite the opposite, in fact."

"Oh?"

"I'm not sure I can explain it, but I'll try. I have had a lot of time to think and pray over the last year, and I feel like my relationship with God is so much more personal now. I understand why people devote their lives to Him. I am happier here than I have ever been in my life, but I want more. I feel this longing I can't explain."

Catherine's brow furrowed. "Can you try to describe it?"

I swallowed hard. "I know you have always been close to Jesus. I haven't had that experience. For most of my life I barely gave God a passing thought. I was too busy trying to survive to think of anything greater than myself. But since I've come here and I feel safe for the first time in my life, something else is happening. It's like there is a small voice somewhere deep down that is urging me to do more, be more."

"Do you think God might be talking to you?"

I nodded shyly. "Can that happen? I don't see visions or talk to angels or burning bushes or anything like that."

Catherine laughed. "Neither do I, but I know in my heart that God guides me. That is how I knew to build this place." She gestured to the building around us. "I think God might be calling you to your life's purpose."

"Really? All of my life, I've been someone's servant. That is all I know. I don't know if I can do anything else."

"Who says there has to be anything else? God calls each of us to serve Him in different ways. You said you are happy here, and I'm glad to hear that. Perhaps you are meant to continue on as a servant here. But allow me to pose one question for you to think about: If you could do anything you want without any limitations, what would it be?"

I bit my lip. I had considered this very thing many times. Could I really tell her? Could I really say the words? I wanted to, but what if she laughed at me? I looked back at Catherine, seeing nothing but compassion in her eyes. I swallowed twice, willing myself to speak. "I want ... I want ..." I took a deep breath, squeezed my eyes shut, and forced the words through my lips. "I think I want to become a Sister of Mercy."

Now that the words were out, I was mortified. What if I had just ruined everything? What if she scoffed at the stupid servant girl and asked me to leave?

But Catherine did none of those things. Instead, a wide grin spread across her face. "Grace! That is wonderful!"

"Is ... is there a place for me? In the order?"

"If you want there to be, there is."

"I wasn't sure, because I don't have the education or refinement you and most of the other women here do. And then there is my past ..."

"Grace, do you think Jesus only called the rich and educated? No. He avoided them and purposefully went where he knew the ordinary people were. He called those whom the rich despised—the tax collectors, the humble fisherman, even a thief. Remember, Judas wasn't always bad. Jesus saw potential in him and he sees it in you, too. He wants everyone to take up their cross and follow him, no matter what they may have done."

I nodded. She was making so much sense. I wanted to be wise like her.

"I want to go back to something you said a few minutes ago. You said you've always been a servant. Being a Sister is the ultimate example of servitude. You vow your life to God and go where He leads. He becomes your master in all things. Only He won't hurt you or betray you like the masters you've known." She thought for a moment. "In many ways, you are better prepared for this life than I was."

I couldn't believe what I was hearing. "What does all of this mean? What do I do now?"

Catherine removed the sheaf of papers the Archbishop had given her from a drawer in her desk. "We'll figure it out together. Have you ever heard of a Lay Sister?"

"No, what is that?"

"It's a type of Sister who participates in the order on more of a basic level. Lay Sisters cook and clean and manage convent affairs so that the other Sisters are free to tend to their duties. For us that would mean teaching, nursing, things like that. Your current role isn't much different."

"Would I be able to continue training the domestics and visiting the poor?"

"Yes, of course. That is the beauty of starting something new. We can define your role however you would like. Your life here should bring you joy."

She handed me a pen and placed the paper between us. "Why don't you help me envision what a Lay Sister of Mercy could look like? I don't want you to feel inferior to the rest of us; that happens in some orders, and I refuse to let it take place here."

Chapter 37

CATHERINE

April 13, 1832
House of Mercy
Dublin, Ireland

It took three months of hard work, but by early spring, the House of Mercy was getting back to normal. The volunteers had grown used to having women in black habits around, and I daresay we three warmed to our roles.

But Elizabeth's was short-lived. She had started showing signs of consumption at St. George's, which we all hoped it was just an ague that would pass. But it was not. Her coughing continued, and at the start of Lent, she began coughing up blood. By mid-month she was in the infirmary and all signs pointed to our little saint meeting her Bridegroom at far too young an age.

Because of this, the mood of House was somber as Easter approached. Then the newspapers began reporting on a particularly contagious form of cholera that had made its way to England and would soon reach our shores, if it hadn't already. Cholera was not an uncommon disease; outbreaks occurred every few years, but they rarely made headlines at all, much less on a national scale like this. Dr. Frances Barker, secretary of the Central Board of Health for Ireland, warned the public to seek immediate medical treatment if they experienced any symptoms. It was critical, he said, that patients seek treatment in the first six hours, because beyond that, there was little hope of survival.

We understood what this meant, even if ordinary people had not yet grasped the seriousness of the situation. The government was preparing for an epidemic and, therefore, so were we. Just as we tried to ease their burden in ordinary times, if the people of Dublin were in danger, it was our duty to help them as we could.

Wishing to remain at Elizabeth's side, I organized our relief response through Sister Anna Maria, and put Grace and Frances in charge of devising a plan to keep the schools running, see to the women and children in the shelter, and protect everyone who lived under this roof. Our health and safety had to come first, or we would have nothing to give to others.

Sister Anna Maria stockpiled all the supplies she could find to treat cholera victims in case the House was requisitioned into a hospital or our Sisters had to minister to people in their homes. Our cellar, usually brimming with canned vegetables and meat, root vegetables and smoked fish, was now home to dozens of bottles of laudanum for pain, castor oil, and calomel to help empty the bowels. Not to mention the gin, brandy, cinnamon, and peppermint that was mixed with water for treatment.

On Easter Sunday, I was dozing in Elizabeth's room when she opened her eyes, coughed, wished me a Blessed Easter, and asked for a priest. Archbishop Murray was already at the House to celebrate Mass, so gave her last rites. Through wheezing breaths and one long coughing fit, she gave her final confession and accepted the holy anointing.

While she was making peace with her God, I was praying for a miracle. We couldn't lose her, not yet, not so young. She was the future of our order and had so much left to give. Why would God allow her to become a Sister of Mercy if he wasn't going to use her tremendous gifts to help others? It was so wrong, just so wrong. I realized in that moment of blind grief, when I couldn't even trust in God, what Mother Mary must have felt like watching her only son die unfairly on the Cross. I had grown to love Elizabeth like the daughter I had never had, and here I was, just two years later, saying goodbye to her on Easter Sunday.

And it was all that horrible Mother Superior's fault. If she hadn't treated Elizabeth like a slave, working her half to death and making her endure conditions not fit for a dog, the youngest Sister of Mercy would be taking her place in the chapel to celebrate our Lord's resurrection, not preparing to meet Him in Heaven. My training at St. George's said I should pray to the Mother of Sorrows for strength and, like Mary, abandon all to God, trusting in his great love and mercy, but in that moment all I could do was wonder if God really knew what he was doing. How could an all-loving being allow such a horrible person to control the lives of women who were dedicated to him? And why did He have to take one of His best daughters instead of her?

Bitter tears welled up from my broken heart, and I leaned my forehead against Elizabeth's cold arm, begging God to change his mind, to let her live.

When I lifted my head again, Sister Anna Marie had gathered all of the women of the house around Elizabeth's deathbed, though at a slight distance, due to her illness. When Archbishop Murray approached her with Holy Communion, they began chanting the Office for the Dead and Dying.

Elizabeth closed her eyes to pray after receiving the body and blood of Christ, and I feared she would never again open them. A few moments later, her lids fluttered and she whispered in a voice so quiet I could barely hear her though my ear was near her lips, "Thank them for me. Their singing brings me such peace."

Her eyes closed again and a spasm rocked her body, forcing her to sit up as she gasped for air between coughs. When her head touched the pillow, she was gone, a soft smile on her lips, despite the violence of her last moments. Whatever she had seen in death must have been beautiful indeed.

Although I wanted nothing more than to drape myself across her body and weep, to sob ugly tears and scream the unfairness of it all, I swallowed my emotions and wiped the tears from my eyes. Standing for the first time in hours, I swayed a little before regaining my feet. Looking out at the grieving women around me, I tried to offer them what encouragement I could. "Today, Sister Elizabeth is reborn again into Heaven with the resurrected Christ, her spouse. Though we mourn, this is the happiest of days for her, for she is with her God to whom she dedicated her life. Therefore, it is fitting that we pray the Easter psalm: 'This is the day the Lord has made.'"

The Sisters responded, "'Let us rejoice and be glad.'"

*****

The next day, the papers reported not on the tragic death of a young nun but on the thousand people who already had been sickened by cholera and the three hundred who had died. The first temporary cholera hospital was opened at Grangegorman Lane Penitentiary and was to be staffed by the Sisters of Charity.

Of course, Father Kelly would be sure they were the first appointed to help. For a moment, bitterness hardened my heart, but then I was struck with inspiration. If he could lobby for permission for the Sisters of Charity, I could do the same for the women of the House of Mercy. Once again, I sought refuge in my office and began penning a letter to the Archbishop, asking his permission for us to serve the cholera victims however we could. I sent it by messenger to hasten a response.

The Archbishop's reply came during dinner. He informed us that a depot was being set up on Townsend Street where anyone seeking cholera treatment could come. It would be ready in a matter of days and we would be the ones to provide aid. Sounding much like the spiritual father he was to us, he left us with sage advice:

"Until then, my daughters, take care that your bodies remain strong. Avoid all intoxicating liquors, which weaken our resistance to disease, but drink a fortifying port wine with your mutton chops and be sure to get plenty of nourishment and sleep. I understand that you have hearts of service, but you will do the people of Dublin no good if you are too tired to treat them or are felled by the disease yourself. I thank you for your willingness to serve those in need. May God bless you with healing hands and consoling hearts."

Chapter 38

ANNA MARIA

May–July 1832
Townsend Street Cholera Hospital
Dublin, Ireland

Ever since the news broke about the cholera epidemic, the streets had been eerily quiet. All public events, including Lord Montague's trial, were canceled or postponed in order to keep the residents of Dublin safe. Only those who had to be away from their homes ventured out.

Townsend Street held an eerie pall as we approached the cholera clinic where we would minister to the sick and dying. Instead of a constant din of voices, seagull screams dominated the atmosphere and the clop of hooves and rattle of wheels echoed through the alleyways long before the rare carriage came into sight. Not even Catherine, who hated the idea of illness and bodily fluids and was loathe to take on the duties of a nurse, or Frances, who usually had advice or wisdom for any situation, spoke. It was as though the weight of our upcoming duties rendered us all mute.

My ears had adjusted to the lack of sound as walked, so the wall of noise when we opened the hospital doors was an aural assault. Hundreds of people formed a queue reaching from one end of the hall to the other. Their voices were punctuated by hacking coughs and crying babies and children.

"Ah, you are here," an eager young man rushed up to us and introduced himself as Dr. Michael Blake, the attending physician. "Just in time. We are about to admit our first patients."

He led us to a large room with dozens of pallet beds arranged in neat rows on the floor. They were separated by a curtain to give each patient a measure of privacy and formed a kind of "room" within the open space. Each room contained only a lamp, a wash basin, and a pitcher. Anything else we might need, the doctor said, was available in a locked room across the hall to keep desperate patients from getting their hands on items they might steal or use to harm themselves.

"You have agreed to work in three eight-hour shifts, is that correct?" Dr. Blake asked.

"Yes," Catherine answered. "When each is over, a new set of volunteers or Sisters will arrive by carriage and the replace those traveling back to Baggot Street."

The doctor wrote something down in book he carried. "When you end your shift, we ask that you change your habit before you leave so that we may launder the old one. You don't want arrive at the convent covered in unpleasant substances. Also be sure to disinfect any items you use in vinegar, and scrub your hands with it before leaving."

Kate sniffed the air. "What is that smell? It's like woodsmoke but with a sweetness to it."

"We are burning all the patients' clothing when they enter to avoid further contagion. An intake nurse will then give them a plain gown to wear that will make it easier to examine them."

Less than an hour passed before the once pristine room stank of excrement and vomit. The four of us divided up the room into quadrants and each of us cared for a block of patients in various states of illness. We held basins for those in the early stages of the illness, whose bodies were rebelling by purging them of all fluids; massaged the muscles of those suffering cramps; gave laudanum and brandy to those in pain; and prayed for and consoled those who were beyond our ability to heal.

Cholera was not an easy death. In addition to the loss of dignity that came with the early symptoms of the disease, as it progressed, patients eventually became trapped their own bodies, able to see and feel, but do little else as their eyes became sunken, their skin withered, and their tongue dried up, making it nearly impossible to swallow. Those who were lucky lost consciousness toward the end, but some suffered severe shock, in full awareness of their death as it happened.

At the end of every shift, as instructed, we changed our habits, disinfected our hands, and stumbled into the carriage. Oftentimes we slept during the ride home and didn't bother getting undressed before falling into bed. One night, I was so exhausted I didn't make it to my room; I fell asleep standing up on the stairs. Catherine eventually discovered me and helped me to bed, only so that we could rise in a few hours to do it all over again.

*****

By July, our spirits were flagging. The nonstop pace had taken its toll on everyone. More than one woman who was paid to help us had taken to drinking the alcoholic tinctures meant for the patients and were dismissed when they were caught. This left us even more shorthanded just as the number of people we were seeing was on the rise. Yesterday, Dr. Frances Barker, secretary of the Central Board of Health for Ireland, announced that more than five thousand cases had been seen in Dublin, and about six hundred people were dying every day.

On top of that, the cost of clothes for the patients who survived, the burial expenses for those who didn't, and the necessities of bedding, medicine, coal, soap, and candles far outpaced the stipend allotted to us by the government, as businesses found a way to make a profit off of people's pain. These added expenses depleted the Baggot Street coffers at a time when our income was at an all-time low, and volunteers dwindled to a core group who lived at the House of Mercy.

But still we showed up every day, despite those who believed we were doing more harm than good. I wasn't aware of this attitude until one of my patients, who was near to recovery, said to me, "I'm so glad I didn't let those silly rumors keep me from coming here."

"What rumors?"

"Oh, you haven't heard? People are saying the government is having people poisoned and then buried alive in order to stop the spread of the disease." She chewed a bit bread thoughtfully. "It's not true though. There's no poison here and I see how carefully that Catherine examines everybody before declaring them officially dead. She wouldn't miss anyone."

I told her I would be back to check on her in about thirty minutes and crawled over the next bed. I had given up walking from bed to bed weeks ago because my joints ached from the constant up and down as I knelt to tend to my wards. Instead, I shuffled on my knees from one beside to another. Unfortunately, that wasn't much better. My knees swelled to the size of tea saucers and were red and sore to the touch, which meant I could barely walk.

That morning, I had found a piece of paper slipped under my door. It was one of Catherine's silly poems, designed to make me laugh. In it, she named my knees cholera and cholerine and begged me to take some time off.

In November, I took her advice and elected to stay behind at Baggot Street to give my knees a rest and help out there. The number of cases was going down, so I didn't feel guilty. One month later, the secretary of the Central Board of Health for Ireland declared that the epidemic was over and awarded us a medal for having fewer deaths than anywhere else in the country. Catherine immediately placed it on the altar and led us in a prayer of thanksgiving for deliverance from this trial.

Chapter 39

GRACE

December 1832
Streets of Dublin
Dublin, Ireland

Returning to the streets of Dublin after the epidemic was a bittersweet experience. Even though the sky was gray, the wind bitter, and the ground frozen, Catherine and I spent several days traversing the city. She wanted to see for herself how the epidemic had changed the city and its poorest inhabitants. My heart leapt with joy each time I encountered someone I knew who had survived, but it also broke when I found a home empty or a family shattered from the death of one or more members. I was gutted to learn Mrs. MacGregor had been one of the disease's victims. I couldn't imagine never hearing her hearty laugh or deep voice again; ministering in the streets wouldn't be nearly the same without her.

One unexpected and joyful change was that so many of the poor recognized and trusted us now, having been patients in the Townsend Street Hospital themselves or hearing about us from a family member or friend. At least a dozen agreed to return to the House of Mercy with us rather than continue their lives in alleyways and sub-par housing.

The docks were an area normally covered by Frances and Kate, so it was a place I had never visited. The buildings there were mostly wooden, often decaying from the wind and salt from the bay. Women hung out of upper-story windows, calling to men in the streets below, or stood in doorways trying to catch the wandering eyes of passersby, occasionally flashing a breast if they received enough attention. Gangs of children ran wild, kicking balls across the alleys and tormenting shopkeepers simply because they were bored.

Inside one boarding house we found a group of three women all laid low with fever, sleeping on thin straw pallets that stank of decay. Catherine stoked the dying peat fire, trying to bring some light and heat to the dank, cold room. I approached the woman who was laying on her side, facing away from me, and knelt down. Her brow was slick with sweat but she was shivering. I pulled the threadbare blanket at her waist up to her shoulders.

That was enough to rouse her and she struck out, mistaking my gesture for a threat. I had made the exact same instinctual movement dozens of times when I was living in similar conditions.

"I am not here to hurt you," I said in a low, calming tone. "My name is Grace. I'm here to help."

At my name, the woman shifted so that she was laying on her back. She scrutinized my face for a long time before saying my name again, "Grace?"

"Yes."

She struggled to sit up. "I know you."

I gave her my arm and she used it to pull herself into a seated position. It was then I could see her clearly. I could not believe my eyes. It was as though the last six years had never taken place. Yes, she appeared older; her hair had lost its luster, her face and neck were scarred, and she would never again have the girlish innocence I had so admired, but there was no doubt—God had performed a miracle; she was alive after all.

"Margaret?" Her name came out of my mouth with a mix of wonder and disbelief.

"Yes," she nodded enthusiastically, then brought a hand to her head as if she regretted the motion.

I hugged her tightly. "I thought you were dead. Praised be Jesus!"

Catherine turned from the fire, where she was heating broth for the women, and looked at me. "Catherine, this is Margaret! Our Margaret!" I cried.

Her eyes widened and she scurried over to us. Kneeling next to us she looked the woman over and declared. "It is. Blessed Jesus, thank you for this miracle."

Margaret recoiled, clearly not recognizing Catherine in her religious garb. I hugged her tightly to me, as I would a little child. "That is Catherine McAuley, whose house we went to that night. Do you remember her?"

"Surely I must be dead or dreaming—Lord what did I take?" she asked herself. "That woman is a nun."

"She is and I will be soon, too."

Margaret blinked several times in rapid succession. "Now I know I am dead. There is no other way Grace Ryan would ever become a nun." She peered into my face. "Are you sure you are the same Grace?"

I handed her one of the mugs of broth. "A lot has happened."

While Margaret sipped her broth, Catherine and I tended to the two other women, who had been roused by our exuberant reunion. They were suffering from the same fever as Margaret, but also had severe cases of the pox. They agreed to come back to the House with us, but only because Margaret knew and trusted us.

Catherine hired a carriage to take us back; there was no way these women could walk the distance. As we traveled, Catherine and I gave Margaret a summary of everything that had taken place since we last saw her.

Once we were back at the House of Mercy and all three women were safely tucked into beds in the infirmary, Catherine and I sat with Margaret, anxious to hear what had happened to her.

"The last time I saw you, you were safe at Catherine's home," I said. "How did you go from there to prostituting yourself on the docks?

"My story isn't all that different than yours or so many others, I'm afraid. Catherine didn't have room for me in Coolock House, so she took me all over Dublin trying to find a place that could offer me safe harbor, but everyone turned us away. It was getting dark, so Catherine bought me a night an inn and we agreed to meet up the following morning."

"A decision I will forever regret," Catherine said.

"What's done is done," Margaret said. "That night, one of the servants from Lord Montague's estate tracked me down at the inn and told me I needed to return to the estate quickly. He said Grace was bleeding and asking for me."

"I was bleeding, but not in the way he made it sound. Lord Montague laid into me when he figured out I helped you escape."

"Oh Grace, I'm so sorry you were hurt because of me."

I waved her away. "Go on."

"When I got back to the house, Lord Montague was waiting for me in the garden. I don't remember much of what he said, only that he wanted to show me the consequences of trying to run away. He hit me several times and eventually I passed out."

I stilled, a memory surfacing of a loud crack, one I initially mistook for thunder. "Did he hit you with his cane, by chance?"

"Yes, how did you know?"

I thought back. "I'm not sure. The whole night is hazy. I remember Mrs. Donahue trying to convince me I really was attacked by robbers in the market. But I know it was Lord Montague who beat me."

"She was probably saying what he told her to so you wouldn't be suspicious," Margaret said. "Where was I? Oh. The next thing I knew I woke up in a small shanty on the bay. A fisherman found me on Sandymount Strand. He said it looked like I had been in the water for a while before I washed ashore. Called me his own selkie, he did."

"So, Lord Montague left you for dead?"

Margaret shrugged. "Him or one of his men. I lived with the fisherman and his family until I was healed enough to be on my way. He offered to take me back to Howth and I let him. What I had no way of knowing was that while I was working for Lord Montague, my da died and my ma answered an ad promising work in America. No one ever heard from her again.

"So now I was alone, with no prospects and no reference, just like you, Grace. I worked in service in Howth for as long as I could, but people were moving away. Once I had a few characters, I tried to find work at the country manors, but the competition was so strong and no one cared about references from a small town. Three years on and I was back to where I started.

"I hopped a cart into Dublin and spent some time at the workhouse before realizing if I stayed there, I'd be there my whole life. By then I was hearing rumors about Catherine and the house she was building."

"My dear girl, why didn't you come to me? I could have helped you." Catherine's eyes were brimming with tears.

"I know that now, but back then I didn't think you'd want me. You see, my heart had grown bitter toward you. In my way of thinking, if you couldn't spare a spot on the carpet or even on your lawn for one night, why would you take me now?"

Catherine began to sob. "I'm sorry. I'm so, so sorry. I looked for you, searched for months."

Margaret said nothing, seemingly lost in thought. After a moment she shook herself and continued.

"Not knowing what else to do, I went back to the shanty to see if the fisherman was still there and he was, only he was all alone—his eldest had joined the Royal Marines, his middle son was lost to the sea in a boating accident, and his wife and child had died. I offered to cook and clean and keep his home while he was away at sea and he agreed. As these things usually go, we fell in love and were wed. Married to him three years I was before a storm blew up, tossed the waves upon the shore, and flattened our home. My husband was killed and I nearly was."

"I remember that storm, don't you, Grace? So many women lost everything that we had triple capacity for months. It nearly ruined us," Catherine said.

"It did ruin me. For the fourth time in seven years, I was homeless. But this time I was in pain from an injury I received during the storm, and tired—so tired—that I no longer cared what happened to me. I took up with the first man who offered to buy me gin, and then I met Lucy and Faith." She gestured to the two women snoring softly behind us. "They knew men who had or could get any form of vice you desired. Honestly, if you hadn't found me today, I would likely have been dead in a matter of weeks."

I sat back, contemplating how our lives had changed so drastically, yet here we were, back together again.

"God had to have had a reason for bringing us back together," I said, more to myself than to Catherine or Margaret.

"He always does," Catherine answered.

Chapter 40

CATHERINE

January 1833
House of Mercy
Dublin, Ireland

"Have you picked a name yet?" I asked Grace.

"You know I have, but I want it to be a surprise," she teased.

"You know it is not usual to keep your name in religion from your Mother Superior."

"What about the Sisters of Mercy *is* usual? Neither you nor Anna Maria even use your religious names," she teased.

"You have a point," I conceded.

My hands were busy with the buttons on Grace's black dress— there were no funds to procure wedding dresses for the novices—but my mind was an hour ahead, anticipating what was to come and how I could make this inaugural profession at Baggot Street as perfect as possible for my "first-born" daughters.

I wanted this solemn occasion to be private between just the women I had known and loved for so many years, myself, and God. The mounting crowd outside said I was in the minority. Relatives and friends of the eight novices who would become Sisters in just over an hour—among them my dear own Kate, Frances, and Grace—were clamoring to bear witness to the momentous event.

A ruckus of riotous proportions rose outside, with shouts and screams for us to let them in. Casting my eyes heavenward, I left Grace and the nervous postulants who would receive the white veil of novices today to see what could be done to calm the crowd.

"The Archbishop is here," Cressida said. She was serving porter and thus had the best vantage to the chaos outside.

"Let him in, but admit no one else," I said. "Lock the door if you have to."

"Or you could acquiesce and let them in," Anna Maria said.

"And put their health at risk with a woman dying of consumption in the next room?"

She followed me around like a puppy as I darted from one task to another. "You at least owe them an explanation." She stopped and waited until I nearly ran into her. "Go upstairs, open your office window and address them. It will do wonders, you'll see."

I glanced around, searching for a clock. "But is there time?"

Anna Maria placed her hands on my shoulders. "You are the Mother Superior. They will not start without you."

Upstairs, I did as Anna Maria suggested. As soon as I pulled back the lace curtains and opened the window, the crowd went wild, yelling and in any other way possible making noise. I feared sticking my head out, lest they throw a cabbage or eggs at me, but there was nothing for it.

"Everyone please," I shouted. "Please calm down." This did nothing to lessen the volume.

A shrill whistle sounded from behind me, startling me so badly my heart nearly stopped. I whipped around to see Grace grinning at me. "That's how we do it in the ancient parts of city," she said.

Feeling slightly more confident that no one was going to throw anything at me this time, I tried again. "Family, friends, and well-wishers, I understand why you wish you join us today."

"Then open the doors and let us in," a male voice yelled.

"I wish I could, but one of our women is very near to dying of consumption, and I do not wish to endanger her health or yours."

Grumbling rose up from the street below.

"I'm sorry," I repeated. "Truly I am. All ceremonies after today will be held in public."

I closed the window before anyone else could object, but that didn't stop one mother from yelling, "I will not allow my daughter to remain a postulant in a convent with such low-born manners that they won't even admit her own mother!"

Still cringing from the mother's rebuke, I rejoined the others in chapel. Once the organ music started either the crowd outside quieted or they were drowned out by the heavenly sound. Seated in a special chair in front of the altar, I watched the very same ceremony I had taken part in only two years before with new eyes. This time I was the one welcoming the future of the order; I was the one whose hands they held as they pronounced their vows, who clothed them in black or white, and who placed the silver ring on their fingers.

No matter how many times I repeated this ritual in the future, nothing would ever measure up to seeing my dear friends take their vows. And the sweetest of all was Grace, who took the name Sister Mary Magdalene as a nod to her past.

*****

I feared the negative public sentiment surrounding our first profession could deter women from entering the Sisters of Mercy, but if anything, it made us more attractive. Other than the particularly loud mother who made good on her threat to remove her daughter, no else had left and we had been interviewing a steady influx of candidates ever since.

By the time summer's heat set in, the House of Mercy held nineteen women in various stages of religious profession and four additional volunteers, including Cressida and Margaret. That was in addition to the fifty female students who lived with us full time and the hundreds of students who ate at least one meal a day while being educated. Every time we admitted a new postulant, Anna Maria asked me where she would sleep and I would quip, "in my lap."

It was such a joy to behold my little community flourishing that I scarcely gave a thought to the costs associated with it, until we ran out of utensils and our meals declined in quality. Grace told me our breakfasts of thin bread with the lightest scaping of butter and dark sugar and a thimble full of milk made the workhouse look like a high quality inn. I couldn't deny that the steaks contained more gristle than meat or that the leg of beef with onion sauce wasn't fully satisfying, but we did what we could with what we had.

If anyone dared to complain, I reminded her that our Lord and Savior was poor as well, and by depriving ourselves, we were imitating him as well as the poor we served in his name. I must have said it a lot because some of the girls started to finish my sentences. I stopped saying it altogether the day Cressida replied, "At least Jesus could multiply the loaves and the fishes," and Margaret added, "and turn water into wine."

*****

Lord Montague's trial date was set for the first week of August. That much we learned from the newspapers. What we didn't expect was for a court official to deliver subpoenas for Grace, Margaret, and Cressida to testify as witnesses. For several minutes after they were served, we sat in the parlor, staring at the summonses. Margaret kept running her fingers over the large wax seals on her document and Cressida played with the ribbons on hers.

"It looks like we will be visiting Four Courts in a few weeks," I said, forcing cheer into my voice.

"I don't know if I can do this," Margaret whispered, sounding like she was going to cry.

"I don't think you have a choice," Cressida retorted, her fear translating as anger.

"Why would judges want to talk to us?"

"Because we know things that can help them."

"Just tell them what you know," I advised. "That's all anyone is asking of you. If you'd like, we can practice so that you're more comfortable."

Margaret nodded uncertainly.

I looked over at Grace, who wore a pensive frown. "You are very quiet." I tapped her foot with my boot.

"I'm thinking," she said, continuing to stare off into the middle-distance.

"About what?"

"What is best for the Sisters."

"What do you mean?" Margaret asked.

"Everything I say, everything I have done will reflect on all of us. If I testify, you could lose everything. How will it look when it comes out publicly that one of your Sisters has a past like mine? You may be able to look beyond it and see who I am now, but many people will not."

"You have to appear," Cressida said.

"Yes, but not necessarily as a Sister of Mercy. I could leave the order tomorrow. That way I would be giving witness as an ordinary citizen who just happened to work at the House for a while. It's not what I want," her voice wavered, "but it may be what is best for everyone."

I grabbed Grace's shaking hands. "I will hear of no such thing and that is final. We will handle whatever may come."

"Yes," Cressida said, brightening a little. "Jesus was the object of ridicule and public shame and a few of his disciples stayed loyal to him. We will do the same for you."

"You've been paying attention," I said, impressed at her use of Biblical metaphor to defuse the tension.

"There are even three of us," Margaret noted. "Catherine would definitely be the Blessed Mother."

"I would say Grace is the disciple Jesus loved," Cressida added playing along.

"Oh, no," Grace countered. "*I'm* supposed to be Mary Magdalene!"

Chapter 41

GRACE

August 1833
Four Courts Building
Dublin, Ireland

Many events and places in my life have overwhelmed me, but nothing so much as standing beneath the double dome of the Four Courts. I was frozen in place by awe, even as hundreds of people passed me by, some nearly colliding with me, others giving me a wide berth. The voices of barristers, judges, witnesses, reporters, and members of the pubic blended together in a low hum that echoed off every surface and seemed fill the space, though it had no physical form.

To look straight up at the mosaic ceiling made me dizzy, so the best I could do was stare at the friezes and paintings below. To me, it was proof that someone like me did not belong here, that I was far too humble for so grand a place. But Catherine explained that the outsized nature of the stacked domes was meant to represent the Heavens and man's littleness in comparison to God.

We strode quickly toward the Court of the King's Bench, trying to ignore that nearly all heads turned to see two Sisters and two lay women in a place so clearly reserved for men. A smattering of other women—all likely called as witnesses like Margaret and I were—interrupted the sea of black suits and robes with dresses of gray, brown, or dark mauve, but even they seemed curious as to why we were here.

I had hoped that inside the courtroom we would find order and quiet, but it turned out to me more of the same of what we'd experienced in the quadrangle. Catherine led us to where the Crown's Counsel sat and let him know we were present and ready to testify when called. He introduced himself, thanked us, and showed us where to sit, several rows behind him.

"This is the second day of the trial; we gave our opening speech yesterday, and the constable and corner gave their testimony," he said. "Today, we anticipate calling about a dozen more witnesses, including the three of you. When you hear your name called, please come forward and stand where indicated, behind that podium there." He pointed toward it.

"Remember, your role is simply to answer the questions posed to you honestly. Don't worry about what your testimony may mean to our case; that is for the judge and jury to decide. If you get nervous, take a deep breath, look at me or Catherine, and answer as best you can. You'll be fine."

We sat where directed and immediately those around us started whispering and nudging one another. Margaret, Cressida, and I leaned in close, our heads nearly touching, and rehearsed our testimony. Soon, the crowd fell silent as the jury of twelve men in black suits and powdered white wigs entered, followed by the four judges, three of whom who looked exactly the same as the jurors, save for the black robes with white fur trim at the throat and wrists worn over their suits. One wore red robes bordered in grey fur, with a tie around his throat and a large gold chain over his shoulders. He must have been the Chief Justice.

Lord Montague was led in and took his place opposite the King's Counsel. I won't pretend to understand the court proceedings that took place before my name was called. Barristers for both sides spoke with the Chief Justice and then the first witness was called.

Then it was my turn. I made my way to the witness stand in a daze, doing my best to ignore the scandalized tittering that followed in my wake. It wasn't often that a nun testified in a courtroom. Only when I faced the King's Counsel, Lord Montague, and his barrister did the magnitude of what I was doing fully hit me. My stomach dropped, my palms grew damp, and I had to swallow down bile. My hand immediately went to the long black rosary at my side, and I stroked the ebony and ivory cross for comfort.

"Please state your name for all present" King's Counsel requested.

"Sister Mary Magdalene of St. Zita, though I was born Grace Ryan."

"And what is your relation to the defendant?"

My eyes strayed to Lord Montague. The last several years had not been kind to him. His twinkling blue eyes had lost their luster, his beard and hair were shot through with gray, and his face was gaunt, as though he had been ill or hadn't had enough to eat. He did not meet my eyes, keeping his gaze firmly on the Chief Justice.

"I worked in service to him and his wife for three years."

"And during that time, did you ever witness Lord Montague raise a hand in anger to the deceased?"

"No. Our employment in his house did not overlap for long, less than a month."

The barrister feigned surprise. "What then makes you believe that Lord Montague was capable of killing Bess Bannon?"

"Objection!" Lord Montague's barrister yelled. "Speculation."

The King's Counselor turned to the Chief Justice. "My question goes to establishing a pattern of violence with his servants, especially women, My Lord."

The Chief Justice considered both arguments, eyes shifting from one man to another until finally resting on Lord Montague. "I'll allow it. Please answer Sister Magdalene."

I followed the Chief Justice's gaze. Lord Montague's expression was neutral; when he finally looked at me, his eyes dared me to speak the truth.

"He was often violent toward the females in his employ." I went on to recount how he had forced me into a sexual relationship with him, hit me when I told him I was pregnant, beat me the night Margaret went missing, and many other times. I recounted what I knew of his abuse of other servants, some of whom were in the room to give their own testimony.

"Was the day you were dismissed the last time you saw Lord Montague?"

"No, sir. I and several other women rented a house on Merrion Square from him for a time."

"Why, if he was violent toward you, as you say, would you enter into a business transaction with him?"

"We knew things about him he wouldn't want made public, as did he about us, so the agreement was our way of assuring one other's mutual silence."

"What kind of things?"

This was the question I dreaded. I wanted to avoid details if at all possible, so Cressida and I could not be charged for our crimes. I took a deep breath and told the truth, broadly. "I knew his finances were not what he broadcast to the world and that many of the things he did to make money were not legal."

"Such as?"

"Objection!" Lord Montague's barrister barked, his face rapidly growing scarlet. "Not pertinent to this case."

For once, I agreed with him.

"The witness's answer will establish a pattern of illegal activity," the King's Counselor stated, not a crack in his placid demeanor. "If he was willing to break the law in other ways, murder is not out of the realm of possibility."

"The defendant is on trial for murder," the Chief Justice reminded them. "Whatever other crimes he may have committed are not relevant unless they are somehow related to the murder of Miss Bannon. Mr. O'Brien, your objection is sustained. Please redirect your line of questioning, Mr. Fitzpatrick."

"You were there the night Miss Bannon died, is that right?" the lawyer asked me.

"Yes, sir. She died our arms."

A ripple of shock and pity traveled through the room as a low buzz.

"Who is the other person of whom you speak?"

"Cressida Smith. She is here in the courtroom."

"And did you know who inflected those mortal wounds on Bess Bannon that night?"

"No, sir, but we had our suspicions."

"Objection!" Lord Montague's barrister shot to his feet.

"My Lord, I haven't even asked my question yet," the King's Counselor pointed out in a frustration-tinted voice.

The Chief Justice bit back a smile. "But you were going to ask what those suspicions were, am I correct?"

At the barrister's nod, the Chief Justice continued. "I will admit to being curious as to the answer myself. Because the answer comes from another alleged victim of the defendant, I'll allow the question."

"Sister Magdalene, please tell us whom you and Miss Smith suspected and why."

"Our first thought was Lord Montague. Yes, he was abusive to us, but then there were the mysterious deaths of the other women who lived with us in Lord Montague's townhome. Jane's body was found in the Liffey and ruled an accident, even though she was a strong swimmer. Isa disappeared and was never found, and then Bess turned up nearly dead on our doorstep. It was suspicious, to say the least."

"Objection! Speculation."

"Mr. O'Brien, I have already allowed the witness to speak. Her testimony cannot be stricken from the record now."

The King's Counselor bit back a grin. He knew he had a good showing. "No further questions, My Lord."

I breathed a sigh of relief. My time on the stand was halfway over. But according to Catherine, the cross-examination would be the most difficult part. I prayed a quick Hail Mary to steel myself for what was to come.

Lord Montague's barrister stood. "Sister Magdalene, you testified that you and Lord Montague had an extramarital affair, is that correct?"

He wasn't going to waste any time with niceties, was he? "Yes sir, but it was against my will."

The crowed tittered again and the tension that had begun to seep into the room during my testimony grew into a tangible weight.

"So you claim. But yet, when you were dismissed from Lord Montague's service—without a character, I might add—what was the reason you were given?"

How did he know about that? I started to see where his line of questioning was headed. "Lady Montague accused me of seducing her husband, a charge I denied then and continue to deny."

Mr. O'Brien hummed his doubts about my answer. "You mentioned being pregnant by Lord Montague. What was the result of that situation?"

"I'm afraid I don't understand."

"Did you have the baby? Miscarry? Give it to a foundling hospital?"

I closed my eyes, knowing how much my answer would hurt my value as a witness. "No, sir. I ... I got rid of it." The courtroom erupted in stunned gasps.

"Lord Montague demanded it was the only option," I added quickly.

"By saying you 'got rid of it,' do you mean to say you had an abortion—an act that I would remind the court is considered murder according to the Catholic Church?"

"Yes, sir."

"And yet you stand here before us dressed in a nun's clothing."

"Objection!" Mr. Fitzpatrick yelled.

"Withdrawn," Mr. O'Brien said before the justices could speak.

Sneaky little Judas. The jury had already heard his insinuation, and that could not be withdrawn from their minds.

"Why did you rent from Lord Montague?"

"Objection! Asked and answered."

A muscle in the Chief Justice's jaw jumped. "Sustained. Move along Mr. O'Brien." He waved him along.

"Allow me to rephrase. What line of work were you in when you rented from Lord Montague?"

I had dodged this answer once, but it looked as though my luck had run out. Ignoring my sinking stomach, I took a deep breath and looked at Catherine, tears in my eyes. Of all the things I said today, this was the one that could be best used against her. She nodded encouragement. "I was a prostitute."

The room erupted as though a gas lamp had exploded. After a moment of stunned silence, everyone spoke at once. Onlookers shouted their outrage and jeered at me while the Chief Justice tried in vain to restore order. They only quieted after he threatened to clear the courtroom.

Mr. O'Brien couldn't repress a smug expression. "So, your religious name of Sister Mary Magdalene, after the fallen woman in the Bible, is no coincidence."

"Mr. O'Brien, may I remind you that we are here to hear a murder case, not a religious sermon," the Chief Justice said.

"Forgive me, Your Honour." He turned back to me. "You weren't just any prostitute, were you, Miss Ryan—I'm sorry, Sister Magdalene?"

My brow furrowed in confusion. What a strange question to ask. "I'm sorry. I don't know what you mean."

"Will you please hold up your right hand, Sister?"

Now his question made sense. Lord Montague must have really thought his chances of being convicted were high if he told his lawyer about the Doves. I held up my hand, palm down, so the court could see the scar the brand on my hand.

"Would you please tell the court what that marking on your hand is and what it symbolizes?"

"It is a dove. Lord Montague branded all of us with it in an attempt to control us. It is meant to mark us as the Doves of Dublin."

The courtroom once again burst into chaos. Our reputations were legendary, but this was the first time one of our identities was confirmed. People were pointing now, calling me all sorts of unsavory names. I prayed that the earth would swallow me up, even if it meant a journey to the bowls of hell.

"So, you are telling me that while you appear before us today dressed as a nun, you have had an affair with a previous employer, sought out an abortion, and were one of the most famous prostitutes in Dublin?" Mr. O'Brien was practically dancing with mirth.

"Objection!" The anger in the King's Counselor's voice was so palpable it was almost a living thing.

"Sister Magdalene is a character witness, Your Honour. Is it not my duty to establish whether or not she is a reliable one?"

"Sustained. But watch yourself, Mr. O'Brien."

"I have no further questions, Your Honour."

The Chief Justice gestured to the King's Counselor. "Mr. Fitzpatrick? Rebuttal?"

If there was any justice in this world, he would come up with something to salvage my testimony. When he didn't immediately move to stand, my heart sank. But then, he got to his feet and addressed me. "Sister Magdalene, what does the Catholic Church teach about the forgiveness of sins?"

"Objection! Mr. Fitzpatrick seems to have forgotten again that he is in a court of law, not a church," Mr. O'Brien yelled, leaning toward the Chief Justice.

The King's Counselor gestured for the barrister to calm down. "Hear me out, Your Honour. My reason for asking this question will become clear shortly."

"Continue, Mr. Fitzpatrick, but be careful or I will throw out your entire cross-examination. Sister Magdalene, please answer the question."

I knew my catechism well enough to see where he was headed. We might be saved after all. "That one can repent from any sin through the Sacrament of Reconciliation, and if that person is truly sorry and honestly vows never to commit the sin again, it will be forgiven." I felt like a child reciting answers before the parish priest.

"And what does that mean?"

"In the eyes of the Church and God, it is as though the sin was never committed." I glanced over at Catherine, who was grinning broadly.

"Did you repent of the sins mentioned in your testimony?"

I nodded enthusiastically. "Oh yes, sir. I repented before I was welcomed into the Church."

"And were you forgiven?"

"Yes, sir."

"Have you committed these sins since your confession?"

"No." I glanced over at Mr. O'Brien, who wanted so badly to object again, he was practically vibrating.

"So, you have lived since then without these sins on your soul?"

"Correct."

"Would that we could all be so forgiving," the King's Counselor muttered, just loud enough for the jury to hear.

"Your Honour!" Mr. O'Brien exclaimed.

"Withdrawn. No further questions."

I sat down next to Catherine, tears falling from my eyes. Relief and fear and shame and so many other emotions coursed through me all at once. I laid my head on her shoulder and she rubbed my arm.

"You did well. Trust in God that He will use your words according to His will."

Cressida was called next and testified how she found Bess after she was attacked and the events leading up to Bess's death. Lord Montague's barrister tried using a similar line of attack as he did with me, but because Cressida wasn't a nun, it didn't have the same impact.

Finally, it was Margaret's turn to testify. When her name was called, Lord Montague looked around. As soon as he saw her, his face went completely white. "This isn't possible," he said. "You're dead. I ..."

His barrister hushed him, but Lord Montague continued babbling, albeit quietly enough that no one else could hear him.

"Mr. O'Brien, please get control of your client," the Supreme Justice ordered.

"Yes, Your Honour. He's had a bit of a shock."

Once Lord Montague had settled down, the King's Counselor began his questioning. After asking Margaret to state her name and her relationship to Lord Montague, he asked, "The accused just said he thought you were dead. Why is that?"

"Because he thought he had succeeded in killing me."

*****

The trial continued for three more days, with barristers for both sides giving their closing arguments to a packed courtroom. Our testimony had drawn great attention to the case, and half of Dublin wanted to see how Lord Montague's barrister would try to dig him out of the trench he found himself in. Catherine, Cressida, Margaret, and I followed the case in the papers, where it was covered in exacting detail—including Mrs. Gallagher's attempts to redirect the truth in Lord Montague's favor, just as she had with me so many years before.

When the jury retired to their quarters, the horrible processes of waiting began. Many juries delivered their verdict without even leaving the jury box, but we were not so lucky. In order to convict, they had to be unanimous. It could be anywhere from a few hours to a week before the jury reached a decision.

We were gathered for Prime two days after the jury adjourned when a messenger arrived with an urgent message for Mother McAuley. We finished our prayers and went to see what the fuss was about.

"The jury has reached a verdict," he said before we even had a chance to ask. "They will deliver it when the court is called to session at nine. The constable sent a carriage to take all four of you."

We bade him to stay for breakfast and then piled into the coach. As soon as we started moving, I began to regret we hadn't had the opportunity to break our fast. By the time we were seated in the courtroom, a cold sweat had broken out on the back of my neck. Margaret didn't look much better. Catherine excused herself and returned with two glasses of cold water. I sipped at mine slowly, having learned the hard way not to gulp when my stomach was queasy. Margaret held hers to her forehead while Cressida sprinkled water on the back of Margaret's neck.

As nine o'clock drew near, more and more people packed the already stuffy courtroom. By the time the jury returned and the judges were seated, guards had been called to keep order and ensure no one else was let into the courtroom.

The jury foreman handed a paper to the clerk of the court, on which was written the verdict. After calling each juror by name to ensure all were present, the clerk asked, "Gentlemen, have you agreed upon your verdict? Who shall say for you?"

"Our foreman," they chorused.

"Mr. Foreman, please tell us your verdict."

"Guilty of murder."

Shouts went up from the courtroom, and we were jostled as those present turned to one another or tried to get a look at Lord Montague's reaction. For a brief moment, the crowd parted in such a way that I had a clear view of him. His face had once again drained of color and he put an arm out to his barrister to keep his balance. He really thought his position was going to shield him from conviction and that the testimony of two women wouldn't be enough to discredit him. Our eyes met. He looked like a ghost already hung and dead.

In my imagination, I always thought I would simply give him a smile and turn away, satisfied that justice had been done. But in the moment, I found that I could not. All I could do was look at him with pity. I raised my right hand and made a tiny cross in the air, a sign that I forgave him and turned the final judgment over to God.

Margaret, however, was under no such influence of the grace of God. She made a rude gesture in his direction and grinned. "How does it feel to be the powerless one?" she asked, even though there was no way he could hear her.

The Chief Justice called for order. Slowly, those around us gathered themselves. The excitement in the room was palpable as we waited to hear the punishment meted out by the four judges.

The clerk wrote the verdict down in his book. "This is your verdict and so say you all?"

"Aye," they answered as one.

The judges conferred and the room was so quiet the creak of the benches as people repositioned themselves may as well have been the breaking of tree branches in a storm. Next to me, Margaret breathed in deep breaths, wheezing a little on every inhale and exhale. On her other side, Catherine's lips moved in silent prayer as rosary beads slipped through her fingers. Cressida stared off into the middle distance, as though reliving a long-ago memory.

Soon, the court crier commanded, "All manner of persons keep silence whilst judgment is given against the prisoner at the bar, upon the pain of imprisonment."

He turned to Lord Montague and asked, "Do you have anything to say as to why the sentence of death should not be pronounced against you?"

Lord Montague stood. "I make a plea in stay of judgment on the grounds that I am a peer of the realm. While I cannot officially claim the privilege of peerage as I did so years ago in another case, I remind Your Honours that I have not killed, nor been convicted of killing, another peer. Therefore, I ask you to take my rank and political importance into consideration when rendering your verdict."

I shook my head. The nerve. The man had learned nothing from his ordeal. He truly believed it was excusable to do to us as he pleased because we were of lower rank than he.

The Supreme Justice's face was stony, his eyes as sharp as an executioner's blade when next he spoke.

"There are times when silence serves you better than speech, a lesson you have failed to master. Your plea is denied. In point of fact, I am less likely to be lenient now than I was before you spoke. The punishment of murder is death. You must therefore prepare for that dreadful punishment, which is equal to your dreadful offense. I cannot extend any hope of mercy to you. The law shall take its course."

The four judges all donned black triangular caps, but only the Supreme Justice spoke. "Lord James Montague, you have been found guilty of the crime of murder by this court. We therefore sentence you to be hung by the neck until dead one month from today."

Lord Montague's face went completely blank at the pronouncement. He did not appear to hear anything else the judges said. Gone was his usual swagger as he was led out of the courtroom by the bailiff, replaced by a stiff gait more appropriate for a corpse, which was in many ways appropriate, as he was now considered "dead under the law."

Once the judges had left the room, the spectators all began talking at once. Catherine hugged me tightly. Over her shoulder, Margaret swayed. Cressida reached out to steady her, but was too late. Margaret collapsed onto the floor in a faint.

Chapter 42

CATHERINE

August 1833
House of Mercy
Dublin, Ireland

Grace was right. The fallout from Lord Montague's trial was swift and severe.

The next morning, Father Kelly showed up at the House unexpectedly. But he wasn't there to congratulate us on the trial or helping to bring a murderer to justice. When I opened the door he pushed past me, pressing a piece of paper to my chest.

I followed him into the chapel, calling after him all the while, asking what was going on.

Without a word, he strode to the front of the chapel, past the altar, to the streetside door where the public could access the chapel. He removed a hammer from his cassock, locked the door and swung at the doorknob, breaking it off and ensuring no one could get in without coming through the front doors of the House.

"Father Kelly, what are you doing?" I cried. "Have you gone mad?"

"I could ask the same of you," he growled.

The noise brought Frances and Grace running.

"What is going on here?" Frances demanded, blocking the middle of the aisle so that the priest had to stop and answer her or else physically push past her.

"I have had enough of the nonsense coming from this house. You have all proven to be an embarrassment to the city and to the Church. Beginning now, your chapel is officially closed to the public."

He glanced at Tabernacle, as though considering hitting it with his hammer, too.

"You are not worthy to have Christ under your roof, much less make a profit from him. I may not have the authority to remove the Blessed Sacrament from this place, but I can certainly make sure you don't benefit from it."

"He has lost his mind," Grace said to Frances.

I reached out and grabbed Father Kelly's shoulder, forcing him to face me. "Father Kelly, stop," I commanded.

"Unhand me, you wretched woman!" he yelled.

I faced him down with every ounce of calm I could muster. "We are in a house of God. This is not the place for such discussions."

I slipped past him and Frances and walked away, heading toward the reception room, where we could sort this out in relative privacy. The priest and two nuns followed me.

I closed the pocket doors and pulled out a chair. "Sit."

He did so and the three of us followed suit, facing him.

"Now, let's start over. What is this all about?"

Father Kelly laughed. "You cause a scandal in court, get an upstanding man sentenced to death, and you have the nerve to ask me what this is about?"

"Ah yes, I had forgotten you were friends with Lord Montague. Never mind the fact that he murdered a woman, tried to kill at least two others, and brutally raped and abused several more."

"This. This right here. The insubordinance. The lack of respect. You should be thrown out of the order at the very least."

"The order I founded. How exactly do you propose to do that?" I was more than a little amused by this idea.

"And you, you should be excommunicated, you harlot!" Father Kelly went on as though I hadn't spoken. "You are not worthy of the title Christian, much less to wear that sacred habit."

Grace faced him with admirable calm. "As I testified in court, I repented of my sins long before I took my vows. You have no right to hold my past against me."

"According to your logic," Frances put in, "no one who has ever sinned is worthy of the title Christian. Would you deny St. Augustine his glory as a Doctor of the Church simply because he had a checkered past?"

She had him cornered and he knew it. I replayed what he'd said in the chapel in my mind.

"Twice, you said we shouldn't be able to benefit from our chapel or the Blessed Sacrament. What did you mean by that?" I asked.

"Any group that throws such suspicion and distrust on the Church as you did with your testimony," he pointed at Grace, "should not be allowed the privilege of collecting funds from its people as you do every Sunday."

"So that is what this is really about," I said. "You have been trying from the beginning to funnel the funds we receive from the public into your own coffers. How *is* your new church coming, by the way?"

"That is not the point and you know it."

I made a doubtful sound. "I don't know about that. If the people of Dublin can no longer attend Mass here, where will they go instead?" I pretended to think. "Ah, yes, St. Andrews, your parish. How convenient is that?"

Father Kelly grimaced at me. "Lest you doubt how serious I am, take a look at the letter I gave you. It is signed and sealed by Archbishop Murray himself."

I looked at the paper in my hand, the one I had forgotten I was holding. Skimming over it, he appeared to be correct. The Archbishop had signed off on the closure of the chapel. But as far as punishments went, this one was not too bad. Still, I wouldn't let him know that.

"How exactly do you suppose we will make up the income you've taken away from us?" I asked.

"You are clever women—too clever for your own good. I have no doubt you will think of something." He stood. "Enjoy your victory while you can. The Sisters of Mercy will not be around much longer if I have any say in the matter."

*****

In the weeks following, both Grace and Margaret suffered a severe case of scruples regarding their testimony. In addition to blaming themselves for the closure of the chapel, they each came to me separately, asking essentially the same question. "How can I possibly live with myself knowing that my words helped sentence a man to the gallows?"

I tried to put myself in their situation when offering them solace. Their logic was sound, but they overestimated their role in the outcome. Yes, their testimony was important. But even without it, the court likely would have convicted Lord Montague on the evidence of his cufflink being found in Bess's stomach. She wouldn't voluntarily have eaten it, nor would he have any reason to make her swallow it. Combined with the testimony of the other domestics, they had a strong case. Grace and Margaret had simply confirmed what the others had said. If they were still concerned, I suggested they meet with Archbishop Murray. It was my experience that he always knew what to say.

While his wisdom helped heal their souls, there was nothing that could be done to bring Margaret back to health. Her courtroom swoon turned out to be much more than shock. The wheezing Grace had heard grew worse and Margaret started having trouble breathing. Dr. Redmond O'Hanlon was called, and he delivered a devastating diagnosis. It was not consumption, as we all feared, but a long-building case of pneumonia, for which there was no treatment or cure.

As though hearing the words set the disease free within her system, Margaret rapidly declined. Within two days, her lungs were blocked and she was wracked with painful coughing fits morning and night. Dr. O'Hanlon estimated she would die before the week was out.

Hoping the sea air would at least provide her friend with some relief, Kate traveled with Margaret to Kingstown. I would have loved to have joined them, but I was needed at Baggot Street more than ever.

While they were gone, the papers reported that Lord Montague had asked the Crown to exercise the "royal prerogative of mercy" and commute his sentence. Reporters began showing up at the House and asking the porters for statements about this development, so I asked them to keep silent. More importantly, they frightened away women who sincerely sought shelter here. They were so persistent that the Archbishop ordered priests from the Carmelite monastery to stand guard outside our doors until the furor subsided.

A week later, when the front bell sounded near dinnertime, I expected to see yet another reporter frantically trying to meet a deadline, but found the Constable standing on the porch instead.

"Hello." The word came out in a whoosh of surprise. "I'm sorry, I wasn't expecting to see you. Please, come in." I stepped aside so he could enter.

The Constable removed his hat and turned it round and round by the brim. "I am afraid I have some distressing news. Is there somewhere private we may speak? I would like Sister Magdalene and Miss Smith to hear it as well."

Immediately, Isa's face flashed in my mind. Had they finally found her? *Good God, please don't let her be dead.* "I will call for them," I said, flagging down the nearest Sister and giving her orders.

The two woman joined us shortly, Grace looking as wide-eyed and frightened as I felt. Cressida, on the other hand, appeared less concerned than I would have expected, though she was picking at her nails, a nervous habit she'd acquired during the trial. Cressida had left the House when the case was over—though she returned a few days a week to volunteer—and she and the Constable had been quietly courting. She had told me just that morning that the announcement of their upcoming nuptials would take place the following Sunday. Perhaps she was just nervous to see him.

"Ladies, there is no easy way for me to tell you this, but I thought you would like to hear it directly from me, rather than read about it in the papers." The Constable still hadn't sat down and was pacing back and forth in a tight four-step path.

The three of us exchanged wary glances. Grace grabbed my hand and squeezed it.

"Lord Montague was found dead in his cell in Kilmainham Gaol this morning."

I gasped in unison with the other two women, my stomach plummeting so hard I feared it would be lying on the rug at my feet.

The Constable stopped in front of us. "We don't know exactly what happened. At first, we thought it was suicide—the result of a guilty conscience—because his wrists and elbows were slashed and the outline of a dove, just like the one on your hands," he gestured to Cressida and Grace, "was drawn in blood on the wall above where he fell."

I shivered, both abhorrence of the mortal sin Lord Montague had committed in taking his own life and in repulsion at the image the Constable's words painted. Grace's face had paled and she looked like she was going to be sick, while Cressida stared blankly at the image burned into her hand.

We sat in silence for a moment before Cressida blinked hard as though coming out of a daydream and looked up at the Constable. "Wait," she said, narrowing her eyes. "You said, 'at first.' Have you changed your mind?"

The Constable cleared his throat. "Yes. We received an anonymous note warning that a letter from the Lord Lieutenant to the Justices in Lord Montague's case was going to be leaked to the press. This letter proved that Richard Wellesley, the first Marquess

Wellesley, had informed the Justices that he intended to commute Lord Montague's sentence, as is his right by law."

"What does that have to do with Lord Montague's death?" I asked, not following his logic. "Why would a man who was about to be freed kill himself?"

"That's the thing. We believe someone else did this to him and made it look like a suicide. It's not uncommon for other prisoners to take justice into their own hands if they feel an inmate deserves punishment they won't otherwise receive. If they found out Lord Montague was going to walk free, they may well have taken action."

"But how would the others know? Has the letter already appeared in the papers?" Cressida asked.

Grace snorted. "Clearly, you've never been in prison. Gossip travels faster than lightning inside those walls. The guards would have been informed almost immediately of the change in sentencing, and one of them likely told a prisoner. After that it would have been a matter of minutes before it was common knowledge."

Her point was certainly valid, but there was one thing still bothering me. "Why do you believe it was someone inside the gaol? Couldn't it just as easily have been someone else?"

"It's possible," he conceded, "but not nearly as likely. Information like a change in sentence is closely guarded, and even if the news had been relayed, there wasn't time for someone from the outside to gain entry and commit the crime."

The Constable bid us farewell shortly thereafter. When we were alone again, Grace spoke up. "Part of me is happy he's dead. Is that a sin?"

I sighed. "That is a question only God can truly answer. A priest could likely give you a better answer than I, but I wonder if you are really rejoicing in his death or simply feeling relief that he is no longer a threat. You have lived in fear of him for years, so it is only natural that when that threat is removed, you would feel a lightness that could be mistaken for joy. I would suggest you examine your motivations, pray for Lord Montague's soul, and if you are still worried, talk to Father Armstrong next time he is here."

Despite giving this advice, the matter of Lord Montague's death would not leave my mind. I didn't feel anything akin to joy over the news, though I could understand why Grace and Cressida might. The stumbling block for me had to do with the Constable. He was awfully quick to brush off my question about a member of the public being the murderer, and I wasn't entirely convinced he had revealed the whole of what the police knew—or at least suspected.

It wasn't until late that night in the quiet hours after Matins that I hit on what had been bothering me. When Cressida arrived earlier that day to see Grace, she was wearing Lord Montague's jade cufflinks as earrings—both of them, not just the one that Bess had swallowed. I hadn't noticed it at the time, but now it struck me as strange that she would want any tangible reminder of the man who had abused her.

And secondly, when she was picking at her nails, I realized she was actually trying to remove something from beneath them. At the time, I wrote it off as dirt, assuming she had been gardening that day, but now I recalled asking her to help in the sacristy. Looking back, I couldn't be sure if it was dirt or blood I saw beneath her nails.

Her fiancé would have been able to grant her access to the gaol, and it wouldn't have taken much to induce a few of the prisoners to do the dirty work for her while she drew the symbol on the wall.

Additionally, the coroner and the constable were the only two who would have had access to both of Lord Montague's cufflinks. She could well have been wearing them as a sign of victory—a silent proclamation that she had won in the end.

I would never be able to prove it, but I would always wonder if the girl once called Wren had exacted her revenge after all.

Chapter 43

GRACE

September 1833
House of Mercy
Dublin, Ireland

I knew this day was going to come—and sooner than any of us would have liked—so it shouldn't have been such a shock when I woke to an eerie rattling, like the bones in a crypt had come to life. I stood on wobbly legs and walked over to Margaret's bed. It was as I feared; the sound was coming from her chest.

When Kate and Margaret returned from Kingstown a week ago, I refused to leave Margaret's side. Catherine graciously exempted me from my normal duties and allowed me to sleep in a special room in the infirmary with Margaret. It was clear she was not long for this world, and after being apart for nine years, I didn't want to miss a moment with her. We talked for hours and I held her through every bout of coughing, even developing sympathy pains in my chest when I inhaled and exhaled, as though my own muscles were taxed beyond their limits.

Now, it appeared the end was near. When Catherine came in after morning prayer to check on us, she took one look at Margaret's pale complexion and turned right back around. When she came back, it was with the priest who had said Mass in the chapel that morning. He gave Margaret last rites and blessed Catherine and me, praying that God would give us both the grace to help Margaret have a happy death and the strength to commend her into God's hands when the moment came.

When the priest was gone, Catherine and I sat on either side of Margaret's bed. Her eyelids drooped and she was clearly worn out by the small amount of activity she had endured. Her chest whistled with every breath.

"Tell me about the angels again," she said.

This was a story I told her often in her first days at Lord Montague's estate, one that I had learned somewhere in my own childhood, though I could not remember when or from whom.

"When God created the world, he assigned a group of angels to every task people would ever need. There was one for preparing food, one for gathering water, one for washing their hair, and so on. When they were cast out of Eden, God recalled most of those angels to His side, with the exception of the guardian angels, who kept each person safe.

"Over time, the angels that used to serve the people began to miss their human charges, so they went to God and asked if they could return to earth. At first, he was adamantly against it, but one day an angel came up with a compromise God could accept. These angels would agree to take on human form and be born just like humans, so that no one would know what they really were. They would dedicate their lives to service of others, so that their human's time on earth could be just a little more like the paradise it was mean to be. To this day, only a select few know that domestic servants are really God's special angels in disguise."

By the time I finished the story, Margaret was snoring, and Catherine, too, was asleep, her head resting on Margaret's lap. I must have dozed off, as well, because the next thing I knew, the soft rumble of voices invaded my dreams until I finally woke to see Catherine and Margaret talking softly.

"I want to show you something," Catherine said to Margaret, reaching down to grab something from the floor. She held up a small hurricane lamp. "When I opened this House, I placed this light in the window of my room in the hopes that you would one day see it and know I had kept a place in my heart and in my home for you. In the intervening years, it has drawn thousands of women to our doorstep. The years we were separated may not have been easy for any of us, but God used them for the greater good."

Margaret smiled weakly. "You're right. Had Smiddy not lured me away from the hotel that night, had I met you for Mass the next morning, everything would have been different. Only God knows what a difference that would have made for all of us."

She barely finished her sentence before a fit overtook her and she coughed hard and long, the spasms in her chest forcing her upright. I put an arm around her back and Catherine braced her shoulders so she could focus all of her strength clearing her lungs. Margaret gasped for air between spasms, making a whooping sound that chilled me to the bone.

"Better?" I asked, when she finally quieted.

She nodded.

"Do me a favor," she whispered to Catherine.

"Anything."

"Don't let that light go out—ever."

Tears rolled down Catherine's cheeks. "You have been the driving force behind everything I have done from that Sunday to now. What am I going to do without you?"

Margaret smiled. "You are going to go on, just as you did before you found me. My time here may be finished, but yours isn't."

She coughed again, this time even more violently and took longer to catch her breath. During that fit, her fingertips and lips took on a blue cast that remained even after she settled.

Margaret lay silent and still for a while, catching her breath. Once she had, she took my hand, "Grace, I promise to watch over you like one of our domestic angels. You'll never be alone, no matter what happens. I love you so much. You are the best gift God ever gave me."

I squeezed her hand. "I love you, too." Tears choked me, cutting off everything else I wanted so desperately to say.

Catherine and I both lay down on the bed beside her and wrapped her in our arms. Slowly, she succumbed to sleep. There were no more fits now, just a gradual increase in the rumble in her chest until it was all I could hear. She gasped one final time, and then there was silence.

"*In paradisum deducant te angeli,*" Catherine whispered in Latin. "*In tuo adventu suscipiant te martyres, et perducant te in civitatem sanctam Jerusalem. Chorus angelorum te suscipiat, et cum Lazaro quondam paupere æternam habeas requiem.*"

May the angels lead you into paradise; may the martyrs receive you at your arrival and lead you to the holy city Jerusalem. May choirs of angels receive you and with Lazarus, once a poor man, may you have eternal rest.

"Amen," I intoned.

Epilogue

GRACE

Our first three years as a religious order were only the beginning of a grander adventure.

Never one to be still for long, after a few weeks rest, Catherine was back in action once again, drafting the first Rule and constitutions of our order. The following year, in 1834, she founded a seaside retreat for Sisters who were exhausted or ill in Kingstown. This was the first of several "foundations" she would place in the care of Anna Maria, giving her the title of Mother Superior.

Over the next five years, she, Anna Maria, and the other Sisters of Mercy founded seven additional convents in Ireland and two in England, in addition to two "branch houses" in Kingstown and Booterstown.

On June 6, 1841, we received official word that Pope Gregory XVI had approved the Rule and constitutions of the Sisters of Mercy as a religious congregation with very few changes to what we had submitted. In a letter to Catherine, he stressed the importance of our simple vows, which allowed us to continue to minister to the people of Dublin:

The Sisters of Mercy have long been called "the walking nuns" as a term of derision, implying they are lower or less than orders whose solemn vows bind them to the work of prayer within cloister walls. It is my will that "the walking nuns" embrace this title for all its name implies: They are the ones who bring the spirit of Christ to the least of their community through the spiritual and corporal works of mercy; they imitate most closely the traveling of Jesus and his disciples across the Holy Land to heal the sick and spread the Good News of the Lord; and their footsteps form a path for future generations to follow, no matter where in the world the call of mercy may lead them.

I hereby give the Sisters of Mercy the Papal blessing, recording and enrolling them among the ranks of religious orders approved by the Catholic Church. With God's blessing, may they continue to serve in love and compassion and prosper for many years to come.

Unfortunately, Catherine's aging body couldn't stand the rigorous pace she insisted on keeping. Beginning in 1840, she was frequently ill and by autumn of the next year, it was clear she wasn't going to regain her strength, as an "old man's cough," as she called it, had taken root in her lungs and would not let go.

On November 11, 1841, we gathered around her bed to chant the Office of the Dead and Dying by candlelight, for it was clear she would not live to see another dawn. One by one we approached her deathbed to say a final word or offer her a blessing. Sometimes she was the one to comfort us, compassionate to the last.

When it was my turn, I asked if she had any final instructions for our congregation. Pulling me close to her, she said quietly, "Be sure they have a good cup of tea when I am gone," referencing the day she comforted Anna Maria with tea laced with whisky.

She squeezed by hand and said, "You will survive this grief. You will go on as you always have, taking one day in hand at a time. Remember that the legacy of our Institute is charity. If you keep that top of mind, you will be certain to do God's will."

In the quiet hours of the night, she woke from sleep long enough to utter the words, "'Tis come to a close." Moments later she was gone, her soul at home with the God she loved so dearly.

Though not present for Catherine's final moments, Anna Maria arrived at the House of Mercy in time to help me prepare Catherine's body for the funeral and lower her into her coffin. According to her wishes, Catherine was "buried in the ground like the poor," the first of many Sisters to buried in the newly-consecrated cemetery in the back garden of the House of Mercy. Catherine had made clear she wanted no elaborate decorations to adorn her final resting place, so a small wooden cross bearing the words, "May she rest in peace," was all that marked her grave,

As for me, I continue to serve the Sisters at the House of Mercy. In the quiet moments between prayer and work, I have made it my mission to chronicle Catherine's life and work, so that future generations may know the story of the kind-hearted laywoman and caregiver-turned-nun who set out to educate women and children and ended up changing the world.

AFTERWARD

The following is a summary of historical events that took place after Catherine's Mercy ends.

Anna Maria Doyle went on to serve as founder and Mother Superior of Mercy convents in Tullamore and Kells and founder, Mother Assistant, and Mistress of Novices in Derry. She died in Derry on September 11, 1866, at the age of 65.

Though she did not live to see it, the growth of Catherine's order was swift. In May 1842, a small group of Sisters of Mercy crossed the Atlantic to found a convent in the Canadian province of Newfoundland, the first in North America. Following close on their heels, Frances Warde brought the Sisters of Mercy to the United States in Pittsburgh, Pennsylvania, in 1843. Three years later, another group of Sisters arrived in Perth, Australia, in 1846; and in 1850, a group settled in New Zealand. Glasgow marked the first Sisters of Mercy convent in Scotland in 1849.

Sisters of Mercy nursed the wounded and dying alongside Florence Nightingale during the Crimean War, greatly influencing Nightingale's later seminal works on nursing as a profession. They also nursed wounded and dying soldiers in the American Civil War and later during the Boer War in South Africa.

Today there are more than six thousand Sisters of Mercy worldwide (as well as about three thousand lay associates), serving in ministries such as education, health care, social work, spiritual guidance, pastoral services, and social justice.

Catherine McAuley is on the path to sainthood in the Catholic Church. After a long process that studied all aspects of her life to ensure "with moral certainty" that she lived the "virtues of the Christian Life to a heroic degree," Catherine was declared Venerable by the Church on April 9, 1990, and granted the title "Servant of God."

To be declared a saint, her life and legacy must pass through two more stages of scrutiny, including having two miracles attributed solely to her intercession. To date, several alleged miracles have been reported, but none has yet withstood the rigor of Church scrutiny. When the first miracle is verified, Catherine will be given the title "Blessed." Upon confirmation of the second, she will be named a saint.

AUTHOR'S NOTE

How do you begin to tell an entertaining story with a potential saint as your main character without veering off into hagiography? That was the question I faced when writing this novel. I didn't want to only focus on Catherine's good points—which would be natural when chronicling the life of someone so virtuous. However, that meant I would have to make up her negative personality traits, because the only records we have are biographies that idealize her. That is where the "fiction" in "historical fiction" comes into play.

Biographies dating from just after Catherine's death—especially Mother Austin Teresa Carroll's *Life of Catherine McAuley: Foundress and First Superior of the Institute of Religious Sisters of Mercy* (1866) and the most recent *The Path of Mercy: The Life of Catherine McAuley* by Mary C. Sullivan (2012)—show us that Catherine was a level-headed, intelligent, fiercely independent woman. While she took her work and her vocation seriously, she liked to have fun (she invented a nonsensical club for the enjoyment of the Sisters and was known to write humorous poems) and detested too many rules and too much rigidity. A few of her more famous quotes are, "God preserve us from serious nuns" (a close approximation of a quote by her favorite saint, St. Teresa of Avila), "be sure to dance every evening," and "be careful not to make too many laws, for if you draw the string too tight it will break." (Fun fact: The opening quote of this novel, "Comfort comes soon after a well-received trial," is actually attributed to Catherine McAuley herself.)

What we don't know was what she was like when she was in a bad mood, not feeling well, tired, or just plain sick of the women she lived with—those things which humanize her. This is where I have given her traits such as impatience, an argumentative nature, mistrust, and even a tendency to believe overmuch in her own worth and mission. These felt like the most natural complements to her known virtues and also fit best with the story I was telling. They are not reflective of the actual person, as we may never know those details.

Fiction Based in Truth

Catherine's Mercy is not only Catherine McAuley's story, however. It is also that of Margaret and Grace, both of whom are completely fictional characters. The only basis in reality either one has is that Catherine really did turn away an unnamed servant (Margaret in this book) who came to her asking for help because she was in fear of her virtue from a harsh master. All that is known is that Catherine never saw the servant again, and her decision haunted her for the rest of her days. No one knows why she made that seemingly uncharacteristic choice, which is why I made it the basis of my short story, "Consequences," upon which this novel is based.

The reality behind Grace and Margaret's lives is very much steeped in history. Their jobs, negative experiences with their master, and Grace's decline into poverty are based in fact. Grace's time at the workhouse is also based on actual records of the House of Industry in Dublin. The Doves of Dublin were inspired by a real-life group of Irish prostitutes called The Wrens of the Curragh, a group of nineteenth-century Irish women who lived communally on the plains of Kildare and supported themselves through sex work. The Doves' branding and murders are completely fictional, though the branding was inspired by actions of modern-day pimps and a ritual endured by some female members of the recent NXIVM cult.

Lord Montague is a fictional character based very loosely on Lord William Vesey-Fitzgerald, 2nd Baron Fitzgerald and Vesey, and Anglo-Irishman who was well known for an affair with his mistress, Mary Anne Clarke. He also ran for Parliament in 1828 against Daniel O'Connell, to whom he lost by a large margin. Lord Montague's trial was based on information found in the book, *Murder Trials in Ireland, 1836-1914*, by W. E. Vaughan.

Daniel O'Connell was a real person, and his Catholic Association and its related membership rules are historical. He began the Association in 1823, and it really took off in the following three years. In 1826, a group of Catholics, the Forty-Shilling Freeholders, voted against their landlords' wishes for the first time, supporting the Catholic candidate for Parliament. By 1828, the Catholic Church took over O'Connell's group and O'Connell was elected to the House of Commons. However, because of the Penal Laws, he was not allowed to take his seat in Parliament. This greatly angered the people, and Protestant leaders quickly saw it could lead to Civil War. So, they passed the Catholic Relief Bill in February 1829, which repealed the remaining Penal Laws and allowed Catholics to sit in Parliament.

William and Mary Callaghan are also real people with whom Catherine lived for nearly twenty years. Upon William Callaghan's death, she inherited what is estimated to be between $1 million and $5 million today. The House of Mercy that she built with this money still stands at 64A Baggot Street Lower in Dublin. While many of the rooms have been modernized, three rooms are preserved closely to how they would have looked in Catherine's time: the chapel, a drawing room that contains items from Coolock House (which also still stands), and Catherine's bedroom, which holds some of her personal effects. In the basement are the Mercy archives, which preserve Catherine's letters, many of her possessions, and artwork and other materials from the early days of the Sisters of Mercy.

Anna Maria Doyle (also called Mary Anne Doyle) and Elizabeth Harley were Catherine's real companions in founding the Sisters of Mercy. The outline of their lives is true, although I have taken liberty with a few details for ease of reading, such as omitting one of Anna Maria's brothers and continuing to call her by her birth name even after she took her religious vows and was known as Sister Mary Anne.

The ceremonies experienced by Catherine, Anna Maria, and Elizabeth while at St. George's are abbreviated versions of real-life Catholic rituals used when a woman becomes a nun. They are based on vows taken by Benedictine monks and my own experience witnessing the first vows of a Carmelite nun.

Catherine's life was so full of people—many of whom had the same first name—that it quickly becomes confusing. For ease of reading, I left out many of the priests who shaped her life, early volunteers at the House of Mercy, and names of actual Sisters of Mercy. For ease of reading, I have narrowed the priests down to Father Michael Blake, Father Edward Armstrong, and Father Mathias Kelly—the latter of whom really was an outspoken opponent of Catherine and her ministry—for the exact reasons mentioned in the book. The volunteers are represented by Kate, who really was Catherine's niece and one of her first helpers; Kate's real name was Catherine, but I chose to call her Kate to distinguish her from Catherine McAuley. The Sisters are amalgamated into Grace and Frances Warde, the latter of whom was a real Sister of Mercy and a dear friend of Catherine.

Necessary Changes

Every historical fiction novel bends the truth in some way in favor of telling a good story.

William Callaghan died on November 26, 1822, but I moved his death back to March 26, 1822, to fit the timeline of the story. The discussion William overheard between Mr. Powell and his wife is said to have taken place in 1821, but I moved the reveal of it to 1824 for dramatic effect. William's note to Catherine is fictional, but the words of his will are authentic.

Grace's botched abortion is based on true stories pre-Roe *v.* Wade found in a *Washington Post* article titled, "When Abortions Were Illegal—and How They Got That Way," which was published on June 24, 2022.

Catherine bought the land for the House of Mercy on June 22, 1824, but I moved the date back a few months to suit the story. The deed was officially signed on December 14, 1824, but I moved it to the following year because, according to my timeline, Catherine would have been in France on the actual date.

The cornerstone blessing took place in July 1822, a month later than it is in this book. The ceremony that takes place around it is loosely based on the Blessing of the Cornerstone of a New Building, found on Catholic.org in the prayers section.

Catherine did indeed study in parts of Ireland and in France for two years, though exactly what she learned there is not recorded.

Grace's descent into poverty is based in actual travails of the people of Dublin. The first House of Industry was established in Dublin by an act of Irish Parliament in 1703, and it was built south of the River Liffey and St. James's Street. There were places of relief for the poor in North Dublin as early as 1772, when the first workhouse was reformed and split into three sections: the workhouse where the poor were located, a hospital for the mentally ill, and a foundling hospital reserved for children. In 1838, the House of Industry on James's Street was renamed the South Dublin Union Workhouse. The formal system of workhouses in Ireland that we think of today (and may link with the Magdalene Asylums of the Sisters of Mercy— although Catherine was not involved in those abuses) were not established in Ireland until March 1840.

Father Mathias Kelly was one of the most outspoken of Catherine's critics. He and Catherine went round and round throughout their lives, with him inquiring into every detail of the running of the House and barging in unexpectedly one day to confront Catherine and demand she either start a religious order or turn the House over to the Sisters of Charity, despite the trust that Catherine had created to prevent just such an occurrence. Archbishop Murray came to her rescue every time, though he was in favor of the religious order.

Anna Maria Doyle first met Catherine in spring of 1827, a few months before her sister (also named Catherine) died in the Presentation convent. I moved Anna Maria finding out about her death up to August to better emphasize the shared experience of Anna and Catherine in both losing their sisters and how their grief drew them closer.

The opening of the House of Mercy took place on September 24, 1827, and is celebrated to this day as "Mercy Day," at Sisters of Mercy-founded and -sponsored institutions around the world. The events of the day hold true to accounts of the opening, including the school being started immediately, women applying for shelter that same day, Daniel O'Connell providing the feast, and Catherine leaving a lamp burning to signal to the women of Dublin.

The Presentation Sisters actually reached out to Anna Maria Doyle twice to try to persuade her to join them, but I have combined the two instances so they aren't repetitive.

Strange as it may seem, William Callaghan's Christmas night attack on Catherine because of his daughter's conversion, and his subsequent death, were historical events.

Catherine's consideration of the constitutions of other religious orders with the input of her volunteers is based on fact. The depiction of their time at St. George's is based on the scant details extant in biographies of Catherine and Anna Maria. The religious rituals they experienced in each stage of their training are based on those used by the Catholic Church for hundreds of years, even to this day. Very little information about Elizabeth Harley exists, other than that she was among the three founding Sisters of Mercy and she died soon after.

The general timeline of the volunteers' ministry, including starting at Dublin's hospitals and then ministering in the streets, follows actual events, as do those of the Sisters after their return to

Baggot Street. The chaos while Catherine was away is real, as well, as is the strange story of Hanna Fulham—one of many historical events you couldn't make up. The Sisters' service to the victims of the cholera epidemic is well documented, as is the public's fickle response to them.

While Lord Montague's trial is completely fictional, Father Kelly really did close the public chapel at the House of Mercy, although in 1834 rather than in 1833, as it is in this book. The best motivation historians can attribute was that it took money away from his parish, St. Andrews.

The "good cup of tea" or "comfortable cup of tea" that is referenced in the epilogue was long a part of Mercy lore and appears in the earliest biographies of Catherine. However, nowadays Mercy experts are beginning to believe it is more myth than reality, so it is no longer portrayed as fact, as it was only a few years ago.

The account of Catherine's final hours, her death, and her burial are all in keeping with early accounts of these events.

ACKNOWLEDGEMENTS

I'm usually not one to demonstrate my faith publicly, but because of the nature of this book, I feel that I must first and foremost thank God for giving me the opportunity to tell Catherine McAuley's story, as well as Catherine herself, who has guided me in so many ways during my Mercy tenure. I feel so blessed to be able to use my talents help others get to know this amazing, groundbreaking, independent, and compassionate woman.

Thank you to my agent, Amy Collins of Talcott Notch Literary, who first saw the potential of my short story, *Consequences*, to become a full-length novel and encouraged me to expand it beyond the story of servant Catherine turned away and explore Catherine's wider contribution to history through the founding of the Sisters of Mercy. Thank you as well to everyone at Chalice Press who was involved in publishing this book: Rebeca Seitz, my acquiring editor; Elizabeth Nelson, my editor; Brad Lyons, my publisher and line editor; Sherri Emmons my copy editor, and everyone on the production, marketing and publicity teams. This book would not be here without you.

Also much deserving of my gratitude is Nancy Dixon, who was my companion during that fateful week in Ireland when we didn't have any idea we were doing research for this book; we thought we were simply gathering information for a fundraising project! Thank you as well to Sister Mary Reynolds, Sister Lisa and everyone at the House of Mercy who so kindly hosted us, fed us, and told us everything they knew about Catherine's life. And I must not forget Sister Jeannette Noonan, who was our guide that week and took us to the best pubs in Dublin.

I must also acknowledge the late Mary Sullivan, who wrote the official modern biography of Catherine, *The Path of Mercy*. In addition, I owe a great debt of gratitude to all of the Sisters of Mercy for keeping Catherine's memory and mission alive all of these years. My life has been much enriched by your examples.

Courtney Marquez and Sister Claudia Ward, thank you for being early readers of the short story that was the basis for this book, along with everyone who read *Consequences* in the brief time it was available, especially those who said they wanted more.

While *Catherine's Mercy* is a work of fiction, I hope it will spread Catherine's story far and wide and be a tiny contribution to her cause for canonization. Any errors or mischaracterization are my fault entirely and are not meant to be reflective of the true woman behind the character.

ABOUT THE AUTHOR

Nicole Evelina is a *USA Today* best-selling author and biographer who writes historical fiction, nonfiction, and women's fiction. Her writing tells the stories of strong women from history and today, with a focus on little-known figures of women's history and literature.

Nicole has worked for a Mercy health care organization for twenty years, so Catherine's story is near and dear to her heart. In 2012, she was fortunate to be given the opportunity to visit Ireland and walk in Catherine's footsteps. She stayed at the House of Mercy, toured Coolock House and St. George's convent, and even knelt on the kneeler where Catherine took her vows as the first Sister of Mercy.

When she's not writing, Nicole can be found reading, playing video games, and enjoying theater, dance, and music. She lives in South Bend, Indiana, with her boyfriend, four cats, a dog, and a snake.